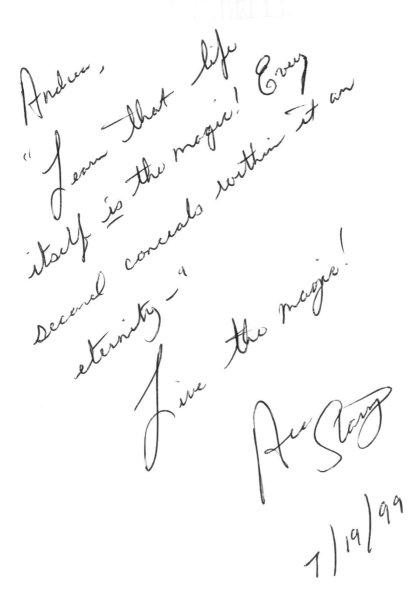

Andrea,

"Learn that life itself _is_ the magic! Every second conceals within it an eternity—"

Live the magic!

Ace Starry

7/19/99

What People Are Saying About THE MAGIC LIFE

The very first reader of the Internet "sneak preview" responded with an e-mail which simply stated: ***"I could not put it down!!!"*** Another reader was so moved that she sent the author a check for $100.00 in gratitude! Here are more of other's amazing, praising words:

*"An **excellent** story. Well written to hold the reader's attention, while weaving in the timeless truths of purposeful living. I'm reader 45. I hope that you reach 45,000 or more!" -- Van J. Walther, age 45, Loveland, Colorado*

*"... I ended up reading something like 13 chapters, and **stayed up much later than I should have**. Today, I stayed at home to work from here, and so far, all that I have accomplished is finishing your book. Thanks for the time and effort you put into it ... **I really enjoyed it"** -- Dave Campbell, age 49, Phoenix, Arizona*

*"What **an astoundingly great novel!** I hope that you are able to publish it. If you do, I own a small bookstore and would be interested in carrying it. If you don't have a publisher, perhaps I can help you find one, as we deal with several. Best of luck to you, **I was thoroughly entranced and changed by the story."** -- Loren Larsen, age 25, Durham, North Carolina*

*"Well, I just **finished the whole story straight through**. I am in total agreement with the first person who read it—**I couldn't stop reading it** ... It was **extremely philosophical** ... very refreshing and inspiration read and it really did make my day! I hope you get this published soon. ... BTW, I was on verge of collapsing into a sleep-deprivation slumber before reading this and **when I started I couldn't stop** ... It was just that much of a good read. Oh yeah, write more ... your style is **totally cool**. (-8" -- anonymous*

*"I was never much of a student. I'm one of those guys who used to go to class, sleep, kid around and "earn" my C's. Your novel however, has **inspired me**. **I couldn't stop reading** it. **I read the whole thing at one sitting** - yes, my butt is sore, but it's a good sore. It's like one of those muscle aches after a satisfying workout. You seemed to workout two of my main muscles, my heart and my brain. Thank you." -- Mike Habte, age 20, Springfield, Virginia*

*"It is **quite a wonderful novel especially for people who have never really followed their heart but wish they had done so**. In my case, **it has given me renewed vigor** to pursue some of the things I've always wanted to do but, for one reason or another, I never did. For that, I am deeply grateful to you." -- Noel Kalicharan, age 45, Princes Town, Trinidad*

*"I just finished reading your novel, and must say that it **more than lived up to the claims** on its web-site. I would go as far as to say that it was **one of the best books I have ever read..."** -- John M. (information withheld by request)*

*"This was a good time in my life to read this story. I had begun to question "why" I was doing what I did for a living and some other things about my life. It's funny but reading this particular story helped me resolve some of my personal issues. I do what I do for a living (higher education) because I like it and I'm good at it!! It's not about money for me; it's about helping students. Also, you helped me resolve some things with my dad's illness. Are you sure you aren't a psychiatrist? ... **I don't really have the proper words to express to you how refreshing this "insight" is**, it is indeed a special talent that you have. Well, Ace, **I could go on for "pages" with praise for this special story** and a very special writer. It is indeed a privilege to "meet" you! I hope that you will continue with your endeavors." -- Roberta Thurmond, age 39, Chattanooga, Tennessee*

*"I wanted to let you know that my mom read your story [too]. She **loved it!** She said it had been a long time since she read **something that could make her laugh, cry, feel happy, just feel good!!** She feels **you touch on all emotions**. She wants to know if you are famous (and of course I told her I would ask)."* -- Roberta Thurmond, age 39, Chattanooga, Tennessee (after letting her mother read it)

*"So, it was no coincidence that you and your book came into my life... Your words inspired great emotion in me today: I cried tears of sadness and pain that I thought I had already cried out, opening my soul even more; **I laughed, I smiled, I felt awe, wonder and amazement,** I felt gratitude. So thank you, Ace Starry, for participating in my life. Thank you for re-minding me of what I already know; **thank you for inspiring, uplifting and shifting me...**"* -- Judee Pouncey, age 54, Tallahasee, Florida.

*"**I truly did enjoy** your book and definitely believe you should get it published. I can also see it as good movie material (I do that to every book I read). I pretty much neglected my cat and my boyfriend today so that I could finish reading it."* -- Linda R. (information withheld by request)

*"...I am **so in agreement with your philosophy** that I have put a link on my homepage."* -- Barbara G., Catasauqua, Pennsylvania

*"I have read your novel, and it's really good. ... like many of your other readers, **I whiled away a morning reading it straight through.** Thoroughly enjoyed it, too, and **will recommend it to my friends.** All this time I've lived in Austin and I've not been to the Pecan Street Festival yet. Laziness, maybe. Anyway, maybe if I go, I'll have a look for Max. :-)."* -- Buddy Brannan, age 24, Austin, Texas

*"I have informed my husband that it is **a 'must read'.** It **may change the entire course of his life,** however. He always wanted to be a journalist like his grandfather. After reading your book, he may decide to scrap marketing and go back to school!!!! Follow that elusive dream of his!"* -- Geri Goldenberg, age 43, Wayne, New Jersey

*"I just this moment finished reading your novel. It was, well, novel. I really enjoyed it, and I wish you all the success in getting it published. **It really does hook you in.** I started reading it two days ago, when I read the first half dozen or so chapters. But **last night I couldn't put it down,** but had to give up around 1 am. So I came into work this morning and finished it. It is **a wonderfully crafted story.**"* -- Russel T. Gould, age 37, Fairbanks, Alaska

*"I found THE MAGIC LIFE to **be original and creative, a fresh innovative approach** to fiction."* -- Robynn Clairday, age 38, Bloomfield Township, Michigan

"You wrote a great book!" -- Lisa Jablonski, age 36, Manhattan, New York

*"I have just [spent] a whole afternoon reading THE MAGIC LIFE from start to finish. I would otherwise have been wasting it doing something else other than what I should be doing, which is work. Hopefully it will teach me how to stop wasting my life and get on with living it. **You are truly a star.**"* -- Barry de la Rosa, age 28, London, United Kingdom

*"You have given a gift. Your words of encouragement and hope, intricately woven into a well-structured novel, enraptured me. It was **very entertaining**, while pulling on the very core of existence. The clarity and conciseness makes your book an easy read for anyone. The message is clear and the **impact is empowering.** More importantly, I appreciate how your use of the 'paranormal' doesn't play off cheaply to your readers. The reconciliation in the final chapter allows your audience to embrace those events even more. Thank you for your gift."* -- Tim Roebuck, age 25, Virginia Beach, Virginia

THE MAGIC LIFE

THE
MAGIC
LIFE

A Novel Philosophy

Ace Starry

RARE
BIRD
PRESS

Rare Bird Press, 240 Pennsylvania Avenue, Yonkers, NY 10707

Printed in the United States of America
First Printing September, 1998

ISBN: 0-9665281-6-6
Library of Congress Catalog Card Number: 98-86217

Dedicated to my loving wife
Kristin
You are the one.

ACKNOWLEDGEMENTS

A special thanks goes to those who gave selflessly for this book to become a reality: among them, my agent, Bob Silverstein; Connie and Herman Woebke; Mark Dexter and Image Systems, Judee Pouncey; my father, John; my mother, Amy; and my three brothers, Kirk, Stuart, and Carl.

In the spirit of THE MAGIC LIFE, I am taking this opportunity to thank the many teachers who have appeared throughout my life. Some were teachers by profession, while many were people who may not even know that they had a profound effect on me. Although some have passed from this life and others have new names and may not even remember me, still my interactions with them played an important part in my life, learning and loving. Therefore, I would like to thank the following: my grandparents, the Headley Family, Sam and Mackenzie, Carlos and Christiana Torres, Charlie Wolfson, Pam Laswell, Tom and Linda Costello, Susan and Scott McNeill, Mary Rahmes, Shannon Starry, Tom and Ann Remlinger, Mike and Jackie Kelly, Pam and Jack Lyles, Randy Plutowski, Carole and Peter Brannan, Ron and Mike Starry, Jean Hickman and family, Clair Haycock, Larry Haycock, Aunt Kay, Chord and Shirley Starry, Tony Escamilla, Paul Miller, Tom Moloney, Mike Goldenberg, Peggy Wheeler, Ron Warfield, Cynthia and Alex Rossi, Martha Absolon, Stella Martinez, Sylvi Lots, Bill Wright, Cameron Scott, David Garza, Dawnetta Denham, Gloria Garrett, Ray Smilor, Gary Kadenhead, Frank Cross, Paul and Heidi Toprac, Rick Marcellin, Allison Howell, Charlie Nobles, Anthony Campbell, Angel Gunn, Cid Galindo, Greg and Lanai Wolfe, Lee Walker, Masahiro Ota, Annette Mertens, Dr. Neil and Beverly Isco, Larry Roy, Sam Martin, Tim Hagan, Mark Kroenecke, Scott Hamilton, Dave Williams, James and Ben Weaver, Early Hudson, Harry Yearsly, Judy Yearsly, Russell Bruce, Steve Shaw, Tim Simpson, Muhammad Ali, Sanford Perlis, Joyce Ann Anners, Matt Chuck, Gordon Ross, Liz Carmody, Janet DeRuvo, Joe Wesson, Annette Gould, Wendy Thompson, David Painter, Tom Hannigan, Dr. Fred Norman, Dr. Charles Lauterbach, Russel Gould, Loren Michaels, Tim Glancey, Sheri Shriner, Jeff Kelly, Meredith Patterson, Jan Alford, Ann Bentley, June Holt, Barry Gillingwater, Susan Lee, Tricia Kokotan, Roland and Carol Lamontange, Bonnie Jost, Mackie Gilcrest, Angelique Goodenaugh, Cynthia Santos, Deb Shottenfeld, Sandra Langston, Joyce Navarro, Jan Lane, Joyce Oliveras, John Severance, Nick Senofski, Sheran Stepanian, Lynn Warren, Susan Ziegel, Kim Ward, Les Keaton, Connie Bunton, Bob Evanecki, Brad Pol, Brenda Mahoney, Joan and Paul Rao, Marsha Soper, John Barrera, Jeff Molinda, Christie Stewart, AJ Games, Cassandra Vouches, Maureen Bartel, Dr. George Zenner, Tony Mannen, MaryAnn Anderson, Dan Mink, Fran Tanner, Pat Wooliver, Pam Nielsen, Becky Porter, Pam Conant, Gradon Stanley, Mike Allison, Tim Driscoll, Shelly Malberg, Jerry Mottern, Kevin Price, Linda Swafford, Terri Sampe, Jeff Osborne, Carol Allred, Jim Langley, Barbara Henscheid, Bill Ingram, Coach Dennis Almquist, Ed Chupa, Coach Jerry Kleinkopf, Elfriede Reinsdorf, Jackie Figeroa, Rocky McClymonds, Sharon Bratcher, Nancy Allen, Karen Popplewell, Lynn Correll, Sherry Sirucek, Jerry Randolf, the Thiebert Family, John Toddman, Gene Turley, Jim Ferguson, the Ward family, Duane Stans, Coach Bill Ingram, Teresa Stradley, Tom Kennedy, Leslie Grant, Bob Packard, Kelly Sturgill, Sara Sterling, Greg Dobbs, Bill Benkula, Wiley Dobbs, Steve Baisch, Steve Schultz, Barbara Storey, Cheryl Greenup, Tammy Goertzen, Sheryl Hurt, Kelli Johnson, Suzy Moore, Darl Gleed, Kim and Kenya Skinner, Kathy King, Reed Harris, Karma Florence, Jim Lucas, Paul Finchamp, Steve Smith, Kathleen Smart, Carl Sandmann, Susan Anderson, Caroll Engstrom, Coach Terry Johnson, Coach Gerald Mayes, Mike Hanks, Deedee Rogers, Jill Blincoe, Thomas Nagel, Mike Albert, Denise Culley, Brent German, Matt Heidemen, Brock McBride, Ray Pena, Ruben Saldana, Patricia Kilmartin, Terri Hansen, Marty Barts

CONTENTS

Chapter	Title	Page
1	*"Pay Attention To Fables and Dreams – They Are The Fabric That Weaves The Universe."*	... 1
2	*"Look For Meaning – In Any Amazing Coincidence."*	... 6
3	*"Be On The Lookout – For Life's Magical Opportunities."*	... 27
4	*"Nothing Will Happen – Unless You Make It Happen."*	... 45
5	*"You Can Only Find The Answers – When You Know The Right Questions."*	... 56
6	*"Access The Child Within You – And Learn What You Already Know."*	... 66
7	*"You Make The Choice – To Be What You Are."*	... 78
8	*"Life Is Full Of Happiness and Sadness – Whenever Life Is Full."*	... 86
9	*"If You Don't Create Your Own Future, – Someone Or Something Else Will Create It For You."*	... 100
10	*"A Sunrise Or A Sunset – Is Simply A Matter Of Perspective"*	... 111
11	*"The Card One Player Chooses To Discard – Often Completes The Winning Hand."*	... 118
12	*"The Path To True Happiness – Is A Trail Blazed By Your Own Heart."*	... 123
13	*"Everything Has A Value – But Only You Determine Its Worth."*	... 134

(Contents Continued)

14 *"Enthusiasm Is The Grease –*
    That Moves Life Over The Rough Spots."   ... *145*

15 *"Without You – There Is No Magic."*   ... *151*

16 *"No One Can Predict The Future –*
    But You Can Create It."   ... *154*

17 *"Just Begin Your Quest –*
    The Universe Will Rush In To Help You." *159*

18 *"Enjoy The Time You Spend –*
    With Family And Friends."   ... *178*

19 *"The Trick's Not To Make A Living Out Of Magic –*
    The Trick Is To Make Magic Out Of Living."   ... *188*

20 *"Remember, My Friend – The Illusion Is The Reality."* ... *200*

21 *"Opportunities Often Disguise Themselves*
    As Tribulations."   ... *208*

22 *"If You Want Things To Change –*
    You've Got To Change Things."   ... *221*

23 *"In Each Of Us Is Hidden – The Ultimate Magician."* ... *226*

24 *"When Your Heart Beats To The Rhythm Of The Universe –*
    Listen To Your Heart."   ... *235*

25 *"Each Second Conceals Within It A Lifetime –*
    Every Minute An Eternity."   ... *241*

26 *"Nothing Is Impossible – Absolutely Nothing."*   ... *244*

"Pay Attention To Fables And Dreams –
They Are The Fabric That Weaves The Universe."

Chapter 1

It all started with the nightmares.

Is this a dream? Am I asleep? Is this really happening to me?

Strapped in a straitjacket, I find myself stationed uncomfortably on a hard metal chair, completely confined. Two uniformed police officers stand over me, staring down at me. One of the men in blue forcefully tugs on the jacket's straps, verifying that they are secure. The second policeman jerks my feet up off the floor, almost pulling me from my chair in the process. Then holding my shoes by the heels, he allows the other officer to lock a pair of inversion boots tightly around my ankles. Next, I hear a distinct tearing sound as one of the officers, using his teeth, rips off a couple yards of duct tape from a large gray roll. Together, the two meticulously wrap the tape around the boots and over the buckles, making absolutely certain the boots won't fly open once I'm hanging upside down.

Unable to move either my arms or feet, I attempt to see just how tight the straitjacket is by wriggling back and forth in the steel folding chair. There is no give, no slack at all.

"Ha, ha, I guess I've gained a few pounds," I chuckle nervously to the officers, trying to relieve some of the tension in the air. However, their obvious lack of response makes me even more uptight.

THE MAGIC LIFE

The pressure from the heavily starched white canvas is constricting my ability to take a full breath. My breathing is forced to become short and quick. As a result, I begin to hyperventilate slightly. Soon my lungs are begging for more oxygen, causing my heart to pound strenuously against my chest.

Desperate to calm my pounding heart, I whisper to myself, "Don't panic. Concentrate on what you are doing. Focus on the escape."

It isn't working – just the opposite. Claustrophobia is taking hold of me. As my blood pressure increases, I begin to feel light-headed. The blood, pulsating against my eardrums, changes the dull thumping in my chest into a sharp throbbing in my head.

Concentrate, Jim! Panic and you could die!

Gradually the driving bass notes of some dramatic theme music replace the thudding in my ears. Over the loudspeakers, I hear the deep-voiced master of ceremonies announcing to the crowd, "Ladies and gentlemen, children of all ages, you are about to witness one of the most daring escapes of all time. Even the late, great Harry Houdini never attempted anything like this! After being strapped into a regulation straitjacket and shackled by the ankles to a piece of rope, our magician, the amazing James Carpenter, will be attached to this two-hundred-foot extension crane. Whereupon, the rope will be set on fire, the crane will be set into action, and our magician will go way beyond Houdini!

"He will be hoisted upside down, two-hundred feet into the air. Remember, the only thing holding him up there will be a four-foot length of burning rope. Check your watches, ladies and gentlemen. The rope will burn through in approximately three minutes. If this daring escape artist does not release himself before the rope burns through – he'll either have to learn to fly – or he'll plunge two-hundred feet TO HIS DEATH!"

The crane starts up. The music builds toward a crescendo, quickly drowning out the dull roar of the crane's diesel engine. After repositioning my chair to face the crowd, the police officers attach one end of the rope to the inversion boots around my ankles and the other end to the hook of the crane. With a wave from one of them, my beautiful assistant, her golden hair blowing in the breeze, steps up onto the platform carrying a fiery torch.

Strutting across the stage in fishnet stockings, her long silky legs draw all the attention away from me. She leans forward, extending the torch, which is now accompanied by a tremendous whooshing sound of the wind-blown flames. Almost in slow motion, I see the flame jump from the torch to the diesel-soaked rope, quickly igniting it. Within seconds the rope's roaring like a blast furnace.

I unsuccessfully struggle to take a full breath, coughing slightly after inhaling some of the diesel smoke. *"Concentrate. Try to relax,"* I repeat to myself in silence.

With a sudden jerk the crane kicks into high gear and the cable hoists me upside down, by the ankles. Looking downward, I see the ground pulling away rapidly, surprised at how quickly I'm pulled higher and higher into the sky.

Twenty feet – I see the people in the audience very clearly from this height. Some have their arms crossed firmly, some applaud and cheer; others simply stare, their mouths wide open. Beginning my struggle against the straitjacket wrapped so tightly around me, I attempt to force my arms away from my body – the attempt is in vain. The jacket doesn't give a millimeter.

Sixty feet, and still rising – my body weight pulling down heavily on the hemp causes the rope to start untwisting slightly. Spinning slowly in a circle, I become aware of every motion, every slight twitch and pop of the burning fibers.

"Get out of this," I say to myself. *"You've got to get out!"* Wrenching sideways, I feel the rope make a sudden lurch down, frightening me. Time is ticking by as I make my way skyward.

Eighty feet – losing my sensation of the crowd, my concentration now turns to the wind. With each gust it sways me slightly back and forth, creating red-hot flames and billowing a continuous cloud of black smoke into the blue sky. My eyes follow a small rainstorm of flaming diesel whipped away from the rope by the blustering air. Falling toward the earth, each droplet disappears, consumed by the flame long before smashing into the pavement below, leaving only a tiny trail of smoke as proof of its existence.

One-hundred feet – with all the blood rushing into my head, I feel a kind of euphoria. Losing the upside down sensation, I feel as though the world around me is inverted. For a brief moment my mind begins to wander, contemplating the vastness of the space around me and suddenly I feel very alone.

"Concentrate, I've got to focus!"

One-hundred-fifty feet – my struggle has now become a test of mental clarity as well as physical strength. My thinking is unclear. My arms are beginning to fatigue. Perspiration breaks out on my head and neck. Short of breath, I am starting to panic. My twisting back and forth becomes violent. I can't get out!

One-hundred-eighty feet – my enraged twisting yields a positive result as at last the sleeves gain some slack. With the extra space comes the ability to take a full breath and the sense that I'll be okay. I just need to force my shoulder out of place for a moment. Pressing my right shoulder fiercely against the restraint, I feel a pop that goes along with a sharp, but temporary pain, "Aaarrrgh!!" For a moment my shoulder is slightly separated; however, I now have the necessary room to get one arm out of its sleeve. A heavy sigh of relief – just a few more seconds and I'll be out.

Two-hundred feet in the air – my arms are almost free; another distinct snap – not my shoulders this time. A burning ember brushes my cheek on its way down. I gaze up. Time stands still for a moment. In horror, I watch as the rope separates. The small end of the burning rope, still attached to the crane, makes a flip skyward as if waving good-bye. The top of the crane pulls rapidly away from me.

"Oh my God! The rope is broken!"

I feel the sudden rush of momentum – downward. A terrifying falling feeling envelops me. The pavement races up to meet me head on. The crowd is screaming.

I scream, "Aaaaaagggggghhhhhh!"

Falling, falling … I close my eyes … falling.

With the sudden lurch of the mattress beneath me, I practically felt myself hit the bed, waking up drenched in a cold sweat. Confused and lost for a moment, there in the darkness of my own bedroom, I could almost hear the faint echo of my own scream. But, as my eyes adjusted to the moonlight filtering though the blinds, I slowly regained my bearings and composure, realizing that it was all simply a bad dream.

Somehow, during my sleep, the bed linens had become entangled around me – evidently the cause of the nightmare. After turning my night table lamp on, untangling myself took only a moment. To my misfortune, I discovered that during my nightmare I'd actually ripped a hole through one of the sheets. It must have happened while trying to free myself. *"The unconscious mind is a powerful force,"* I thought, perturbed that I'd have to go out and buy another set of designer sheets.

Taking a drink of water from the glass on my nightstand, I relaxed, trying to reassemble the details of the nightmare. However, they were not very clear. I found that by the time I was completely awake, I had forgotten much more of the dream than I remembered.

It had been a long time since I'd had a nightmare. I couldn't really remember the last one, and I was sort of glad that I didn't remember this one. They happened a lot, right after my father died, but that was when I was just a kid.

That was a long time ago.

Why was I having nightmares again? Why now?

"Look For Meaning –
In Any Amazing Coincidence."

Chapter 2

The next day was one of those warm, humid, autumn days in Austin, the kind that makes Texans wish for a change of season – boring, even monotonous weather, but nearly perfect for the Pecan Street Festival. Occurring twice a year, in both the spring and the fall, this outdoor festivity with all of its artsy-fartsy paintings and peculiar handicrafts was something I always welcomed. For the past six or seven years I had made a point of attending at least once each year. However, this fall, as I wandered through the street perusing the different vendors' booths, I couldn't help noticing that many of the arts and crafts were the same as the last time I attended. The festival, like most of my life, was beginning to look a lot like the year before. I, too, found myself wishing for a change of season.

Then I heard a voice, like that of a Shakespearean actor, booming out into the wandering crowd of festival goers, "Ladies and gentlemen, children of all ages, step right up. The show is about to begin. Come see the incredible, amazing, astounding Maximillion as he attempts miracles beyond the concepts of human imagination!"

His words sent a chill up my spine, but not the kind that is a foretelling of something ominous, more the feeling you get when you're experiencing something extraordinary – like goose bumps. I was intrigued by this deep and thundering voice of possibilities. Led by my own curiosity, I weaved my way through the crowd until finally coming to a clearing at the street corner.

There, standing on top of a rather large, dusty old theatrical trunk, projecting all the enthusiasm of a ringmaster on the opening night of the circus, was the magician. Waving a silver-tipped magic wand in the air while shouting his patter out to the crowd, this engaging street conjurer made quite a striking impression. He was attired in a classic black tuxedo with tails, including a red satin vest adorned with sequined lapels, which sparkled brightly in the afternoon sun. On top of his head, tilted just slightly to one side was the mandatory black top hat, the kind that pops open with the flick of the wrist. He also sported the standard, well-trimmed magician's beard and mustache.

From the streaks of silver-white at his temples, or the salt and pepper coloring of his facial hair, I would have guessed him to be in his late forties or maybe even fifty. But perhaps because of his physical condition, or from his youthful manner as he played to the crowd, he seemed to be much younger than the smile-wrinkles around his eyes, or the years of wisdom hidden behind them.

Indeed, he had all of the trappings of a truly magical man. Well, not really a man, more like a riddle, an enigma. Half of him seemed fairy-tale wizardry – the other half, performer-reality. He looked as if he could really do magic – not just tricks – I mean real magic. I think it was his eyes; he certainly had the eyes of a magician. At times they sparkled more than his lapels. There was something about his smile, too. When he smiled, it was with a rather mischievous grin hinting that, behind those mystical blue eyes and that sly smile, he might be up to something devious.

One thing about his appearance, though, did strike me as peculiar – kind of out of place. I noticed a small silver chain dangling around his neck. Where there should have been a medallion, or perhaps a crystal of some sort, attached to it, instead, pinned to the chain with a simple safety pin was a small square of tattered white cloth. The material looked to be nothing more than a small piece of an old rag or the corner of an old handkerchief. However, I concluded from observing the magician's interactions with the strange necklace that it was possibly much more.

THE MAGIC LIFE

At times, while he talked to his audience, the magician would rub this threadbare piece of cloth between his thumb and fingers, as if it were a good luck charm or magic amulet. Sometimes he would hold the piece of cloth and whisper to it. Perhaps this was just a nervous habit or (if I let my imagination get the better of me) perhaps the cloth contained his secret to some awesome powers over science and nature. Maybe this strange talisman contained his secret to the mysteries of life. Whatever it was, I knew that the cloth was important to him.

"Hurry, gather round, while the good seats are available," the magician proclaimed as he walked up to spectators who were intent on walking by and dragged them by the arm over to a predetermined spot. The magician was a true master at drawing himself a paying crowd. The unsuspecting onlookers would pause and sometimes laugh out loud, knowing that the fun was about to begin. Rarely did people seem unsure about joining in. But if they were, with a smile and a wink, the charming conjurer would always make them relax, kick back, and stay awhile.

"So, did you two call ahead for a reservation?" he quipped as he grasped a middle-aged woman and her son, adding them to the circle.

"Was that smoking or nonsmoking?" he asked, just for a laugh, of a little round-bellied boy who seemed more intent on eating his chocolate ice-cream cone than watching a magician.

He took one of the attractive young girls by the arm, asking, "Would you like to stand next to somebody famous?" Then he said in a rhyme, "You are, sweetheart ... me! The amazing, incredible, astounding ... Maximillion Vi!"

His resonant voice and cunning wit quickly attracted a sizable audience with two hundred or more people, young and old alike, now forming a circle around this unique street entertainer. I almost had to consider myself lucky; being one of the first to get there, I now stood at the front edge of his crowd.

For his opening Maximillion Vi performed silent magic that truly was wonderful to watch. Like an elaborate dance, he pulled cards and silver coins out of thin air. Objects that he borrowed from the audience would vanish, only to reappear under his hat or in a spectator's pocket or purse.

The younger children enjoyed the show most of all – the kids, who had pushed their way through the crowd to the front row and now knelt or sat on the asphalt, pointing and poking one another, their eyes wide open in amazement. Most were hypnotized by the bewildering magician, as if he were a Pied Piper ready to lead them off to a better world.

I, too, more than enjoyed his clever deceptions, the wonder and mystery of not knowing all the answers. In those mystical moments I became a child again, lost deep in the wonders of magic, trying to take it all in: the magician, the crowd, the sunshine. I recalled when I was the little boy, watching my first magician, clinging tightly to my father's hand. Just like the children kneeling in the street, I would have also pushed my way up to the front of the circle; because, when I was a little boy, I wanted nothing more out of life than to become a famous magician. Of course, those were just the dreams of a little boy.

Watching the magician perform, recalling those memories, I flashed back to my own childhood, in Springfield, Missouri, back to the time when I first decided to be, or perhaps discovered that I was going to be, a magician.

My father had taken me with him to the smelly old junkyard, to help him dump a load of garbage. Dad loved to visit the junkyard; I never could understand why. The smell alone could almost kill a small boy like me. But Dad was always on the lookout for something of value. *"One man's trash is another man's treasure,"* he'd say. That particular day, while we were unloading the *trash* from the pickup, my nose held with one hand, Dad spotted a potential *treasure*, a dilapidated old trunk lying in amongst the junk. With a little luck and a few hundred hours of sanding, he said that stinky old trunk could eventually become a coffee table, one with a *new* avocado-green imitation-antique finish.

The trunk was padlocked shut so he couldn't open it, but Dad picked up one end and gave it at shake. We could hear something inside, but couldn't tell what from the sound. The mystery alone made the trunk irresistible to Dad, and even caused me to forget the junkyard stench for a while. Dad used to say, "Curiosity is a sap running deep in the Carpenter's family wood." After offering the junk dealer five dollars for it and the dealer countering with ten, eventually they settled at seven. The dealer didn't know it, but Dad would have paid a lot more than seven dollars just to find out what was hidden inside. Mom often said that that was the "sap" he was referring to. We endeavored to open the trunk right then and there, but the lock was rusted solid. Dad decided, after beating on it with a tire iron for a short while, that even though both of our imaginations were working overtime, we'd simply have to wait until we got home.

Upon returning home, my father immediately dug a hacksaw out of his trusty toolbox and hacked off the rusted semblance of a lock. Opening the trunk, we were greeted by a puff of musty air. What we found inside may have been a little disappointing to my father, but was certainly a treasure to a seven-year-old boy. There inside, in almost mint condition, were several old magic tricks, an old bouquet of feather flowers, and three books on magic.

"Well, look at that. I guess destiny wants one of us to become a magician," Dad said as he tossed me one of the books. At that moment, I truly believed that fate had placed those objects into my hands, almost commanding me to learn the art of legerdemain.

For some time after that, I remained enthralled with the art of magic, mastering the three tricks in the trunk: the linking rings, color-changing scarves, and vanishing billiard ball. I read those three books until the pages practically fell out and went on to read several more books from the library about famous magicians like Houdini, Thurston, and Blackstone. But I never really became much of a magician. Frozen in time for just a moment, I wondered, "When did I give up that childhood fantasy? If I hadn't become an accountant, could I – would I – have ever become that famous, astounding magician of my childhood dreams?"

As soon as I began questioning myself, my positive energy dwindled away, my thoughts drifting elsewhere. I couldn't help thinking about my job, "Should I be wasting time playing games at the festival? Back at the office, I had unfinished work and I'd feel guilty Monday if I didn't get it done over the weekend. Maybe I should just forget about spending the day..."

The magician began examining the crowd saying, "I will need another sucker ... uh ... volunteer ... a gentleman, a strong man." He turned and looked squarely at me, almost as if he were reading my mind. "You will have to do," he said, and before I could disagree, he grasped my arm and briskly walked me into the center of his circle. Somehow I knew that I would end up being the butt of the joke, making a fool of myself in front of the crowd, but I just couldn't find it within myself to say no.

"Allow me to introduce myself, sir," Maximillion said as he reached out and graciously shook my hand. "I am the amazing, incredible, and astounding ... Maximillion Vi ... rhymes with "*free*" ... which unfortunately is also what you work for as my assistant today. You may call me simply '*Amazing*' for short. Your name is?"

"James, James Carpenter, you can call me Jim for short," I said, giving him a firm handshake along with my feeble attempt at wit.

Smiling a curious smile, he pulled his eyebrows down as if he were going to ask me a question. His expression gave me a strange feeling, as though he knew me from somewhere before, or as if he'd wanted to meet me for some time. Then something magical really did happen. While we were shaking hands, the magician reached up to the chain dangling around his neck, took the small piece of ragged white cloth between his thumb and fingers and began to rub it briskly. "James, James Carpenter?" he said with a slight question.

Suddenly, a tingling sensation came over me, "chills" just as I had when I first heard his voice. Only this was much stronger: a positive energy, a feeling of excitement, a zest for life. This fantastic insight that life was truly magical, exhilarated me. At that moment I became acutely aware of my surroundings: the sun, the smiles, the magician. My vision even seemed to sharpen. Faces became brighter and clearer as I surveyed the audience: majorities and minorities, young and old, fat and thin, all laughing and smiling, all enjoying this unique moment. The magic was universal and in that magical moment (regardless of age, race, or background) they all became children again – fun loving and carefree, freeing themselves from their pasts, and suspending their disbelief to enjoy the illusions.

Why should I feel guilty about taking a day off? Everyone else was having fun. Why couldn't I? Somehow, I knew I was being given this opportunity to experience some of life's real magic. I deserved a little magic in my life, too. Right then I decided, for the next few moments at least, to just put away troublesome thoughts about my job, close the accounting books, and simply enjoy the magic. Amazingly, all of this went through my mind in that one short moment when the magician touched my hand and rubbed the small white piece of cloth.

As abruptly as I had entered into this heightened state of awareness, I was pulled back into the present. Lost for just a second, I suddenly realized what Max was saying.

"Would you please act as the official timer for this act, Jim?" Max asked.

"Sure," I replied.

"Does your watch have a sweeping second hand?" he inquired, pointing to his wrist.

The question made me glance at my wrist only to discover that I was no longer wearing my watch. "I could have sworn that I was..."

"Here, I guess I could let you borrow mine," Max said as he reached into his pocket and pulled out a watch – my watch!

My chin almost dropped to the pavement. The crowd also realized that he was now holding my watch and they laughed aloud. I couldn't help chuckling too, awestruck that this man had taken off my watch without my having a clue. Deciding that maybe I should check for my wallet, I reached for my back pocket...

"I was possibly going to pay you for helping me out, but all you have in here is a couple of bucks," Max said, grinning. Again the artful pickpocket had duped me. He stuck my own billfold into my hand, then asked politely if he could borrow a one-dollar bill.

"Folks, let me demonstrate how easy it is to drop a dollar into the hat." Saying that, Max tilted his head forward. With a quick snap from his neck, his top hat, like a gymnast scoring a perfect ten, did one complete revolution and landed open end up on the street in front of him. He held the dollar two feet above the hat and released it, the bill slowly drifted down like a feather into the hat. "See how easy money goes into the hat," he said. "Well, it comes out a lot quicker." With a snap of his fingers and a wave of his wand, the money defied gravity, shooting out of the hat and back into my wallet!

I did a double take. "You know Max, you could make a heck of a living doing that," I said, under my breath.

"I do make a heck of a living doing this," he whispered as he stuck his foot into his hat. With a kick up, the hat made an aerial flip and landed perfectly back on top of his head. "Magic, I mean," he said, not missing a beat.

"The trick," he whispered to me, "is not to make a living out of magic. The trick is to make *magic* out of *living*." He then winked and grinned, letting me know that I could trust him. It worked. For some reason, I did trust him, the same way a child might trust Peter Pan.

"Well, Jim, have you ever seen one of these?" Max asked assuming an air of importance as he turned around dramatically pulling a white canvas straitjacket out of the trunk.

"Yes, I have," I answered, not considering that I hadn't actually seen a real straitjacket – only pictures of them.

"It makes me very nervous when volunteers answer yes," Max said as he looked all around the audience with this wide-eyed worried look.

They laughed.

"Of course, Jim, you mean that you have seen them in pictures – not up close – right? ... Please agree, or I get really nervous."

"Well, yes," I agreed, but somehow I had a strange feeling that I actually had seen one before.

"We are now going to test your strength," Max said. "I asked you when you volunteered so graciously if you were indeed a man of constitutional fortitude and resolute dedication, did I not? ... Oh, I didn't? Oh well, you'll just have to do since you are standing here in the middle of my circle."

With that he placed his hands on my shoulders and whispered a few strange words to himself, which sounded Latin or ancient – that is, what I could hear of them. Placing one of his hands over my head, he gazed intently into my eyes. Next he pressed his index finger to the middle of my forehead, and began rubbing the small white piece of cloth with his other hand.

Then Max spoke to me. "You are now hypnotized," he said. "Your arms," Max pulled my hands straight out in front of my body, "they are steel!" Again he rubbed the cloth pinned to the chain about his neck. "They are beams of solid steel and cannot be bent – steel, Jim!"

As he said this, I indeed felt my arms become rigid and stiff.

THE MAGIC LIFE

Could I actually be hypnotized? I attempted to discreetly move my arms. Not wanting to say anything out loud, so as to ruin his act, I just wanted to see if I really couldn't move them. I could not. I tried harder; still I couldn't move. Realizing that I was no longer in control, I started to panic.

As if sensing my pending hysteria, Max again placed a hand on my shoulder, winked, and in a steady reassuring voice said, "Don't worry; you are always in control – always. Nothing will happen unless you make it happen." He had read my mind. Immediately, I was comforted and relaxed. After all, what choice did I have? I had just started to enjoy myself, when I discovered how I was to become the butt of the joke.

"Your arms are frozen in front of you," he said, as Max proceeded to place the straitjacket – on me!

The straitjacket was a coarse white canvas contraption covered with frayed leather straps and scratched steel buckles. The jacket showed years of wear and tear. Looking it over, I was sure it had been escaped from many times. I could also tell that it was highly improbable – no, make that totally impossible – that once strapped in, I would ever be able to escape.

After he had my arms strapped around my back, he gave the straps a couple of tugs and asked, "Does that feel like a real straitjacket?"

Once again, without thinking, I answered, "Yes."

Max rolled his eyes, raised one eyebrow, and made a face at the crowd asking, "How do you know what one feels like?" Once again they laughed and I laughed along with them; however, I really didn't feel like laughing. For some reason unknown to me, I was overcome with a feeling of *deja vu* like I'd been in this predicament before. The feeling wasn't pleasant at all; in fact, it was disturbing.

I know I must have looked somewhat ridiculous, but one little boy was laughing so hard that the crowd began to laugh at him. He kept pointing and laughing, almost falling over. The boy's laughter became infectious. Before long everyone in the crowd was enjoying the laugh-fest, everyone but me. Max had me totally strapped into the jacket – all except for one strap – the strap that buckles up underneath the crotch. Suddenly we all realized why the little boy had been laughing so hard.

"There is one strap left, ladies and gentlemen, and we call that strap – everybody say 'Oooohhhhh,'" said Max.

Everybody went, "Ooooooooohhhhhhhh."

"... the strap of death," Max said as he pulled the strap way up between my legs. There I was, standing with my arms crossed and strapped behind me, struggling to move an inch, probably looking like some deranged lunatic, getting a strap-of-death *wedgie*. The crowd went wild.

Max walked over to an attractive woman in the crowd and asked if she would assist us. She was a little bit anxious about the whole thing, saying that she didn't want to end up looking like me. Who could blame her?

Max reassured her that she wouldn't be put in the jacket, then snapped his fingers as if to un-hypnotize me. Stepping behind me, he unbuckled the straps to free me from the jacket. As I was pulling off the jacket, Max walked the beautiful woman by the hand to the center of the circle and introduced her to the audience. "Kristin, this is everyone," he said. "Everyone, this is Kristin." Then handing the jacket over to Kristin, he stated, "Just for the fun, I think that you two should put the jacket on me."

With that he pulled off his tuxedo coat and satin vest, tossing them into the trunk. He placed his hands and arms into the straitjacket, which Kristin held open for him, and instructed me to step behind him and strap him in as tight as was humanly possible.

"With pleasure," I responded.

Pulling the back straps taut, I could tell that Max was holding a deep breath, expanding his chest. All he had to do was release his breath and the jacket would be loose.

"Come on James, you can make it tighter than that, can't you?" Max yelled to the crowd.

"If you weren't holding your breath I could," I replied, trying not to sound too arrogant. With that comment Max let loose a puff of air that allowed me to tighten the jacket an extra two inches, as tight as his rib cage would allow.

Then Max asked me to pull the arm straps around his body and also tighten them as far as they would go. Practically hearing the compression in his voice, as if it were now even difficult for him to take a breath, I wondered if he would, in fact, be able to escape. So, feeling a touch sympathetic, I pulled the arm straps secure, but not too tight.

"Is that all the strength that you have?" Max lectured. "Put some muscle into it, James. Besides, don't you think the show will be better if I don't get out?"

"Okay, if that's the way you want it," I responded, now pulling with all the force I could muster.

Then in a comedy falsetto voice, Max said, "Yes, by George, I think he's got it."

The crowd laughed. Looking at him now, there was no way in the world he'd ever get out of that straitjacket. He didn't even have room to sweat.

Max walked to the center of the crowd and in a loud deep voice said, "Now, ladies and gentlemen, as you can see, I am truly strapped in the confines of a regulation straitjacket. There is virtually no humanly possible way for me to escape."

"Uh uh," came the voice of the little boy who had been laughing so heartily earlier in the performance. He was pointing at what Max had so eloquently referred to as "the strap of death," hanging precariously between the magician's legs, still unbuckled.

"Son," Max quipped in his theatrical voice, "didn't anyone ever tell you that it's not polite to point – especially in that direction." The crowd roared. Max, smiling that devious smile of his, turned his head slowly in the direction of the young woman, Kristin.

"Kristin?" Max asked with a sheepish grin. "You are probably wondering why I asked you to come here?" he said, swaying back and forth to make the strap swing. "Don't be shy. Just reach down between my legs and grab whatever you find dangling there." Again a chuckle from the crowd and Max continued, "This strap doesn't have to be as tight as the others."

Tears formed in my eyes from holding back the laughs, at this farcical scene. Kristin, bending down behind him, reluctantly reached between his legs; Max would squirm just as she reached for the strap, swinging it out of her reach. After several failed attempts she grabbed it and began buckling the crotch strap together.

"You sure are taking your sweet time, Kristin. You're enjoying this way too much!" Max teased.

The crowd began yelling, "Tighter, make it tighter!"

"Go ahead and pull it tight," Max said and then whooped, "Waaaaaaiiiit, not that tight!" Kristin ignored his antics and buckled the strap tightly. After which she stood straight up signifying that she had indeed strapped the escape artist in firmly. Max then acknowledged, "Let's give Kristin a big Texas round of applause. Thank you for being such a good sport, Kristin, and helping us make the world a little happier, and certainly a safer, place. I want you all to know that y'all are enjoying this a lot more than I am."

The crowd applauded for Kristin as she smiled and took her place back amongst them. Max moved back into the center of the circle, calling to the audience, "Ladies and gentlemen, does anyone happen to know the world record for the escape from a straitjacket? Houdini could escape in less than one minute. The incredible Loren Micheals could escape in less than forty seconds, The Amazing Randi in less than thirty. However, the world record for the fastest escape from a regulation straitjacket happens to be ... eighteen seconds. And do you know who happens to hold that record? – I ... don't know either.

"Today, however ... I – the incredible, amazing, astounding Maximillion Vi – will attempt, for the first time in Austin, Texas – for your sheer and utter enjoyment – NO SUCH THING!"

Then Max remarked in exaggerated Jewish accent, "I can't get out of here in that short of time. This is really tight! What do you think ... I can do miracles?"

Strange that he would ask such a thing. He could do them; miracles, yes, that was exactly what the audience expected – exactly what I expected. Only moments ago Max had seemed omniscient, capable of miracles. Now in the straitjacket, he appeared to be a mere mortal like the rest of us. However, I had the distinct feeling that his distressed-mortal *look* might be just that – for appearances.

Max continued, losing the accent this time, "How about if I escape in a reasonable amount of time? Is there a reasonable person among us, who could suggest a reasonable amount of time for my liberation from these bonds – the likes of which, even the great Houdini never felt?"

A few persons in the crowd started to shout out times.

"Fifteen seconds."

"Ten seconds."

"I said reasonable," Max grumbled.

"Thirty seconds," I said, thinking it was reasonable.

With that he turned back to me and asked, "What time did you suggest?"

"Thirty seconds," I repeated.

"What's that again? Louder, for everyone's benefit, Jim," Max said, leaning closer to me as if I had stumbled upon the proper time.

"Thirty seconds!" I shouted out.

At the same time Max yelled, "TWO MINUTES!" overpowering my voice, ignoring my suggested time. "The man says I should attempt to escape in TWO MINUTES!"

As the crowd laughed, I was beginning to understand the real magic that Max Vi held. People loved him – *that* was the magic.

Max continued, "Very well ... I will attempt to escape from this straitjacket within the constraints of a two-minute time limit – even though such a release may appear to be a virtual impossibility.

"Ladies and gentleman, I have to ask you to trust my official timer, Jim. Jim, you are going to have to keep me posted. When one minute has passed I want you to yell out ... One minute! ... Got that? At one minute and thirty seconds I want you to yell out..." He made a motion for me to fill in the blank.

"One minute and thirty seconds!" I shouted.

"And at one minute and forty-five seconds, James, I want you to yell out..."

I took the bait and yelled out, "One minute forty-five seconds?"

"Wrong!" Max said, making a loud obnoxious sound like a buzzer on a game show. "GZZZZZZ... No James, when I reach one minute and forty-five seconds, I want you to start counting down. Fifteen ... fourteen... thirteen... Got it?"

"Got it." I replied.

Max announced loudly to the crowd, "And everyone will start counting down with Jim, right?"

A few of the more vocal ones shouted back the answer, "Right." But the response was not overwhelming and certainly not satisfactory to Max Vi.

He repeated, "And everyone will start counting down, right?" almost reprimanding the crowd.

"Right!" the crowd yelled.

"And should I escape in those last few seconds counting down four, three, two, one, everyone will burst into a thunderous round of applause! Right?"

"Right!" The crowd screamed back like a cheerleading squad.

"Screaming and cheering – RIGHT?" Max yelled back even louder.

"RIGHT!" was the crowd's overwhelming response.

" ... REACHING FOR YOUR WALLETS!" Max yelled, raised one eyebrow, paused for effect, breaking the rhythm. Some started to respond, but after they realized they'd been led down this path, the crowd laughed.

Max then became serious, almost solemn, stating, "If I do escape and indeed you do appreciate the show, please show your appreciation by placing your spare change, ones, fives, tens, twenties, municipal bonds, stock certificates, car titles, expensive jewelry, or deeds of property inside of my hat." He paused. His eyes took on a steel gray concentration and he inhaled a deep breath. Turning to me, he stated that he was ready to start.

"On your mark ... Get set..." I paused to let the second hand sweep to the start position. Max stood poised. "GO!"

The incredible Max Vi shrugged his shoulders, grimaced, clenching his teeth while twisting violently back and forth. I looked at my watch; time was passing quickly. Thirty seconds and the magician's struggle didn't reveal so much as an inch of slack. The straitjacket held firm.

"The first order of the day is," Max announced already half out of breath, "the strap of death."

With that announcement, Max, still secure in the jacket, sat down on the street and kicked off his shoes and socks. He quickly worked his way into a kneeling position and reached for the crotch strap between his legs with the back of his feet. Slowly, like a contortionist, he pulled the strap up with his toes and unbuckled it. To watch him stretch his body to the very limit, almost made me hurt. Amazing!

Glancing again at my watch, I saw that one minute had already expired.

"One minute!" I yelled out just as he had instructed earlier.

"Not yet! Wouldn't you know I would have to find the one person with the Quartz Acutron watch," Max grumbled for a laugh. With that remark, the incredible Max Vi stood up in his bare feet, breathing deeply to regain his strength.

His face remained tense and contorted, until with one long slow breath he suddenly relaxed. All of the jerking and struggling stopped. His face became poker-playing deadpan. Determined, painstakingly he lowered one of his shoulders. He stared straight ahead with intense concentration. I checked my watch. He was still a far cry from freedom.

"One minute thirty seconds!" I yelled.

His hand barely moved under the jacket. Sweat dripped from his forehead. The seconds ticked by. Max concentrated all of his efforts into moving just one hand.

"Fifteen ... fourteen ... thirteen..." I shouted, and the crowd joined in.

"Twelve... eleven ... ten..."

I couldn't see any movement at all on the part of Max. My heart began to pound. He was not going to get out.

"Nine ... eight ... seven..."

I heard a popping from his shoulders that caused him to wince in pain and groan aloud.

"Six ... five ... FOUR..."

His arms flung free from his body and over his head.

"THREE ... TWO..."

A quick strong jerk and the straitjacket burst up high into the air.

"ONE."

Max Vi was free!

The crowd exploded into an ovation. With a quick sigh of relief, I began to applaud and cheer with them. Max waved the straitjacket in the air with one hand, reached over and grabbed his hat with the other. Turning in a circle, he exclaimed, "If you appreciated the show, please show your appreciation!" The crowd responded in kind, with people digging out money from pockets, purses, and wallets. Parents entrusted their children with the change or dollars, instructing them to place it inside the magician's hat. I observed one grandpa, so pleased with the show that he presented his grandson a crisp ten-dollar bill to add to the pot.

Having completely regained his breath and now showing no signs of his momentary struggle, Max said, "I would like to thank you – all of you – by leaving you with one last miracle."

Then he turned to me, instructing, "Jim, if you would please, collect the rest of the money. When you are finished just place the hat and money inside this old trunk." He walked over to the trunk full of props and pulled out a large red satin sheet, closed the trunk and returned to the center. Holding the sheet behind him and above his head, turning around in a circle, he called to the audience, "Ladies and gentlemen, please take this one small bit of magic into your lives. *Learn that life itself is the magic! Every second conceals within it a lifetime, every minute an eternity. Learn to live each moment of life as if it could suddenly disappear.*"

Max then lifted the sheet above his head, covering his entire body. Pausing for a moment of silence, he then just simply vanished. There is no other way to explain it. He faded into nothingness, the satin sheet casually drifting to the street below as though he had slowly evaporated.

The crowd was silent. We all gawked at each other, expecting that he would somehow appear in the next instant, but after an awkward minute he still did not. A few people started a rather weak round of applause, but the illusion had been too astounding, too real, too stunning, almost to the point of being surreal. He had been standing in the middle of the street, surrounded by a crowd of people! There was just no way his disappearance could have happened beyond black magic or witchcraft.

An aging white-haired woman walked forward, and placing a dollar into the hat she broke the silence, saying, "You two fellows put on one heck of a show." Her gesture of good faith started a new round of applause and brought a new stream of money flowing into the hat. Somewhat confused, I couldn't resist a quick bow to the crowd. Even though I knew it was wrong, I couldn't help wondering what would happen if I just took his props, money, and straitjacket and became the magician of my childhood dreams. Where was Max Vi anyhow? Maybe he had vanished for good.

The crowd slowly disintegrated, just like the magician, soon transforming into a constant flow of people wandering through the busy festival thoroughfare. Only one other person remained standing in the same place after the crowd had dwindled. Standing alone at the back of the walkways was Kristin, the beautiful woman who had assisted in the show. She strolled up to me, smiling.

"You are part of the act, aren't you?" she asked.

"No, I really wasn't. I was just a volunteer, like you, that he pulled out of the crowd," I replied.

"Well, where is he?"

Knowing that I didn't have an answer, I just laughed, "I suppose he'll show up for his money sometime."

"Why don't you and I just take off with it?" she joked, taking me by the arm. "Come on, buy a lonely girl a drink."

Even though it was the best offer I'd had in ages, I just couldn't leave before seeing that the magician had his money. "That is tempting, but I think that we can manage without taking away his hard-earned cash," remembering just then what I was supposed to do with the money, "Wait just a minute," I said. Then I walked over to the magician's old trunk, unlatching it to place both the money and hat inside as I'd been instructed.

Startled, I jumped back, as up out of the trunk popped Max, "Congratulations, you've found me! I was beginning to think that you'd never open this darn thing."

Right in front of me stood the amazing Max Vi – truly a magician's magician. "How on Earth did you get into the trunk?" I asked.

"What makes you think it was on Earth, James?" Max asked rhetorically, "Sometimes the questions aren't as obvious as the answers. That's why I suggest that people don't dwell too much upon questions. You see, it's more often the questions themselves that keep you from seeing the answers. Just concentrate on the reality, not the illusion, and you will see that the answers are always right in front of you. Your life will give you the answers. That is, if you stop confusing yourself with too many questions."

"I don't understand what you mean," I said.

Max answered, "Well, isn't it amazing that I am here, in the trunk? Isn't it amazing that you were here today, and the only one who found me. There is a meaning in it, James. There's meaning in any amazing coincidence. The question itself is the answer. It's magic! And, Jim, it's only magic if you have a question."

I just stared at him mouth open, perplexed and maybe even slightly flustered by his strange double-talk. Then I asked, "Is it real magic, or is there some sort of a trick to it?"

"One man's *trick* is another man's *treasure*," he replied. "If you really have to know, I'll tell you. I always tell my good assistants. But, before I tell you, I must warn you that by telling you the secret, the magic itself will disappear. Once it does, then only real magic can bring it back." He paused, looking at me for some semblance of understanding.

Although I didn't understand most of what he had said, I realized in my heart that I really didn't want to know the secret. He was right. Knowing would spoil the fun, so I shook my head no-thanks.

"Good choice, Jim," Max continued, "a lot of the time, people come up to me and demand to know how I do these amazing things. I wonder to myself, 'Why do they have to ask?' Isn't it enough to see it happen? If we enjoy the magic then what is the purpose of asking how? If we were all magicians, then where on earth would we find magic? When the sun rises, sometimes isn't it just enough to feel the warmth – to see the sunlight spilling over the countryside? Do we have to know that it is a fusion reactor, spewing photon particles across space? Sure it's nice to have a weather forecast. But sometimes an unexpected shower can be revitalizing – don't you think? Imagine just how boring life would be if you and I did know all of the answers. Too many of us spend too much time looking for the secret, '*the how,*' when the answer is the magic itself, '*the why.*'"

Kristin approached, breaking Max's spell by saying, "Jim, I'm afraid you've gotten more than you bargained for. Two things that I have learned in this life are: one, that you never ask a magician *how* he does his tricks; and two, you never, never, ever ask *why*." With that she threw her arms around Max, and they embraced with a short, but affectionate, kiss and hug.

"Jim, allow me to introduce my assistant and wife – the incredible, loving, tolerant, Kristin," Max said with a wink.

Now, I truly felt like the fool. "I should have guessed when she offered to run away with me," I said.

"She always does that. It's part of the test," Max said nonchalantly as he pulled on an old football jersey, the number "zero," over his tux shirt and began to pack up his tricks.

23

THE MAGIC LIFE

"Test?" I asked with more than a touch of that Carpenter curiosity.

Before he could answer, a couple of youngsters who had watched his act reappeared, asking Max for his autograph. The magician cordially responded by digging in his trunk for some of his black and white promotional photographs. After getting his signature on them, the kids ran down the street ecstatic with their new treasure. Max then lifted the hat full of money; weighing it in his hands for a second, he announced, "One-hundred-seventeen dollars and forty-seven cents. Would you check that for me? You are an accountant aren't you?" Max asked. "You account and I'll tell you about the test."

The sun was just setting; the festival was winding down and many of the booths were closing shop. At Max's request, I started doing what I was supposed to be good at, counting money.

"James," Max began, "every year I perform the escape and vanish seven-hundred seventy-seven times. Sounds amazing doesn't it? Actually I use that number just to make the story interesting. Really, I have no idea how may times I do that particular act each year, probably somewhere around fifteen, I suppose. Well, anyway, I have been doing that act since I was about a year older than you are now. How old are you anyway?"

"Twenty-eight," I replied. He laughed and pointed to my handful of bills, knowing I was in the middle of counting and that his questioning would prove to confuse me. It did; I lost count. But I just chuckled and started over. "Well, I will actually turn twenty-nine in a couple of days," I added.

"Exactly," Max stated, "I started the escape act at thirty years of age. Anyway, I have been performing around the world, in twelve languages for about twenty years. Each and every time, I have a volunteer, like yourself, assist. In all of those shows, in all that time, I have met only three other people who demonstrated the same qualities you possess. But unfortunately all three failed the test.

"Meeting you here today was no accident. Fate threw you into my circle for a reason." He then placed his hands on top of mine to make me stop counting the money and said, "You can feel it too, can't you? I've been looking for you for a long time – James," he said, "you are the one."

Pulling his eyebrows down into a serious look right at me, he stated, "I want you to take this money home with you and count it. Bring the money back to me next spring, if and when you decide to come to the festival. If you can't come, or don't wish to, then you keep the money for yourself. I know it isn't very much to a yuppie guy like you, but you might have some fun with it, just the same. Maybe you'll take a good-looking girl out for dinner."

Why would he give me the money and ask me to return it the next year? What did he mean by the qualities that I had? I was curious to say the least.

"I've got everything put away. Should we disappear?" Kristin asked.

"Wait a minute," I said. "What do you mean? What do you want with me?"

"One second, sweetheart ... I think that James is truly the one," Max said, pushing both the money and hat back into my hand. "James, if you want to learn the true secrets of life's magic, then you must first accomplish a great feat."

"What feat? What do you mean?" I asked.

"James, you must be patient and observant. If you are patient, in time, life will reveal its greatest secrets. If you are observant, you will learn to recognize them. James, always be on the lookout for the magical opportunities in your life. The magic life will be yours only if you explore them. This could be one of those magical opportunities. Every second conceals within it, a lifetime – every minute, an eternity."

"Great for you," Kristin called to me, "I look forward to seeing you next year." She then walked over to me, reached out and took my hand in hers. Standing directly in front of me, smiling her nearly angelic smile, she gazed up at me and said, "Thank you, Jim, for participating in my life."

With that she rose up on her toes and leaned her face forward to kiss me. Naturally, I closed my eyes as I felt her warm lips softly press against my own. The moment was very fleeting. Kissing her softly, I felt her warm touch slowly vanishing. Her hands seemed to vaporize in my grasp, leaving me holding nothing but air. Suddenly, I was aware of the cool wind and the empty streets as I opened my eyes to discover that I was standing at the curb, alone – not a trace of Kristin or Max. The sun was now below the horizon and the evening breeze whispered around me. I stood there for several minutes staring down at my watch in disbelief – it was late evening. I wouldn't have believed that any of it had ever happened, but, like an experience out of the *Twilight Zone,* there in my left hand was the magician's top hat filled with dollars and coins.

As I made my way back across town, to the parking garage, I played the strange scene over in my mind. I could visualize Kristin and myself strapping Max into the jacket; I could see the agony on his face as he pulled himself free. I could see him vanish under the cloth. But I couldn't see how it was possible. It all seemed like a dream: the feelings, the small white piece of cloth, the test.

What did he mean when he said I was *"the one?"*

"Be On The Lookout –
For Life's Magical Opportunities."

Chapter 3

The next morning I awoke to the blaring of some loud, unintelligible rock and roll mixed with the annoying buzz of the alarm-clock radio. Dismayed to find that the weekend was already history, I sleepily rolled out of bed and stumbled into the shower. Wouldn't it be great if I'd just dozed off after working too late once again on a Friday evening – that I might somehow wake up back in my office to find myself gawking up at the clock with the whole weekend still ahead of me? Eventually, I succumbed to the shower's warm water and the illusion vanished. Reality set in – Monday morning. Yuck.

Wrapping a towel around my dripping body, I climbed out of the shower and strolled into the kitchen to make my morning cup of Java. It was still there. After staying up half the night counting it over and over, it was now lying in proper little stacks on the kitchen table. The cold hard cash was confirmation that the weekend's strange event was not a dream, and certainly not an illusion.

Yes, of course, the incredible and amazing Max Vi was right – precisely twenty-one dimes, one-hundred and eighty-four nickels, five-hundred-seventeen pennies, one-hundred and ninety-two quarters, thirty-eight one dollar bills, one five spot and one ten. Exactly $117.47, just as the magician had predicted. *"Some kind of trick,"* I thought. *"Who does he think he is, Nostradamus?"*

Picking up the magician's top hat from off the table, I tossed it to the floor. Then balancing the hat with my foot, I tried to flip it up onto my head, the way that Max Vi had – close, but no cigar. The hat's brim ricocheted off my head into my spice rack. The oregano crashed to the counter, spilling everywhere.

"Maybe I'd be more coordinated after my coffee," I thought. As I began to wipe up the mess, I couldn't help but notice something odd. The spice jar had tumbled onto an open magazine, landing face down on a Coors beer ad. The ad that used to read "Coors is the one" now appeared to read *"You're* the one." Exhaling a quick breath, I chuckled sort of nervously as that icy chill rushed up my spine.

Just a coincidence, my imagination was probably just getting the best of me. I looked at it again, more closely. The words didn't actually look like, "You're the one." They really looked more like *"Coor're* is the one." And I practically had to squint to make it say that – yeah, my overactive imagination again. That's all. Even though I had rationalized the incident away, still, seeing the words written made me a little uneasy. I couldn't help thinking about what Max had said. *Me? The one?* Right.

Oh my God, maybe the one who was going to be late for work! I hadn't noticed how much time I'd spent messing around with all of the stuff. I was no more *"the one"* than Max was a CPA – whatever *"the one"* was supposed to be. And this "one" had to get to work pronto.

I rushed though the morning traffic, still, I arrived to work five minutes late. It was the wrong Monday to show up late. Mr. Braeback, the office manager, had already moved everyone into the conference room for a surprise reprimand concerning the art of vanishing paper clips, disappearing pencils, and evaporating staplers. I considered just skipping the meeting altogether and stealthily making my way to my office cubicle. However, fear, as well as guilt, forced me to choose the more honorable course of action. I opted to slip into the meeting late, attempting to go unnoticed.

I thought that I had it made, opening the back door just enough to squeeze through and into the meeting without catching old "Back-breaker's" attention. But before he finished his less than clever repartee, he looked straight at me and snarled, "James, I would appreciate a little more effort towards timeliness on your part."

So much for my sneaking in unnoticed. The entire group turned to give me the third degree, as if they were perfect angels plucking their harps and I was Satan himself, interrupting their concert with an off-key accordion.

"Yes sir," I replied, plastering a plastic smile on my face. Outside, I played the good employee and accepted my reprimand with quiet dignity as I found a seat. Inside, I was once again disheartened with my job. The meeting dragged on and on – same old stories, same old windbag. It gave me acid indigestion. Would I ever get back to my desk and to some real work?

When the meeting had finally died, my motivation had died with it. Consequently, the balance of the morning was spent alternating between wishing that I'd just stayed home in bed and daydreaming about becoming a magician – actually, the greatest magician that the world had ever known. The numbers across the computer's ledger sheet blurred as I pictured myself sawing a beautiful lady in half and levitating a grand piano into the air. Maybe I would have lions and tigers in my act or catch a speeding bullet in my teeth. No, to be really great I'd have to make the Statue of Liberty disappear, like David Copperfield. Wait, I've got it, something different – I would make a battleship disappear from the high seas and then make it reappear in someplace like Central Park!

It was really quite the daydream till Braeback walked up to my desk, glared down at me over his bifocal glasses, tapping his watch. "Timeliness, James," he snapped.

Reality set in. As if by some evil black magic I was right back where I had been before my mystical weekend – no one special, just good old James, the bean counter. Hell, I was no one important.

Then again, maybe I shouldn't be so hard on myself. After all, I was good at my job – I had a brass recognition plaque to prove it. I wasn't exactly *unhappy* with work; I had received ample promotions, earned great money, and made plenty of friends.

But I felt alive when I was in front of that festival crowd – as though I didn't belong within the audience. I belonged in front of the audience. When I pictured the old woman, who had believed that I was part of the magician's act, I knew we gave her something that no one could ever take away: a moment of true magic, the magic of enjoying life, forgetting the everyday drudgery. She felt the magic of living; I knew it.

Perhaps I should have listened to my father. "Follow your heart," he would always say. He encouraged my magic when I was a little boy, especially the world famous *"cut-the-rope-in-half trick."* One trick that I would torture him with daily. He used to just sit and watch patiently, smiling, waiting for me to say, "ta da!"

"That's great!" he would say. "Now put it back together and you'll really have something!" He would go on to say that he knew my destiny was to someday become a great magician. Of course the next day he'd say it was my destiny to be a great surgeon, mechanic, or great banker. "Son," he'd say, "as far as I'm concerned, you can be anything you want to be ... except unhappy."

Dad was always happy. He really knew how to enjoy life, such a joker. I certainly missed my old man. It's easy to miss someone who is always happy – funny how you can remember certain things. When I was very young he once told me, "James, it's better to die a happy pauper than a miserable rich man." Too young to understand the word, "pauper," I mistakenly thought that he had said "papa." So, I asked him if he was a "happy papa." After a laugh, he told me that he was indeed my "happy papa." That's when my childhood nickname for my dad became: "Happy Papa." He died, my happy papa, when I was just thirteen – I guess I never really got over his death. Funny how I remember that so clearly.

My mother, brother and I were left miserably poor. When father died, being the oldest boy, I felt that I had somehow inherited the burden of responsibility to raise our family. At Dad's funeral, my Uncle Ray put his hand on my shoulder and said, "You have to be a good soldier and take care of your mother now." But Mom was the real soldier, in fact, the General; I never stood a chance against her.

"Hard work puts food on the table – not daydreams," Mom used to say. I know she resented Dad for leaving us behind; hell, I resented him, too.

She'd come home from work completely worn out, but never too tired to tell us how tired she was and to divulge her secrets to success. "If you don't work hard, nothing hardly works. The squirrel that doesn't save anything for winter will starve. Luck stands for labor under correct knowledge. An honest man works an honest day." It was a steady stream of platitudes.

Bless her heart. She did work hard to see that Carl and I got through college. I finally got my CPA. My brother Carl – well, Carl chose to follow the old man's advice. Now he carried forward the family tradition: poverty – a family tradition that I could've lived without. However, Carl always followed his dreams. He was an actor and swore that he'd never leave the theater. Actually, I don't know if he'd really been in *the theater*. He spent most of his time doing odd jobs to support his *theater* career. Still, he had occasionally impressed us with a television commercial and even though he didn't earn much, he was persistent. Someday, I believed, his persistence would be rewarded.

Mom was right; hard work had paid off for me. I had over forty thousand dollars in investments, a lakeside condo practically paying for itself in tax deductions, a Volvo, and a top-of-the-line music video system. Yet, I had to keep asking myself, "Why am I so miserable?"

Mom kept saying, "You'd be happy if you'd just find yourself a nice girl, settle down and make me a grandma." Sometimes she didn't hesitate to add a "Goddamnit!" Maybe she was right about making her a grandma, one problem – I couldn't do it alone. Sure, I'd had relationships and I'd been through the dating scene, however, with very limited success. Never seemed to find the right girl – or when I found the *"right"* girl, she thought I was the *"wrong"* guy. Definitely I was carrying a deficit in the relationship column. That went for friends, too. Most of my college buddies were now married with children. Once they were married, they moved on to their "married" friends, leaving me behind – almost friendless.

In the midst of my brooding about life, a wonderful memory from the past came walking in the door – Gina Lee. Gina was one of those women blessed with the total package: a great sense of humor, a golden heart, a good head on her shoulders, not to mention a *heavenly* body. I really was not going to mention that. Her looks were the kinds that make men sigh and women gag when she wasn't looking.

Gina walked right up to my desk and stopped, flirtatiously saying, "Good morning, Jim. Did ya miss me?"

THE MAGIC LIFE

Gina and I had some history, both of us growing up in the same part of Houston, attending the same high school and junior high. In fact, Gina was my very first date, the junior prom (what can I say, I was a slow starter). Memories like that stay with a person. I was so shy, I remember hanging up the phone a dozen times before I actually dialed all the numbers. When I finally did ask her out, I was so nervous that I had to read from a written script I'd laid out on my bed in front of me. But in spite of my canned speech and shaky voice, she said yes.

"Good morning, Gina," I replied, smiling too, yet trying not to reveal my enthusiasm about seeing her first thing in the morning. (And I certainly wasn't going to tell her that I might have missed her.)

She began to fumble through her purse looking for something as she said, "I've got a little something in here for you."

Not even realizing what she'd said, I found myself thinking back to that first date. Boy, I had such a big time crush on that beautiful little blond girl. Meeting her parents, I was absolutely terrified. I just knew that her father wouldn't like me. Gina had warned me that Mr. Lee had played football in college and was darn proud of it. Athlete I was not. Back then I was something of a ninety-eight-pound weakling. Of course her dad was the one that answered the door that night. Gina was being fashionably late (probably so that she could make that grand entrance walking down the stairs). Good in theory, but it left her dad and me attempting to make small talk. Wouldn't you know it, right off the bat he asked me if I played on the football team. Like an idiot I told him that I preferred debate. Unfortunately, not the right answer – not even close. Not that he chastised me. Instead, after that statement, he chose to pretty much just ignore me.

"How was your weekend? Did you go to the Pecan Street Festival?" Gina asked, her manner suggesting that she might have seen me.

"Yes, I did as a matter of fact," I said, slightly embarrassed by the thought that she might have seen me locked up in the straitjacket, but semi-wishing that she had.

"I wish I'd seen you there; we could've had a lot of fun together," Gina said still in a search through the purse.

Even though talking with her dad was strained, conversation always came easy with Gina. We really seemed compatible. And even though the prom date had ended with an unexpected and rather abrupt handshake, I still maintained a high school crush on her. For a while she even shared my locker. I wanted to ask her to go steady, but I was just too darn shy. Privately though, I fantasized that maybe someday after college I'd even marry her. Gina went to Europe the summer after the junior prom, and we lost touch before anything could really develop between us. My senior year, Gina was a cheerleader and started dating the captain of the football team. How could I compete with that? I didn't even try. So we just drifted apart.

I hadn't seen her since high school, that was, until my first day of work at Lee, Fellers and Gadheart. Not having any idea that her family had moved to Austin, I was clue-less that her father was the "Lee" in the accounting firm that I had joined. When I saw her after all those years though, my heart still skipped a beat. Fate had thrown Gina and me together again. For a moment I thought that we might even start dating, possibly rekindle our high school romance.

However, it was not to be. One of the other accountants, Mark, informed me on my first day at work that Gina was completely hands off. Anyone making a pass at her would be terminated. He wasn't kidding. He showed me the actual memorandum. In plain English it meant that if I valued my career – which I did – then I would simply have to continue to fantasize about her in private. Since Mr. Lee, the boss, already had pegged me as a loser back in high school, I knew that I would never be able to ask her out now.

To make my life even more wonderfully difficult, Gina was always stopping by my desk – just to say hello – whenever she was on the way in to see "Daddy." Four and a half years of dropping by my desk, saying hello, giving me cards, telling me jokes, and flirting had made me crazy about her all over again. Once again, I'd just have to fight off those feelings.

"There it is," she said with a smile as she pulled out a small red envelope and laid it down in front of me.

Curiously, I picked up the envelope, semi-relieved that she hadn't seen me looking like an idiot at the festival. Looking over the envelope, I spied my name, carefully hand-scrolled in calligraphy on the front. "What's this?" I asked.

THE MAGIC LIFE

"It's just a silly card. Don't read it until you go home," she said, stopping me from tearing it open. Then, quickly changing the subject, she asked, "Did you see the magician at the corner of Sixth and Lavaca Streets?"

I nodded an immediate, "Yes, he was great!"

She continued to describe the magician's act, "He did the most incredible things, didn't he? When he cut the girl in the audience in half, I thought that I would just die. Do you know how they do that?"

"I didn't see him cut anyone in half. We did – I mean, he did a different act," I said, not knowing if I had just made a Freudian slip. (Perhaps I secretly wanted her to see me performing with the magician.)

"Was that you? You're the one, the one that I saw in the straitjacket thing," Gina said, "I thought that was you, but I didn't know for sure. There was such a big crowd and we were way in the back and couldn't really see. We didn't stop and watch because there were so many people. The girls I was with wanted to move on. Besides, we'd seen him earlier. If I'd only known that that was you," she slapped me gently on the shoulder, "I would've stopped and taken a picture."

Before I had the time to express my slight embarrassment about being in the straitjacket, Mr. Lee, her father, the boss, came marching around the corner. "Well, good morning, Gina darling. Did you remember to bring me the journal that I left on the desk? Good morning, James. How was your weekend?" Mr. Lee asked, acknowledging my presence, but not really waiting for an answer.

"Yes, Daddy, I did," Gina replied to his question. "See you later, magic man." With that she turned the corner and walked with her father down the hall, into his office. As she looked back over her shoulder, I could have sworn that she winked at me. Then as her father closed the office door, I heard her say, "Daddy, guess what? It was him. James is the one..." With that the door to the office closed. I couldn't help thinking that it was strange to hear those words again.

"The one?" I asked myself.

Quite taken aback, I now gazed down at the ruby red envelope in my hand. The card was a totally unexpected flirtatious gesture. Oh sure, Gina and I had had our intense ten or fifteen minute conversations, and sometimes we even exchanged those "looks." One year at the company Christmas party we were alone and in an empty office, talking about what we found the most attractive in the opposite sex, and she told me that she liked a man who could dance. Well, I'd had just enough to drink that I pulled her in close and began a slow seductive lambada – "the forbidden dance." Just as I did, I overheard her father walking toward the office, talking to someone. That ended the "forbidden" dance. The thought of losing my high-paying job actually had me shaking as he entered the room, but he didn't suspect anything. Turned out he just wanted to introduce a new client to his daughter.

I was so relieved that we didn't get caught that, well, from that moment on, bound by my own fear, I became determined to honor Mr. Lee's orders: "Anyone so much as lays eyes on Gina – he is standing in the unemployment line!"

Why did she keep flirting? Was she just naturally a flirt?

Then it dawned on me – my birthday. I had completely forgotten. That was why she had given me the card. At five minutes past ten o'clock I would be twenty-nine years old. Unbelievable. *What happened to my twenties?* Not that twenty-nine was *that* bad, not like the dreaded thirty-something. At least there was one more year to live. Looking down at the card, I smiled. Even though I was absolutely dying to open it, I placed it in my breast pocket next to my heart, deciding to wait until I got home as Gina had requested.

Soon I was absorbed in my work and the hours flew by. Gina had since come and gone with a short, flirty hello, good-bye. When lunch time rolled around, a couple of the other CPA's came to my desk, offering to take me to Bennigan's restaurant for a birthday lunch. I thought their company would be better than eating alone, so I agreed to go. However, by the time we had deciphered which car to take, just where we would all sit, and whether or not we needed separate checks, I was ready to re-think the disadvantages to dining alone.

We were nearly all seated in the restaurant and I had just about resigned myself to having a boring time when Gina suddenly dashed in. "Do you mind if I join you?" she asked, waving at the group.

"That would be great," I said, standing up and suddenly feeling a whole lot better about the luncheon.

THE MAGIC LIFE

Mark Silverberg was about to sit down next to me, but Gina lowered her eyebrows giving him *a look,* accompanied with a pleasant, "Don't you think we should sit, girl, boy, girl?"

Mark was agreeable to taking a different seat, allowing Gina to slip in next to me. This was perfectly all right with me, however, even though his actions were practically sanctioning it, Mark stared back at me with one of those cold looks of his own as if to remind me, "You'd better be on the lookout for Daddy."

The conversation started off kind of slow at first; all anyone wanted to talk about was work. Having promised myself to avoid that mundane subject as much as possible, I asked Mark, the wild one of the bunch, about his weekend. Mark had something of a reputation for getting crazy and I hoped his lurid tales would stir up some clever conversation. No such luck. Mark non-enthusiastically replied that over the weekend he had come into the office and worked a few extra hours. This was the only conversation. This was followed by a long silence from everyone. *Were they really all just as bored and uncomfortable as I was, only being polite because it was my birthday?*

Determined to break the almost deadly silence, looking for some sort of icebreaker to start conversation rolling, I asked if anyone besides Gina had witnessed the incredible magician at the Pecan Street Festival.

The answer sounded like a skipping record. "No ... no ... no ... no."

Then like a breath of fresh air into the stench of boredom, Mark suddenly spoke up saying, "Speaking of magicians, would you all like to see a magic trick?"

I was aghast that such a sudden burst of creativity could evolve from this group. *We're not magicians. We're accountants for God's sake!* Quickly I blurted out, "Yes, I'm sure we'd all like to see the trick, Mark." Anything, I thought. Everyone else seemed equally enthused to get some semblance of conversation rolling.

"Okay, it's not very good, but it's something you can do with matches," Mark mumbled nervously. He clumsily pulled a pack of matches out of his pocket and proceeded to tear out seventeen of the matches, counting them out and crisscrossing them on top of one another as he did.

"I will pick up six of these matches and leave nine," he said, then scooped up six of the matches. "There you have it." The remaining eleven crisscrossed matches formed the word "nine". "How's that for an accounting miracle?" he asked.

"That's great," I said, secretly hoping that the one trick was both his debut and finale. Yet, I applauded his effort to change the subject to something other than work. At least he was making an attempt.

We both realized that his attempt had succeeded when Karen, a slightly chubby, quiet associate, slurping her bean soup, asked, "Don't you know a trick, James? I heard that you did magic when you were a kid."

"How did that get out?" I asked, "That was a long time ago and I really don't do it anymore."

Gina chimed in, "James and I went to junior high together, and he used to be quite the magician, if I recall. I seem to remember that you won the junior high talent show, didn't you, Jim?"

"The junior high talent show? That *was* a long time ago. How did you remember that?" I asked of a memory I had long forgotten.

"Oh, only because you beat me, and I was a wicked baton twirler," Gina stated, laughing at herself. "Too bad for all of you that I don't have a baton to twirl, but you can still do a trick for us, can't you, James?"

"Well, it's true, I did a couple of tricks when I was just a boy, but it's been such a long time. I don't know if I could remember any," I said. All of a sudden, I realized why Mark had been shaking. The thought of actually doing something with the whole group watching my every move was somewhat alarming, even frightening. "The eighth grade talent show was an awful long time ago," I said, hoping to get out of it.

"Oh, I thought I overheard something about you doing magic at the festival last weekend," said Karen. "You are *the one*, aren't you?"

Again, there it was "*the one.*" As she said it, I felt that strange tingle come over me. It was as if something was telling me that I should at least give it a try. Something the magician had said came back to me, *"Always be on the lookout for the magical opportunities in your life. The magic life will be yours if you explore them."* Deep inside I knew they all wanted, just as desperately as I did, for this lunch to be fun and exciting. Maybe this was one of those "magical opportunities" Max had been talking about.

37

"Come on James, show us a trick! Pleeeease," Karen asked.

They were all trying so hard to make it enjoyable for me and I was *"the one"* letting them down; my reluctant attitude was making the event a miserable failure. That was about to change.

"Well, I do know this one trick that I used to do at the dinner table when I was a boy," I said. "Does anyone have a quarter I can borrow?"

Karen applauded, "Yea!" as Mark quickly fished in his pocket, pulling out a quarter. He handed it to me, joking that he expected interest at twelve percent compounded *"quarter"*ly.

Everyone laughed, including me, as I took the quarter from his hand. "I will make this quarter vanish in the same way that it has been done for a thousand years," I proclaimed, placing the quarter on the tablecloth in front of me. And in spite of my stage fright, I was actually excited about the idea of having a good time.

"I know how I make quarters disappear," Mark chimed in, "I spend them." Wonder of wonders, everyone laughed again.

Setting the quarter in the center of the table, I then placed the salt shaker over the top of it, covering it completely. Next I unfolded my napkin and wrapped it around and over the salt shaker so that I could lift up the wrapped-up salt shaker and show the not-yet-vanished quarter. "Watch closely," I said, my voice beginning to crack a little. "Make sure I can't slip the quarter from under the shaker and napkin. If you'll all just say the magic word, it will vanish."

"Abracadabra," said Karen.

I lifted the napkin and salt shaker to reveal the still un-vanished quarter. "Everyone has to say the magic word or it won't work," I added.

"Abracadabra!" the table responded, including the waiter who had stopped to watch and now found himself repeating the magic words.

Then I pressed my hand down sharply upon the napkin, which had earlier retained the shape of the salt shaker underneath – but no more. "You all have more magic than you know – the salt shaker, not the quarter, has vanished." Indeed it had vanished into thin air, thanks to a little sleight of hand I'd learned years ago – a sleight allowing me to drop the salt shaker into my lap while I misdirected their attention to the quarter.

"I can't believe it!" said Mark.

"That was incredible," Karen added.

Sighing with relief that it had actually worked, I grinned all over. However, checking to my right, I discovered that Gina had caught me. Glancing down into my lap, from her vantage point she could see the salt shaker where no one else around the table could. The secret was exposed. Well, so much for trying to be magical. I was about to throw in the towel and say, "Well, you caught me." But, just when I thought that I had been foiled, Gina surprised me by not telling anyone else. In fact, the opposite, she just smiled and very convincingly said, "James, you are amazing!"

Then she did something that I really didn't expect at all. After suggesting a quick round of applause, without looking down, she reached into my lap secretly taking the salt shaker, and slyly placed it into her purse, saying, "Stand up and take a bow, James."

So, I did. Saying in my best Elvis impression, "Thank you very muuuch."

"Where is it?" they asked. "Tell us how you did it," came at me from everyone. I realized at that moment that I had done it; I had truly made them believe in the magic.

Gina, in the meantime, had nonchalantly placed her purse, now containing the saltshaker, in the middle of the table saying, "James if you're really magic, you'll make it appear somewhere else."

She was great; I couldn't have planned it any better. For once I picked up on my queue, saying, "Okay, how about if I make it appear in your purse."

Gina opened her purse with a look of surprise that should have garnered an Oscar. "I can't believe it!" she said pulling the salt shaker from the purse.

The rest were as astounded by the silly trick as I was by their reaction.

Mark stood up saying tongue-in-cheek, "Come on people, let's give him the standing 'o'!"

At that given moment I enjoyed a gratifying sense of wonderment in my life, the same feeling that I had when I first publicly performed magic as a teenager. The experience brought back my lost memory of standing on the stage at Ludlum Junior High, the night I won the eighth-grade talent show.

THE MAGIC LIFE

On stage that night I wasn't a bit nervous. I recalled looking down at the trophy in my hands, a moment in my life that I'd completely forgotten. Even though the trophy was just six inches tall, gold-painted plastic, I remember it felt like ten feet of solid gold. And now, even though it was just a lunch at Bennigan's, it may as well have been Carnegie Hall. That's the positive feeling I got.

Soon everyone was engaged in casual conversation, joking, laughing and enjoying lunch. Just before time to go, the waiters and waitresses appeared with a cake lit up like a miniature forest fire, singing some absurd happy birthday song, and making me wear a dorky paper dunce hat. No one even noticed Gina reaching over, squeezing my hand. I hadn't felt so silly in years. But it felt great, childlike – I was truly satisfied knowing that the real magic was the transformation of this lethargic group into an energetic party – not just by a simple trick, but by changing my attitude.

As we left the restaurant, I really didn't get the opportunity to tell Gina thank-you and, unfortunately, when I got back to the office she was nowhere in sight.

The rest of the day passed rather quickly with five o'clock arriving before I knew it. Mr. Lee stopped by my desk on his way out to tell me to call it a day and go home. "By the way, Gina reminded me that it's your birthday today," he said. "How many years is it now?"

"Only twenty-nine," I answered.

"Well, you're not quite out of the running yet then," he said adding, "you know what they say – a man trades in his dreams for security at age thirty."

After that depressing remark, he asked me if I had seen his daughter and I answered that I hadn't seen her since earlier in the day. Mr. Lee turned around and was off to catch the elevator, concluding an episode of casual conversation longer than any I'd ever had with the boss. He never really spent much time talking with the underlings like myself, so I should have felt privileged, I suppose. Instead, I was slightly disappointed, because, for just a minute there I thought he might reach into his checkbook and pull out a birthday bonus. Maybe he felt that his words of wisdom were bonus enough. Though I didn't really believe that everyone "trades in their dreams for security at age thirty."

After packing up some work to finish at home, I walked through the office toward the elevator. Almost all of the workstations were empty, all the office doors shut. I felt like a tumbleweed blowing through a ghost town. It always amazed me how quickly the office emptied at the stroke of five. Just waiting an extra few minutes, I always avoided the mass exodus, making a clear easy shot to the elevator.

As I waited for the elevator I pulled the birthday card from Gina out of my pocket, gazing at it until the doors opened. Stepping in, I pushed the button for the garage floor. Just when the doors began to close, to my surprise, Gina rounded the corner calling, "Hold please." When she discovered it was me in the elevator, her face lit up with a smile. As I shuffled the card into my briefcase, I too, found myself smiling, wishing that I would somewhere find courage to punch the button, stop the elevator between the floors and passionately embrace this beautiful woman.

Could I? That was exactly what I was going to do! My heart started pounding; because, just for a moment, I believed I really could.

"James," she said, interrupting my fantasy, "we made a pretty good team, today. Don't you think?"

"Yeah, we sure did," I said, "I wanted to say thank you, but I didn't get the chance. I had a good time. Did you?"

"Yes, I did," she answered, "And you're welcome."

She glanced up at me and our eyes collided like two shooting stars unwilling to change their course. This was the opportunity that I'd been waiting for. The appropriate thing to do would be to continue gazing into her eyes, clutch her tightly, tell her I loved her and kiss her with all that passion I'd held back over the years.

Just once, I wished that I could listen to my heart, but instead I simply rode the elevator silently, watching my golden opportunity dwindle with the diminishing of each lighted number as we passed each floor descending to the garage. Upon reaching our final stop, the chance was gone; we said our standard "have a nice night" and then parted.

Wishing that I was someone else, someone less timid, I trudged over to my car then paused briefly before opening the door to watch Gina pull away. Somehow I always felt better after I saw Gina safely on her way. Putting the key into the car's lock, turning it, and slowly pulling the door open, I had unsettling thoughts. If I kept thinking about Gina this way, I was going to get myself into big trouble. *I'd better just stop it.*

With that thought, I tossed my briefcase onto the passenger seat and spied the ruby red card, still unopened, falling out onto the seat. I'd completely forgotten about the card when she entered into the elevator.

I tore open the envelope. The card read:

"You're the one who makes my day,
When I'm feeling kinda blue,
The one I want to know,
Much better than I do.
Happy Birthday"

And it was signed, "Love, Gina."

Why did she do have to go and do that? I just stared at the card. I must have opened and shut it fifty times. She had written, *"Love."* It wasn't *"love ya"* or *"with love."* It was just *"love."* I felt like such a kid — silly, I guess.

Then I recognized it. There it was again. *"You're the one."* As I realized that I was seeing the words I felt that familiar tingle streak up my spine. Suddenly I became uneasy. I had this strange feeling that I was being watched. Cautiously, I peeked up out of the corner of my eye into my rear-view mirror to check the back seat. Not really afraid, but somehow, for some unknown reason, I half expected that magician to materialize in the seat behind me. However, nothing happened, nothing at all. On that account, by simply reminding myself that it was my 29th birthday, I relaxed with a sigh. The stress of growing old was probably just getting to me.

Giving the card one last look before placing it back in my pocket, I nonchalantly turned the key and listened to the purr of the Volvo for a second before heading back to the condo. There, in my standard evening routine, I stopped and picked up my mail before entering, slapped the button on the answering machine, and made a beeline to the refrigerator. The electronic voice informed me that I had two messages. The first was a happy birthday from my brother, giving me a few jabs about getting old. The second was from my mother asking if I liked the tie that she'd sent. I couldn't really say since it hadn't arrived yet, but I could guess it would be nice and conservative. All in all a good birthday, so I popped a *Budget Gourmet Dinner* into the microwave, kicked off my loafers, and turned on the TV.

After eating a little dinner, watching a little TV, and catching up on a little work, I hit the hay. *So, this is twenty-nine?*

Before long I was fast asleep and found myself in that place between space and time – dreaming. In this dream I'm only thirteen years old, standing on the gymnasium stage after the eighth-grade talent show. The show has already ended and they have presented the awards. Proudly I display the first place trophy, which I can't believe I've won, as a reporter for the local paper snaps a picture. Most of the attendees have already made their way home, leaving the basketball court littered with empty metal folding chairs and scattered with discarded Xeroxed programs. Only a few straggling kids, ones who took part in the show, and the parents of the stragglers remain. Mom and Dad step up on the stage to congratulate me with Carl riding Dad piggyback style. I'm holding the trophy proudly as my father gives me a bear hug. Mom readies us for a picture, telling me to turn the trophy so that she can read the inscription through the camera. As I turn the trophy, it slips in my hands and I accidentally drop it over the edge of the stage. We all watch as, in slow motion, the trophy smashes onto the hardwood floor below breaking into a thousand pieces.

With the smashing of the trophy the dream suddenly changes, and now seems somehow familiar, a scene I've dreamt before. Full grown, I am sitting on a hard metal chair, two uniformed police officers strap me into a straitjacket; one of the officers locks my ankles in. Now I remember – yes – this is the dream where I escape from the straitjacket while hanging in mid air. But something doesn't feel right. Something is wrong.

The straitjacket fits very tight, and for a moment I struggle. The police officer looks up at me, and for the first time I see his face – Mr. Lee! He smiles a smile that chills me to the bone, saying, "Well, James, you're not quite out of the running yet – you know a man trades in his dreams for security at age thirty," My heart starts to pound; something is definitely wrong with this dream.

A beautiful blond woman steps onto the platform carrying a burning torch. I can feel the heat coming from the torch and hear the sound of the wind-blown flame. Once the woman is close enough for me to see her face, I know her – it's Gina! "Good luck, magic-man," she says, lighting the rope on fire. "We make a great team, don't we?" Then she smiles, blows me a kiss, turns and walks off the stage.

The music starts and I can hear the master of ceremonies. Something is different here, too. "Either this man will have to escape, learn to fly, or drop two-hundred feet to his death." I know this voice, it's the magician; the MC is Maximillion Vi. *"James, you're the one,"* he laughs as he engages the lever which starts the crane in motion.

"Wait, I know this dream; I don't get out. I don't escape! I fall!" I am frantically shouting, "No! No! Stop, stop!" But the music becomes too loud, overpowering my cry for help as the sound of the crane's engine kicks in. My ankles are jerked suddenly, and I am hoisted rapidly into the sky. In a panic, I twist back and forth upside down, trying to free myself from the restraint. Higher, higher. Too late, the rope snaps and I am falling, "Aaaagggghhh!!"

Next thing I knew, I hit the bed again with a thud. My heart still racing – what a nightmare. The images faded fast before I could piece them together exactly. However, this time I did remember most of the dream – something to do with escaping from the straitjacket, falling, and the magician telling me, "You're the one."

"Nothing Will Happen –
Unless You Make It Happen."

Chapter 4

L ooking over at the dining table at the $117.47, I realized that I'd better make a trip to the bank soon. Having all that cash just lying there wasn't doing any good for anyone. At least in the bank I'd gain a few months' interest before the Spring Festival.

All of the strange coincidences, strange comments, and even stranger dreams had me riled up, bound and determined to not just forget and go on with life. After all, it wasn't as if $117.47 was a lot of money to me. I really didn't quite get the point to his strange experiment, however, he certainly had gotten my attention with his mysterious methods. Enough so, that I vowed out loud, "Upon my father's grave, I will return to the festival in six months if nothing more than just to see the look on his face when I return the money, plus interest." Under pressure I always tended to get a little over-dramatic.

Curiosity being one of my strongest suits, rather than worry about it, I thought, *"Why not take a little initiative and find him? Why wait?"* Pulling out the phone book, I looked under magic and magicians. Maybe just a long shot, but I might find the old Max Vi master magician listed in Yellow Pages. I riffled through the sections for both magicians and entertainers. No such luck. Only three magicians were listed in the local book: Fingers the Magnificent, Bimmy the Clown, and the Incredible Martini. Now I felt my creativity, driven by my insatiable curiosity, challenged. *How does one find a magician when he really needs one?*

I decided to try calling each of the magicians to see if they had heard of Maximillion Vi. Bimmy the Clown didn't answer. Neither did Fingers the Magnificent, but I did leave a message after listening to some recorded foolish banter about fun for all and thrills of a lifetime.

The Incredible Martini, however, was there.

"Martini's Magical Mystery Show," he answered.

"Hi, my name is James, perhaps you can help me. I'm looking for a magician," I stated.

"Well, I'm a magician and I work cheap," he chuckled.

"No, I'm afraid I misled you. I meant that I am trying to contact a magician by the name of Max Vi," I said. "Would you, by chance, know him or know how I might find him?"

"Well, I don't know of anyone going by that name, but if it's a show you want, I'm reasonably priced and really quite good, I might add. Humility, though, is not one of my best qualities. It's so hard to be humble when you're omniscient, you know. Anyway, I do this one trick in which I eat a lighted cigarette, swallow a fish, and then..."

He sounded so enthusiastic, I almost hated to interrupt. No use for him to work so hard. "I'm sorry but I'm not looking for a show; I just have something I'd like to return to him," I said, cutting off his sales pitch.

"Well, if you're sure that that's all you need, let me tell you. If you really want to get in touch with a magician just click your heels three times and ask, 'What is the number for the Society of American Magicians?' If he isn't a member, then he's probably not much of a magician anyway," he said.

"Do you have that number?" I asked, "I didn't even know there was such a thing as the Magician's Society."

"Sure, just a minute," he said, and I could hear him put down the phone and search for it. Picking up again, he continued, "Hello, yes, I've got it right here. It's area code 317-243-0774. If this magician you're looking for is among the living, then chances are that he's a member and they'll be able to help you find him."

"Thanks, I really appreciate your help."

"You're welcome and have an absolutely magical day!" he articulated like a true performer. Hanging up, I found myself thinking that he was really a nice guy in a crazy sort of way. However, I knew that I wouldn't be able to get in touch with anyone from the Society of American Magicians at this late hour. It was already past eight o'clock. Anyway, did I really want to make a long distance call just to find out where this magician came from? I could write the society a letter from my office or wait until spring. Then the timer went off on my microwave, and putting the question far behind me, I settled in for a dinner of Salisbury steak, mashed potatoes, and evening news.

The days that followed passed more like years as the winter cold and flu season came and went. The extremely plodding pace I credited mostly to the monotony of my bleak existence, the same each day: work, television, sleep; work, television, sleep. Some days I would really mix it up: sleep, work, television. Once in a while, I did manage to create a little mental diversion by further searching for the elusive Max Vi. However, all attempts to find the magician were futile. When he vanished from the street festival, he really vanished into thin air. I'd contacted practically every professional magician in the state as well as the Society of American Magicians, and the International Brotherhood of Magicians, but to no avail. This particular magician was at the very least an unknown, maybe a figment of my imagination, or perhaps he just plain didn't want to be found.

There was one bright spot in my searching: I may not have found Max Vi, but I uncovered an old friend. The search, reviving my interest in the art of magic, prompted me to take a weekend to visit my mother's house with a distinct purpose – a scavenger hunt. My mission was to go though the attic looking for that old box of tricks I had collected as a boy.

Mom wasn't too enthusiastic about me rummaging through her attic, but eventually she consented and said she'd even accompany me (whether I wanted her to or not). Reaching the pull rope, I pulled down the access cover. A mixture of dirt and bits of insulation pelted our faces as I did. Taking care to properly unfold the collapsible wooden ladder attached to the back of the attic access, Mom determined she'd go up first. We both agreed that the ladder might fall apart if we both got on at the same time. Her real concern, of course, was that if she fell, hopefully I would be there to catch her. I didn't have the heart to tell her that if she fell on me, it would probably kill both of us. However, she didn't fall, and we both made it into the attic without incident.

Inside, the attic was piled high with cardboard boxes full of old dishes Carl and I used in college, clothes long gone out of style, and books which we'd always planned to take to the Church rummage sale. Everything was covered with a thick layer of dust. Mom moved a couple of boxes and an old lamp, declaring, "We're going to have to do some house cleaning I see. Well, Jimmy, if what you're looking for is anywhere, it'll be inside of here." Pulling off a dust cover she revealed the old trunk that Happy Papa had bought from the junkman for seven dollars. The imitation-antique finish that Dad had so meticulously applied years ago had now become authentic. "Remember this old trunk your Dad painted?" Mom asked, "I put your kid's stuff in it after I made Carl's room my sewing room."

"Yeah, I remember this old thing, all right," I said.

Opening it and looking in, between the Snoopy piggy bank, Mad magazine collection, and miscellaneous junk, I spied something else I hadn't seen for a long time – my old junior high scrap book.

"I thought I'd lost this," I said, clearing a place to set it down.

"What's that?" asked Mom, pulling up a stool next to me, adjusting her glasses.

"It's my old scrapbook, from junior high," I said, opening the front page and reacting with a smile at some pictures of Carl and me. In particular I laughed at one showing us attending a Scout meeting with Dad the night we'd entered our hand-carved, wooden race-car into the derby. We lost, but our car, "the original silver-bullet," sure looked good. The photo showed Carl holding up the wheel that fell off as it came out of the starting gate. There were a lot of great pictures with Dad and me: where he taught me how to shave, even though I didn't need to; the time he decided to be Dracula on Halloween; and when he'd taught me how to drive a tractor.

Turning the pages, I discovered photos of my friends from junior high school along with some bad poetry I had written and even a blue ribbon I'd won for a drawing I'd entered into the county fair. All of these were memories I had often recalled and cherished as time went on. However, when I opened a page near the center, it was like opening a floodgate. A river of untapped memories rushed in. As if by opening up the center of the scrapbook, I'd opened up a section of my subconscious which I hadn't accessed in many years.

These pages were filled with my tribute to magicians of the day. Here were cut outs, pictures and articles from magazines or newspapers – anything that had to do with magic. I'd forgotten how into magic I really was. There was a picture of Blackstone when he had been performing in Houston; pictures from Doug Henning's, *The Magic Show,* on Broadway, cut from a Time magazine article. There were even pictures of me performing magic shows for my parents and their friends.

There was one article that stood out from all the rest – one that almost jumped off the page. It was an article about a relatively unknown magician performing a death-defying stunt. The picture showed the magician hanging from a crane, attached to a burning rope, while bound in a straitjacket. The headline below it read: Magician Tim Glancey Goes Beyond Houdini. The origin of my nightmare was suddenly as black and white as the words that described his act. I recalled how as a teenager I had dreamt about repeating that very stunt. Only three people in the world had ever done it. I remember telling Happy Papa that I wanted to be number four.

Anxious to see what other memories I'd long forgotten, I enthusiastically turned the pages forward. Jumping ahead in the book, I noticed the pages became blank. I'd stopped putting things in the book long before it was full. There were as many pages left empty, as were filled. Making my way backward through the blank pages, I came upon the last two additions to my scrapbook. On my left hand side was an old newspaper article, the paper brown with age: "Young Magician Brings Magical Talent To Ludlum Jr. High."

The picture below the headline showed me holding my trophy, next to some other kid I didn't recognize holding second place and a little blond girl wearing a sequined leotard holding third. "Winners of the annual talent show from left to right, James Carpenter 1st Place, Elsworth Cecile 2nd Place, Gina Lee 3rd Place." Gina was so cute. I didn't even remember this picture. On the opposite page was my last entry. It was the photograph that Mom had taken of Dad and me on the stage that night just as I recalled in my dream, Dad standing next to me, Carl on his shoulders, the trophy in my hands.

THE MAGIC LIFE

"That was a night I'll never forget," said Mom, standing up, "Come on, Jimmy, I'm going down to the kitchen. I'll fix you some lunch."

"I'll be right with you," I said, but then I realized that she wanted me to go down first to catch her if she fell. So, I helped her down and then returned to scavenge some more. I never found the tricks that I was looking for, but there in amongst my high school memorabilia and dust-covered year books I found the neglected copy of the book that I'd once practically worn out as a child, *The Amateur Magician's Handbook.* Reopening that book also reawakened many magical memories of my youth.

After my lunch with Mom, I packed most of the things I'd found back into the trunk. Before taking the long drive back to Austin, I tossed only the magic book in the seat of my car, thinking I'd let Mom be the curator of the memories since she'd done such a great job of it over the years.

Other than that one episode at Mom's house, my continual search for Max over the winter months was mostly wasted energy. Maybe I should have listened when he said, *"too many of us spend too much time looking for the secret, when the answer is the magic itself."*

Persistence was on my side, however. The day of reckoning was close at hand. Tomorrow, I would at last solve the mystery of the vanishing magician, and answer the riddle of, *"You are the one."* For tomorrow was the Pecan Street Festival.

I wouldn't have been surprised to find that Max was just a part-timer who only did magic at the fall and spring festivals. But regardless of his stature among magicians, I knew that I would finally solve the $117.47 mystery. Somehow I would manage to get $117.47 out of the bank and delivered to him, complete with 7.5% interest compounded annually and in return I would find out what he meant by "you're the one." I admit I was a little curious as to the possible reward such a commitment on my part might bring – I really didn't expect any reward of the monetary kind. The answer to the questions *who*, *what*, and *why* would be enough to make me happy.

Sitting there in my office cubicle that Friday, I was totally useless – stupid with anticipation the entire day – eagerly awaiting the festival weekend ahead. I felt like a kid waiting for Santa Claus. Sure, I knew that Santa would arrive eventually, but if I weren't sleeping with at least one eye open, I could miss him.

At last it was almost quitting time. The clock hanging above the door just wouldn't cooperate either. It seemed to move slower than ever before. Staring at that frozen clock for five minutes, I had long since put my work away. The minute hand moved in painstakingly slow motion up to the twelve position, finally striking five o'clock. The weekend was here! I almost shouted out loud. Of course I didn't really yell out loud, but just for once I would have liked to yell out like Fred Flintstone does as the Friday five o'clock horn goes off, "Yaaa ba Daaa Ba Dooooooo!" That sure would wake 'em up. I didn't yell it, but I did manage a stifled "Yesss!" Just as I did, Gina walked around the corner.

"Hi, sexy," she said teasingly as she kissed her two fingers, touched my arm and made a sizzling sound, "sssssss." I hated when she did that, only because I genuinely loved it. She had begun to tease me excessively lately. And I recently came to the conclusion that she did it because she sensed that I was trying to play shy and act not interested in her. You know, the hard-to-get guy. I did have a real struggle though, keeping back a heartfelt smile whenever she called me sexy. Who wouldn't?

Even though I had had a couple of those "close encounters" with Gina over the few winter months, I knew that my best interests were still served by just admiring from afar. Occasionally, I weighed my crazy thoughts, thoughts telling me that I would give up everything just to be with her, foolish and outlandish thoughts that I could only dream. Many times I had wished that I had the guts to run away with her. The idea sounded like something that my father, Happy Papa, would have done.

"Hello, Gina," I said, trying to hold back a radiant smile but not really accomplishing it.

"You're sure in a hurry to get out of here. Have you got any big plans for the weekend?" She asked.

"As a matter of fact I do," I replied. "I am going to the Pecan Street Spring Festival. What about you?"

"Oh, I haven't got any plans yet, really," she said, hinting for an invitation from me. Never any good at that sort of thing, I didn't pick up my cue. Tired of waiting on me to make my move, she just flat out asked, "Why don't you take me with you? ... Unless you have a date or something."

I was, of course, stunned. Light-headed, bumbling, semi-paralyzed, breathless, my worst nightmare had come true; she was offering, and I had to turn her down. I couldn't believe my rotten luck, I wanted to go, but I certainly couldn't go. I had to think about my job, my livelihood. I wasn't allowed to date the boss' daughter. It was as simple as that. I told myself over and over, time and time again; some things in life one has to give up for security.

"Well, I, uh..." I groped for something to say, "I'm sorry but I can't. I mean, uh, I have to meet someone."

Disappointment fell on her face. At that moment I realized that she had taken a sincere risk in asking me. She was vulnerable, going out on a limb to make the move because she knew that I probably wouldn't. I felt awful. I'd let her down and I hated the feeling that it gave me.

Unfortunately, I just didn't hate it enough to lose my job over it.

"Oh, I didn't know that you were dating someone," she said apologetically.

"No, you don't understand. I'm not dating anyone," I said, worrying that she might give up the chase if she thought that I was taken. "I would love to go with you some other time, but this weekend I am going to meet with the magician, uh – friend of mine. He ... well, it's a long story. But, I am going specifically to see this guy. I have been waiting six months just to talk with him."

"Is it that same magician from last year?" Gina asked, showing some relief on her face.

"Yes, one and the same."

"Okay, well, maybe then we can do something some other time, like next weekend," she said. "I forgive you. I know how you magicians are about sharing secrets."

"Yeah, maybe next weekend we could do something," I replied, not even realizing then that I had made a date. Picking up my briefcase, I headed to the elevator, leaving her waving a fingered good-bye.

"Have fun, I'll see you Monday," she called out, standing there wearing her cute little Mona Lisa smile. "Don't miss me too much."

As the elevator closed, after checking to see that the elevator was empty, I clobbered myself in the head with my briefcase. "I'm such an idiot,"

I said out loud to myself. "I've been waiting for years to date Gina again and look at me now; I am a true idiot," I thought. Why not date the boss' daughter? She asked me, I didn't ask her. Why shouldn't I be happy? Why not just quit? I hated my job anyway.

Then, without any warning, the elevator lights flickered and went dark. In the blackness with a sudden jerk and a loud grinding sound the elevator halted. My heart stopped, too. "Oh shit," I whispered. For a few long seconds I stood frozen, knowing at any second the elevator would go crashing nine stories down. My knees were suddenly weak. I wouldn't know what hit me because I was scared completely senseless there in the dark.

"God help me!" I thought. Then the familiar chill rushed up my spine and a warm feeling of calm came over me. Just like when I was a child and used to run to my father because I was afraid of the dark. He would hug me and the fear would vanish. When I got this tingle, the fear vanished and was replaced by a calming feeling, a feeling that everything would be all right.

Then a strange thing happened. There in the darkness, I could feel a presence, someone standing there. And this strange presence talked to me just as plain as day, not even in a whisper. It was just as substantial as a real person's voice, one who was standing right in front of me, saying to me, "Don't worry, it's just you and me in here."

"What the...!" I shouted, jumping back, crouching into the corner of the dark elevator, and pulling my briefcase up in front of me to protect myself from any possible attack.

"And nothing is going to happen to you unless you make it happen. Remember, *nothing ever happens unless you make it*," said the voice.

I wasn't really scared. Oh, maybe just a little, more just a sort of a natural panicking from the sudden appearance of something unknown in the dark. It was pitch black in there now, but I knew that when I had entered I had walked into an empty elevator alone. The elevator had made no stops and I knew that I was absolutely the only person on it.

"Who's there?" I demanded, now trembling, cold with fear. Then abruptly, the elevator surged making a deep whir; the interior lights blinked on and it continued down to the garage. With the interior lights now on, I found myself still quite heart-poundingly alive. Still squatting, crouched down in the corner of the stark elevator, I was positively alone. Looking up, I scrutinized the ceiling to see if the ceiling hatch was open or if there were evidence that someone had entered and quickly exited. To my relief, but further confusion, there was no hatch in this elevator. Nobody could have gotten in or out.

The elevator descended slowly and normally. Thereafter the doors opened at the garage floor. Noticeably shaken by the episode, I crept out of the elevator and slowly peeked around the corners, half expecting someone to leap out at me. At the same time, I also prayed that nobody would be there to observe my embarrassing state of quasi-panic. All clear – whew. Straightening my tie, I took a deep breath and walked briskly to my car. Everything appeared normal. Several people were nonchalantly getting in and out of their cars, totally oblivious to me and my quandary. And the elevator – the elevator seemed to be working perfectly again.

Maybe I just imagined the whole thing; I'd heard that the mind was capable of creating lifelike hallucinations when one is hysterical with fear. Maybe I had suffered an auditory hallucination when I thought that the elevator was going to fall. Maybe something was triggered when I clobbered myself in the head with my briefcase, who knows. Yeah, that must have been it … I was certainly not one to believe that I was hearing voices for no evident reason, and I wasn't going to listen to some kind of ghost – no matter how authentic he sounded.

"Nothing is going to happen," I heard it plain as day, "unless you make it happen." Just a one-time panic attack. That was a sufficient enough explanation for me.

I drove home, checked for messages, popped in the old frozen dinner and opened up the *Amateur Magician's Handbook*. Tonight I was determined to teach myself a trick that I had long wanted to relearn, "the cut-and-restored rope" trick. This was one of the tricks that I had done in the talent show so many years ago, but couldn't begin to remember how. Maybe I would get a chance to show it to Max Vi tomorrow. As thoughts about the magician entered my mind, I couldn't help thinking about the eerie elevator incident.

"*Nothing will happen unless you make it happen.*" Thinking that the voice sounded somehow familiar to me, I tried to place it. Was it the magician? It was Maximillion Vi – I knew it.

"You Can Only Find The Answers –
When You Know The Right Questions."

Chapter 5

Saturday morning I awoke early in order to get to the bank before driving downtown to the festival. My dramatic side had taken control; I wanted to present the elusive magician a hat full of cash and not have to write him a check. I felt it was more the way that he, Max Vi, might have done it. Not really knowing what to expect, I was a little anxious. However, I was still very eager to see him. After all, I'd built him up to be so much in my mind. Whatever this meeting brought, one thing for sure was that it would brighten my somewhat drab existence – my so-called life. Believe me, I needed a little excitement in my life.

By the time I withdrew the cash, drove down to the festival, and wandered around town looking for a place to park, it was already two-thirty in the afternoon. Due to a practically perfect weather forecast, I was caught up in what became the largest turnout in festival history. Traffic was awful for Austin, so congested that traveling just five or six miles took me almost an hour. The real trick was finding a parking space once I was there. After a long search, driving up and down the streets, I finally gave in and paid five dollars in disgust. Then I headed out hastily toward the corner where I had last watched the magician performing six months before.

On the way to his show my heart raced. I felt high-spirited, giddy, like a kid going to the circus for the first time. As I approached that same corner, sweaty palmed, nervous with anticipation, I couldn't see him, but I could hear the boisterous laughter of the audience. There must have been two or three hundred spectators gathered at the spot, maybe more. The crowds were always much larger in the spring, but today was packed unusually tight. Briefly, I saw him hop up on his old trunk, above the crowd, and I could once again hear his loud bass voice booming over them and listened as it muffled when he stepped down, disappearing into the huge circle of people. I breathed a sigh of relief. It was Max Vi, all right. He was for real.

Max seemed much more ordinary than I remembered, and I began to have second thoughts about the psychic nature of our first meeting. Deciding not to stress the supernatural experiences when I saw him, unless he brought them up, I resigned myself to just having an ordinary conversation with him. However, just in case we did get a chance to talk a little about magic, I had brought a couple of my new magic tricks with me. Perhaps he could show me a few tricks of his own or something. I really didn't know what to expect, but most important I was going find out what he had meant when he said, "*You are the one*," before he conveniently disappeared. Maybe I imagined the whole vanishing thing. I don't know.

It would have been impossible for me to get up close to the front to see him, so I decided to wait out of the sun, eat a corn dog, and maybe drink a cold one. Then after the crowd had dispersed a little, I could rush up and quickly intercept him before he started the next show.

While I was sitting on a bus bench next to the food booths, waiting for the crowd to clear, a cute little blond-haired, blue-eyed boy wearing a blue tank top and red shorts, sat down beside me to eat his lunch. He hadn't a care in the world. How lucky he was to be just a kid, I thought. Totally absorbed by the moment he concentrated on, what to him was, the most important thing in the world – getting the right amount of mustard on his corn dog.

Since I had already devoured my overpriced corn dog, I was left sitting there with nothing to do really. After practicing magic for several hours the night before, I felt up to an audience of one. Once I'd started reading about the "cut-and-restored rope," it was like riding a bicycle. How to do it, came right back to me. Since the opportunity was presenting itself, I decided to perform just this one trick for the little boy.

THE MAGIC LIFE

Until this time I had been holding the magician's hat, but I decided to wear it to free up my hands, and besides, it helped me look the part of a magician. "Hi, there young man. What's your name?" I asked the little boy.

"I'm not supposed to talk to strangers," the little boy replied, looking over at the man next to him for approval.

His remark kind of took me by surprise. How unfortunate it is that we live in a world so full of fear. "Well, you don't have to talk to me since I am a stranger. But, I'm going to do some magic, and you can watch. No one ever told you not to watch strangers, did they?" The boy shook his head *"no"* without saying a word. With that, I dug the piece of rope out of my pocket, outstretched it and tugged it, demonstrating that the rope was real. Then I reached for my trusty scissors and cut the rope in two.

"Now, say the magic word," I said, seeing that the boy had decided that I was no longer a stranger, but rather a magician.

"Please," said the little boy.

I had to laugh – after all, it was better than my routine. "Please is a good magic word," I said, "but the magic word for magicians is 'abracadabra.' Can you say 'abracadabra?'" I asked.

"Abercadaber," replied the little boy.

"That's right," I said, "abracadabra." Then, with a little *"presto-digitation,"* also know as sleight of hand, I made the two halves of the rope appear to restore to one solid piece.

"Believe it or not, I learned to do that trick when I was about your age," I said.

The young boy's eyes became as big as the light bulbs that just flickered on inside his head. "How did you do that?" he asked, mouth wide open.

A surprising round of applause came from behind me. I hadn't realized that several other people standing near the food stand were observing me. A couple of older women, their full cups of beer held by their teeth, were just clapping away, some of the beer splashing out as their heads bobbed in time with their flabby arms. I was slightly embarrassed by the attention; but I couldn't resist tipping my, I mean, the magician's hat to take a big bow. It felt wonderful to be the magic man.

"You're pretty good," said one of the men standing there watching, "Here, Jimmy, give the man a dollar." With that he bent down, gave the young boy a dollar, then gently pushed him back over in front of me.

"Is your name Jimmy?" I asked, kneeling down to the young lad.

"Yes," he said shyly, looking up for approval from the man who just gave him the dollar.

"That's my name, too," I said.

"I assume that you are Jimmy's father," I said to the man and he nodded a *"yes"* and rubbed the boy on the head.

"Thank you very much for the dollar, but I'm not a professional. I was just practicing," I said returning the dollar to the boy. "You can keep it."

"Well, I think you're as good as any of the others that I've seen here before," he said. "Tell the man 'thank you' for the show, Jimmy."

"Thank you, magician man," said the little boy.

"Come on, Jimmy, what do you say you and I go find your mother?" With that the father picked up some packages full of handmade crafts and artistic trinkets, and plodded off. The boy, holding his father's hand, skipped along.

As he was walking away, the kid pulled on his dad's sleeve and I could hear him say, "Dad, can I be a magician when I grow up?"

"Son, he replied, "you can be anything you want to be." With that he disappeared into the crowd. It was a beautiful moment for father and son, bringing back memories of my own father. *"You can be anything you want to be, except unhappy."*

Then, I realized that the crowd had thinned substantially around the "real" magician; he must have finished his show. Putting the rope and scissors back into my pockets, I headed back through the crowd to see the magician. As I approached Max Vi yelled out in that same booming voice that I remembered so well, "Ladies and gentlemen, children of all ages, gather round..."

Darn it, I was too late to catch him in between acts. He had already started another performance. Since there were so many people, the crowd formed a circle before I arrived. Quickly though, I weaved my way through the crowd, walking right up to the front so that he'd be sure to see me. I didn't know quite what to do, but I had great expectations. Whatever happened, it would be a surprise. Maybe he would make some clever remark, which would somehow convey that he knew that I would be back all along. Or he might bring me up on stage and introduce me to the crowd. Perhaps he would just wink at me or nod and smile, letting me know that he would see me after the show. I thought that he might possibly drag me into his show again as the assistant. I expected everything – anything – but I was not expecting what happened next — which was nothing. Absolutely nothing.

He just looked right past me, as if I were just one of the hundred spectators who had come to see him perform. I smiled and waved his hat to attract his attention, but he just kept on with his performance, ignoring me, as though I didn't exist. He looked square at me, but did nothing to signify that he remembered our deal. Nothing at all. I felt a little sick.. For the last six months I had anticipated something special, something exciting, and now he didn't even know that I existed. Dumbfounded, I stood there and watched him perform exactly the same act as six months before, practically mouthing all the jokes and one-liners. Obviously I had wasted way too much time thinking about this guy.

He still rubbed his little white cloth to hypnotize a spectator. He selected some guy out of the crowd at random, as he had me, and strapped the straitjacket onto him. Although I enjoyed seeing the show this time as a spectator, I felt cheated; his assistant was stealing *my* act.

Looking through the crowd, I even spied the magician's wife, Kristin, standing across the circle from me waiting to be called upon to help. I'd never forget *that* kiss. I waved at her to get her to look in my direction, but it was futile. All their eyes, including hers, were glued upon "the amazing Max Vi."

All too soon, the show was over. Max had escaped from the jacket and vanished from under the cloth, to the utter amazement of the crowd. Of course, he left his unsuspecting assistant to pass the hat, and of course the money filled it to the brim. However, this time the collection was going to be almost twice what the magician expected. Because; when the assistant passed the hat my way, I sadly pulled the money out of my coat pocket. Despondently, placing the money into my magician's hat, I handed it, hat and all, to the now slightly puzzled, but still smiling, assistant.

"When you see Max again, which you will, give this to him and tell him that it's all here, plus interest. He'll figure out what I meant," I said, turning to leave. I couldn't face him. Not wishing to publicly acknowledge the now painfully obvious fact, I was insignificant. Just ol' James, the bean counter. If I had been *"the one"* before, it was now past history. He didn't even remember me.

I didn't get it. Perhaps the magician had become so accustomed to people just spending the money that he took it for granted that I wouldn't show. Maybe he'd forgotten about me the minute I walked out of sight. Anyway, I'd suffered enough rejection for one day. Feeling like an abused dog, I just tucked-tail and headed home.

On the drive to my condo, I couldn't help brooding again. I was sick and tired of nothing happening in my life. I expected something magical. Somehow I had believed this magician would tell me that "I was the one." For some reason, I wanted to believe that I was the missing key to the secrets of the universe. That I, through some magic power, would somehow be able to solve all of mankind's problems or that I would lead the people out of their daily darkness. Maybe I would solve the pollution problem, or discover a cure for cancer or aids. At the very least, I thought that maybe I would unlock the secret of making myself happy.

Why? Why was it that I had dreamed up this perfect scenario? Why did I have to have a let down when it didn't happen? Why did he lead me on some wild goose chase? Why did I imagine all of those things? The voices? Why didn't I just keep the money and take Gina to the festival? Why am I such a stupid jerk? I wanted to believe in fairy tales, so I guess that I deserved it. I know better. If it sounds too good to be true – it probably is. Hard work is the only magic that really works.

As I pulled into my garage I was steaming mad. *"The nerve of that guy,"* I thought. I don't know what kind of game he was playing, but I was going to write to the person in charge of the festival and make sure the same magician never worked there again. He must be some kind of a nut. What kind of guy gets his kicks from giving people false hopes? I was really mad, getting madder by the minute – I wanted to break something.

I opened my door, walked inside, and slammed it shut behind me. Stomping through the living room to the kitchen, I checked for messages; of course, there weren't any. Then, boom, all of a sudden, like a nuclear shock wave, it hit me. I stumbled backward as I looked into the living room, almost falling to the kitchen floor, tripping over the dining chairs. My heart stuttered a beat. Out of the corner of my eye I had just caught him – Max Vi. There he was, sitting on my couch, his feet propped up on my coffee table as if he owned it, reading my *Wall Street Journal.*

"Jesus Christ!" I said, not knowing whether to be scared, joyful or angry.

"No, just me, Max," came the response from the amazing Max Vi who didn't flinch a muscle. He just sat there, smiled and said, "I hope I didn't startle you too much."

"How did you find me? How did you get in here? Why are you here?" I questioned, stunned, practically gasping for breath.

"Come now, I'm a magician," Max replied. "We never tell our secrets."

Just staring at him with my mouth open, I would've assumed that I'd be furious – I mean at the concept of a stranger sitting in my house uninvited. It was unnerving. However, he simply looked at me as he had the first time, smiled and winked. A tingling shock wave bolted through my body – the Pied Piper effect all over again. I trusted him, not even knowing why I did.

"But I thought that you didn't remember me. I gave the money to the ... ", I began to stutter.

Before I could even start questioning, he started answering, "His name was Burt, but Burt isn't like us. You see, you and I have a lot more in common than Burt and I. You and I have destiny to fulfill.

"I was certainly glad that you didn't take advantage of my offer to spend the money. I was slightly disappointed, however, that you left before I got a chance to talk to you – even though I absolutely understand your doubting me. Just don't let it happen again. Remember, I have a reputation to keep up.

"James," he continued, "it was just an act. I pretended to not see you. It's extremely important to the audience that I, as a magician, remain somewhat mysterious. It is absolutely necessary if there's going to be suspension of disbelief. You see – they must see me as someone very special, almost above a normal human being. This helps create the illusion. Probably the way that you felt, when you first saw me – right?" he asked with a smile and a pretense of arrogance.

He knew he was right. He motioned for me to sit down by patting the seat next to him. As I sat down, confused, I could feel a thousand questions coming into my mind, but I was unable to utter a single phrase.

"Remember, I am going to teach you *all* of my secrets. Or that is, you'll learn all of my secrets if you choose. James my friend, you are *the one*," he said as he leaned forward and touched my arm. As he did, I felt that tingling chill run through me from the point of his touch.

"What does it mean?" I asked. "Are you for real? Why are you here?"

"James," he replied, "It means that you must learn to be *the one, the one* that you really are capable of being. James, you must learn that you are not just James Christian Carpenter, the accountant. You are not just good ol' James the Beancounter. You are a potential wonderkin, a muse, a changer of the world. We are going places, you and I. You'll be changing things, and things will change. As for your two other questions, I am for real, as real as you make me. I am here because you want to learn. Just like you are here because I want to teach. That's pretty much the way life works. Teaching and learning are two of the three most important things in life."

"What is the third?" I asked, not even knowing why I had.

He continued, "The third element is the most crucial. It, however, is the one element of life that cannot be taught or learned. It is that which you must acquire naturally, somehow find, or create on your own."

I was a little confused because his statements weren't really answers, but more like walks around an answer, like a politician would do. It was, however, so unbelievable and fascinating that I clung to his every word, without interrupting.

He leaned back, reached up into the air and a tobacco pipe appeared at his fingertips. "I don't smoke it," he said. "I just like to hold it when I tell a story." He stuck the pipe into his mouth, bit down on it, and cocked his head up to one side as if he were going deep into thought.

"Let me tell you a fable, James," he said, removing the pipe and pointing it in a gesture. "Fables have been known to change the course of history, you know. You should always *pay close attention to fables and dreams,* Jim, *they are the fabric that weaves the universe.*

"This fable starts off like every other really great fable: Once upon a time — there was a king who ruled a larger than average kingdom. On the scale of one to ten, his kingdom was a seven. But the king was not satisfied. He was ruler of all he surveyed, yet he knew that beyond his horizon there must be more, more realms to conquer, more kingdoms to overthrow. One day a stranger arrived from a distant empire and requested an audience with the king. The king, not familiar with the land the stranger called home, was exhilarated by the prospect of expanding his domain.

"He, therefore, decreed that the stranger be brought before him shackled in irons. His soldiers found the man, secured him in chains, and brought him to the king. The king proceeded to torture the stranger, demanding that he reveal which direction he had come from and how large an army protected his city. Even after great torture, the stranger refused to tell. Frustrated, the king had the stranger thrown to the lion's den where he was torn asunder and devoured.

"Several months later an army marched from the distant realm into the kingdom, and in the cover of night overthrew the ambitious king. The king was led to the chopping block for his treachery against the stranger whom he had sent to the lions. 'Just tell me one thing before you kill me,' begged the king as he was about to be beheaded. 'How did you know that I was here?'

"The conquering king answered, 'It is really very simple. I send out men bearing friendly greetings in all different directions. If and when our men don't return – we know that our enemies lie in that direction.'"

Max stopped and placed his pipe in his mouth.

I tried to figure out what he was getting at and then gave up, "I don't get it. I'm afraid that I'm just kind of slow."

"Don't feel bad. There's not really a lot to get. It's just that sometimes it's not what we don't know that gets us into trouble. It's rather what we don't know that we don't know. You see, the king knew that he didn't know the location of the stranger's kingdom, but what the king didn't know was that his actions were revealing his own location. If he had simply freed the man he would have been better off. The king couldn't have known this, because he didn't know that he didn't know. Sometimes there are no answers to the questions because we don't know any of the right questions," Max said with a grin and then he asked, "Does that mean anything to you?"

"I suppose that, since I don't even know what questions to ask, it's better to just consider you as the man bearing friendly greetings and know that I'll reach the other kingdom in good time," I laughed a little, because I had the feeling that I really did understand – another chill crept up my spine.

"Indeed, you are *the one*," he said, as he covered the pipe with his hands, making it vanish. He then sat back in his chair and put his hands folded behind his head.

"Can I at least ask you a question of what I know that I don't know?" I asked.

"Sure, you can always ask questions. That doesn't mean that I'm going to have the answers, because I don't know what I don't know either. But you go ahead and ask. If it's a good question, I'll try to give you a good answer." He then sat up and leaned forward to look me right in the eyes.

"Okay, here goes. Who are you?" I asked.

"Not a bad question at all. In fact, a very good question. However, it is more important for you to answer it than it is for you to ask it," he said, pulling on his salt and pepper beard while rubbing the piece of white cloth which dangled from the chain about his neck. "Who are you?" he asked.

This seemed quite profound coming from this mysterious man sitting in my house uninvited. He was absolutely right. "I don't really know – do I?" I replied, and again the tingling. The phone rang and broke my almost mystical thoughts. Knowing that the machine would answer it after two rings, instinctively, I leaped up. "Just a minute let me get..." I said as I turned for the kitchen.

The instant I had my back toward him, I realized I was making a mistake. I had that feeling you get when you lock your keys in the car and realize it as you see yourself shutting the door. It was too late to stop and go back. Something inside me told me that he had finished his conversation with me. Sure enough, when I turned and looked back he was gone. He had vanished again and I had the depressing feeling that I probably wouldn't see him for another six months.

"Access The Child Within You –
And Learn What You Already Know."

Chapter 6

I picked up the phone and blurted a rather abrupt, "Hello," as if I were almost mad at whomever called. I couldn't help blaming the caller a little for my taking my eyes off the magician. Perhaps if I had just kept my eyes on him, watching him every minute, he wouldn't have vanished. However, my anger was quickly diffused when I discovered, much to my pleasure, that the caller was my ever-optimistic younger brother, Carl.

It had been a long time since we had last talked and I was anxious to hear from him. Carl was always the bearer of good news, whether or not there was even good news to bear, he was probably the one person that I would have to forgive for interrupting – something about that damn positive attitude of his.

"Guess what?" he asked.

"How in the heck should I know what?" I said. "Are you coming into Austin?"

"No, but you will be able to see me," he replied. "You have to guess."

"You bought a billboard on I-35? Okay, I give up. What are you up to now?" I asked.

"Well, all right, if you give up. Remember a couple of years back when I told you that I was auditioning for the situation comedy about an accountant who meets an alien?"

I kept on listening.

He said, "Remember, you helped me research the part – of the alien. Get it?"

There had been thousands of auditions. He had informed me that he had been on hundreds, but almost never cast. The only reason that I recalled this particular audition was that he had asked me to help him with a little character research, using my background as an accountant to help him get into the part. Specifically he had said that, "For once my accounting career was going to be put to good use."

"Yes, well, I sort of remember, but I thought the idea was canned by the networks, wasn't it?" I asked, trying to remember precisely what happened with the show.

"Well," he continued, "it was dead, but they gave it mouth-to-mouth resuscitation, and it is going to be alive and breathing on the Fox network next spring! We start production of actual episodes next Wednesday and we will go on the air by mid June. I'm afraid that I've finally done it. I'm going to be a TV star!"

"That's fantastic! It's unbelievable," I said. "I'm envious, I knew that someday if you kept slugging it out that eventually all of your hard work would pay off. I knew you would be a success. Have you called Mom and told her the news?"

"I just found out this morning," he said. "I wanted to tell you first though, because you always believed in me – not that Mom won't be happy that I'm substantially employed in any fashion. You and I know that Mom would have still been happier if I had become a dentist or something real."

"Don't be too hard on her; Mom just wants what she thinks is best for you. Now you are getting the chance to prove to her that you knew what was best all along," I said, knowing his feelings were absolutely on target. Mom probably wouldn't even begin to express any pride in Carl or his work. More likely she would even be a little bit sarcastic, saying something like, "Well, it took you long enough; now you can start earning a living." She wasn't actually mean, just a little bitter about life in general. Oh, hell – who was I kidding? She was a lot bitter.

Carl and I talked for at least an hour about his new show and how his character was stereotyped as a rather boring nerd accountant. If he only knew how exciting some of the real accountants down at my office were, he wouldn't have called it stereotyping. He would have called it extremely realistic. I could only imagine what life would be like for an accountant that really met an alien. "Sometimes I feel that I'm the alien in our office," I said.

When we finally hung up the phone, I realized that I had completely forgotten to tell him about my alien visit of sorts. With all of the excitement about his new part, I had neglected to tell him about the magician and his strange disappearing act. Looking at the door, I wondered if the magician could have made it out in the time I took to pick up the telephone. Sure, it was just a trick.

Of course, the magician had vanished leaving yet another strange riddle for me to solve. Now I was supposed to figure out the question of the ages: "Who am I?" It was a very pertinent question – a coincidence – since I was currently having an identity crisis. Usually, I would have laughed off such a question as simply sophomoric, but the truth was that I was not very satisfied with the person I thought I was.

Maybe I was just like my brother, I thought – an actor playing the part of a boring accountant. Bingo! Another tingle ran up my spine. This tingle-chill thing was getting to be far too commonplace. The phenomenon seemed to happen whenever I was thinking about something to do with the magician. Again the chill, like a response to my very thoughts, enveloped me. Strange, maybe I was losing my mind. Should I pay attention to this sensation? Or was my imagination getting the best of me? Maybe, just maybe, there was something going on here that was beyond the bounds of ordinary everyday occurrences.

Maybe I should explore the possibility of a psychic phenomenon. Then the answer came to me, *why?* Just as Max had said, sometimes we look for the answers and the answer is to be found in the question. If it were psychic or not, did it really make any difference? It was as real as I wanted it to be. I was convinced that he was really here, sitting in my home. He really talked to me. I really saw him perform, and I really got goose bumps practically every time I thought about something he had said. Go with the flow, Jim, just go with the flow. Maybe I just needed to relax, sit back and wait.

He did say to have patience. Well, I was willing to give patience a try, at least for the night. I curled up with a good magazine and lay down in bed to read. When my eyes finally got too tired to read another word, I clicked off the light and drifted off, fast asleep.

I was dreaming that I was at the spring festival again, watching the magician perform. Only this time, I am just a little boy and can't see over the people standing in front of me. They are all laughing out loud, but I can't see what they are laughing about. I try to slip in between the people, pushing my way to the front, but they just won't let me squeeze by. They are too big and overpowering. I feel helpless. Turning to look for help from the older man next to me, I find my father, exactly as I remember him.

"Son," he says with a smile, "would you like to see a great magician?"

"Of course I would, Happy Papa," I reply.

He then hoists me to his shoulders and I look over all of the people. The magician who is standing in front of the crowd performing is not Max Vi. The magician is me! I am the one performing for the crowd. I wave at myself and smile.

Then the dream changes direction like only dreams can; I am no longer at the festival, but crouched down in the corner of the elevator at work. Everything is running in slow motion. The elevator stops and the doors open. In a macabre scene like in an old episode of *The Outer Limits*, Max Vi walks on wearing a white tuxedo, holding a black rabbit in his hands. The doors close and we start rising very rapidly. I can hear the whir of the motors kick in.

"Well, James, do you know the answer to the riddle yet?" he asks, almost shouting against the background noise of the whirring elevator motor.

"Who am I?" I ask, as the elevator races higher and higher.

"Yes, do you know who I am?"

"I thought I was supposed to answer who I am, not who you are."

"It's one and the same, answer or question. You and I have more than a lot in common. I am you," he states.

Suddenly, I realize that I am strapped tightly in a straitjacket, seated on the hard metal floor of the elevator. "You aren't me, I am James C. Carpenter. I am the son of my father and mother. I am my brother's brother. I am just a man, not a magician!"

"Then who am I?" he questions.

Confused and angry, I can feel the gravitational force pressing down hard on my body and face. The elevator grinds loudly, about to reach the limit of its ascent. It does reach that limit – suddenly my stomach enters my throat, for a second I am weightless as the elevator turns silent and begins falling downward. Now there is no elevator at all; I see Max suspended in space and I am falling away from him. I am still trapped in the straitjacket, falling.

"YOU ARE...!" I shout at him.

The action woke me from the deep sleep and the dream instantly vanished. The shouting was unnerving, so real that I thought I might have actually shouted out loud, but I wasn't about to let it get to me. *I'm a big boy now and nightmares are only frightening when you are sleeping.* Still, I wasn't that anxious to get back to la-la land, so I sat up and drank a sip of water from the glass on my nightstand. Not wanting to forget what happened in this dream, I sat there with my eyes open and relived it for a few minutes, almost getting up to get a pen and paper. But I decided my bed was too comfortable and I was really too sleepy. Besides, I really didn't want to wake up completely.

Who am I? I wondered.

I'm a lot of different things. I'm an accountant; but really that is what I do; that's not who I am. If you take away what someone does, then what's really left? I was born who I am without any action of my own. I guess that who I am is as simple as being. I am just my father and mother's creation, just a product of their genes and one passionate night. Is that who I am? Is the rest just a by-product of my surroundings and the changes caused by living day to day? Is who you are limited to what you are given in the way of mind and body at the moment of conception? Are those the limitations that define *who*? Does that mean that I have no control over who I am? I thought about it for a few minutes. It all seemed pretty fatalistic, pretty negative, I mean not having control over who I am. But, to think of it in the terms of being born male with two arms and legs, with brown hair, and a moderate amount of intelligence, I really didn't have much to say about it. No one really gets to say much about it. A depressing thought, but I guess I was fortunate to have been born whole with as much going for me as I have. So, thankful for what I had, I rolled over to get back to sleep.

The next morning I awoke somewhat refreshed, not remembering any more dreams after the one nightmare about the strange elevator ride. Feeling almost invigorated by my midnight's conclusions, I was ready for a great new day armed with at least a few answers for old Max.

I did know who I was: just an ordinary guy with a few dreams. I had wanted to be a magician when I was a kid. So what, I wanted to marry the boss' daughter, too. I wanted to be like my father or like my brother and follow my dreams. But, I was also something like my mother, hard working, dedicated, and I wanted some of the good things that my hard work would allow. I was intelligent and not ashamed of it. I had achieved a reasonable amount of security and I was damn glad to have it. Sure I had a few regrets, but I knew one thing for sure. I knew who I wasn't. I was not Max Vi, not a piece of fiction or some kind of illusion. I was, at least, a real person living in a real world.

My morning shower, electric shave, and the drive to the office were pretty much uneventful. I decided to write down my thoughts on who I was as soon as I got into the office. If I had to wait for another six months to see this disappearing magician, and then answer his questions – I figured I better have the answers written down. Otherwise, I might just forget who I was. That kind of sounded silly, *I might forget who I was*.

Traffic was light, so I arrived early at the office. When I got to my desk, I pulled out the pencil drawer to get out a pen and pad. A surprise was waiting for me. In my pencil drawer I found a single, freshly cut, red rose. I picked it up and inhaled its wonderful fragrance. I looked for a note, a card … but nothing. The flower had to be from Gina. Who else? However, I'd probably never find out. The rule of thumb is that a man can never ask a girl if she anonymously gave him flowers. Because if she did, she probably won't admit it and if she didn't, then she'll never forget it. It's a no-win situation all around.

I figured to get even. One good rose deserves a dozen I always say (as if I had ever sent a dozen roses to anyone other than my mother). I picked up the phone and called a florist. Asking him to deliver a dozen red roses to her at the office and feeling quite brazen, I had them sign the card, "from your secret admirer." After all, who could it hurt? No one. If she never found out that they were from me, there was no harm to anyone.

At lunchtime I saw the florist making the delivery, and even though I wanted to see Gina's reaction, I decided to slip out for lunch before she got them. That way, if she decided to confront me, she couldn't. I was such a sucker for her that I would probably give it all away with just one look. If I weren't there, she might not suspect that I was the one. Picking up my briefcase, I headed into the elevator, my mind a million miles away thinking about Gina.

Not even remotely thinking about my strange elevator dream – *deja vu* – it happened. After descending a couple of floors, the elevator stopped. When the door opened, Max was standing there – just like in the dream, complete with a white tuxedo and tails. Thank God, he wasn't holding a black rabbit. I would have freaked out entirely.

He stepped into the elevator and smiled saying, "Fancy meeting you here."

"I didn't expect to see you for about six more months," I said, trying to pretend that I was not totally startled by this stranger-than-life specter with the amazing ability to enter into my dreams.

"Well, I was just performing in the neighborhood and I thought I would come up to your office and see if you would join me for lunch," he said.

Attempting to act almost cool, not awestruck as I really felt, I replied, "I think that would be great."

"Terrific, I know where we can go. It will be just the place to celebrate, James," Max said, patting me on the shoulder, "Congratulations are in order."

I couldn't help feeling inadequate whenever he was around. He had a way of transforming me into the little boy of my dreams. I don't know why I put up with all the clandestine mystery. In that instant, I decided that I wouldn't. "Is it really necessary?" I asked, almost thinking aloud, still feeling that he knew what I was going to say before I said it anyway.

"Absolutely, James. If I know you, as well as I think I do, then you have spent the entire night figuring out who you are," he said. "Stop me if I'm wrong. The way I figure it, anyone who is so curious as to wait six months, give up a hundred dollars and a date with a cute girl – just to be asked a question – is going to figure out the answer to the question, or spend the entire night awake trying. By the looks of you, you got a good night's sleep. So I must conclude that you have answered your first question."

"Well, do you want to know the answer to the question?" I asked. Then my intuition stopped me. "Wait, don't tell me. You don't have to; I already know the answer to my own question. It really isn't important that you know the answer, after all it was my question wasn't it?" I said, intuitively understanding the logic to my thought process and unable to believe that it came out of my mouth.

"You really are catching on, James," Max said with a chuckle and a wink.

"Well, where are we going to have lunch?" I asked.

"Now that is a really good down-to-earth question, and I have a good one for you. Do you like pizza?" Max asked.

"You mean there is something that you don't know?"

"Of course you like pizza," he said, "I was just being polite. Even a mind reader, like myself, must maintain a certain decorum in a social setting."

I couldn't help thinking to myself, "I've been bested again." He was simply playing the odds. Hell, everyone likes pizza. It was always as if he knew me. Full of questions, which I would feel a fool to ask, I knew that if I asked questions I wouldn't get answers. And I also knew that I would get more answers without asking any questions. But I wanted to know some things. Where did he come from? Was he real at all? Why was he really on the elevator? Was he some kind of a guardian angel – something mystical? Or were he and I both nuts? He looked real enough. If he *was* a hallucination, he was one hell of a hallucination.

I wasn't about to broadcast my possible psychosis by insinuating that he was some kind of psychic spectacle, but I was really beginning to wonder about the possibility. We exchanged very little conversation on the way to the restaurant. He suggested that we take my car, of course. He probably didn't own a car; he probably never used a car, just de-materialized from one place and re-materialized in another. How else could I explain his sudden appearances and disappearances?

When we walked into the pizza parlor and proceeded up to the counter, he suggested that I order first and that he would pay for both. Ha! I knew it. He didn't know what kind of pizza I liked. But, I wasn't about to ask or he would have told me. So I ordered a couple of slices of pepperoni and an orange drink. All the time, I had this eerie feeling that the person taking my order couldn't see the magician, because the pizza guy looked only at me when we walked up. Maybe Max was only visible to me.

My suspicion was almost confirmed when the he asked, "Can I have your name please?" not even acknowledging Max's presence.

"Carpenter, James Carpenter," I said reaching for my wallet, not sure if I were standing next to a ghost.

"No, let me get it," said Max, "I insist," making a twenty dollar bill appear out of nowhere in his hand.

The man behind the counter completely missed the trick, but then he turned to Max and referring to the tux asked, "Hey, what's the occasion? Are you getting married?"

At least I knew that Max was real, not just a figment of my imagination. Or if he was, at least the illusion was now shared between the pizza guy and myself. After Max finished ordering a couple of slices of combination pizza and a cola, he paid for both and we sat down. He talked. I listened.

"I'm sure that you are very curious about me," he said. "Curiosity is one of man's greatest gifts, but it's just better I teach you a bit at a time – walk before you run, crawl before you walk. I would just like to add that you should learn to swim before you can crawl. Life is full of mysteries, James. But people need to solve their own small individual mysteries before they can move on to solve the major mysteries of the universe.

"James, I have been looking for you for a long time. You first intrigued me with your keen sense of observation; you can see things which others fail to see, feel things that many others fail to feel. When you first approached me at the festival, I observed the way you analyzed the reactions of others. Thinking constantly of the current surroundings, you know where you are at any current moment, unlike most people – you live in the present, not the past or future. You noticed when I first rubbed this cloth swatch," he said pulling the cloth attached to a chain from under his collar.

Then Max continued, "You noticed my beautiful wife, too – but who didn't? You realized that your billfold was gone before I told you, James. But most important and amazingly, you grasped how other people perceive life around them and what they sensed about you. You embody the capacity to cherish life's mystery, not having yet lost all of your innocence.

"However, don't feel too special, James, you are not alone in this ability. All men and women share this ability to live in the now, at one time or another in their lives. You see, children all have it – a natural God-given ability, much like, say, swimming before you can walk. Did you know that a child is able to swim soon after he is born? Swimming is almost as natural as breathing. But if the child learns to crawl first, swimming becomes more difficult – as though there are too many distractions after the baby has discovered his newfound freedom. Learning to swim before you learn to crawl is almost effortless, easy, because there are no distractions.

"If, however, you go even farther and you progress from crawling to walking without yet learning to swim – swimming becomes much more difficult, even somewhat frightening to learn. You learn many of the fears about your limitations as a human being when you learn to walk. You learn, for example, that you can't walk on water.

"Swimming becomes extremely difficult to learn after you have learned to run, as though you've completely forgotten your God-given gift and must totally relearn swimming. If you learn too many other things, then this natural birthright will become almost impossible to remember and relearn.

"But remember, nothing is impossible if you have the proper knowledge, beliefs, training and attitude. This is important James; remember it. Nothing is impossible if you have the correct knowledge, beliefs, training and attitude. It isn't too late for you to learn it all because of *who* and *what* you are.

THE MAGIC LIFE

"You are one of the lucky few who, at your age, hasn't yet lost the ability to see life without sticking yourself into the picture. Reality becomes very clouded and foggy when a person lets his or her individual life affect perception. Your perception is still uncluttered. When most people become *who* and *what* they are, they leave the magic behind, carrying too much emotional baggage and including too many of life's little prejudices. James, inside you're still like a child who hasn't yet picked up all of the misinformation we adults have to cart around. Access that child within you, and learn what you already know – to swim again, James.

"I asked you to find out who you really are. You probably have a pretty clear picture. Discovering who you are is like learning to crawl, leaving behind the security blanket of an infant. No longer is suckling at your mother's breast enough. Now you must learn and explore possibilities. You are, in essence, defining yourself, discovering where you can go, as well as where you can't. This newfound mobility defines for the rest of your life, your limitations. Your very exploration creates your belief system, teaches you boundaries you cannot see beyond. That is who you are. You are a man. You are your parents' son, and you have their form, shape and color emblazoned upon you. Your choice or not – where you stand, as you stand, is who you are.

"Next I ask you to discover *what you are*; that is: learn to walk, not as easy as learning to crawl. But, we all seem to get it after a few tumbles. Just remember, when you learn to walk, a lot of the things that you could do easily as a child may become frightening. In walking we first recognize the limitations of time and space. Deciding *what you are* can impose many restrictions, limits and constraints." He paused, took a drink of his soda, and wiped his lip with his napkin. "I want you to learn to crawl, walk, and soon run, never forgetting your God-given ability – to learn without constraints."

Then over the loudspeaker, "Pizza for Carpenter. James Carpenter, your pizza is ready."

I raised up out of my seat and turned to him. "When I get up to get the pizza are you going to disappear?" I asked, not knowing if he could answer a question straightforwardly.

"James, I think that you have more to digest than just pizza, and for me to be here would only make you concentrate on more questions. Now you know the question, spend this time searching for the answer," Max replied. "Just think about what I have said for a while, discover *what you are*, and I'll be back soon to teach you to run."

"Well, if you're gone when I get back, it has been a pleasure listening," I said. "You really have given me some food for thought."

Even though I knew that he would be gone when I returned, I felt perfectly satisfied with our conversation. I turned back around to see if I could glimpse him walking out the door, but he was gone in an instant without any sign. He was teaching me something at last. As I picked up the pizza I realized what his lesson was. I stopped and smelled the aroma: pepperoni, the spices, and tomatoes. It was great. I recalled what it smelled like the first time, when I was a young boy and my mother made a Chef-Boyardee Pizza for us kids. I could feel the heat radiating off the ovens, and I sensed the ambition of the fellow behind the counter. He was really hustling and overtly friendly, no doubt because he aspired to be more than a pizza pusher for the rest of his life. Almost as if I could read his mind, I sensed that he wanted to be the manager. I saw a girl, not happy with her job, taking an order next to him. Obviously, she wanted to be somewhere else doing something else. Then my awareness of the sounds, smells, and subtle sights all intensified, and I smiled because I really could feel them.

Max had reached me. A chill tingled up my spine.

One more bizarre thing – I was given only my pizza. The pizza guy never even called Max's order ready.

*"You Make The Choice –
To Be What You Are."*

Chapter 7

After quickly consuming a couple of slices of pizza and slugging down my orange soda, I wiped the tomato sauce off my chin and headed back to work. My mind was still swimming from the intensity of Max's discussion. "What am I?" I thought that I had already answered that. I would really need to examine this question carefully since I had thought it was exactly the same as, "Who am I?" That afternoon, I pulled into the parking garage feeling very full and almost drowsy, as though I were in a fog. Somewhere in the misty corners of my mind was the answer to this riddle, but presently the solution eluded me.

After I parked the car, I sat for a moment just thinking, "If *who* I am is that which I was given – so to speak – then *what* am I must include everything that I became." I didn't feel comfortable with the obvious answer. *What* I was, was more than just ol' James, the accountant. The answer, I knew, would take a lot of inner searching. Upon entering the elevator, I hit the button for the 25th floor and breathed a heavy sigh of submission. Maybe I'll figure it out later. I walked out of the elevator, past the receptionist and headed to my desk. The receptionist, glancing up, stopped me before I had traveled all the way down the hall.

"James," she said, "Mr. Lee asked to have you drop by his office as soon as you returned."

"Are you sure he wanted to see me?"

"Oh, yes, I took the message myself," she replied.

Suddenly weak in the knees, I felt the butterflies congregate in my stomach. What did he want to see me for? I had rarely ever been called into his office, except when I messed something up. He was usually pretty reasonable, but I hated feeling like an idiot – pretty much the case whenever I screwed up. After dropping my briefcase and jacket off at my desk, I picked up a pen and yellow note pad and headed back down the hall to his office. When I reached his door I paused, took a deep breath, then addressing Mr. Lee's personal secretary, Molly, I said, "Tell Mr. Lee that James is here to see him."

"Go right in, James," she said, "He is expecting you."

Cautiously, I opened the door, ready for a royal butt-chewing session. Mr. Lee sat behind his big oak desk with his glasses pulled down low on the bridge of his nose, reading some computer spread sheet. He reminded me of Ben Franklin, only with much shorter hair.

Not even glancing up for a second to affirm my presence, he said, "Come on in, James, pull up a chair." He finished what he was doing, and then peered at me over his glasses. After a long pause he turned his eyes toward the window and in a commanding voice, clearing his throat he started, "Hrrmph, I have a problem and I need your help. I think that we have something we need to talk about."

Then, on the credenza by the window, I spied a dozen red roses, my roses – oh my god, Gina's roses! They may have looked beautiful, but I smelled trouble. I felt unsteady, almost faint. I had done it now; he was going to fire me for sure.

Then my brain kicked into high gear, "*Maybe he doesn't know that I sent them.*" Not wanting to play out my hand just yet, I zipped my mouth shut as I reviewed my phone call to the florist very slowly, over in my mind. I'm sure that I had sent them anonymously. Yes, I positively said to sign the card, "From a secret admirer." There was no way her father could have known that I was the culprit who sent them. Perhaps she had just placed them in her father's office. Maybe my visit to his office had nothing to do with the flowers.

"James, do you see those flowers that are sitting behind me?"

So much for that theory. Oh well, I was history. "Yes, sir. They're very beautiful," I said, not knowing how to respond and not yet ready to admit my defeat and beg for mercy.

"Well, they weren't sent to me," he said. "That's why I need your help. I caught someone delivering these to Gina, my daughter. Well, I know that she is sort of a friend of yours, and I think that she kind of likes you. Isn't that right?"

"Yes, we get along fine, uh, very well," I said, feeling like the mouse sitting on the trap nibbling at the cheese, any moment the spring would snap and whaaack!

"Well, I haven't given them to Gina yet, because I wanted to talk to you first. You see, I don't know who sent these yet, because the chicken S.O.B., pardon my French, didn't have the guts to sign his name. That's why I called you in here – to help me out before this thing gets out of hand. I would really appreciate it if you would find out who in the heck this 'secret admirer' is.

"You just don't know Gina's past history with men. The last guy that sent her flowers was a motorcycle gang member, a real bad egg. You know, sex, drugs, rock and roll. Well, not this time. I want to you to find out this creep's name before he gets his grimy paws on my daughter. No sir, I don't want to see her wrapped up with another useless no account bum. If you only knew what it's like being a father to a beautiful girl. I don't know why, but she never seems to want to get involved with anyone with a sense of responsibility. You know, someone with his head in the real world, like you and me."

Dazed, I couldn't believe what I was hearing. Like a bad situation comedy: here was the over-protective father putting his foot in his mouth up to his knee. Luckily, I hadn't spilled my guts when I walked into the room; even though I would've loved to see the look on his face if he discovered I was the scoundrel who sent the flowers. The absurdity of it all almost made me laugh, until I realized what a truly horrible situation I was in. Somehow it lost its humor.

"James," he said, "you know how much that girl means to me. I know that it isn't necessarily in your job description, but I would appreciate it if you could just ask her if she knows who sent them. Once you uncover his name I will take over and check him out from there. If he is some Colombian drug dealer or ex-convict, damn it, I want to find out!"

Not knowing exactly what to do, I took a deep breath and exhaled slowly, thinking to myself, *"Should I tell him that I was the secret admirer?"* I wasn't a motorcycle gang member, I wasn't a drug dealer, ex-con or no account bum.

Considering the situation, I tried to take myself out of the picture. I really didn't know much about Mr. Lee's relationship with Gina. I'd just taken for granted that they were close because they saw each other so often. I really felt sorry for him now; he was so overprotective that he was making himself miserable. And what about Gina? How in the world did she ever put up with him controlling her life that way? Maybe she didn't. Possibly she dated the wrong kind of men because her father was too protective. Thinking back, however, I couldn't even remember her ever dating a motorcycle hoodlum. That did it! I was going to lay my job on the line. He was going to have to let me date his daughter or he could fire me!

"Well, James?" he asked.

My knee-jerk self-preservation reaction took over. "Yes, of course you can count on me," I hated myself, but I had never handled this type of situation before, and I was, well, sort of winging it.

"Jim, why don't you talk to her tonight? It's almost two o'clock now; if you asked her to go out for a drink tonight after work she might spill her guts to you."

I couldn't believe my ears. He was asking me to take Gina out.

"Well, I don't even know if she would go out with me," I said, still in minor shock and absolutely not believing this latest development. He wanted me to date her! Ha!

"Oh, I'll bet that she would meet you for a drink or something like that. After all it's not like it was a date or something."

"Okay, I'll give it a shot," I said.

"Good," he said, standing up extending his hand to me. "Thanks a lot for helping me out, James. I'll make it worth your while."

"Don't worry about it."

I certainly wasn't worried about it being worth my while. Here I was getting him to actually sanction a date with Gina, without even asking his permission – a trick worthy of the incredible Max Vi. We shook hands, after which, I practically danced a jig back to my office cubicle.

Work seemed to be extra tedious after that, with my mind repeatedly wandering to events of the previous twenty-four hours – more excitement than in the last few years combined. It was almost too much to handle. What was I going to do about Gina? And what about Max's question? What about my life? I closed my eyes attempting to concentrate. Feeling a tension headache coming on, I began to rub my forehead.

My hand was joined by a much softer pair of hands slowly rubbing my temples. I opened my eyes and there stood Gina.

"Do you have a headache?" she asked in a sympathetic voice.

"Yes, and that feels great," I said, before it dawned on me what was happening and how it must have looked to everyone else in the office. "I'll be okay," I said, "as soon as the aspirin kicks in." Sitting up straight in my chair, taking her hands in mine, I reluctantly pulled them away from my temples. Inside I was dying. How was I going to forget about the girl I loved, knowing in my heart that she would love me too if we could just leave the rest of the world out of the picture?

"Daddy said that you had something to ask me," she said.

"Oh yes, there is something that he wanted me to talk to you about," I said fumbling for words, "I need to talk to you about something personal."

"What do you mean?" she asked, giving me a rather puzzled look

Stumbling and groping for words, "I don't know what I mean," I said, my heart pounding. I took a deep breath and asked, "I just wondered if you would like to maybe meet me for a drink tonight after work."

"Is that all? Yes, I'd love to," Gina replied. "Any place special?"

"Well, I thought maybe," I said, as my mind raced searching for a place to have a drink with a beautiful girl that you want to impress, "we could meet at the ..."

Before I finished, she interjected, "How about the Lake Austin Palace? Do you know it?"

"Oh yes, it's a beautiful place," I said, knowing of its reputation as a fine restaurant, but never having actually been there.

"What time do you want to pick me up for dinner?" she asked.

She was so forward. I was just asking to meet for a drink and now she had me picking her up for dinner. But, it sounded okay to me! "I guess I could be ready around seven thirty, is that all right?"

"That's just fine. I guess it's a date," she said with a smile.

Guiding my career right down the drain would almost be worth planting one big wet kiss on her lips. I really wasn't that happy with my job anyway. With what was probably a very stupid grin on my face I just gulped, saying, "Okay, I guess it's a date."

After a couple of "see-ya-laters" she waltzed off down the hallway and was gone. Somewhere in my state of confusion, I was lost without a road map. Things were really getting complicated. To get me out of this would take a guardian angel – although I really didn't want to get out of this one. That was the tough part. Maybe it had something to do with what Max had said at lunch. Max had a way of providing answers before I knew the questions. But what did what he said have to do with my situation? The question that he had asked was *"What was I?"* and I knew that he didn't mean the same thing as *"Who was I?"* but I was still confused. They were the same and had nothing to do with my question at hand.

Mark walked up to my desk and handed me a piece of paper. "I think that you better take a look at this, James."

Looking down at the paper; I turned it over front to back only to see that it was blank on both sides. "What is it?" I asked, totally confused as to why he handed me a blank sheet of paper.

"It's your job description after Mr. Lee finds out that you and Gina are messing around," he chuckled.

"Sorry to burst your bubble, Mark, but Gina and I aren't fooling around," I said. "In fact we are going out tonight as a favor to Mr. Lee."

"That's not what it looks like to me and the gang. You may say you're doing the boss a favor, but it looks more like the 'bossanova' to me," he said. "You know what I mean? Not that we blame you – that baby do got back!"

"That's pretty funny, Mark – really good toilet humor. Did you ever think about becoming a *comodian*? Well, I have a lot to do. You'll have to excuse me while I get back to work, or we'll both end up with this for a job description," I said, handing back his blank sheet of paper.

"Hey, sorry if I upset you. I was only kidding around," Mark replied. "I think it's fine for you two to go out; you're perfect for each other. You've been flirting with each other for the last – what – three years? I would just consider my job if I were you. But, then again, she might just be worth *my* job."

"Yeah, thanks Mark. I'm not upset, but I really have to get to work," I said, ending the conversation.

He left and I went back to work. But, because of Mark's joke, I couldn't help thinking about Max Vi's new question: *"What was I?"* If you ask a person *who* somebody is, they will tell you the name of the person, nine times out of ten. If you ask them *what* they are, they will tell you what they do. In that case I guess I'm an accountant. That's it! What you learn is what you are! I am an accountant because I know accounting principles. I learned accounting. What you are is what you learn to be. If I were a dentist, I would have learned dentistry, if I were a teacher I would have learned how to teach. That's what he meant. What you are is that which you choose to learn. *You have the choice to be what you are.*

The thought made a chill shock my spine and I knew that I was on the right track. Max had said to remember that anything was possible with the correct knowledge, training, beliefs and attitudes. I had no control over who I was, but I was in control over what I was. To learn and believe whatever I wished was my choice. Just like the little boy who asked his father. I could be whatever I wanted to be. Again a chill went through me, stronger this time.

Unlike *who I was*, over which I had no choice, I could choose to learn to crawl, walk, run or swim.

Well then, *what was I?* Was I just an accountant? I shuddered. Surely I was more than an accountant; I had learned more in my life than just GAP accounting. Really, I, like Max, was a magician, too. At least I could perform some tricks.

At that moment I realized, *"what"* I was, was just a label. To the kid who was told not to talk with strangers, I was a stranger. He had changed the way he reacted to me, because the label he had assigned to me said that I was a stranger. We all assign labels to everyone, creating what they are. Learning what you are is only part of what you are. I knew *who* and *what* I was somehow was not so important. It is more important that I am, just the existence of me is me. I am a storage of experiences and knowledge. I am a person, a real person. There is more to me than just who and what I am.

Was an accountant all that I was? No, definitely not, I had dreams, ambitions, aspirations, emotions, fears, and regrets … I had love to give … Yeah – I had regrets, all right.

The rest of the day passed rather quickly. At five o'clock I straightened my desk and was about to head out to the elevator. I had opened up my desk drawer at least a dozen times to look at the rose, which was now starting to wilt and about to lose its petals soon if it didn't get some water. Deciding to take it home with me, I was just putting it into my vest pocket when Gina walked around the corner.

"Hi, James, I'm looking forward to our date tonight," she said.

"So am I," I said, feeling very good about seeing her again, "Wait a second and I'll walk you to your car."

We got into the elevator and again I found myself fighting back those feelings. She stood there just a few feet from me. I could smell her perfume, Elizabeth Taylor's Passion. I found myself breathing too heavily, feeling a little light-headed. I wanted so much to embrace her and kiss her. Taking a step toward her, I looked into her blue eyes and said, "Gina." This was it. She looked up at me, and we both knew what was going to happen.

However, nothing was going to happen. Just then the elevator stopped and the doors opened. Several people entered, talking about their jobs. The mood changed; my heart quit pounding. And though I was a little disappointed, I was almost relieved. If the elevator hadn't stopped, would I have kissed her? I quickly recovered from my light-headedness when the elevator doors opened into the garage. As I headed for my car, Gina reached out and grasped my hand, squeezing it with a giggle.

"James," she smiled a sincere smile and said, "thank you for the flowers."

I didn't say a word. I just stood there grinning, watching her practically skipping over to her car. As she drove past smiling like the cat that just ate the canary, she waved and honked her horn. "I really do love her," I said to myself.

"Life Is Full Of Happiness And Sadness –
Whenever Life Is Full."

Chapter 8

After a quick shower and shave, I put on my best silk blazer with a new pair of pleated slacks and *Polo* shirt, better than wearing the old standby, my navy blazer and khaki slacks. Reaching for some cologne, I wondered what would be right to induce the proper mood. Then it dawned on me. What mood? What was going to happen? I wasn't going to be seducing anyone! I was supposed to find out who Gina thought sent her the roses. But I already knew who she thought did – me! And I already knew who did – me!

What would I say to her on this date that wasn't a date? Mr. Lee had already determined that it was just a get together for a drink after work. Yes, I wanted her, but I also knew that I just couldn't throw away my career. Her dad may not have me thrown out on the streets, but I was up for partnership review this year. Although I really cared about her, I knew that it was in my best interests to not see her again; we would have to just be friends. I'd just have to tell her we were only friends. That was that.

I reiterated this plan over and over to myself, all the way out the door, into the car, and driving to her house. However, when she opened her door my mental train derailed and suddenly I forgot all about my terrific non-involvement plan.

She was lovelier than I had ever imagined possible. Wearing a back-less black satin dress, her golden hair was pulled up revealing her soft neckline wrapped by a single strand of pearls. She looked and smelled of sweet seduction. I had never seen her wearing anything like this and I liked it. I liked it a lot. She smiled, turned a circle holding the dress out to her side like a dancer, saying, "Hi there, sailor, new in town?"

My eyes must have been popping out of my head and my mouth gaping open. It was obvious that I'd never seen her looking like this before. All that I could muster was a long pause and a, "Hi."

She took hold of my hand and stepped out of the doorway, pulling the door shut behind her. "You look and smell marvelous, James. I don't know if I want to go eat dinner or you," she said with a chuckle. Then she laughed and added, "Oh, I didn't mean for that to come out the way it sounded. I just mean that you look great."

Obviously I had picked the right cologne.

"You look absolutely stunning," I said, at last able to complete a full thought without rambling.

"Thank you, James. And I want you to know that I think that you are the most handsome man that I have ever met," she said. "Of course, I've never met Mel Gibson, Tom Cruise, or even Mel Brooks, for that matter."

I was glad to see that she still maintained a sense of humor even while she looked ravishing. We both laughed and I opened the car door for her. I was kind of quiet, even for me. At a loss for words on the drive to the restaurant, I felt kind of awkward. I kept thinking things like: I should have washed the car, and did I remember to brush my teeth? I found myself even wondering if my socks matched.

"James, you sure are quiet. Don't be so shy. I'm still just me, Gina. I'm the same person who wears blue jeans and a T-shirt that you always tease at work," she said.

"I'm sorry, I do seem a little nervous, I guess. I don't know why," I evaded, more than just a little nervous. Usually I didn't get this nervous on dates, but I knew that Gina and I really had potential and I didn't want to blow it.

"Well, don't be nervous. I won't bite you – yet," she said, as she pushed up the armrest and scooted across the seat. Then reaching over, she lifted up my arm around her shoulders and kissed me on the cheek. That helped relax me a bit – a lot.

With a surge of confidence from her actions, I said, "Thanks, I needed that." I squeezed her shoulders in close to me. She smiled. Fantastic. Maybe I need to relax, keep my thoughts in the present, not concentrating so much upon the past or future. My thoughts were graced with a tingle up my spine and I knew it was the right thing to do.

We pulled up to the Palace, probably the most chic and ostentatious place in Austin. Just the drive up into the long circular driveway, around the flowing fountains, past the Rolls and Lamborginis to get to valet parking, was an experience for most. If you weren't a state legislator or senator, you normally would have to wait a week to get a reservation. Luck must have been on my side or I wouldn't have succeeded with such little notice.

We approached the uniformed doorman and exchanged good evenings. He opened the doors as if he were presenting royalty. When we entered, I understood why. The restaurant was extremely elegant. Huge windows overlooked the lake; grand crystal chandeliers hung from the ceiling; each table sported a complete service of fine china and crystal glasses in place. All were covered with starched white linen tablecloths, adorned with a different colorful floral centerpiece, and came complete with a smiling waiter in a tuxedo, attached.

A large flowing fountain centered it all, and beyond, the rear windows overlooked the valley with a grandiose view of the lake and the city in the distance. A string quartet was softly playing chamber music in the corner. The scent of the flowers filled the whole restaurant. Our arrangement, coincidentally, was a bouquet of four dozen red roses.

"Oh, James, isn't this just beautiful?" Gina said as the maitre d' showed us to our table. We did, indeed, have one of the best tables with a beautiful view of the city.

"I had heard so many good things about this place, but it's more elegant than I ever imagined. Thank you again for bringing me," Gina said.

We then exchanged some more small talk concerning the ambiance of the restaurant. I was almost afraid that we'd run out of conversation, but the waiter was soon there and I took the privilege of ordering the wine. Gina was somewhat impressed by my expertise. Fortunately, I had prepared myself for just such an occasion, years ago, by attending an adult education class on fine wine tasting. But I had almost never used the knowledge that I had gained from it and up until that moment thought that it was a waste of sixty bucks. The nearest to ordering a fine wine for me was a trip to the Ale House to pick from the ninety-eight different varieties of beer. At the time I took the class I hoped to meet someone like Gina. Who would have thought that it would have taken this long to have the opportunity to order a decent bottle of wine?

I completed all the proper moves, viewing the label, sniffing the cork, trilling the wine, and finally the ubiquitous approval. With all of the formalities that go with such a high class culinary excursion out of the way, Gina spoke up, "James, I want to know more about you. Tell me about yourself."

"Well," I said, wondering if my life would ever be the same after tonight, "I don't really know where to start, or what to say."

"You can start by telling me about your past, I guess. You know that I don't really know much about it, after our one date in high school."

"Well, after high school I went to school at the University of Texas, where I studied accounting..."

"I am not asking for a resume, James; I want to know about you," she said. "Tell me about your family. Let's talk about your dreams and aspirations. Tell me about where you want to be in ten years. Tell me who you really are. What do you want to be when you grow up?"

"And to think that for a few moments I thought we weren't going to have anything to talk about," I said laughing, practically overwhelmed by all of the questions. At the same time I couldn't help being pleasantly awed by the coincidental nature of being asked, *who I was* and *what* I wanted to be.

It was great to see that Gina truly did have an interest in me, the real me. But something inside of me still held back. I wanted to talk to her about the inner me, about my recent experiences with Max, and how it had reawakened my dreams of being a magician. I wanted to tell her about my feelings, that I was missing something in my life, and how I wasn't really fulfilled at work. But, I didn't want to freak her out with the stuff about Max. And I'm sure it wouldn't have been the greatest career move to tell the boss' daughter that I couldn't stand my job.

So, I took a more conservative approach. "I'm just a normal guy: I like sports; I drink beer. But I guess that I'm not stereotypical because I like to go to the theater and the symphony too. I really like a lot of different things," I said, knowing that it probably sounded wimpy and boring. I apologized, "I'm sorry, it just seems so hard to start off talking about myself."

"Well then, tell me about your family, I don't remember if you have any brothers and sisters," she said. "I want to know what I'm getting into here."

"Well, for starters, I guess I can tell you that I have a younger brother, Carl. He hates when I call him my little brother. He is a twenty-five-year-old struggling actor out in Hollywood who actually believes he's the good-looking one. Carl has never really made the big time, but he's done a couple of commercials. He's always doing some kind of play or something, waiting tables on the side to keep afloat. However, he recently landed a part in a TV series, which he says should make him a household name. Who knows? Maybe I'll have a famous brother some day. You would like him; he's a real nut at times. He's a ham, just like my father..." I paused, trying to recall if I had ever told her that my father was deceased.

"What's your father like?" she asked.

"My father died when I was in my early teens, of cardiac arrest. It was rather unexpected."

"I'm very sorry. I forgot," she said, but rather than dwell on a possible *faux pas* she pushed forward. "I don't know what I would do if it weren't for my father. He's the greatest. What about your mother?"

"Oh yes, Mom is still very much alive. She lives in Houston, so I visit her about once or twice a month. Every time I do she says the same thing, too. 'Are you married yet?'" I said and laughed, hoping that I wasn't making any improper insinuations.

"Tell me, why isn't a catch like you married?" Gina asked.

So much for my insinuations. "I guess that no one will have me," I answered. "At least that's what I tell my mother."

Gina leaned forward and asked, "What is the real reason? You aren't one of these guys that is afraid of commitment, are you?"

"Oh, no, I am looking to be committed. Ha, ha. That really sounded stupid. Well, what I meant to say is that sometimes I think that maybe I'm not really happy with myself. I've had a couple of relationships, but they just didn't seem to work out. How can you be happy with someone else if you haven't got it together for yourself?"

Gina answered, "You could let the other person help you get yourself together; I think marriage is all about sharing the good and bad. Too many people wait for life to be perfect before they start to enjoy it. At least that's what I believe," she said. "Besides, you really seem to have it all together. You have a great job. You have great looks. You have a great sense of humor."

"Funny, I tell myself the same thing," I said. "But, somehow I feel that I'm missing something."

"What?" she asked, leaning forward.

About to answer her, out of the corner of my eye, I saw a person approaching the table wearing a white tuxedo. Before I could look up, he spoke and I immediately recognized his voice. Once again I was slipping into the *Twilight Zone*. Every time he showed up, my world became more unreal.

"Good evening, madam and sir. Allow me to introduce myself," he said. "I am the amazing, astounding, and incredible Maximillion Vi. However, you can call me Amazing for short or Max for shorter. I am the house magician this evening. Perhaps you would like to see a little bit of legerdemain, or a paltry amount of prestidigitation, or a conundrum of conjuring. If not, then how about a few magic tricks while you wait for your dinner to arrive?" Max turned his head just enough in my direction to give me a wink without Gina seeing, to remind me that while he was performing I was not to reveal that I knew who he was.

I thought to myself, "*Who he was indeed!*" This was not just a mere coincidence. I might as well just sit back and enjoy. I was just along for the ride now.

"Well, Gina, would you like to see some magic?" I asked.

"You know I love magic. Of course I would," Gina replied.

For the next few minutes he did some of the most incredible illusions and had us laughing all the while he performed.

"Do you like card tricks?" Max asked.

91

"I love them," Gina replied.

"Well, I wish that I knew one," Max replied. "Then we would both be happy. I suppose I could make up a card trick if I had a deck of cards."

"If you're really a magician, just make them appear," Gina challenged. I had to agree. But I knew he was too good for that. Max would not have brought cards up at all if he were not prepared in the first place.

"Don't you have any cards I could borrow?" Max asked, directing his question to Gina.

"No," Gina replied.

"Look in your purse just to make sure," he said.

Pulling her purse into her lap, she opened it up. Lo and behold! Inside was a deck of cards with a sticky, yellow, *Post-it* note stuck to it. The note read: "If I were really a magician, I would make them appear in your purse." Both Gina and I were astounded.

Max proceeded to do some card tricks, each more astounding than the last. After the cards had vanished, he made some little red sponges appear and disappear in Gina's hand. He made coins appear and vanish right in front of our eyes and eventually they passed one at a time through the table and into a goblet, which he held under the tablecloth. He ended by pulling a small black and white rabbit out of his top hat. I was still glad it wasn't the solid black rabbit from my dream. Somehow this bunny seemed more physical and less metaphysical. A good thing since I was trying to get a grip somewhere on the reality of the evening. Not an easy task, the way things were shaping up.

"Magic is like life. It's simply what you make of it. Some people choose to see distasteful deception while others see awe-inspiring illusion. Still there are those, like James, who see magic and life for what they really are," Max stated directly to me.

"What are they really?" Gina asked of Max.

She wouldn't get a straight answer. But I was as anxious as she was to hear what he would say. Even though she was the one asking the questions, I knew that he was really talking to me.

"What are they, you ask?" said Max. "Amazing!"

"That's not much of an answer," Gina said.

"I guess that depends on how really amazing magic and life are, don't you think?" Max asked with a smile and a wink in my general direction.

I could read volumes into what he had said, but now I wondered if I was reading too much into everything. Maybe I was giving more credit to what was happening with him than I should. After all, his tricks were just that, tricks that I had seen other magicians perform in other restaurants. I even knew how he did some of them. A few were very similar to those I'd seen in my handbook and I could probably perform them myself with a little bit of practice and training. Yet, I didn't know how Max got the deck of cards into Gina's purse without my seeing. That was impossible – that one had me stumped.

He then placed his hands out in front of us, cupping his empty palms together. "Allow me to look into the future for this evening." When he opened his hands he revealed a small crystal ball that now filled them.

"Look at that, James," Gina said. "Okay, magician, tell us our future."

If anyone could foresee the future, it was Max, and I was not about to interrupt. I just sat quietly and watched, trying not to put myself into the picture, rather, thinking how marvelous this evening was. Without prejudicing my view (by including all of my own doubts and questions), the events surrounding me did appear really astounding – a significant moment of my life. Gina, Max, the flowers, the fountain, the lake, everything – life *had* created a beautiful illusion for me.

"Oh crystal ball, I wish to see into the future of James and Gina," Max said as he gazed into the crystal. "Reveal unto me – the future that you see ... I see both of your futures are becoming very intertwined. Fate will play its hand tonight, changing both of your lives, forever."

"Will we live happily ever after?" Gina asked.

"*The path to true happiness is a trail blazed by your own heart.* Happiness is up to you," he replied.

"What about sadness, will there be any sadness?" Gina asked.

"I know it sounds trite, but without sadness how would you know how to appreciate your own happiness?" Max Vi replied. "How can you even begin to feel alive if you've never felt real sadness? *Life is full of happiness and sadness – whenever life is full.*"

"Sounds like pretty standard stuff to me," I said. "You know, I expected some better, more well-defined predictions, from one such as the Amazing Max Vi." After saying it, I realized I must have sounded cocky without really meaning to.

"No one can really predict another person's future," he said, giving me a rather harsh look and tone of voice. "But, you can influence it. You can change it. Sometimes you can create it. *If you don't create your own future, someone else, or something else, will create it for you.* Remember, Jim and Gina, the difference is not in the path that one takes, but the trail that one makes."

Gina – like my protector – chimed in, feeling that the conversation was getting tense. "Amazing? That is what you said to call you, isn't it?" she asked.

Max smiled and said, "You can call me anything you like, any time you want."

"How do you do such magical things?" she asked.

"A magician never tells his secrets, right?" I responded before Max had to.

Then Max continued, "Just if you ask him how; the trick to getting the secret is to ask why?"

"Well then why?" Gina asked.

"Let Jim tell you *why*," Max replied. "He knows."

"I've just barely figured out *what*," I said and we all laughed. Only Max and I really understood, but it still sounded kind of funny.

"I'm glad to hear that," Max replied. "It means it's time for you to work on *why*." Then the waiter appeared at his side with the table tray. "I'm sorry, but the time has come for dinner to be served and for me to vanish. Thank you both very much, you have been a perfect audience. And I might add that you make a perfect couple." With that he winked, turned, and walked out of view.

As the waiter set the entrées on the table, Gina looked at me questioning, "Is that the magician from the Festival? The one that you know? I know it is. Aren't you going to give the man a tip?"

"Oh yes, thank you, I nearly forgot, didn't I?" I reached quickly into my wallet and pulled out a ten-spot as I called over a waiter. "Would you please give this to the magician?"

"Excuse me?" responded the waiter.

I repeated, "I would like to give this tip to your house magician."

"Do you mean the quartet?" the waiter replied.

"No, not musician, I meant the magician," I explained. "You know, the man performing magic tricks at the tables, wearing the white tuxedo."

"Sir, I beg your pardon, but we do not employ any magicians. If there was a magician at your table, well, he was not employed by the restaurant," he said.

Gina remarked, "That is so strange, isn't it?"

"It's more strange than you can imagine," I said.

"What do you mean?"

"I believe that it was no coincidence he was here tonight," I said, looking at Gina, wondering if I should tell her the whole story and just how she would take it. "Something really strange is going on here," I added.

"Well, I don't know how, but you're on to me," she said almost boasting. "I admit it; I did it. I knew you liked magic, so when I saw this magician performing last week at another restaurant, I thought that it would be nice for our first date if he came here and performed for us. I offered to pay him fifty dollars, but when I mentioned your name, he said that he would do it for free. That's why I thought you should tip him."

"You? You did? Wait a minute! You said that you saw him last week. I didn't ask you out until today," I said.

"Oh my gosh, that's right. Well, I guess that I have a huge confession to make," she said, looking up into the air as if to ask for divine guidance. "This date was not really your idea; it was mine. I made it all happen. Just as the magician said, I created it."

"What do you mean?" I asked, suspecting that I wasn't the one in control from the very start. After all, all that I had intended to do was just ask her out for a drink. Look what it had turned into.

Gina answered, "I have been waiting for a long time for you to ask me out. At first I thought that you had someone else, then I thought maybe you went gay. But, I know you're not, and I know you like me. I've even tried asking you to ask me out, but you never do. Like when I asked you if you were going to the festival. Finally, I decided that I would just have to get up the nerve and ask you instead," she said. "So this morning, I gave you that one red rose, and I was going to ask you if you got anything special. Then I was going to say that we could celebrate your having a secret admirer by going out. We would come here for dinner and sit at this table with the red roses. When you made the reservations, you didn't know that I'd already made them under your name.

"Anyway, my plan changed a little, when, while you were out to lunch, I received a dozen roses – I sure hope that they were from you. It was Daddy that actually came up with the real plan. After I told him that you sent me a dozen roses, he suggested that he should call you into the office for a little chat. He said that he would pretend that he was mad and that you should help him find out who sent the flowers. And of course the best way would be to take me out for a drink. Now you know why Daddy and I get along so well. He's devious, just like me."

"You mean that your father knew about this all along?" I said laughing out loud. "I thought that I was being so cool in his office. He was great. He was really great! I have to hand it to him. I especially liked the part about the Colombian drug dealer."

She gave me a questioning look. "Never mind," I said. "But I thought he really wouldn't let anyone who works for him date you. Mark even showed me the memo."

"Oh, no, you heard that? Serves me right, I guess … I was the one who made up that rule," Gina said. "That was just so I wouldn't be hit on by every Tom, Dick and Harry with an accounting degree and lead in his pencil. But you're different from the rest; you're the exception. I kept wanting you to ask me out, but you wouldn't," she said, her lips pouting.

"I think that you're about the most cunning, calculating individual I've ever met," I said, shaking my head in disbelief. "Let me restate that. You are the most beautiful, calculating individual that I have ever met. This will have to go down as the strangest date of all time. Maybe even the best date of all time."

"Well, maybe the *second best*?" she said reaching into her purse. "Here I brought something to show you."

Out of her purse, she shyly pulled a small silver-framed photograph, which she glanced at briefly and smiled. When she turned the frame for me to see, I couldn't help chuckling just a little at the two awkward teenagers, frozen for posterity on the Kodak paper. There we were: Gina in her frilly, white, southern-belle gown complete with hoop skirt and parasol, me in my rented gray tuxedo with tails and ruffled shirt, both surrounded by an imitation starlit night – a hundred cardboard stars, covered with tin foil, hanging on strings. "Wow, this is amazing, I've never seen this before."

"You probably don't remember, but when we ordered them we had them both sent to me. Well, I promised back then that I'd give one to you on our next date. Since you never called me, I just held on to it. Eventually it went into my keepsake box. Yesterday, my Mom and I were talking and she remembered it, so I went rummaging through my memorabilia, and well, here it is. That's for you to keep, James. It has taken awhile, but I guess I kept my promise."

"Thank you, Gina," I said, "This is really terrific! I don't really know what to say."

"Well, you could tell me why on earth you never called me," she said punching me softly on the shoulder in jest.

"I am beginning to wonder that myself," I said, cradling the photo carefully for one last look before placing it into my jacket pocket.

Gina paused, waiting for more of an answer, "Well?"

"I don't know, maybe I was shy … maybe I was just afraid that you didn't really like me," I said.

"Why?" Gina asked, "I was nuts about you."

"Well, the one thing that I can remember is that when we said goodbye I was going to kiss you goodnight and instead you stuck out your hand for the old handshake."

"Oh, that," Gina lamented, "I can explain that. It wasn't anything to do with you. It was because of my father. When you and I were on the front porch saying goodnight, I could see Daddy peeking out the living room window," she laughed. "He always told me that good girls don't kiss on the first date. I was afraid that he would embarrass me something awful and I didn't want you to see him either, James. I had the biggest crush on you. I didn't know what to do, so I shook your hand. When you didn't ever call me after that night, I must admit that I was pretty devastated."

"That was a long time ago, wasn't it? I can't believe I didn't call you either, I'm sorry," I said, "but, we're here tonight."

"Well, I'll tell you one thing," Gina said taking my hand across the table, "I did make Daddy promise that he wouldn't be peeking out the window tonight."

"You're too much," I said and we both laughed.

The rest of dinner was fantastic. We had waiters making a fuss over us as we made a fuss over each other. The conversation covered everything from high school days, both of our ambitions and dreams, to Daddy's golf game. Gina was everything that I had ever imagined, exciting, loving, smart, caring and fun. She was amazing. Why did I wait so long? After all the flirting, kidding, and joking back and forth – after years of denial – it was self-evident, I loved her then and I loved her now.

When the time came to call it a night, I knew where I wanted this evening to go. That kiss, the one I had planned on the elevator for a year, was going to finally materialize and I was going to reveal my true feelings.

As we walked out of the restaurant, wrapped arm in arm, looking up to a genuinely beautiful starlit night, listening to the sounds of the gushing fountains, it all came to a crashing halt. The next few seconds passed in slow motion.

Walking over to the valet, handing him my ticket, I heard the screech of braking tires. Turning quickly to the sound, I saw a car jump the curb and the doorman leaping out of harm's way. The skidding Mercedes glanced off the key booth, sideswiping the concrete columns at the entry making a loud, grinding clash. It missed my torso, but my arm slammed into the side mirror as the car passed, ripping my coat from my shoulder and flinging the framed photo out into the street where it shattered on impact. Gina, however, was standing directly in front of the car. It's bumper smashed into Gina's legs which buckled from under her. Gina's body flew across the hood of the car. Her head and body came to a crushing stop, smashing against the car's windshield.

I grabbed my right arm, soaked with blood where the mirror had torn my jacket, and sprinted to the car where Gina lay motionless on the hood.

Her legs were twisted under her body, obviously broken. She bled from the back of her head, which now made a circular indentation into the shattered safety glass. Searching desperately for something to stop the bleeding, I yanked at my coat to take it off only to find my sleeve impaled into the gash in my arm. When I tugged the material, I felt a tremendous pain. I yelled in pain, "Agghh," as I ripped off the sleeve caught in my own muscle tissue. The pain was immense, but taking a deep breath I proceeded to pull the jacket free, screaming at the doorman through my clenched teeth, "Call an ambulance!"

The driver, a woman, cut across the chest and face, stumbled out of the car, toward me. Crying hysterically she sobbed, "Oh, my God. Oh, my God!"

I felt faint, knowing I was about to black out. I tried to pull the glass away from Gina's head without moving her body, pressing my jacket up against the wound in the back of her neck. It was then that I realized that she was not breathing. Everything seemed to be caving in. My vision narrowed as if I were viewing the situation through a closing tunnel. I blacked out.

"If You Don't Create Your Own Future –
Someone Or Something Else Will Create It For You."

Chapter 9

The awful smell of ammonia slapped me in the face. I opened my eyes, shaking my head from the pungency, and tried to focus. Almost a lost cause, but then my thinking cleared a little. An Emergency Medical Team member was waving something in front of my eyes and nose, something to wake me up and clear my head.

"I'm awake. What happened? Where am I?" I asked, still in a daze, but slowly realizing what was going on. My eyes began to focus as my head cleared. Apparently, I had been out cold for more than a few minutes. The EMT's had already bandaged my arm and now worked, bent over the hood of the car where Gina's body lay in a pool of her own blood.

"We're ready to lift this one, Mike," said one of men who was bending over the hood of the car, yelling to the man standing above me.

"Okay, you just sit tight here for a second," he said to me, giving me a pat on the shoulder. He then, in one continuous motion, stood and hurried over to the front of the car. They lifted Gina's rag-doll body from the hood on to a stretcher making sure not to move her spine. One of them came back over to me.

Tears automatically filled my eyes, "Is she alive?"

"She's still alive," assured the EMS man, named Mike. "We'll do everything that we can. Right now we need to transport all three of you to trauma at St. David's. Can you walk?"

"Yeah, I think so," I said, wincing from the pain as I tried to use my arm to help me stand.

"Careful, here let me give you a hand," Mike said as he pulled me up by the uninjured arm. "Is the lady ... is she your wife?"

"No, she's not," I said, trying to hold back my tears.

Escorting me to the front seat of the ambulance, he said, "Why don't you ride over in the front. I'm sorry, but we need all the room to work in the back. Come on." Painfully slow, I walked over to the cab of the ambulance, stepping over what was left of my torn and bloody silk jacket and the smashed photo that lay in the street. Sitting down inside the ambulance, I stared through the small window into the back where Gina lay motionless.

Why? I began to cry as I feared that I might lose her forever. She was slipping away from me before I had a chance to say *I love you.* "Why did it have to happen? Just when I thought that I was going to be happy, they take it all away."

The driver jumped in and turned on the siren, pulling out into the traffic. I turned in the seat so that I could see through the window without turning my head. The EMT's worked frantically on Gina. By now she had tubes stuck into her veins, an oxygen mask on her face, and her beautiful dress was cut off of her shoulders. But Gina was still motionless except for the violent jerks of her head and body as they performed CPR. One of the men shook his head then took out a syringe plunging it into her left arm. By the looks of things, I could tell that she was near death.

We pulled up to the Emergency Trauma Ward entrance where two doctors, several nurses, and orderlies were waiting. Like a well-placed guard, one of the nurses stepped in front of me cutting me off from reaching the stretcher, which held Gina as they whisked her away. Finally inside, I was approached rapidly by a nurse with a pen and a clipboard in her hands.

"Are you the next of kin?" asked the nurse.

"No, I am just her boyfriend," I said.

"Do you know how we can reach the next of kin?" she asked, writing as she spoke.

"Yes, I work for her father. I can give you his number," I said relating all of the information that I could, after which she asked me to sit in the waiting room and said she would have a doctor see me shortly. I remarked that I was fine and that I just needed to know that Gina was all right.

"You're not as fine as you think," she replied. "We need to get someone to set your arm."

That was the first time I noticed my broken arm. "No wonder it hurts so much," I said to myself as I limped my way toward a nearby sofa occupied on one end by a Hispanic woman crossing herself and praying. Leaning back, I rested my feet up on the coffee table, trying to get comfortable. It wasn't working; my head and arm, both throbbing torturously, hurt way too much.

What was actually only ten minutes passed by like an eternity. A nurse finally approached me; I was half sleeping, half trying not to pass out, with my eyes half-closed. Evidently assuming I was asleep, the nurse touched my shoulder and spoke very softly to me. "Mr. Carpenter, the doctor will see you now," she said.

"What about Gina?" I asked, grimacing slightly from the pain, letting out a guttural groan as I did. My heart sank. My bottom lip began to quiver, and I wasn't sure if I wanted to hear what they were going to tell me. My fear – that they would tell me she was dead.

"Maybe the doctor can tell you about her condition when you talk with him," she replied.

I really didn't expect her to know what was happening anyway. But I would be damn glad to finally get in to see a doctor. The nurse led me into a sterile room and had me sit on one of those cold steel examination tables covered with paper. She then took my blood pressure and pulse, asked me a few questions about dizziness and nausea, wrote a few notes into my file and then trotted out the door, completely emotionless the entire time.

I was expecting a long wait, but the doctor appeared almost as soon as the nurse had shut the door. "Hello, James, I'm Dr. Zenner. I'm going to have to pull that bandage off and take a look at your arm. First let me..."

"What about Gina? Is she going to be all right?" I asked in a state of panic, biting down on my lip (a bad habit which surfaced whenever I was under stress). If he didn't give me an answer, I just knew it was because Gina had died and since I wasn't a relative, I was not notified.

"Which one was Gina?" he asked.

"The girl brought in with me … in the black dress," I said, nearly panicked. Realizing too late that, by the time the doctor examined her, the dress was probably removed and, anyway, what she looked like was far from his mind.

"I'm not sure, just calm down, both women are alive. Was she the one driving the car or the pedestrian?"

"She was the one hit," I said and tears rushed down my cheeks. I was not crying; I just couldn't stand it any more. "Just tell me, is she going to be all right?"

"James, she is receiving our best possible care. She is listed critical right now. That means that she has suffered life-threatening injuries. She has had a severe head trauma and has not yet regained consciousness. Both of her legs are broken, she has severe lacerations about her neck, and she has lost a large amount of blood. The best advice I can give you is to pray and wait."

I hadn't realized that during our conversation the doctor had removed part of the bandage and was giving me a localized anesthetic. After re-bandaging he walked over to a cabinet and pulled out a couple bottles of pills. "I'll assume that you are going to be staying in the waiting room for a while. These pills will help with the pain, but no driving while you're taking them. Take two every couple of hours," he said as he gave me a paper cup full of water and two pills. I didn't know if they were pain pills, or tranquilizers, or what, but at that point I hurt too much to care.

"The nurse will wheel you down to X-ray now and we'll get a picture of the break in your arm, so that we can set and cast it. And try not to worry, I'll keep you posted on the Lee girl's condition, just as soon as I return." With that he scratched a few more notes in my file and left.

In the quiet I sat there, the only sound was the rustling of the paper that covered the cold metal table I was sitting on. It's just an illusion, I thought. It's got to be just an illusion.

The nurse entered a few minutes after that. Beginning to feel light-headed and nauseated again after I had taken the pills, I guessed that they were starting to have an effect. Calmly, the nurse asked me to accompany her to X-ray. However, when I proceeded to get down off of the table and stand, my legs collapsed under me. My vision went spinning and then dark. I was out again, like a light.

Next thing I remembered, I could feel the cool soft sheets against my skin and the pillow under my head. The air had that very recognizable hospital smell. I felt a little dizzy and drowsy, like the feeling that you get when you fall asleep on a late night road trip trying to stay awake to keep the driver company. I felt the need to be awake and I attempted to sit up – disoriented. But still, somehow I figured out that I was lying in a hospital bed in the dark. When I tried to move, I realized that my right arm was very heavy. I couldn't bend it. Then it all started to come back to me; I had broken my arm and it was in a cast.

The room was void of light. I had no idea what time it was, what day it was; I could barely remember who I was...what I was. There in the dark silence I remembered. "Gina," I said aloud and sat up in the bed. What about Gina? I reached around groggily to find a light or the nurse's call button. Then a voice out of the darkness, I recognized. Soothing to my ears, commanding and calming, it was the voice of Max Vi.

"James, she's going to be all right," he said.

Peering into the black void, I squinted my eyes. I could almost see him standing in front of me in the darkness. Then the lights flashed on, the brightness hurting my eyes. Not Max, but rather, a nurse was there to take my blood pressure. "Yes, we could use a little light," she said. Then she took my vital signs silently and recorded them on the chart. "You just get some sleep, and we'll talk about it in the morning," she said, clicking the lights back out.

Too tired to comment further, I shut my eyes once again. My head spinning in a fog, I drifted slowly off to sleep. Dreaming again, Christmas Day 1968, and we are just finishing opening the presents. I see my father sitting in his Lazy Boy recliner, his feet propped up on the simulated-marble coffee table, Kodak Instamatic in hand. Everyone is so happy, the best Christmas morning I remember. The music on the reel-to-reel is playing Elvis Presley's "Blue Christmas" – the joyful scent of the Christmas ham baking fills my every breath.

Carl has already made quick work of his gift wrapping, the remains of which now blanket the room like remnants of an early morning snowball fight. Carl cheers, "Look Daddy!" getting exactly what he wanted, a "Robotron," a remote-controlled robot that goes forward and backward with hands that change to missiles firing ten feet at the touch of a button. Why he wanted that, I hadn't a clue. Still, he is pleased as punch to run it back and forth over the tiled kitchen floor.

Still wrapped in its red foil wrapping, my big present is sitting on the coffee table. The label says: "To Jimmy, From Happy Papa." I tear at the paper with a vengeance to reveal that my dream had come true also. Inside I find the Blackstone Jr. Magic Set, my first real new magic kit. Having seen a commercial on TV, I begged my father to get one for me – seventeen tricks guaranteed to amaze your family and friends.

"You are going to have to give us a show after dinner," says my father, peeling one of the oversized navel oranges which Santa always left in our stockings.

"Say thank you to Happy Papa," says Mother.

"Thanks, Papa," I reply and I run over to him, giving him a hug – so real I can feel the rough tickling of the wool on his sweater.

Then just as dreams always change, without any foreshadowing at all, we're suddenly sitting at the dining table. Mom brings out the main course, making a big production number just as she always had before Dad died. "Presenting the star of the dinner, ta dah! You think I'm a ham, this is a ham!" she exclaims. She was so much happier, so full of life when father was alive.

Dad stands up; he picks up my plate to serve me a slice of ham. Fear and pain come over his face, a look that I'd never seen from him before. Dropping the plate back down to the table with a clank, he bends over grabbing his abdomen in pain. Carl and I both look quickly over to Mom for some kind of reassurance.

"Are you all right, dear?" asks my mother, almost nonchalantly.

"Sure, it's just some extra acid, nothing a few Rolaids won't fix. Don't worry yourself," says Father.

Now the dream shifts time and place again. Now I am sitting in the hospital waiting room again. In my lap is my talent show trophy. My mother is seated across the hall from me. Carl, still just a little boy, is on her lap, eyes closed, mouth open, sitting upright but asleep.

"Mrs. Carpenter," says the doctor as he enters into the waiting room.

"Yes," replies my mother, as she stands up, carefully laying my brother back down onto the couch. Mom and the doctor walk across the cold gray room to the other side. I don't take my eyes off the doctor's mouth. Not actually hearing him, I can read his lips and make out the words he is saying perfectly, "I'm sorry, Mrs. Carpenter."

"I'm sorry, Mrs. Carpenter," he says.

"What about the show?" I shout, jumping out of my seat, the words echoing over and over. The trophy falls from my hand slamming against the hardwood floor, breaking into pieces.

"*She* is dead," my mother says crying, my dream confusing the two realities.

"No, *she* can't die. I love her. We have to do a show for Papa," I explain. "We have to do a magic show for Happy Papa!"

"There aren't going to be any more magic shows," she says. "There is no more magic."

With that I opened my eyes.

There, wearing his white tuxedo, sitting calmly at the foot of my bed, was Max. Not yet noticing that I was awake, in his hand he was holding the chain he generally wore around his neck, rubbing the small white cloth nonchalantly between his thumb and forefinger. Having turned on the small lamp on the table next to him, he was quietly reading a magazine. When he heard me stirring he stood up, turned, and set the magazine down.

"Are you awake?" he asked.

"What are you doing here?"

"I figured that you could use a guardian angel about now?"

"I knew it. And am I glad to see you," I said.

"Tell me, will Gina, will she be all right?"

"Jim, no one can predict the future," Max said.

"You can. I know you can," I said, knowing that he could, but refused to tell me.

"I can tell you that whatever happens has a purpose," Max said, "The purpose is to help you to discover your *why*. Whenever an individual is ready

106

to discover the *why* to his existence, he suddenly is given an opportunity. Usually that opportunity is in the shape of a tragedy or challenge. If she needs to die in your world for you to discover why, then she will die."

"But, I don't get it," I said. "I just don't understand, why?"

"Jim?" he asked. "Why are you alive? What is your reason for being? You can't go through your life just existing. You have to have a passion. You have to know what drives your vitality. This is how you will learn to run. Jim, you need to discover your reason to live – why you are, who and what you are."

"Don't you understand? It's Gina," I said. "She's my reason to live. With her I can have meaning in my life." Maybe because I was so tired or had been through so much, whatever reason, tears flowed down my cheeks.

"James, we all have a reason for being, it's similar to a contract which we make with ourselves before we enter this life. Life is the struggle to meet the terms and conditions of that contract with yourself. There are two ways to complete this contract. The first way is when we have completely fulfilled our obligations to ourselves the contract simply ends. The second is when, because of circumstances beyond our control, occasionally we are unable to fulfill our obligation. Then life steps in and lets you start over. The forces in charge of life always take the necessary steps to meet their end of the bargain. Understand that this includes creating any necessary tests, trials and tribulations.

"If your reason to live dies, you will die, too," Max said, now standing at my side. "But, if you go on living, then whoever or whatever died was not really your reason for living after all."

I was tired; I felt so sleepy; I wanted to sleep.

Max then reaches over and takes hold of my left hand, which is not in a cast.

"Here Jim, I want you to have this."

He places the silver chain with the pinned piece of white cloth into my hand, closing my hand tightly around it. "This piece of cloth is all the magic you will ever need to bring Gina back. If you believe in its magic, you can know *how*. But you must first find your *why* for being. Without understanding your *why* you will never know *how*. There is no *how* to life's magic if you don't understand *who* you are, *what* you are, and most importantly *why* you are."

The room is becoming foggy. Somewhere in the fog, Max fades into nothingness. Clenching my fist over the necklace, I realize I'm asleep.

The next thing I knew, I opened my eyes to a sun-filled room. The brightness of the sun shown through the sheers, the drapes now pulled back by a nurse who had awakened me. Feeling something in my hand, I looked to see if it was there; but I was not holding the necklace – only the corner of the sheet. It must've been a dream.

"Good morning, Mr. Carpenter," said the nurse. "How are we doing this morning?"

This nurse was someone that I didn't recognize. I felt a little bit groggy, but not so much that I didn't remember the night's events.

"How's Gina? Is she going to be all right?" I asked.

"What was her full name?" asked the nurse.

"Gina Lee," I replied, hoping for a square answer.

"I'm sorry, but you're going to have to ask the doctor."

I knew the answer before I even asked the question. Then I had another question. "How did I get in here? What's wrong with me?"

"Well, let me see if I can tell," she said as she picked up the chart, "It says here that you were admitted the day before yesterday for a broken arm, bleeding ulcer and a related reaction to a drug. Did you faint or something?"

"I guess I did – you mean that I have been out for two days?" I replied in confusion, but not expecting an answer. "I don't remember."

"Well, you've been sleeping awhile. Of course you were admitted after four in the morning, so it's only been a day really. The reaction probably wasn't too bad, because the doctor seems to have treated it with simple medication," she said. "He will be making another round at four thirty; you can ask him all of your questions then. Meantime, several people came to see you and left you cards and flowers. You seem to be a pretty popular guy at work."

I looked over at the credenza where there were two bouquets of flowers and several cards propped up against them. "Could you please hand me the cards?" I asked.

"Certainly," she said as she picked up the cards and handed them to me one at a time.

Opening them was a little difficult. However, once I got used to the fact that my right hand didn't work very well in the cast, I was able to rip them out of their envelopes ungracefully. The first card had a magical motif and was signed from the gang at work. "Wishing you a magical recovery," it said. The second card, a more plain vanilla "get well soon" variety, was signed simply: Mr. Lee. I wondered if he were still here; I wondered if Gina were still here. I had been out for almost two days.

The doctor walked in, quickly picking up my chart and asking, "How are you doing?"

"I'm all right, but I need to know how Gina Lee is doing," I said.

Not even looking up from the chart, he asked, "Is she a relative or friend of yours?"

"She was with me, uh, ... on a date, when she was hit by the car. We were both in the accident. Please, I've got to know. I've been out for two days and the last I knew she was in intensive care, and they didn't know if she would live."

"Jim, let me be straight with you. Gina is alive, but she is hanging on by a thread. I really didn't give her as much credit as she was due. With an injury to her head that severe, she should not even be alive."

"Thank God she is alive," I said. "Can I see her?"

"Jim, she hasn't regained consciousness, and I am very sorry, but to be absolutely truthful with you, it is highly unlikely that she ever will," he said.

My heart stopped. I experienced that same indescribable emptiness that I had felt when my father died. It suddenly became painfully obvious why all that her father had written on his card was "Mr. Lee." That he could have written anything at all was a wonder. *She is dead*, I said to myself, and my eyes filled with tears. I started to say something, but my mouth became dry, quivering, and I found that I couldn't speak.

"I'm sorry, Jim, in your condition, I really didn't want to tell you. But you do have the right to know," he said. "As for you, the medication we are giving you seems to have done the trick. You should be able to leave here within a couple of days. We just want to keep an eye on you for a while and monitor your progress."

"That's what they told my father, too," I said, and I guess that the doctor said a few more things to me, but in my almost catatonic state I really didn't care and didn't know what. I couldn't hear him anymore, completely unaware of anything going on outside of my own thoughts. Oh, I was aware that the room was now empty; I was empty.

"A Sunrise Or A Sunset –
Is Simply A Matter Of Perspective."

Chapter 10

Picking up the third get well card, one of those cards with a beautiful picture on the cover, but nothing written on it, I looked it over. The picture was the ocean view of a sunset. I opened it up. Inside, hand-written, was the question: "Sunrise or sunset?" It was, of course, signed simply: "Max." I had no idea if, or when, he had delivered it. I almost became angry with him for giving me some sort of puzzle to work on. Right then, I was in no mood for games. Sure, this one was simple enough. He meant that I had to make a choice. Either this was the beginning of a new day for me, or the end of one. I had an answer to give him this time. It wasn't the beginning or the end. It was the middle. "Figure that one out, Max," I said to myself, as I tossed the card spinning into the white wastebasket on the floor next to the other bed.

The door opened and I could hear the rustling of a paper bag. In walked my mother, bless her heart, bearing gifts in one of those mall shopping bags they give the customers around Christmas time. No doubt filled with something that she knew I really didn't need, but, once I got that something, I'd be darn glad I had it.

"Jimmy, I got here as soon as I could. It's such a long drive that I had to find a hotel. And since I'm not going to drive back tonight – I had to find someone to watch Felix," she said, setting the bags on the end of the bed and giving me a peck on the cheek. Felix was her mangy looking cat, who couldn't possibly have spent the night alone in that big old house. Because I knew how much she babied that cat, I had to be a little sarcastic at times, but really I was just glad she had the company.

"Mom," I said, "you didn't have to get a hotel room, you could have stayed at my place. Besides, I'm really okay; you didn't have to come up. I'm going to be fine. Anyway, that's what the general consensus is around here."

"Well, I know how you are about taking care of yourself. If you're in trouble, then I'm going to be here. If all that you'd done were just broken your arm, I wouldn't have come up to Austin. But, I've already talked to the doctors, you know. They told me that you have an ulcer, like your father. I was so worried; I just wanted to know that you are really all right," she said.

Even though she was really worried, Mom was tough. It would probably take a major disaster for her to let go with tears. But I could see through that tough exterior. She was on the verge of letting the river flow when she started reminiscing about Dad. She always started by wiping the bottom of her eyelids.

"I'm glad that you're here, Mom," I said, trying to put her at ease. "How have you been?"

She relaxed, starting a lighter conversation, "Well, I have been thinking about quitting my job, and going to one of those travel schools that I've been hearing about on the television. My friend, Pam, who is working at Dillard's, she's doing it. I hear the travel business will be one of the big opportunities for the next twenty years. I figure that I have just about that much time left," she said.

Whenever we talked anymore, the subject was always very superficial or in some way involved her final departure. I knew that if I didn't steer her conversation in the direction I wanted it would be heading for disaster. We would either spend the next two hours talking about how her life just passed her by (because she was too busy raising two sons) or else I'd be hearing about Felix's last trip to the vet to get rid of sand fleas.

"How's Carl?" I asked, wondering if he'd ever called her about the TV show.

"I will never understand that kid," she said. "He's just like your father; I don't know if he'll ever amount to a hill of beans. I told him I'd be happy to send him back to school if he would come back to Houston and study something real as you did. But you know him, he just asked me for some money, to tide him over till he gets his next – whatchacallit – gig."

"But last time I talked to him he told me about a part on a television show," I said, feeling out of the loop.

"Well, he had, but you know how those things go. One day he is on top of the world and going to make the big time, and the next he's living out of a dumpster. I wish that you'd have a talk with him when he comes up," she stated matter-of-factly.

"He's coming up? When?" I asked.

"Well, it should be within the next week or two, as best as I can calculate. Carl admitted to me, when we last talked on the phone, that he was broke and had enough food in the icebox for a week or two. When he asked me for some money, I told him he'd have to come and get it. I'll buy him a one-way ticket home. But if he wants to return to California, then he'll just have to hitch-hike or pay for it himself."

This was true mother, master manipulator. But I knew Carl better than she did. Carl wrote the book on counter manipulations. If he were coming to Houston, it was probably because someone there was making a movie and he was looking for a part. In actuality the call was just a ploy to pressure my mother to buy him the ticket to Houston.

Suddenly mother spied the flowers. "Who sent you all of the nice flowers and cards?"

"The cards are from some friends at the office. I don't know who sent the flowers yet. Is there a card in them?" I asked.

Leaning over the flowers, Mom picked off the little cards sticking out of the bouquets. She opened them and read them aloud. "This one just says from all of us at Lee, Fellers, and Gadheart wishing you a speedy recovery." Then a smile blossomed on her face. "This one says with love, from Gina."

"What did you say?" I asked. "Let me see that!"

My mother, not knowing about the entire accident, continued nonchalantly, "Have you finally met someone and not told your mother? What's wrong with you? I'm so ugly that you don't want to introduce me to my future daughter-in-law? Oh look, there is some more written on the back of the card," she said as she pointed to the back of the card I was now holding.

I didn't know what to say to my mother, not really wishing to talk about Gina. But when I read the back of the card, I knew I would have to tell her everything. Written on the back in Mr. Lee's hand, "Dear Jim, Gina ordered these to be delivered to your desk after she figured out that you sent hers." I fought hard to hold tears back, but tears fought harder against me.

"What is it?" Mom asked.

For the next hour and a half, I cried on my mother's shoulder telling her the whole story about the flowers, the office incident and the date. Mom said she was sorry for being so indelicate; she hadn't even considered that there was someone else involved in the accident. The hospital staff, of course, hadn't told her anything other than that I was involved in an accident, and I had developed a bleeding ulcer.

"Have you been able to see Gina yet?" she asked.

"They told me that only family would be able to see her until her condition is upgraded from critical."

"I know hospital rules. We can get in to see her if her family will let us. Have you talked to her father?"

"Mom, you're forgetting that I've been unconscious myself; I haven't talked to anyone but you."

"Well, let's give him a call," she said. "Where's the phone?"

"I was unconscious when they gave me the room; they didn't give me a phone."

"Well, I'm going to the desk to call him."

"Thanks Mom – Mom, I love you," I said as she walked out the door. That was my mother, always in control of the situation, never hesitating for a moment.

I wondered what I would do if I could see Gina. I wanted to tell her that I loved her even if she couldn't hear me. I wanted to tell her that I would be waiting for her and that I was not giving up on her. Just then the door opened, in walked Mr. and Mrs. Lee, followed by my mother.

"Boy, that was sure quick," I said.

"They were at the desk when I was making the call," said my mother.

"How are you, James?" Mr. Lee said to me.

"I've been better," I replied, not knowing what to say next.

Never had I seen Mr. Lee look so awful either: his eyes, puffy and bloodshot from lack of sleep, and his clothes, a mass of wrinkles as though he had slept in them the last week.

"Yes, so have I – so have we," he said, pulling his wife in tight next to him.

"I see that you got the flowers," said Mrs. Lee.

Mr. Lee added, "I had them brought up from the office." He ran his fingers over the petals of one of the flowers then continued. "Gina really cared about you; I want you to know," he said with a sniffle. "I told the nurses that you could visit any time you want. So you're on the list as far as that goes."

Though he acted strong, I could tell that he'd already drained all his tears and by now was completely numb. I was probably lucky to have missed out on the past thirty-six hours.

"I'm not going to give up on her," I declared.

"I know," he said.

A nurse popped her head into the somewhat crowded room. "I'm sorry but you are going to have to call it a day. Mr. Carpenter is in need of some serious rest and relaxation, and visiting hours were up twenty minutes ago."

"Well, Jim, I guess we'd better be going. For the first time in two days, we are going home, but we'll be back in the morning. So, do you need anything?" asked Mr. Lee.

"I can't really think of anything, but thank you both for coming to see me. I'll see you tomorrow," I said, as they walked out the door arm in arm.

After the door shut, my mother said, "Well, they seem like very nice people. Terribly sad about Gina ... I met her family at the company barbecue when you began working there, do you remember?"

"Mom, I'm kinda tired," I said, and I was tired.

"I haven't even given you your presents," she said, "I'll just set them here and you can open them when you feel better. I am going to the hotel and go to bed, but I'll stop by in the morning before I drive back to Houston."

With that she leaned over and gave me a kiss on the cheek and a hug. It felt good.

"Good night, Jimmy, I'll see you tomorrow."

"Good night, Mom," I said as she headed out the door.

Immediately, I pressed the button to summon the nurse to find out which room Gina was in. Rolling out of bed, I thought I'd just jaunt down the hall, only to discover it was a bit breezy. My rear was hanging out of one of those hospital gowns. Where in the heck were my clothes, and who in the heck undressed me? I searched the credenza drawers; the top one was empty, in the bottom they'd stashed my clothes. When the nurse entered, I was just pulling on my pants.

"Mr. Carpenter, you are supposed to be getting some rest," she said. "Is there something I can do for you?"

"As a matter of fact there is, I would like to visit my girlfriend, but I don't know her room number," I said, ready to put up a fight if she refused to tell me.

"I'm sure that we can arrange that," she said, much to my surprise.

I followed her to a main desk where she punched up Gina's location on a computer. "She is still in intensive care on the third floor, that is room 312. But she is..."

Not wanting to wait around to hear that I would have to wait till the morning, I bolted down the hall to find an elevator. The nurse halfheartedly called out for me. Judging by her feeble attempt, she was on my side.

When I finally found 312, I peered in through the glass. Gina was lying inside, on a bed with several machines rolled up on carts, monitoring her. Next to her bed, a nurse was sitting in a chair reading a book. As I opened the door, I recognized the steady beep of the heart machine. The nurse looked up at me, inquiringly.

"I'm sorry for disturbing you," I said. "But, I have to see her. She was with me when the accident occurred."

"I understand," said the nurse. "Why don't you take a few minutes alone with her? I'll be sitting just down the hall at my station. If you need me for anything, or if you hear any change, you just push this button, all right?" she said cordially, as she pointed to the cord with the button on the end.

"Thank you. I won't be very long."

Looking at her just lying there – like that – confirmed the tragic reality. Up until then, it had seemed like a bad movie. Now it was a slice of life. Just lying there in silence, her bandaged head was held by a shiny steel viselike contraption. Tubes were running out of her mouth, nose and arms. Plastic packages of plasma and blood hung next to her. Her eyes were closed, black and blue, and her mouth was dry and slightly open. Until I got down close to her face I couldn't even detect breathing. Kissing her cheek lightly, I prayed that somehow she would open her eyes and everything would be all right. But she just lay there in silence.

"Hi, I was just in the neighborhood, so I thought I would drop by," I said nervously, feeling confused, awkward over the situation, wondering if I had the guts to say what I wanted to. "I have a few things that I need to tell you. I don't know if you can even hear me or not, but I want you to know some things. So if you can hear me, then here goes nothing.

"Mainly, Gina, I want you to know that … I love you, and I'm sorry I didn't get the chance to tell you. Finally I realize that I've loved you for a long time. I'm just sorry that it took me so long to figure it out. I wanted to kiss you every time we rode down on the elevator. I just want you to know that, because I don't want you to give up and leave me here alone.

"I feel as if I have been wasting my life. Now that I've discovered what a fool I've been, it's too late to do anything about it. Well, I promise you that if you come back to me things will be different. I'm not going to let a day go by without living life to its fullest. I'm not going to wait around while life passes me by," I said as tears pushed to the edge of my eyes. "You have to fight for me. I don't want you to leave me, don't you see, I have no life if you're gone." Tears filled my eyes and overflowed down my cheeks.

Picking up her left hand, I held it to my wet, tear-covered cheek. Her hand was still warm, but otherwise lifeless. I held on tightly, praying that she would somehow be all right. I needed my guardian angel now.

*"The Card One Player Chooses To Discard –
Often Completes The Winning Hand."*

Chapter 11

The itching was driving me crazy. I was back at work, sitting at my desk, trying to get a pencil under the cast to scratch, but it just wouldn't cut it. I'd sure be glad to get the stupid thing off of me. It seemed as if ages had passed by since the accident, but it had only been nine weeks. Today was the day I'd get the cast removed. Other than that, things appeared almost normal at the office. Mr. Lee was back working again after a three-week leave of absence; however, he seemed rather distracted. He acted differently towards me now – in that he would talk to me a lot, mostly about Gina, sometimes about business. Often times it seemed he just wanted to talk to me, because we had developed a common bond. Surprisingly, we did think a lot alike – he, too, thought that most of the people in the office were totally boring.

I had visited Gina vigilantly, at least once every day, sometimes twice. As soon as I left work and in the afternoons on the weekends I'd go to the hospital and just sit with her for a while. Sometimes I watched a portable black and white TV that I brought with me, but most of the times I took books and magazines to read aloud to her. I wondered if she knew I was there. Someone had to be there for her. Even though the Lees stayed much of the time, I could imagine how lonely she might be. If she were aware of what was happening around her, but unable to respond – how awful – I didn't want her to suffer that.

Sometimes I would swear that she moved, but her body was always motionless. It was as if she was in another place, another dimension. I wanted to believe that someday she would make the trip back, but my hope, like that of everyone else, faded with the sun of each passing day. I held on mostly because I didn't know what else to do.

I hadn't heard hide nor hair from the amazing Max, as if my throwing the get well card away had severed our relationship. I was beginning to regret that I had; it would be nice to see him again. I guess that since things were getting back to status quo, my life was boring again.

Mr. Lee walked up to my desk. "Good morning, Jim," he said.

"Good morning, Greg," I replied. Since the accident he'd asked me to call him by his first name. At first I felt peculiar, but by now quite natural because we had come to know one another as real people, friends. I had learned a lot from Greg. So often we see people every day and say "hi" and "bye" without ever knowing what else they have to say to us – possibly something meaningful and important.

"I wanted to let you know that we are moving Gina home tomorrow, but you're still welcome to come and visit as often as you like. We've hired a full-time nurse, since the doctors say that her condition will allow it," he said. "We think taking care of Gina at home would be a lot easier for us. Anyway, Linda and I would like it very much if you came over for dinner this weekend. It's sort of a welcome home party for Gina, but it will be just us."

"Yeah, that'd be terrific," I said, but I wasn't really sure. I hoped that it wouldn't turn into an all-night candlelight vigil. Mrs. Lee could be very remorseful at times, often managing to blame herself. I sometimes wondered if she didn't partly blame me. After all I was the one that …

"You just name the time and I'll be there," I said.

Filling me in with all the necessary details, he then walked down the hall to his office. I had spent a number of evening meals with the both of the Lees. However, all of them consisted of takeout food in Gina's hospital room. They were really nice people, the Lees. I know why Gina loved them so much, and I knew why they loved her.

THE MAGIC LIFE

I wasn't sure if I liked the idea of taking Gina out of the hospital. The move would be better for the Lees, but I wasn't sure that I would feel comfortable visiting her at their home. But this way her parents could spend more time with her and I knew that she would want that. It really didn't make much of a difference what I thought anyway.

No sooner had I gotten back to being productive, than it was already time to head over to the hospital and get the damn cast off – quitting time for me. The rides down the elevator were not nearly as eventful without Gina around. In fact, they could be downright depressing. Sometimes I even hoped for Max to appear; however, I figured that he was out of my life for good, too.

When I got to the hospital they sawed my cast off. The skin under the cast was as pale as a white onion, and smelled just about as bad. But, I rejoiced seeing that everything still worked. Afterwards, I stepped upstairs to visit Gina. She was lying in the bed, on white linens, with the curtains wide open making the room well lit. She had fresh flowers on the nightstand, fresh makeup on her face, every hair in place, and a calm peaceful smile.

I'd made a habit of dumping the stagnant water in the flower vase and adding new whenever I visited. Turning to pick up the vase, I saw movement from the corner of my eye. I heard a voice as plain as day, "Hi, Magicman." Startled, I quickly turned around only to find that she was still motionless. She hadn't moved one inch – only in my overactive imagination. I tried closing my eyes and opening them again, shaking my head. Nothing. She was still the same: peaceful, calm, and quiet.

Auditory hallucinations – I had had them before. That's what they were. Sometimes, I wanted to hear something so bad that I was willing to believe the hallucinations were real. Taking the flowers out of the vase, I poured the old water down the bathroom sink, and refilled it with new. When I returned to the room I saw her. I stood frozen for a moment. It was so strange. Gina was sitting up on the edge of the bed. She turned to me, smiled and said, "Jim, you have to let go. Live *your* life; don't die with me. Find the magic."

Startled, I dropped the flowers and the vase smashed against the floor; water splashing and glass exploding out across the white tile. I blinked from the crash and looked back to the bed. Gina was still asleep. She hadn't moved. It was just me – my overactive imagination. My heart was pounding, but I wasn't afraid.

A nurse rounded the corner. "Is everything all right in here?"

"I just dropped the vase that I was refilling," I explained.

"Don't worry, we'll get a janitor in here to clean it up," she said, before she headed back out the door in search of the janitor.

I sat down on the side of the bed with Gina and looked into her silent, still closed eyes. "Was that you talking to me?" I asked Gina, looking for a response, a signal of any kind.

"What did you say?" came the voice of the janitor from behind me.

"Nothing," I said, startled a little, turning to look at him.

"Well, it sounded to me like you were talking," said the janitor, a smiling old black man who looked to be in his seventies. "And you can bet; she is listening," he said mopping up the water and picking out the glass to discard in a separate bucket. "I've been here for a long time; sometimes I talk to them, and sometimes they talk back. They're just doing their best to tell me things they want me to hear."

"Has Gina ever talked to you?" I asked, wondering if there was any substance to what he said.

"No, I can't say that she has," he said. "Maybe she doesn't have anything to say to me." With that he finished mopping up and started to say good-bye. "You have a nice evening now, both of you." Then he remembered something. "Here," he said. "I have a present for you."

He reached into his pocket and pulled out a piece of paper. "This might be just the thing you need. *The cards you set in the discard pile are often the cards someone else needs to make a winning hand.*"

"What?" I asked, not understanding.

"You know, one man's trash is another man's treasure," he said.

Thinking that he was giving me a piece of trash that he had found, I laughed.

As he headed out the door, I looked down at the crumpled paper in my hand, a card that had been tossed into the trash at one time. It read "Sunrise or Sunset?" It was so odd that he would have the card that I had thrown away. Were psychic forces at play here? I looked out the door, but the old man had gone. I looked down at the card and got a tingle. Max was not out of my life.

Then I thought about the hallucination with Gina sitting on the bed. Maybe I seriously needed to consider seeing a shrink.

"The Path To True Happiness –
                    Is A Trail Blazed By Your Own Heart."

Chapter 12

I hadn't yet figured out my "why" – my reason for living. However, if forced to choose, Saturday mornings certainly ranked high on the list. I slept in late, a little after 9:00, then got up and made my Kona coffee, which I really wasn't supposed to be drinking (doctor's orders), but actually I only used a little to flavor the cream. After filling my favorite cup, I sat back in my comfortable recliner to watch some heavy-duty cartoons, drink my hot, coffee-flavored cream and, well, just veg out. Sure it was boring, but at least it wasn't work.

I was sipping my cup of coffee, totally engrossed in an episode of *Teenage Mutant Ninja Turtles* when the doorbell rang. No doubt somebody selling something or else those Jehovah's Witnesses coming to tell me about the end of the world. Nobody else ever rang my doorbell on Saturday morning.

Walking up to the door, I noticed through the window a taxi idling at the curb. I opened the door; there stood Carl with a suitcase in each hand. "Hey bro," he said. "I hate to ask, but ... I'm a little short on cab fare."

"What a surprise – it's great to see you!" I said, giving him a hug and handshake – the kind men in our family were taught at puberty, one arm hugs and the other hand shakes. It was our way of showing we cared without that embarrassing affection. Not even thinking about it, I reached into my back pocket and pulled out my wallet. "How much?"

"Oh, just a couple of bucks for the tip, I had enough for the ride," Carl said.

I handed him two dollars. He dropped the suitcases in place, jogged over to the guy in the cab and handed him the money, saying, "Thanks for waiting, man. Take care, Travis."

"What's happening? What brings you to Austin?" I asked, picking up one of the bags while Carl made his way back up the walk, picking up the other.

"Well, since I had nothing else going on, and Mom paid for a ticket to Houston, I figured I might as well come and visit you."

"Come on in. What's shakin'? Have you got a movie going on here?" I asked, pointing at the two suitcases. "It looks like you plan on staying awhile."

"I know I should've called, but…"

"Don't sweat it, you know you're always welcome to the extra bed. Just chuck those in your room. Do you want to join me in a cup of Java?"

"Sure, that doesn't sound too bad, creamer and sweetener if you've got it," he said as he tossed his bags in the back room and returned in less than a second.

"Believe me, I have plenty of creamer," I said.

While I fixed him a cup of coffee, he made himself at home, grabbing the remote control and flipping the channels on the big screen television. Lying there in my big easy chair he asked, "When did you get the big screen?"

"I've had that TV for almost a year now. I guess it has been a while since you and I have seen each other," I said, handing him his coffee cup.

"Yeah, but you're looking pretty good for your age. You're almost the big 'THREE-O', aren't you?" he asked, reaching out to pat my stomach, making the insinuation that I was gaining some weight.

"I'm not in that bad of shape," I said, looking down at the few extra pounds of spare tire around my midsection, "considering my job."

"Yeah, one bad thing about working in an office all day, you never do get any exercise, do you?" he said.

"Sure, I get to work out down at the club, once in a while after work. Or there's always the weekends. Of course, I'm usually so mentally worn out by the end of the week that I settle for watching *Mutant Ninja Turtles* and eating a bowl of Cheerios for my workout."

"I noticed that you don't have a cast on any more," said Carl.

"Yeah," I said, "I'm sure glad to get rid of it."

"Well, I'm sorry I missed it. I wanted to write something obscene on it so that everyone at your office would be shocked," he said. "So tell me, what's going on down at Pee, Smellers, and Badfarts?"

"As usual, things are pretty dull," I said. "I'm sure that you wouldn't be interested in any of it. But now, you tell me about what's going on in tinsel town. You're the one who has all the excitement in his life. I want to hear how Carl Carpenter is about to make the big time."

"Don't I wish. More like big time washed-up. I've never gone this long without getting a callback. I was so broke that I actually came up here so Mom would lend me some money," he said. "Hell, I had to eat."

"Mom told me all about it quite a while ago. I guess I should've just sent you some money, but I didn't know if Mom was exaggerating for effect. You know how she is. Besides, she said that she was going to buy you a one-way ticket home, and I selfishly wished for a chance to see you. I guess I thought that you must have gotten something going when we didn't hear from you within a week or two," I said.

"Well, I was just being stubborn. I wasn't about to let Mom win. When I finally got kicked out of my apartment for late rent and had to spend a couple of nights in my car, I decided that it was time to swallow my pride and give in to Mom. She made it quite clear that there were plenty of strings attached to my bailout. Since you know about the travel deal, then you probably already know about my having to have my *discussion* with you."

"What? I don't know anything about any discussion," I said, and I really didn't know anything at that point. However, it was becoming clearer as we talked.

"Well, according to Mom, you are going to straighten me out about finding a real job," Carl said.

"Oh yeah, now I remember."

"But, I have news for you," he said.

"Hey, Carl, I am not going to push any of my life on you. What you choose to do with your life is your business, not mine," I interrupted. "You know that I won't try to tell you how to live."

"That's hardly the attitude that I expected from you," he stated. "I thought you would tell me that it was time for me to put away my childish ways and grow up to the ways of the real world."

"I have always supported you and your dreams, Carl." I said. "I'm not about to be the one to take your ambitions away. I realize how important they are to you, and personally, I don't think that you'd be happy at anything else."

"Well, I don't know what to say. I was expecting you to lecture me with the old *real world* pep talk. After talking with Mom, I really wasn't expecting you to be on my side at all," Carl said.

"Carl, if you're waiting for me to tell you about the real world, I have to say that, to me, the grass looks greener over on your side."

"Well, I guess it always does, doesn't it?" he replied.

"What do you mean?" I asked, realizing that he probably envied me and my life as much as I envied his.

"Well, it's just that I'm ready to throw in the towel," he said. "I've done all that I can. I've finally decided that I am just being stubborn and stupid, I'll never make it as an actor and it's about time I faced up to it."

"What?" I couldn't believe what was coming out of Carl's mouth.

"You heard me right. I'm going to give up and get a real job. That's the reason I came back home. That's what I wanted to talk to you about. I wanted to find out what I need to do to become an accountant."

"But is that what you really want to do?" I asked.

"Look, Jim, I really haven't got any other choice. I haven't got enough money to get me by for two days in LA, let alone however long it takes to find something substantial. I thought that I had the sitcom all sewn up and I guess I just quit looking. I know that there's no time to relax in this business. Well, I relaxed, got caught in the old squeeze play and tagged out."

"You've been there before, Carl, why are you giving up now?" I asked, not believing this. Carl had always been so optimistic about everything, living on a shoestring for months, yet still positive that the big break was just around the corner.

"I'm tired of knocking on the door and nobody answering. I feel like I've been taking advantage of you and Mom for the past eight years," Carl said, hanging his head, fumbling with the TV remote.

Carl didn't know it, or expect it, but I was going to give him a different pep talk. I didn't want him to give up his dreams. It was already difficult for him, and Mom never made it any easier. Maybe it was time for me to make it easier; maybe I could help.

"That's not the old Carl that I grew up with," I said. "Carl, you're the last one that I'd ever expect to just give up. Let me tell you something. For the first time in my life, I am extremely disappointed in you. You may not know this, but I have envied *you* and *your* lifestyle for years. I always wished that I were the risk taker, the one who could follow his heart. Don't you see, Carl? You're the one with the guts in this family. You have always lived life to its fullest, believing in yourself and what you are doing. You follow your dreams in spite of what others think or say.

"I know that it's sometimes difficult for you, but if you give up your dream, I'll lose part of my dream, too. You have to make it; someone needs to have a full happy life in this family. Don't let Mom kid you either, she needs it too. You're just about the only excitement she has. She *has* to worry about you. If she didn't have to dig up that money for you, what would she do? What reason would she have for getting up in the morning? Don't let her make you think that you've been putting *us* out. Not at all – we enjoy hearing and talking about Carl, the struggling artist's exploits and adventures. We don't want you to starve to death; I know that you'd rather starve than ask for money, but it'd be different if we had something else going on in our lives.

"If anyone is a failure here, it's me. I'm the one living someone else's life. I became what I am because of what others expected of me. You are what you are because of you: your dreams, your ambitions, your passions. You're a born actor. I'll always regret that I didn't follow my dreams, like you did.

"Remember what Dad used to say, 'If you find a job you like, you'll never work a day in your life?' Well, the opposite is true, too. Find a job you hate and, believe me, you work every minute," I said, stopping to take a breath, realizing that I'd been talking way too long. "Whew – that was much more than I ever planned on saying."

Carl said with a laugh, "I can't believe this. You are trying to talk me out of quitting?"

"You're damn right I am," I said. "You know, I've learned a lot about life in the last year. Since the accident I realize what a mistake it's been for me to live this safe life that I lead. I never take any risk at all. I was falling in love with someone, but never told her. Now she's gone. Story of my life, and I don't feel very good about it."

"I'm sorry, Jim, Mom told me about that," he said.

Quickly changing the subject back to Carl, I said, "You don't have to make the same mistake, quitting just because it's getting tough. Look at all of the work you've put into it. How about that? You can't just throw the years away. You've got to just keep knocking on doors. Who knows, the next door that you knock on could be that door that swings open."

"But what if I never make it?" he asked.

"Then so what? Do you need to make it? Or do you need to do it? There's a difference you know," I said. "The difference is that the people who *need* to make it are the ones who eventually give up. The people, who need to *do* it, have a passion for doing it. They never give up, because they've found out why they exist – their reason for living."

As I spoke, I realized where all of this newfound wisdom was coming from. "When I was younger, I wanted to be a magician; I wanted fame; I wanted to make people laugh and I wanted to amaze them. Along the way somewhere, I traded my dreams and ambitions in for security. Now, I'll never live my dreams; I'll play it safe, just as Mom advises. You come up here and see all of my material things, all these yuppie toys. Well, let me tell you, I would trade them all in for an ounce or two of self-respect. Carl, believe me – you think you are unhappy now? You could trade in your dreams for security, but there's no guarantee that you'll be happy about it. A very wise man once told me, *'The path to true happiness is a trail blazed by your own heart.'* And when it's all said and done, happiness is what life's really about."

Carl looked at me somberly and said, *"Above all else, to thine ownself be true."*

"What's that?" I asked.

"It's Shakespeare, from 'Hamlet'," Carl said. "It was a father's advice to his son."

"Sounds like pretty good advice to me, like something Dad would have said to you right now," I reiterated. "Look, Carl, if you still have the passion for theater and acting, and I believe you do, then I'll give you the money to get back on your feet. Following true passion eventually makes people successful in whatever they attempt. You have that true passion. Success will eventually come your way. I know how hard it is for you to keep trying with Mom discouraging you all of the time. Maybe I can counterbalance by cheering you on."

"I couldn't take your money; you've worked hard for it," he said.

"Carl, if you want, I'll charge you interest. I'll look at it as an investment, and I'm sure it's a damn good investment, too. When you make the big time, you can support me for a while."

Carl hesitated for a moment, but sensing my resolve, the worry left his face as he said, "Thanks, Jim, you have no idea what you've just done for me." He practically leapt over the sofa to me to give me a bear hug and shake my hand. "You are so right – about everything – thanks.

"I really do love acting; I practically live for that stuff. Hell, I work other jobs just so I can act. If you only knew how thrilled I am to get up in front of a crowd and listen to their applause, or get a laugh out of a hopeless line. I can't believe I was actually going to give it all up. You are one hell of a brother, and I'll pay you back, I promise," Carl said, getting a little teary eyed.

"I'll write you a check for two thousand now and buy your ticket back to LA. If you need some more after that's gone, I have a few more bucks stashed away that I can manage to part with," I said.

I wasn't certain if Carl would actually ever be able to pay me back. But if he got started again, I knew that he was every bit capable of supporting his career. He'd been on his own for the past four years – with only a few hundred bucks from Mom now and then and a few fifty-dollar donations in his birthday cards from me.

To show my faith, I wrote him the check and I could immediately see the relief on his face. My search for security had been good for something after all; sure made me happy to help ol' Carl out. Maybe my reason for living had something to do with helping Carl fulfill his dreams – his contract with himself. But, I wondered about me, *was I too late in the game?* Had giving up *my* dreams made it too late for *me* to change game plans?

Then for some strange reason, I thought back to the card that Max had given me while I was in the hospital. *Sunrise or Sunset?* What do you know, I was right. It wasn't the beginning or the end; it was the middle. It's always the middle; a beginning to one thing is the end to another. The reality is that one man's sunset is another man's sunrise; the sun is continual. It's simply a matter of perspective – just a matter of where you are on the earth, where you are in time. Wow, that was really profound! I couldn't believe that I'd thought of it without help.

Then my thoughts returned to a more earthly plane. What would Mom say if she knew that I was undermining her plan to get Carl off of the "Mother-Carpenter welfare system," her name for lending Carl any money?

"There's one thing that you must promise me," I said, "not really strings attached, just hairs."

"What's that?" he asked.

"You'll have to tell Mom that I tried to talk you into becoming an accountant, but that it didn't work."

He'd always paid her back every cent. So why'd she do it then? I mean why did she always try to stop Carl from pursuing his dreams? If she really wanted him to be happy, then she'd just have to understand his need to live his "why." Maybe it was because she saw her dreams collapse when Dad died. I didn't know.

Carl and I spent the rest of the morning talking about the Hollywood scene and what he almost did for the new sitcom. He told me that after they shot the first episode, he could tell the show was going to flop. "It was just plain boring," he said.

"It sounds like you made it *too* realistic," I added. He looked at me peculiarly, like he didn't quite grasp my meaning. "I mean most of the accountants that I work with are uninteresting. That really sounds bad – I don't mean to stereotype them as dullards, but I just don't seem to fit in."

"Jim, you never did fit in with that group," he said almost scolding me. "And what I don't understand is why you don't quit and do something else. You've been complaining about your chosen profession since your first accounting class in college."

"Sometimes I wonder about it," I said, "especially lately. I just don't have the drive that I used to. I feel as if I'm in a hurry going nowhere. I'm almost thirty years old and I really have nothing to show for it."

"You have a lot to show for it," he said, with a wave of his arm to the TV and stereo system.

"Yeah, I've got all my stuff, that's for sure. But I really don't have anything that makes me proud of the last ten years. When I graduated from college and passed the CPA, I was proud. But, I guess that I was doing it just to make it, because now that I've made it, I feel like there's no reason to do it."

"Well, then quit," Carl said.

No doubt he really meant it. If Carl were me, he would quit. Like our mother in one respect, when it comes time to do something you should just do it – you don't debate it to death. Too rash for me. "I can't just quit," I stated bluntly.

"Listen to yourself," he said. "You were telling me moments ago about the glories of living up to your dreams, but you aren't going to take any of your own advice. Practice what you preach, Jim."

"I'm too far gone. I've worked real hard to get to where I am," I said. "I can't just walk away from all of that education and expense. Besides, Mom would kill me."

"Mom hasn't killed me, yet," he said, "And besides, she always liked *you* best. Working hard, to get where you're at, isn't necessarily positive if you end up in some sort of living hell."

A bit dramatic, but his advice was starting to get to me. I wanted to be like him and Father, but I knew I was forever stuck being *who* and *what* I was. "Carl, I don't know how to do anything else but accounting. It's what I am," I said.

Rationalizing made me think of what Max had said about learning to walk before learning to swim. I must have forgotten how to swim. I had learned accounting, and now was drowning in my success.

"You are smart – you could learn to do anything you want to. I know that," he said.

Now the shoe was on the other foot. I could feel it coming, the old "unreal world" pep talk. I thought I'd head him off at the pass. "But, I'm almost thirty years old. I can't just quit and start over," I said. "That's just ridiculous thinking."

"Don't think of it as quitting and starting over. Think of it as if you're in the middle and you've changed directions," he said. Then Carl's face lit up. "I've got it! Why don't you become a professional magician?"

My spine tingled when he said it, but I wasn't listening to what both my intuition and life were telling me.

"Because!" I said emphatically.

What a fine crafted argument that was – if he only knew how many times I'd wished to become something else, besides an accountant.

"I know it's what you really want to do. Wouldn't it be great? Ha, you could move down to LA with me, and we could be roomies," he laughed. "Best of all, we'd have a big screen TV."

"Well, we'd probably have to sell it, along with everything else, just to make the rent," I said.

"So what," he said, "as if we can't live without a TV. It's not like they have any good shows about accountants and aliens on anyway. Ha, ha! Besides, didn't I once hear someone say that if you have a passion, eventually you would find the way to succeed?"

"I guess I can dish it out..." I said.

"Tch..tch..tch, but you can't take it," Carl said shaking his head back and forth.

"I don't have to take this from you," I said in jest, picking up one of the cushions off the couch and chucking it at him. "You are the little brother and I am the big brother."

Carl, imitating a little kid, said, "You better be careful, or I'll tell Mom."

"You better be careful, or I'll stop payment on the check," I said tongue-in-cheek. "Just kidding," I added, because I really didn't want him to feel any strings were attached to the loan.

Carl and I were always very close. We spent most of the afternoon just "BS"ing and downing a few brews. By evening we'd both loosened up enough that I even told him all about my strange encounters with Max Vi. He told me that, even though it was too weird for him, he thought it must be doing me some good – the positive change in me was evident. I wasn't buying it though; I couldn't see any real change. I knew *who* I was, *what* I was, but I was still hanging on to walking. I guess because I didn't know *why*.

*"Everything Has A Value –
But Only You Determine Its Worth."*

Chapter 13

Sunday morning I saw Carl head back home on a plane. Once he'd decided to continue pursuing his acting career, taking a vacation seemed meaningless. I guess that's what a passion makes you do. I really admired his attitude. Although we did have fun for one night, I wished that he had stayed longer.

When I got home from the airport, I called Mom to discuss what had transpired between Carl and me. In spite of my reservations, I decided to tell her the truth – that I talked him out of a "real job." She took it rather well, saying that she was glad it was my money, and not hers, going down the toilet. For Mom – that was taking it rather well.

Three days had passed since I'd last seen Gina and I was anxious to see her again. It had become sort of therapeutic for me, allowing me to think aloud about life and its *why*. And although it felt a little strange at times, talking out my troubles to her, I sometimes found I could work my way through many of them. Besides, I truly believed that if she were listening she'd know all about the real me after she came out of the coma.

Anyway, tonight was the special Sunday dinner at the Lees and I was to arrive at around five-thirty. Although it was a little early for dinner for me, the Lees seemed to be the type of family that had enjoyed (or maybe endured) a ritualistic six o'clock Sunday dinner for the past thirty years, never missing it once.

Thinking that it would probably be a pretty formal affair, I put on a business suit, and proceeded to drive to the Lees. On the way I couldn't help thinking about the first night that I saw their house. I hadn't been back there since the accident and as I walked up to the door I almost experienced a flashback. What I wouldn't have given to go back in time and live that night over again. The moment I saw Gina open the door, I would've just kissed her. Right then and there, I would have told her that I loved her. Who knows, maybe the delay would've changed the time-line just enough to keep her from being hit. As I stood at the door, I thought about not taking those little opportunities that life gives you, and the unforeseen consequences. But we don't ever know what we don't know.

Mr. Lee opened the door. "Come on in, James, get in out of the heat and into some cool air."

As always in Austin in August the heat was sweltering. My wearing a coat and tie made it doubly hot. Just the short walk up the walkway from my car to the door had me drenched in sweat. But the cool air of the entry hall as I stepped into it was revitalizing. Their home was every bit as luxurious as I had imagined, open, airy, decorated with fine art pieces, and luscious plants. The marble entryway, vaulted ceilings, and huge spiral staircase that wound its way around a dramatic crystal chandelier were almost overwhelming. Their house must have cost a fortune to decorate, but it wasn't *too* pretentious. Surprisingly, it felt quite comfortable, even homey.

"Have you been working?" asked Mr. Lee, noticing my suit. Mr. Lee was only wearing shorts and a sport-shirt. Suddenly I realized I was overdressed for the occasion. I recalled he always wore slacks, even at the company picnics. I'd never pictured Mr. Lee in shorts – actually he looked pretty good for a middle-aged accountant. For one thing, I didn't expect him to have tan legs – which he did. Not that I really spent a lot of time wondering if his legs were as white as mine were – I was just surprised that they weren't.

"I just thought that I'd dress for dinner," I said, handing him the gift-wrapped bottle of wine that I'd purchased just for the occasion. "Here, this is for the chef."

"Well then, that belongs to me, I suppose," he said, cradling it with a chuckle. "Tonight we are having barbecued spare ribs and I'm the man with the secret sauce. So you'd better like ribs," he said, showing me his homemade barbecue sauce mixed in a Mason jar. Then he turned and yelled towards the kitchen, "Linda, James is here."

"I'll be out in just a minute," she called back.

"Let me get you a drink, James. What'll it be?" he asked, as he walked into the living area to the wet bar.

"Do you have any beer?" I asked, feeling self-conscious about even drinking beer. "I'm really not much of a drinker." (Alcohol was another thing the doctor advised me to shy away from.) Besides, after the way Carl and I had pounded a few the night before, I wasn't feeling much like drinking anyway. And it probably wasn't a good idea to booze it up over at the boss' house anyway, even if we were on a first name basis.

"Well, let's see. I have six different flavors. What kind do you like? Lone Star, Budweiser, Coors, Miller, Miller Lite, or Pearl," he said, almost sorry that he didn't have more choices. "I guess that I need to get some good imports in here. But, most of my friends aren't much for beer," he added.

"Well, I'll just have a Lone Star," I said, showing my good Texas upbringing. Mr. Lee quickly exhibited his southern hospitality, getting one out for himself as well, making me feel right at home.

"Do you want a glass?" he asked.

"No thanks, that's all right."

He handed me the beer saying, "Well, you look very professional, but at least take your coat and tie off. It's too hot to dress for dinner today. I guess it's my fault, I should've warned you that we're never too formal 'round here," he said, with a touch of a Southern drawl. He really was a different person away from the office.

"I guess I've just never seen you without a suit on," I said. "I sort of took it for granted that you always wore one." I could even picture him sleeping in one, but I didn't mention it.

"Well, work is something else," he said. "Anything that I can do to keep from thinking about work is mandatory when I'm at the house. And Linda makes me live up to that promise."

"Are you talking about me again?" Mrs. Lee asked as she came waltzing into the room.

"Hello, James, it's good to see you again. How have you been?" She was always so cordial and proper. She gave me one of those proper hugs which included an air kiss to avoid getting lipstick on my cheek.

"I've been doing fine, Mrs. Lee," I said.

"Oh, please, call me Linda," she said.

"Okay, Linda," I replied, feeling a little uncertain.

She sat down and motioned for both of us to follow suit. We all sat in the comfort of the high-ceilinged, wood-paneled room, Linda and myself on the huge dark green leather sectional. Mr. Lee sat in his personal domain, the matching leather recliner (the remote control was on the table next to it). There was something of a pregnant pause for a few seconds, one where I felt that no one was going to say anything – as if we really didn't have anything else to talk about other than Gina or work. Work would be okay, but I didn't know if it was my place to bring up Gina or if they would.

It was Mr. Lee who filled the silence. "What do you think about the Cowboys this year?" he asked, referring to the football team, the Dallas Cowboys.

Not really keeping up with sports, I wasn't one to make any real intelligent conversation about football. "I really haven't been up on what's happening, since they fired the coach," I said. (At least I knew that much, and I certainly wasn't going to tell him I preferred debate this time around.)

"Well, I think that they're in for another great season. Linda and I have season tickets. It's a nice way to get away on the weekends and go to Dallas, even though they always win. Maybe you and I could go up to one of the games this year," he said. "You probably need the getaway as much as I do."

"That would be great," I said. "It's been a long time since I've been to a pro football game."

"Greg, James didn't come here to talk football. He came to see Gina. Come on James, I'll show you to Gina's room, and Greg can go cook the ribs," she said as she stood up from the sofa, motioning for me to follow her down the hall.

"All right, I'll get those ribs going," said Mr. Lee. "I think the fire's hot."

Mrs. Lee led me down a hall, past a few rooms and eventually to the door. "This wasn't her old room," she said. "She had the apartment with the separate entrance out the back, upstairs. We put the nurse in her room. We wanted her to be down here in the guest room in case anything happened – we wouldn't have to carry her down the stairs." We walked in. "Gina, there's someone here to see you," she said, just as if Gina were going to answer her, just as she had for years before.

The room was very alive, bright and cheerful with family pictures. The shelves displayed various knickknacks. The bedspread was a brightly colored floral print. Instantly I had to agree: home was a much better place than that drab hospital. Though there was really no way of knowing for sure, Gina seemed comfortable being home. She lay there in her silent sleep, looking like a little girl who had just tuckered out from playing too hard and lay her head down for a quick nap. There were no tubes sticking out anywhere and no noisy machines beeping a constant reminder that her life was insecure. The cold, sterile, hospital feeling was gone. Seeing her this way was warm and comforting.

We both paused in silence and looked at her. The tendency at first was to want to whisper when we talked in the same room with her, but we'd all grown accustomed to the idea that we weren't able to wake her. So now, we talked out loud.

"I think she's glad to be home," said Linda.

"Yeah, I'll bet that she is," I said. "How often does the nurse check on her?"

"She checks on her hourly," Linda replied.

"Is that enough?" I asked, wondering if she were getting enough attention, but knowing that the Lees would make certain that she was.

"According to the doctors, she could remain in this condition for a long time to come. We just have to treat her as we would a sleeping baby," she said.

Then I noticed that Mrs. Lee had been crying. It wasn't apparent in her voice, but her mascara had run just a little and had given her away. She quickly picked up a tissue from the desk dispenser and wiped away the tear. Realizing that I'd noticed she said, "Oh James, it's so hard not to cry."

"I know," I said, not knowing what else to say.

"I'm going to go check on Greg now. I'll leave you and Gina alone," she said.

As she stepped out, I felt awkward with this new situation. Before it seemed so natural to talk to her and to read to her. Now I was wondering what her mother would think. I was feeling a little lost.

Looking at Gina lying so still, I picked up her warm, motionless hand. "Hi, Gina," I said. "I've been missing you lately. I'll bet that you're glad to be home. It's pretty here; I really like your room. A little too feminine for me, but I'll bet that you like it better than that old hospital room, don't you? I'm beginning to feel kind of strange talking to you. I think that if you answered me, it would be easier for both of us." I paused, waiting for an answer; I thought for a moment that she would speak – but nothing.

"Well, I'm not going to give up on you. You're going to come back. I know it. Max told me one time that all I needed was patience, and he would teach me the secrets of the universe. So I figure, if I wait around awhile, I'll eventually learn what's keeping you away, and I'll bring you back.

"My brother came to visit me yesterday – yeah, I was surprised, too. I couldn't believe it, but Mom had actually talked him into quitting his acting career – the very thing he lives and breathes. And do you want to hear something really strange? I talked him out of it – me, mister real world conservative talked him out of quitting. Can you believe that? Not only did I talk him out of it; I gave him the money to do it. I know it doesn't sound like the ol' James you know – it didn't sound like the James I knew either. Maybe it was the old James, only now he knows himself a little bit better."

Then Mrs. Lee walked back into the room with the nurse. "James, I would like you to meet Joanne, our nurse."

"Nice to meet you," I said, shaking her hand.

She smiled back politely. "I'm afraid that I have some necessary duties to tend to. You'll both have to excuse me and Miss Gina," said the nurse. The way she sounded, those duties were something that demanded privacy. Even though I wasn't about to argue, for some reason Mrs. Lee thought that I wanted to stay, so she took me by the hand and led me out.

"Come, James, let's go into the dining area and talk while Greg finishes those ribs," said Mrs. Lee. She took my arm and we strolled into their dining room where the table was set up buffet style, plates and silverware on one end – food on the other.

"Oh, are we ready?" Mrs. Lee asked Mr. Lee, who was just entering from the patio with a mile-high tray of barbecued ribs.

"Those smell wonderful," I said, my mouth watering as my olfactory nerves overloaded with the delectable aroma of South Texas barbecue.

"That's my secret sauce," said Mr. Lee.

"Well, just help yourself. We aren't really very formal tonight," Mrs. Lee said to me. "You can start, James."

When we had finally gotten our plates filled, Mr. Lee decided that we should all eat in the family room. He commented that the dining area was just too formal for him and besides that the chairs were damned uncomfortable. Mrs. Lee disagreed with him at first, chastising him for saying "damned." However, the comment about the comfort of the chairs did win her over and she granted permission to eat in the family room. "That's okay," she said, "but we're not going to watch television, Greg. We're going to talk with James."

Ribs are somewhat difficult to eat daintily, and I knew that somehow I was going to drip some of the secret sauce all over my white shirt. All I have to do is wear white and I'm sure to slop something all over it. I was right. It only took me a minute before Mrs. Lee was heading to the bar for some seltzer water to help me remove the stain. The ribs were delicious though, and to ruin my shirt was almost worth it. The conversation started out light. Surprisingly, we didn't talk much about Gina.

"When I was your age, James, I had so much to look forward to. Now don't get any ideas, but I was just about thirty when Paul Coetrack, Geoffrey Fellers and I decided to leave the firm that we were working for and start our own. You probably don't remember Mr. Coetrack, I think he was gone before you joined the firm. He was such a feisty son of a gun that we could hardly work with him. And he really didn't like Gadheart joining the firm. I often wonder what ever happened to Paul. He probably became a soldier of fortune or something like that," he said with a chuckle.

"Anyway," he continued, "what I was getting at is that you're so lucky. You're young, and you've got everything going for you; you're whole future is ahead of you.

"Funny how life turns out, when I was a boy, I wanted to be a pro football player. I was quite the football star in high school. But, when I got to college, I was just plain too small to play with those big guys. Oh, yeah – I tried out for the team, even though nobody had given me a scholarship. In those days they didn't have very many athletic scholarships for football players – not like they do now. That was cold country, Minnesota State. As a freshman and sophomore I played first string, but I was cut after the first week my junior year, and you know what? I was lucky – that I was. I was only one hundred and seventy-four pounds. The average player was over two-twenty. It was then that I realized I'd better learn to live within my limitations. I decided, with the help of a few prodding sessions from my father, to study business. You see, I don't believe that the mind has any limitations, like the body. The only limitations you have with the mind are the ones that you set for yourself.

"It was actually my first accounting professor, Dr. Headley, who taught me that. He was a great man, and smart, let me tell you. I was way in over my head in my first accounting class. Like most newcomers to accounting, I didn't know a credit from my asset. I'll never forget the time, after just royally flunking his midterm, that I went in to his office to talk to him, to see if I could some way persuade him that I was worthy of a "D minus" and not an "F." I'll never forget that talk. It really changed the way I look at life.

"'Everything in life has a value,' he told me. 'And that value is dependent on three things. The first is how much it took to create it. Was there time, effort, and substance involved? The second is how much do people want it, or what the perceived value is. And the last and most important is – believe it or not – what day it is.' I really didn't understand the *what day it is* statement. 'However,' he said, 'because it's Tuesday, I'll give you the D minus.'

"Well, I really liked this old professor for that. And I learned that he was right. Old Headley was a good teacher, and I decided to become an accountant because of him. In our work, we are constantly trying to determine the true value of things. That value usually depends upon what something costs to make and how much one is willing to pay for it. You understand that don't you?"

"Sure," I said. "That's pretty basic."

"Well, *what day it is* could mean that there is a time value to something, like time value of money. You know, a dollar today will be worth a dollar plus interest tomorrow. And, of course, we know that fresh bread will be worth a lot more hot out of the oven than if we wait a week to sell it," he said, pausing to see if I was catching on.

"So, why was your test worth more since it was Tuesday?" I asked with a chuckle.

"James, I asked myself the same thing," he said as he tore apart a biscuit, using it to mop up some of his barbecue sauce. "I knew that it hadn't appreciated in value. So the way I figure it best, he meant that the value of something is pretty flaky to begin with. One day, for example, a stock can be worth a hundred dollars; the next day the bottom can fall out or vice versa based on someone's comment. Value is based upon the perception of something, you see. It's not based upon a truth. Putting a value on something is pretty much a judgment call that we make on a daily basis. When it comes right down to it, its real value is often dependent more upon what day it is than anything else. James, *everything has a value, but only you determine its worth.*"

"James, you will have to excuse Greg," Mrs. Lee chimed in, "He is into *Zen and the Art of Accounting* lately."

"Don't give me a bad time. James needs to know the finer points of accounting if he's going to become a partner," he said, and the words quickly brought my ears to full attention.

"Partner?" I asked, surprised, yet well aware of the kind of money which one could make from participation in the firm profits. Partner meant a lot. Just looking at their house made me practically drool.

"Well, we're in the process of promoting, and we have chosen three associates who are going to make partner this year," he said. "I was supposed to wait until next week to tell you, but I don't think that anyone will be too upset, since I am the boss."

"Congratulations, James," said Linda.

"Thank you," I said. "I really don't know what to say."

"You don't have to say anything. Just let me tell you a few of the perks that you'll get. For instance you get an individual office, no more cubicle. You don't have to attend the staff meetings anymore. You get to boss a couple of associates around, and you get participation benefits. That means about twenty grand more a year. That's something to celebrate, don't you think?"

"Yes, that's great!" I exclaimed, excited about the prospect of a new improved life. Now maybe I wouldn't be so bored with my job. Maybe this was the change I needed.

"Let's open up a bottle of champagne, Linda, and make a toast to our newest partner," said Mr. Lee. He then walked over to the bar and pulled out and uncorked a bottle of Brut champagne. The cork popped and the champagne flowed. Filling four glasses, he passed one to each of us and left one sitting on the counter of the bar.

He raised his glass, saying, "Here's to you, James! Your value has increased tonight, and may you determine your worth tomorrow."

That night I dreamt about going to the Lees. In the dream, Gina answers the door dressed exactly as she had been that evening, lying in bed. She looks marvelous; she is vibrant, alive, smiling at me. However, the dream is macabre, disjointed – something just isn't right. "James, we're so glad you're here," she says, "Daddy's been waiting. He's got a surprise for you." She then kisses me on the cheek and leads me by the hand.

"Come on in, James, I have something for you," says Mr. Lee, motioning me to come in. His back is turned to me so that I can't see what he is holding. "There was a big promotion on these over at the firm, so I picked one up for you," he says. Then he turns around, holding up a straitjacket, the arms opened up for me to slip in.

The dream repeats the same as the previous nightmares with Mr. Lee strapping me in the straitjacket and then attaching my ankles to the crane. Gina again lights the rope on fire while the voice of Max Vi announces, "He'll either have to learn to fly, or fall to his death..." It ends, of course, by my being dragged into the sky by the ankles, confined and confused. Panic overtakes me 200 feet in the air and once again, I find myself falling, falling, screaming.

THE MAGIC LIFE

With a thud against the mattress, I woke up, sweating and heart pounding. The same nightmare. Why did this memory fragment from my past become this nightmare? Why was I still having a recurring nightmare about it? Why?

"Enthusiasm Is The Grease –
That Moves Life Over The Rough Spots."

Chapter 14

Three weeks had passed since my big promotion, and I was getting pretty settled into the new office. Not much to see really, very starkly decorated: one plant, one chair, a small file cabinet, two decorator pictures on the walls beside me, and my diploma and certificates hung on the wall behind me. A little claustrophobic at times because the new office had no windows, I hated to admit it but I even missed the old teeny tiny cubicle a little. At least there was always somebody walking by the 'cube.' Here, there was nothing except my work to pass the time. With the exception of the phone ringing, or someone coming to visit (which was a rarity), I had virtually no contact with anyone.

The small desk clock, included in the company-provided desk set had now replaced the huge wall clock. Still, I was doing better financially after depositing a paycheck, which included my new bumped up salary. Even after taxes, my check was substantially more than I made before the promotion. I just had to think of new ways to spend all that cash. I suppose I could buy a few more yuppie toys; I always wanted one of those chairs that had a built-in stereo, or maybe I'd get a boat.

There was one huge advantage to having my own office: I could close the door and take a nap if I wanted. Since nobody ever came down the hall to visit, I could take a lot of naps if I wanted. Who was I kidding? Really

THE MAGIC LIFE

I wasn't the type. I had never actually slept, but I must admit that the location had provided a significant amount of daydreaming.

Just a few weeks remained before the Fall Festival, and I was looking forward to seeing Max again. Wondering if my days of being tutored were over, since I hadn't heard from Max or even dreamt about him for months, I figured that he'd just given up on me. If Max were going to teach me the secrets of life, he'd better get started; because I sure hadn't learned them on my own. Maybe I'd let him down in some way and that was why I hadn't heard from him. But, I still wanted to see him, and I knew he would be performing at the festival. Therefore, if I wanted to see him, I could in just a few weeks.

One major obstacle for me to overcome before the festival was something that I dreaded – vacation time. I know that sounds stupid, but I never know what to do on a vacation. Last year, I simply went to Houston and visited my mother, a fiasco. Although I had been given two weeks off, after only four days, I was so crazy that I came home and vegged out in front of the TV. This year I had asked if I could just work and take my money in cash instead of a vacation. The director of personnel informed me that vacations are to help us become more productive, not to help us make more money and work ourselves to death.

I'd thought about taking a trip to Europe. Even though I could afford it, traveling alone would be kind of a drag. Instead of talking to strangers on one of those all-day bus tours, I'd probably be better off just secretly working at home and not getting paid for it. Whatever I was going to do, I had only four days to plan, because personnel also informed me that I had to schedule the two weeks off before next Monday or lose them.

The phone rang. I answered, "This is James."

"Hey, Bro, what's this I hear from Mom about you getting a promotion?" asked Carl enthusiastically. From the tone of his voice, I could tell he was back on the right track again. I knew that it wouldn't take him long once he decided to get after it.

"Hey, Carl, it's good to hear from you. Yeah, I got the big partner promo. But to tell you the truth, work's still boring as ever. Tell me, what's happening in tinsel town?" I asked.

"I've got a few things going. I just shot a pudding commercial – the high point of my career," he said sarcastically.

"Well, I'll have to look for it," I said.

"Don't expect to see it in Austin. It's only playing in the Midwest. But, it'll pay a few bills. The exciting news is that I just got a part with a dinner theater group out of Newport paying $650 a week for the next six weeks. I can't believe it," he said.

"That sounds like a lot of money for a dinner theater part, isn't it?"

"Yeah, normally it would be about $300, but the play is being underwritten by some corporate foundation. We don't even have to have an audience, and we still get paid!" he said.

"Sounds like a good steady cash flow for a while."

"Yeah, steady employment, can you believe it? It's not quite a real job like yours, but real enough for me. Anyway, I'll be able to send you some money. And guess what I am playing?" he asked.

"A mutant scorpion?" I replied. He knew that I hated his guess-what game, but still, he kept on doing it.

"Funny," he said, "quite funny, in fact I think that you *should* give up your day job. You should be a comedian."

"Well?" I said. "You ask a stupid question..."

"I'm playing the magician in *Carousel*," he blurted out. "Isn't that a funny coincidence? First I get the part of an accountant, what you are; now I am a magician, what you should be."

"Ha, that is a real knee slapper. That is *'Hee-Haw'* hilarious," I said, with all of the sarcastic enthusiasm I could muster. "How was I supposed to know that you were playing a magician?"

Carl just blew right past it without comment. "Anyway, we're just finishing up rehearsals, and we start production next week. I've got a comp ticket for opening night, waiting for you, if you can take off for a day to come watch. It would be great for you to get away for a while, don't you think?" he said.

"Carl, I think that you really are a magician! I was just trying to figure out what to do for my vacation. What would you think about me visiting you for a while?" I asked,.

147

"Tell me when your flight arrives and I'll take care of the rest. It's been a long time since you came out to California. I just rented a little house out by Venice Beach, really cheap, a little out of the way, but a lot nicer than that rat hole I had in Hollywood. Since I will be performing nights we can spend the days doing the tourist thing," he said, "We'll have a great time."

Knowing I could afford to stay in a hotel if I didn't like the accommodations, the more I listened the more excited I became. He was a damn good salesman, ol' Carl. According to my father, *enthusiasm is the grease that moves life over the rough spots.* He always said that if Carl's enthusiasm were oil, we'd be Exxon. If anyone knew how to have fun, it was Carl, all right. "I think it's a plan," I said, jumping on his well-lubricated locomotive.

We continued to shoot the bull for a few more minutes ending with me telling him I'd call to let him know when I was arriving. He informed me that I'd have to call his answering service, because he didn't have a phone yet, but not to worry, that one would be installed soon. A home telephone was a luxury most struggling actors couldn't afford. Carl was no exception. I was surprised that he said, "yet." Although most considered telephones a convenience, Carl viewed them as an intrusion upon his sanctuary. However, I often wondered if intruding on his sanctuary was rationalizing his not being able to afford a phone.

There was just one other thing I had to deal with in order to take a vacation: I'd be away from Gina for a week. Seeing her at least every few nights since she moved home, and more often when I could, had become part of my routine now. Even though she was still unconscious, I just knew she could hear me. She needed me to be there. Maybe I would just spend a few days in California.

The day dragged on, the alarm on my wristwatch announcing five o'clock with that little "beep-beep, beep." Since I didn't have the big clock to watch anymore, I was compelled to set my watch alarm to prevent my working any longer than necessary. Heaven forbid, I ever accidentally worked overtime. Straightening up my desk and putting a couple of things into my briefcase, I was about to head out the door when Mr. Lee stepped in front of me.

"Are you calling it a day?" he asked.

"Yeah, I wanted to get to the store before I went to visit Gina tonight. I wanted to buy a book to read to her. Is there something you need for me to do before I go?" I asked, noticing that he had a rather puzzled, or perhaps a troubled, look on his face.

"Well, not really something you can do for me. James, sit down for a second," he said, as he pulled the door shut behind him. I hated whenever someone who wanted to talk pulled the door shut. It reminded me of the long sermons that my mother used to preach when she thought I was going to get a girl in trouble. He had that look, too: he didn't know where to start, but figured that he'd better clear the air. That was the look.

I sat down and he sat on the corner of the desk in front of me playing with the pencils in the pencil and penholder. Having never seen him fidget like this, I asked, "What's on your mind?" I hoped that I would be helping him out of his predicament. We had become close enough friends that whatever he had to say, he could say to me.

"Jim, this isn't really easy for me. I want you to know that Linda and I have truly appreciated your devotion and attention to Gina. In the past few months, you have become like one of the family to us. We're only concerned for your well being, Jim. We don't know if Gina will ever come out of her state. If she does, we don't know if she'll ever be the Gina that we knew. The doctors say that both are very unlikely," he said.

I didn't like the sound of the way this was going. "What are you getting at, Greg?" I asked, knowing that I was not going to like the answer waiting for me.

"We think that you're spending too much time with Gina. Jim, you're still young and have your whole life to live. I know that you love her, son, but you have to do what is best for you. Linda and I have talked it over; we both like you so much that we want to see you move on. I want you to be happy again. Someday you will find somebody and have a family, and ..."

My eyes filled with tears, but I held on to my dignity. We were both men, and I was not about to cry like a little boy. "I know that you mean well," I said. "But I'm not ready to give up on her."

There was a long pause before either of us spoke.

THE MAGIC LIFE

"I know you, James; you'll never give up. You're that kind of person," he said. He was right; I was prepared to live the rest of my life this way if I had to.

"I know that she'll make it," I said, but deep doubts were creeping in, just like the tears that now were backed up so heavy in my eyes that they were pushing over the eyelids and about to spill down my cheeks. I wiped my hand across my eyes, so that I could prevent the possible flood.

"Jim, we've decided that you shouldn't visit her anymore. We think it's better for you this way," he said, putting his hand on my shoulder.

"Don't do this to me, Greg – I love her," I said, and a lone tear made it past the dam and down the spillway.

"I know that, and I know this isn't easy for you. It wasn't an easy decision for us either," he said. He stood up and walked toward the door.

I wanted to die. "Can I at least tell her good-bye?" I asked. "I wouldn't know what to say, but I had never had the chance to tell my father good-bye, and it still hurts me."

"Yes, of course you can," he said, and then he was gone.

I thought that I had gotten over the hurt, but now I knew that I had repressed it. She had been taken away from me once before, only I refused to let her go. Now she was being taken away from me again. I couldn't let it happen. I needed her.

"Without You –
There Is No Magic."

Chapter 15

The warm evening, along with the burnt-orange and red sunset, was just bidding farewell through the bedroom window as I sat down on the edge of Gina's bed. The colorful sunset filled the room with warm tranquil tones, cascading through her hair, and painting a calming warm glow on her face. Gina lay in her bed in a peaceful, serene repose, wearing a cream-colored satin nightgown. The Lees dressed her every day and changed her to pajamas or a nightgown every night. They wanted to believe that everything was the same. I wanted to believe it, too. But it wasn't the same for me anymore; she was gone. The time had come for me to say good-bye.

As roses had played such a significant role in our past, I'd bought her a bouquet of the deepest reds that I could find. Removing one, I placed a single red rose in Gina's hand and closed her sleeping fingers around it. Running my trembling hands through her sunlit golden hair, laying my face close to hers, I could smell the scent of her strawberry shampoo, and feel the warm soft touch of her cheek against mine.

"I am going to kiss you, and you are going to open your eyes," I whispered, pressing my lips softly to hers, feeling her breath faintly beneath my own. As I gently kissed her, I pushed a faint gasp of breath toward hers, hoping that somehow she would magically reawaken and we would live happily ever after. She did not.

I swallowed hard and brushed away the stray tear that I had left behind on her cheek, knowing that she was gone forever. That tear would be my last tear for her.

"Good-bye, Gina."

After a long somber drive, I returned home and I decided to pour myself a strong drink. For the first time I could recall in my life, I felt justified drinking alone. I didn't turn on the TV, rather I sat on the couch, accompanied only by my drink and depression, and stared at the blank screen. Eventually, I reclined and stared up at the ceiling for a while. After laying there for at least an hour or more, feeling sorry for myself, wondering why I was getting such a raw deal out of life, the alcohol took over and I was asleep.

Never before had I experienced a dream that made me cry in my sleep. The dream starts off with the memory of the junior high talent show. Once again I am just a kid of thirteen. Just as then, Dad is carrying Carl piggyback up the stairs, then Mom lines us all up for a picture.

"You're going to have to give me a show at my birthday party," Dad says to me as Mom tells everyone to say *"cheeeeeesse."*

Dad is jogging around with Carl on his back for a few minutes then sets him down, saying, "Carl, I'm afraid I'm out of breath." He rubs his arm for a moment. And with pain and angst spreading over his face, he grabs his chest, and he drops hard to the floor.

"John!" Mom yells.

In the hospital waiting room, I see the doctor talking to my mother across the room. I am too far away to hear, but I see him mouth the words. "I'm sorry, Mrs. Carpenter, but your husband has passed away."

"No!" I shout, "We have to do a magic show for Dad, he can't be dead."

Mom pulls me in, hugging both Carl and me, saying, "There isn't going to be any magic show. Without your father there is no more magic."

We are now attending my father's funeral. The scene exactly as I recall: the misty-eyed relatives, the pale-colored flowers, the gloom-ridden black clothes. Puffy-eyed and weak from not eating, we all look like hell. Papa's death has taken a toll on all of us. They never say anything directly to me, but I overhear them. "He was so young," they say, "I can't believe he died like that, so unexpectedly." "What is she going to do with those boys?" As they lower the casket, my mother, brother, and I are all standing next to the grave. Mom can't seem to stop crying. Carl's crying, too. But I'm done crying, I've run out of tears.

Uncle Ray is holding Mom up. Mom is holding onto Carl on one side, hugging him closely against her hip. I am standing next to Carl with my left arm over his shoulder. In my right hand, dangling at my side, is the talent show trophy. Still fresh in my mind are the words my mother had said at the hospital, "There is no more magic."

"Without you, Happy Papa, there is no magic," that said, I toss the trophy into the grave watching it shatter against the hard wood of the coffin, six feet below.

I awoke, tears coming into my eyes as I painfully remembered why I gave up that childhood dream. My life was as empty as the pages of my scrapbook that followed that fateful day.

"No One Can Predict The Future –
But You Can Create It."

Chapter 16

The emptied bottle of Chivas Regal that lay, bone dry, on the living room floor was justification enough for my pounding head. I woke up on my couch, having never made it to the bed the night before.

"What time is it?" I mumbled to myself, reaching up to feel if my head was still there or if it had been replaced by a bass drum. A woodpecker had taken up residence in my ears. My mouth tasted like paste, the kind you used when you were in kindergarten to glue papers to the desk. The kind that if you ate it, it would just stick you up good, not kill you. To top it off, my stomach had moved back to Ulcerville – over rough roads in an old U-haul truck. Struggling to concentrate on my watch, which lay on the floor, along with my tie and one dirty sock, next to the empty bottle – my eyes focused in disbelief.

"Oh, my God, it's nine-thirty!" I said and jumped up quickly – too quickly. The booze had not yet left my system, and my head began to swim again. Sitting back down, or rather letting my body fall into the couch, I got a whiff of my arm pits. I smelled awful; I was sweating pure alcohol.

Reaching for the telephone, I dialed the office. Since I was now a partner, I had the privilege, when calling in sick, of simply calling the main desk to leave a message. No longer did I have to endure the twenty-question game from Mr. Braeback.

"Good morning, Lee, Fellers and Gadheart," said the receptionist in a voice almost perky enough to make me barf.

"Good morning, this is James, please inform everyone who needs to know that I am not coming in today. I'm a bit under the weather," I said. In these situations the less said, the better.

"Okay, James, I will. Mr. Lee asked if anyone had seen you earlier," she said.

"Well, you can tell him that I won't be in today," I said.

"Have you got the flu?" she asked.

I really didn't want to answer any questions; I didn't want to be awake at all. "Well, yeah, that's fine – tell everyone that I have the flu," I said, not used to telling even the whitest of lies to play hooky from work. Rarely did I ever miss work, even when I really was sick. I'll bet that I had more unpaid sick leave than anyone in the company.

"Okay, I will. You take care of yourself and get better," she said.

"Thanks, good-bye."

"Good-bye."

I had planned to start picking up my mess from the night before, but instead I opted to drink a glass of water and take an aspirin. Then I dragged my body into the bedroom, removing my pants and pulling my shirt off on the way. Falling into the bed with a thud, I was hoping that I could just sleep it off.

Next time I opened my eyes, it was two in the afternoon. Dry and parched, I stumbled out of bed into the kitchen for another glass of water. My head was not drumming anymore, but I still smelled like a wet horse biscuit. I poured myself a bowl of cereal, Cheerios of course, and turned on the tube – some soap opera. I just couldn't take it. I wasn't up to watching people with problems less than my own. Besides, the guy on the screen looked worse than I felt. So, I flipped to the sports channel to watch the old-timers play a little golf. That was about all I felt up to, watching senior's golf. Even watching baseball sounded too strenuous.

After an hour of just sitting there, staring at the television and thumbing through a few magazines (which I'd already memorized from cover to cover), I made a rash decision: I would buy my ticket to California – now. I needed to get out of Austin. Leaving town was the one way I could see not thinking about Gina – out of sight, out of mind. I had to get the hell out of town as soon as possible. Picking up the phone, I made a reservation for an evening flight – that evening. "California, here I come." Then, only because it was my duty and I was not one to shirk my responsibilities at work, I called Braeback.

"John Braeback here," he said, sounding like a drill sergeant with a bad case of hemorrhoids. I shouldn't say such mean things, but I really didn't like the guy.

"John, this is James Carpenter," I said. I'd never called him by his first name, but calling him John gave me a feeling of authority, and I kinda liked it.

"James, I hear you have a case of the flu," he said. "What can I do for you today?"

This new semblance of decency, too, was only due to my now being a partner. In the past he would have demanded to know which doctor I was going to and how much of my work would have to be handed out. He then would've spent fifteen minutes telling me just exactly how much my illness was costing the company, etc.

"About my vacation," I said, cutting to the chase.

"Yes, you have to schedule your time soon, because you are going to go past the deadline for this year's scheduled week off," he said.

"Well, how about if I start my vacation tomorrow?" I asked. "Is that soon enough for you?"

"This is pretty short notice. I don't know if I can get anyone to cover for you," he said. "You know how short-handed we are."

"I also know you're a very capable man," I said, feeling my authority affecting him. Otherwise, he would have just given me a flat "no" for an answer. "You'll figure something out," I said. "I have faith in you."

"Well, I guess, we can have Mark..."

I didn't even let him finish the sentence. "I'll see you in a couple of weeks. If anyone needs to talk to me, I'll be unavailable. There are no phones where I'm going. I'll have to call in," I said, knowing that it was going to be uncomfortable for him, but I really didn't care. He'd made me uncomfortable plenty of times. I was not in the mood to show pity for the man. In reality, I would have probably been a little more empathetic, if I hadn't had quite so much to drink the night before.

"I'll have to check this out with Mr. Lee first," he said, putting up a little resistance to my newfound authority.

He didn't know that Mr. Lee was my ace in the hole, but I decided to let him know. "Yeah, why don't you talk to Greg about it. If he has any problem, which he won't, tell him to give me a call before he leaves today. I'll be flying out tonight."

"Okay, I'll just do that," he said.

I could tell he thought I was bluffing by calling Mr. Lee by his first name. He didn't know what I knew: Greg would guess the reason I was leaving town was to get Gina out of my mind. Hell, he would've probably suggested a vacation himself – if he'd thought of it.

"Well, I'll talk to you in a couple of weeks," I said, hanging up the phone, not even waiting for him to say good-bye. I was sick and tired of putting up with playing the part of the dweeb, living like a groundhog, afraid of my own shadow. Even though I might regret it later, I wasn't going to let this jerk push me around anymore – time for me to think about myself for once.

I went into action. Planning to come back baked like a five-hour roast, when I packed my suitcases I made sure to include extra sunglasses, suntan lotion, and swimming trunks. Just as I zipped up my last suitcase, the phone rang.

I picked it up and said, "Hello."

"Hello, Jim, this is Greg. I just talked with Braeback. He told me that you were wanting to take off for a while."

"Yeah, I have some vacation time I need to use up; and to tell you the truth, I think I need a vacation right now," I said.

"I just called to tell you that I, well, I just want to say that it's all right with me. I know that we can manage here for a while without you. And if you need the time, I think that it's a good idea for you to get away for a spell," said Greg.

"I thought that a few days away might help me clear my head. I appreciate your calling," I said.

"I just wanted to make sure that you're okay," he said.

"I'll be okay."

"Where are you going?"

"I'm heading out to California. I have a brother who lives out there. We haven't had a good visit for a while."

"That sounds like a good idea. Well, are there any of your projects we need to take care of while you're gone?" he asked.

We lined out all the work details easily since I kept a detailed work plan on file. Most of my work was ahead of schedule anyway. After we got the work specifics out of the way, he told me to have a good rest and said he'd see me when I returned. I told him to give my best to his wife and Gina. Replying that he would, we said good-bye and hung up the phone.

For once, I was taking control of my own destiny. Maybe this was what Max meant when he said, *"No one can predict the future, but you can create it."*

"Just Begin Your Quest –
The Universe Will Rush In To Help You."

Chapter 17

The voice over the loudspeaker announced, "Flight ten-thirty-four to Los Angeles is now boarding at gate eighteen. All passengers with boarding passes for rows twenty and higher please begin boarding. This is second call for flight ten-thirty-four to Los Angeles."

I looked down at my ticket to check my seat assignment again – a window seat, over the wing. Hurry up and wait some more.

"Passengers holding seats for rows ten and higher should now board for Los Angeles."

Slowly, I meandered over to the line. Why were people in such a hurry to be the first in line anyway? The plane would take off at the same time. Hurrying to get off after landing, I could kind of understand, but rushing to wait in line made absolutely no sense. I slowly made my way through the check in, down the chute to the plane, and found my assigned seat.

Quite a few seats were left empty on the flight, after all the passengers finished boarding, and the two seats next to mine were both vacant. Great, I could stretch out and relax. While the flight attendants did their little safety song and dance, I pulled out the flight magazine and started studying the crossword puzzle. Watching the stewardess, I always thought that they should name a dance "the stew" and have you dancing and pointing the way they do to demonstrate the exits. Just an odd random thought.

Shortly after, we were taxiing down the runway, ready for takeoff. Since I was a little superstitious about flying, I liked to get the takeoff out of the way. The way I looked at it: fifty percent of all airplane accidents occurred during takeoff, the other fifty percent happened during landing. I was fine once we were in the air.

My superstition had manifested itself in a strange way. During takeoff or landing, I always wore my sunglasses (at least I'd have a little more protection for my eyes if we were going to crash). Stupid, I know, but it's just one of those little rituals you try once and you end up sort of becoming addicted. Not unlike the flying aces who would kiss their mascots before takeoff thinking they would be shot down if they didn't. Since I performed this rite once before and survived, I was cursed to repeat it over and over.

Putting down the magazine, I donned my sunglasses for takeoff. As the plane began to gain speed, I watched out of my window. It was just starting to rain, developing a cloudburst. Raindrops began pelting the runway as we accelerated. Takeoff was a little rough due to the sudden change in weather, a bit bumpy while traveling down the runway, but it was smooth as glass once we got the 727 off the ground. Breathing my sigh of relief, I removed my sunglasses as I looked down at Austin. As the plane turned and headed west higher into the clouds, I could see the university, the state capitol, and even the hospital all diminish one by one and eventually disappear over the horizon.

Sitting there, I couldn't help thinking about some of the odd habits which I had internalized over the years. Many actions are just automatic – we don't think about doing them, we just do, like my putting on the sunglasses during takeoff and landing; I was certainly well programmed, a creature of habit. If I did it once and was successful, I saw no point in ever changing. No wonder I was so set in my ways. If any aspect of your life becomes comfortable, why would you change? Is change really a good thing?

After I dug the airline magazine back out, I continued on my crossword puzzle – seventeen down, three letters for "absolute value." The center letter I felt fairly certain was the letter "a," it was also the second letter in eleven across, which coincidentally, I had as "magic." Its definition was "necromancy." Then it dawned on me "absolute value" is *the maximum*: "m" "a" "x." *Max?* When I thought of Max, the chills, always accompanying my thoughts about him, returned as well. I almost felt him looking over my shoulder. Certainly he wasn't on the plane – I would've seen him get on. That was unless he was on the plane before it landed. Looking around to see if he were on the plane with me, I had the tingle again.

When I boarded I really hadn't looked that closely. I really had a strong feeling about this. If there was such a thing as ESP, I knew he was on that plane. There was no way that the crossword puzzle would just happen to join the words "Max" and "magic." This was no coincidence. Something was going to happen, I was going to get another visit from my guardian angel. It was about time – another tingle – now I knew for certain that Max was on the flight with me!

I sat there waiting for Max to magically appear. Maybe I would see him sitting out on the wing in the rain as in an old *Outer Limits* episode. Or maybe he would walk up as a steward or something. I just sat there and waited, ready for him to appear. Waited, waited, and waited for him to appear. However, the only person who appeared was a flight attendant asking if I wanted a drink.

"Why not?" I said, realizing that my imagination was working overtime again. "I'm officially on vacation as of this moment."

"Well, what will you have?" she asked.

"How about a Tequila Sunset?" I said, actually meaning a Tequila Sunrise.

"Do you mean a Tequila Sunrise?"

"*One man's sunrise is another man's sunset.* Yeah, it's the same," I said with a chuckle to myself. "What time will we be in LA?"

"We should be landing in about two hours, eleven-thirty Pacific time," she said.

"Thank you," I said, taking hold of my drink and miniature tequila bottle. I poured the whole bottle into the mix. That was going to be a potent one – it was. The color of the drink reminded me of the sunset in Gina's room, the night I said good-bye. I wondered if I'd ever see her again. The purpose of this trip was to start fresh, to get her off my mind. If it took all of the tequila in California, that's what I would do. Taking a large gulp, I put on the headphones and, letting my mind wander, headed for the land of forgotten pasts.

After flipping the channel selector up and down for a while, I settled in to some classical music. I'm not really much of a classical fan, but I was tired and I thought a little Beethoven would be relaxing. Maybe I could catch a couple of Z's before we got into Los Angeles. Carl would want to go out for the rest of the night. That is, if he got my message, and was able to pick me up. If he didn't show up, all the more reason to have a little sleep under my belt. I'd have to rent a car and find a hotel on my own. Who knows how long that could take in Venice Beach, in the middle of the night, in August?

Yawning, I leaned my chair back as far as it would go, which wasn't far. I knew I couldn't really get comfortable – unless, I had one of the pillows like the guy across from me had. So, I pushed the button for the stewardess and she snagged me one. Propping it up against the window, I turned sideways to lay my head on it, closing my eyes to listen to a little Mozart.

A hand touched me on the shoulder. Thinking that it was an attendant, I opened one eye at first; however, I quickly directed my full attention to the person standing in the aisle when I discovered who it was. Max Vi leaned over to me and said, "Isn't this a coincidence? I was just thinking about you and here you are. Do you mind if I sit?"

I almost had to pinch myself to see if I was awake. Pulling off my headset, I looked around. Yes we were still on the plane and unlike the last time I'd seen him I was wide awake, maybe a little sleepy, but not dreaming. His clothing caught me off guard. Max was standing there wearing a navy business suit and red tie. He seemed a little out of character. But no matter how he dressed, he still looked mystical. He still looked like a magician.

"Where did you come from?" I asked, smiling.

"Up there. A better question might be: 'Where are you going?'" he responded in his counter-questioning style, with a laugh.

"Max, I've been through a lot since we last talked. I've wanted to talk to you. I need to talk to you. I'm not really in the mood to play word games. Right now I have some real questions I need answered, not asked," I said.

"Fair enough," he said. "I'll answer straight for once. I'm sitting in first class; I got on the plane late, and when I was walking back to the restroom, I saw you. I almost didn't wake you, but since we hadn't talked in such a long time, I thought you might like to continue our program now."

I refused to believe *that*. I wanted to believe that he was tracking me all this time, that he'd been hiding, waiting until I was on the verge of sleeping so that he could appear in my dream. His explanation was so rational it let the wind out of my sails.

"I had a feeling I would see you. Look, my crossword puzzle, the words 'max' and 'magic' are intersected," I said, showing him the magazine.

"I'm glad to see that you are busy tapping into the current of life. The past, present, and future can be found in almost anything around us. A person can open a book to any page, turn a card from a tarot deck, or read the horoscope from the Sunday paper. Each item could seem to reveal life's most intimate secrets. But, it's simply the individual tapping into the universal flow of life around him. Those signs are always there to guide you, if you are open to taking direction. You never see them if you spend all your time looking for them. However, they will *always* show themselves when you need them."

I had so much to tell him, but now I didn't know where to begin.

"Well, what else do you want to know?" he asked.

Feeling the fool because I wasn't sure what questions I was supposed to ask, I chose to explain what was happening to me instead. "I think I've discovered my reason for living," I said.

"So tell me, what do you think that reason is?"

"I was put on this planet to love someone – wasn't I?"

"You mean to love Gina, don't you?" Max said, softly, somewhat apprehensively, fearing I might be wounded by just the sound of her name.

"Yes, and now I've been told that I have to give up – that I should quit loving her and move on with my life. Do you have an answer for me? Am I supposed to quit loving her? How do you ever stop loving someone?"

Max turned to me and said, "Do you remember when I told you the three things of real importance in the world? The first one was to learn, the second was to teach. The third one was something that I said couldn't be taught or learned. It's something that you must discover on your own. Jim, I was talking about what we call, in life "love." Of everything that exists in this world nothing is more important. There are a million sayings, a million *more* songs, all about this mystery of life called love. 'Love is magical.' 'Love is blind.' 'All you need is love.' It's as if nothing else matters in the world, when you're in love; and nothing else matters in the world when you're not. Do you know why there is so much written about this one aspect of life?"

"Not really," I said without much thought.

"Because it is everywhere. Love is universal, timeless, space-less; it crosses every border, language and culture. I'm sure that you've heard before, that there are many different types of love."

No lightning flash there. "Everyone knows there are different kinds of love. The love one feels for a brother is not the same one feels for his wife and so on," I remarked.

Max continued, "Exactly. However, there are two extremes. The first extreme is an immature type of love, a taking love. Not immature in the sense that you like someone before you love them. I mean a love that revolves around a give and take situation. When a person finds gratification from being with someone else, sexual gratification, or even sharing one's life with another, this is that type of love. This is the love in which a person must receive a benefit in order to continue loving.

"The second extreme is a more mature love, the all-giving love. This love is unconditional; meaning that when I give my love, I don't expect or need anything in return. This is a higher kind of love, but don't take higher to signify better. It's not better; it's simply different. The more advanced a love, the more difficult to achieve, but not necessarily the better. We all are in different positions in life, allowing us to love in different ways. To say that one love is a better love than another is like judging a beauty contest. Something like comparing roses to tulips, who can determine which is better? It's really determined in the eyes of the beholder. Neither one is better. They are both beautiful. But some people prefer one flower to another.

"Anyhow, the love that I am referring to was perhaps the love that Christ or Gandhi had for mankind. When someone is driving a spike through your hand, crucifying you, or assassinating you, this kind of love allows you to ask that they be forgiven – not to curse them to damnation as most of us would. This is the same love that is given by parents to a crying child. Love for one's child extends far beyond all of the pain and suffering a child can give. In this kind of love, understand, giving is the key. And giving unconditional love is the key to becoming your true self.

"You asked me if you ever stop loving someone. The answer is determined by the kind of love you share. Grieving for a lost love is missing what you expected in return. You will eventually lose that love. However, if you love unconditionally the answer is no. Unconditional love will last forever, never expecting anything in return, yet always receiving the gratification that only unconditional love can provide."

Max paused a moment, then asked, "Have you ever heard of Abraham Maslow?"

"I don't know, but the name sounds somewhat familiar," I replied.

"Well, he was quite an expert in the field of psychology. He said that there exists a hierarchy of different needs in mankind, and that these different needs were ranked in a particular *'filling'* order. In other words, a person has to fill his base needs, such as the need for air and water, before he or she begins to fill the next higher need, say for food. After which he or she can move on to such needs as the need for sexual gratification, and a need for the sense of belonging. Anyway, Maslow believed that at the top of mankind's needs, was the need for self-actualization. This is the equivalent to the quest of discovering your *why* for existence. Once you have filled all of your needs, according to Maslow, you become whole. Once you are whole, only then are you able to love all of life with a mature and giving love. Only after you have satisfied all of your own needs do you discover the one remaining need. That is the need to fulfill the needs of others. What else matters if you have fulfilled all of your own needs? Jim, what kind of love do you feel for Gina?"

"What you are telling me is that I love Gina in an immature way," I said, feeling that what he said made a lot of sense, but it really wouldn't make any difference in the way that I felt toward her.

"Jim, I said that those were the extremes, meaning that your love can exist in many points along the spectrum of love. Love can be fifty percent giving and fifty percent taking, twenty percent giving and eighty percent taking and so on. No one type is better than the other. Whether love is better to give than to receive depends upon what you need, where you are in your life. For the most part I imagine that your love has been a totally unselfish love for some time now, not really deriving much pleasure from receiving."

"No, I suppose I have been giving and not getting ever since the accident."

"Do you feel good about giving for the sake of giving alone? Or do you expect to get something in return? Maybe you don't expect something in return now, you're just unconsciously banking on the future repaying you." Max asked, "Would you love her as much if you were certain that she could never give anything back? That is the question to determine the level of love."

When I thought about his question I was confused. All along, I loved her and hoped she would return to me, some sort of reciprocation of my love. Was that wrong?

"How can you love someone if she doesn't return the love?" I asked.

"Nothing is wrong with wanting love to be returned. Nothing's wrong with giving and expecting something in return. These needs for something in return are simply needs along the hierarchy. However, when you feel that you have all the love that you need, feel completely loved, giving becomes enough. Not just enough but even more satisfying. Do you understand? Giving becomes satisfying because you are happy and fulfilled in all of your other needs. Once fulfilled, then you will have the ability to attain the highest love, an unconditional love for life.

"But don't confuse even that love with your *why* to life. The love of life is only available to you once you have learned and are living your *why*. How can you fill your needs if you don't even understand what they are? Once you truly know your *why*, then you will find it easy to fulfill all of your other personal desires and needs. Then you will be at the top of the hierarchy, ready to give back an unconditional love to life," he said, "and beyond that, the possibilities are truly magical."

Max pulled out the steel chain from under his collar and rubbed the piece of cloth between his fingers, as if he were searching for an answer that he couldn't find. Perhaps if he rubbed the cloth, he would be given divine guidance.

"Why does it have to be so difficult?" I asked. "Why does it have to hurt so much?"

"Before any dream is realized, life tests everything you learned along the way. Life doesn't do this because it is evil, but rather because it wants you to master the lessons you learn on your journey. The closer you get to the dream, the tougher those tests become."

"Like my grandfather used to say, 'It's always darkest, just before the dawn,'" I said.

"Absolutely true, but remember that *brightest days, from darkest night, begin with just one ray of light.* Believe me, James, your sunrise is not that far in the distance.

"James, the lesson of unconditional love is the most difficult lesson to learn; because, as I told you before, it can't be taught. Being the most difficult to learn, it includes the most difficult tests. However, remember that the more difficult the test, the greater the reward."

"I give up. I don't know my purpose to life. Just tell me what it is and I'll do it," I said, at my wit's end. I was tired of worrying about it. "Without Gina, what's the point?"

"If you abandon this test, this pursuit of your *why*, it won't be because of Gina's love. An unconditional love will never keep a person from pursuing his or her own destiny," Max said, "You know who and what you are. Now, James, follow your destiny. Find out *why* you are."

I enjoyed and understood everything that he was saying. But in my search for meaning to my existence I was still lost.

"Jim, for most people, the question of why they are doesn't exist. Many people discover *who* and *what* they are without any need for what they don't know they don't know. They don't know that they are missing a *why*. *Why* seems to be difficult for most. Maybe I can help you with some examples of people who discovered why they are. When a person discovers why he exists, he usually becomes a huge success, because the match is perfect. Life opens up its doors to the person who knows what it expects from him.

"Abraham Lincoln, he knew his reason for existence. He was destined to be a great leader of political thought. He learned it early on. Many great composers understood that music was their reason for existence.

THE MAGIC LIFE

Mozart could have never been anything else but what he was. Many athletes realize that they are destined to be winners and live to achieve that success. For example, do you suppose that Muhammed Ali didn't know for a second that his future was to be the world champion of boxing? I imagine he had a doubt now and then, but you can bet any insecurity didn't last very long.

"And just because you're good at something, doesn't necessarily mean it's your reason for living. Consider Christopher Reeve. He was a good actor, great as *Superman*, but his life's contract demanded passage to another plane."

I interjected, "But I'm just a normal guy. I'm not a boxer or composer. I'm not even a very good accountant."

"James, Abe Lincoln would have been a mediocre farmer, Cassius Clay a mediocre store clerk. That's why so many people are just, as you put it, 'normal guys' like you. They know *who* they are and *what* they are. They just haven't discovered *why* they are. Don't misunderstand me. Just because you find out *why* you are doesn't mean that you instantly become famous either. Fame is not in everyone's picture. Do you know Annabel Rosa Saldana?"

"No," I replied.

"I didn't expect that you would, but maybe you should. She runs a foster home in Almedia, California. Discovering her why was extremely difficult for her at first, too, but now she has encountered and embraced her *why*. Once a mediocre housewife and average lawyer, now she's a remarkable social servant, because she has encountered her life's true significance.

"And that doesn't mean your *why* has to be something altruistic, or even worthwhile for anyone other than yourself. Mrs. Saldana exists to help others in her very own special and unique way. Even though she isn't rich and famous, she has found the one thing that always accompanies living out one's own *why*. She is happy. That is the reward; anyone who learns to live her *why* and to love life unconditionally, will be happy."

"So if I discover my *why* I will be happy?" I asked.

"No, you can discover your purpose and refuse to live it. Once you discover and accept it, you will have learned to crawl, to walk, and finally to run," he said. "But if you live it, to the fullest, every moment, life will indeed be gratifying. It's then that life will reveal all of its secrets.

"On the other hand, people who discover their *why* and don't live it are usually the most miserable and unhappy people in the world. Only after you begin to experience your *why*, can you learn to truly live. Really think about this while you are vacationing. Question some people who live their *why*. You will know who they are. You need to discover your *why* before – well, let's just say that you need to do it soon."

"What? Why do I need to hurry?" I asked, sensing that he was going to tell me something and then he decided not to worry me. Max was holding something bad back from me, some sort of negative consequence if I didn't discover my *why* soon.

Then a flight attendant tapped Max on the shoulder and said, "Sir, we are about to land. I am going to have to ask you to return to your seat."

"I guess I had better be going back to my seat. Just concentrate on the world around you; stop searching for questions. The answer is as close as me," Max said as he stood up.

Still with no answer to my question, I knew that he would just vanish into thin air again. "When will I see you again?" I asked.

"Soon enough, you just work on *why* for now. *Just begin your quest and the universe will rush in to help you*," he replied, before walking through the curtained-off first class area.

"What do you mean?" I asked, but he didn't get a chance to even hear the question.

Not long after Max had gone, the attendants readied the plane for landing and we were soon on the ground, taxiing into the concourse. Having been so distracted by seeing Max, I completely forgot to put on my sunglasses for landing. Maybe now I could drop that foolish habit, I thought, with a chuckle to myself.

Anxious to get off the plane, I was more anxious to see who picked up Max or if he was taking a taxi, or whatever. Although I really didn't care how Max left, I just wanted to see him leave, to know if he did it in a normal way. I just wanted to be sure that he didn't just disappear. To end my suspicions, I needed visual verification of his departure.

"Please remain seated until the captain has brought the aircraft to a complete stop and has turned off the fasten-seat-belt sign," said the stewardess over the intercom. I sat waiting until we stopped, hoping that everyone else would, too. However, at least twenty people wanted to get off of the plane just as much as or more than I did. The line down the aisle backed up rapidly before the plane had even come to a full stop. Since I was sitting in the middle of the plane, over the wing, I had to wait just like the rest of the working class stiffs flying coach. And by the time I had gotten out of the plane and into the terminal, there was no sign of Max anywhere. Only the crowds of deplaning passengers filled the aisles. Even if he were there, I wouldn't have been able to see him. There were too many people. I was never going to determine if Max were real or just an illusion.

Standing there just looking around, wondering if Carl had gotten my message, it dawned on me. If Carl were working a show, he was probably not going to be able to pick me up. Maybe I should try to find a hotel, I thought.

"Continental Airlines passenger, James Carpenter, please pick up the white courtesy phone, James Carpenter."

With all of the commotion going on around me, I could barely tell what was said over the loudspeaker, either James Carpenter or A. Bartender. The rest I kind of just figured out from past experience. Making my way to one of the white phones, I picked up the receiver. I didn't have to dial anything. An operator simply asked me for my name, told me thank you, have a nice day, and then punched up a voice mail recorded message.

None other than the great Carl Carpenter explained, "Hey Bro, I won't be able to get there at eleven-thirty, but I will come pick you up eventually, don't sweat it. I should be there before twelve-thirty. Just hang loose. Get a drink in the bar or something and I will be there sooner, if not later. Don't let the Hare Krishnas sell you any flowers and don't eat the hot dogs. They'll make you sick. Rumor has it, they're made of real dog meat. Other than that – I'll see ya soon. Hasta la bye bye."

To hear him joking around and in such high spirits was good. Not only was he acting like his old self, he was acting semi-responsible. He wasn't there waiting for me when I deplaned, but he was acting something like a mature adult. He had gone to the trouble of leaving a message for me and he was actually coming to pick me up. This was great. My spontaneity was going to work for once. Usually, anything I tried off the cuff (especially where Carl was involved) was a disaster. Things were going to turn out all right. Hearing Carl, I felt like we were really going to have some fun; and right now I could certainly use some fun.

I strode down the hall to the baggage pick up. Miracle of miracles, all of my luggage had made the trip with me, too. How long would this lucky streak last? Picking up my bags, I went back to the bar. Not really in a drinking mood after my recent binge, I just ordered a Coke and a sandwich, one of those that pops into the microwave and the bread comes out tasting like rubber. Surprisingly, it tasted pretty good – for rubber.

I sat there at the bar, ate my *Goodyear* sandwich, drank my Coke and watched the people come and go. How many of these people knew their *why*? The bartender? No way. He was into the moment. Just staring up at the television hypnotized, he was holding his wet bar-towel in one hand and eating pretzels with his other. *"His purpose in life could be to eat pretzels and watch the Entertainment Channel,"* I thought.

When that Carpenter's curiosity finally got the better of me, I inquired, "Bartender, do you mind if I ask you a question?"

"Why not? Everyone else does," he said. "And call me Kirk, my name is Kirk, like captain of the Enterprise."

"Well, Kirk, you can call me James; my name is James Carpenter. It's a pleasure to meet you, Kirk," I said.

"Sure, now can I get you another Coke or do you want something else?" he asked, picking up my empty glass from the counter. I nodded a yes, so he filled the glass with ice and Coke.

"Kirk, may I ask you a rather strange question?" I said.

"I'm a heterosexual; so if this is a some kind of a pick up line, forget it," he said almost apprehensively.

"Oh, no. I'm as straight as the next guy."

"Well, around here the next guy is usually a fruit," he said laughing, "Not that I care what they are, doesn't make any difference to me; I'm secure in *my* sexuality. So what's the question?"

"Do you have a purpose to your life? I mean besides bartending. That's not really my question. What I mean is – well – I've been doing a lot of soul searching for some time, trying to find a meaning to my life, a purpose for my being who and what I am. I'd just like to know if anyone else has a problem finding out their true purpose in life."

"Wow, that's a doozy of a question. Usually when people ask something like that they are drinking tequila or scotch – not Coca-Cola. That's a tough one. I guess that I haven't spent a whole hell of a lot of time thinking about what my purpose in life is. Kind of depressing, now that I think about it; I don't even know if I have a purpose," he said.

"Well, did you ever dream of being something else besides a bartender?" I asked.

"Oh sure I did. I'm like practically everyone else in Los Angeles, I wanted to be famous at one time. I'm no different."

"So, what made you give up and become an airport bartender?" I asked.

"Not wanting to spend most of my life looking for work! I got so I didn't enjoy doing acting, the pressure of not knowing where my next meal was coming from. I needed to settle down and grow up," he said. "Besides, this job suits me better; I like a steady paycheck. I don't make a lot, but I get to meet a lot of interesting people, and I can watch a lot of sports."

"How long ago did you quit acting?" I asked.

"It's been a long time. Let's see, I guess that I was about twenty-nine, or thirty. That was about twelve years ago. Huh, time sure passes when you're having fun."

"Yeah, it sure does," I said.

"Well, James, how about you? What's your story? Are you some kind of a writer, a psychiatrist, or what?"

"I'm an accountant, actually."

"I would've never guessed. And I'm pretty good at guessing what people are," he said. "Take him, for example," he said, pointing to a man in a gray pinstriped suit reading a Wall Street Journal. "You might guess that he's some kind of stock broker or financial wizard, right?"

"Sure, he has that look," I said and probably would've bet on it.

"To my trained eye, I would say he's a salesman, probably sells insurance, or maybe medical supplies," he said, sounding pretty sure of himself.

"How are you sure that he doesn't work in finance?" I asked.

"I just am, trust me."

Deciding to call his bluff, I walked up to the man and asked. "Excuse me, I'm sorry to bother you, but the bartender and I have a bet going. We'd like to know what you do for a living."

"Is that the guy?" he said pointing to Kirk. He then snickered a little, smiled and said, "I sell insurance."

I thanked him for the information and walked back over to the bar where Kirk was waiting.

"Well, what does he do?" Kirk asked.

"You were absolutely right. He's an insurance salesman. How did you know?" I asked.

Assuming the role of Sherlock Holmes, Kirk said, "Elementary, my good man, simple deductive reasoning: First he was reading the Wall Street Journal. If he were a financial analyst he would have either read the paper first thing in the morning or at work, not at midnight. Second he wears pull-on shoes, the sign of a salesman. All the big shots or number crunchers wear lace ups. Last he ..."

Then the man who we had been watching joined us at the bar, and interrupted Kirk. Pulling up a stool next to me, the insurance salesman asked, "So how much did he win?"

"We didn't bet any money," I said.

"You're one of the lucky ones then; Kirk has been pulling that stunt off and on for about a month. He's a quite a character, this guy," he said.

"James, allow me to introduce the man who used to be my good friend and fellow airport lizard, Ronald. Ronald, this is James, who is in search of the true meaning of life," said Kirk, who, turning his attention to Ronald, asked, "Ron, do you want the usual?"

"Yeah, I guess I can have a quick snort before the wife gets here."

"One Heineken comin' at you," said Kirk.

Ron asked, "So, James, you want to know the meaning of life?"

"Not really the meaning so much as the purpose of *my* life," I said.

"Well, what do you do for a living? Wait, let me guess. You're a writer!"

"That's what Kirk guessed, too. Why did you come to that conclusion?" I asked.

"It's usually some type of creative person who's in search of the meaning of life. You don't look like an artist or a musician. You don't have an earring or a tattoo. Consequently, you must be a writer."

Kirk, who had returned with a full mug of beer to set down in front of Ronald said, "I'll bet you ten bucks I can guess what he does."

"Yeah, I'll bet you ten bucks you *can*," said Ronald.

"Believe me when I tell you, you won't believe what this guy does," said Kirk.

"What is he, an accountant?" asked Ronald.

Laughing, Kirk exclaimed, "I can't believe it! You guessed,"

I, however, was not really amused as they were. "What's so funny about being an accountant?"

Kirk replied, "That's just it – nothing," both enjoying a hearty laugh at my expense.

"So tell me, just what is an accountant supposed to look like?" I asked.

"Take it as a compliment, James; you don't look like one. Accountants are kind of well, you know, boring. They wear brown polyester suits, have Coke bottle thick glasses, and store a sharp pencil behind their ear."

"Come on guys, give me a break. Accountants aren't like that – they aren't *that* bad."

Then the realization struck me; we really were that bad. I knew two older guys who actually did wear brown polyester suits to the office. One of them even had the thick glasses. Laughing a hearty laugh, I said, "They're not all that bad. They don't all have sharp pencils behind the ear, ha! Some of them have dull pencils behind the ear. Ha, ha. Hey, wait what am I laughing at? I am an accountant!"

We all had a good laugh over the stereotypical accountants, bartenders, and insurance salesmen. Ronald and Kirk were funny guys. And we had a great time guessing people's occupations, but whenever we asked we were almost never right. For example this one gorgeous woman who looked like she just had to be a model, turned out to be a mortician. *What* someone was, certainly was not limited by *who* they were.

Then Carl walked up to the door, looking around not yet seeing me. "Actor," I said, "He looks so much like an actor, I'll bet ten bucks that he is an actor."

"You're on, amigo," said Ronald, who was feeling a little loose from the effects of the four beers without dinner (his wife was late), "But he can't be a waiter or busboy who is trying to be an actor. He has to say and be employed as a real actor."

Keeping my back turned to Carl so that he wouldn't see me, I got a ten out of my wallet and said to Kirk, "Here, you hold on to the money until we find out what he does."

Ronald followed suit, handing Kirk a ten spot. Then he walked up to Carl, who, in jeans and a white T-shirt, really looked more like a *Happy Days'* reject than anything else, "Excuse me, sir," inquired Ronald, "would you mind telling me what you do for a living?"

"Why?" he asked, "Who wants to know?"

"We're just having a little bar room contest and we're trying to guess people's jobs," said Ronald.

Not letting me down for a second, "I'm an actor," said Carl.

"Well, I'll be damned," said Ronald. "Now how in the hell did you figure that one, James?"

"He's my brother," I said, waving to him. "Hey, Carl."

"Jimmy, long time no see. What's goin' on? Are you taking these guys' hard earned cash?" said Carl, shaking my hand, seeing Kirk approach with the money.

"You win. No one said anything about a relative," Kirk said as he handed me the money.

"Foul, I call foul!" said Ronald not really caring about the ten, but laughing because he had been taken by the same stunt that he and Kirk had played for the past month.

"Fellas, this is my brother Carl. Carl, these two airport lounge lizards are Ronald, and Kirk."

Shaking hands they told Carl he didn't really look like me. Carl laughed and said, "Thank God!" Ronald then gave Carl his business card. (I had never seen an insurance agent who didn't hand out his business card.) Anyway, I offered to buy Ronald his next beer. But he insisted I keep the money that I had bilked him out of. We all joked around a while with Carl and me ending up staying for another beer. It wasn't long before some woman came walking up to the bar and Ronald said, "I'll wager ten dollars I can guess what she does for a living."

"Yeah, I'll bet you can. She looks like your wife to me," I said.

"You are good. You, my good fellow, are a veritable magician," said Ron, who picked up his briefcase, pulled another business card out of his pocket for me, said goodbye, and disappeared down the concourse arm in arm with his wife.

"He looks happy," I said.

"He's one lucky guy," said Kirk. "I don't know anyone who enjoys his job and life more than that guy right there."

"As an insurance salesman?" I muttered, thinking that would be a fate even worse than being an accountant.

"I don't know why, but the man really enjoys selling. You should hear him talk about closing a deal or making a presentation. Ronald Costello was made for that business," said Kirk. "Ron doesn't make a lot of money, but he loves his wife and family, and really likes what he does. You asked *me* about the meaning of life, well Ron has life already figured out; he seems to have it made."

The time eventually came for us to give our regrets to Kirk, who jokingly informed us that it was closing time and said he'd certainly be glad to get rid of us. Carl and I closed up our tab, and meandered toward short-term parking. Bantering back and forth, we eventually reached our speeding "chariot," Carl's pride and joy – a bright yellow, 1971 Triumph Spitfire. Even though it was actually a heap, having spent more time on blocks than on the road, Carl loved his sporty pint-sized car. The joke in the family was that Carl's car looked fast "just sitting there." I was happy to hear that it wasn't currently in the shop. However, glad as I was to see the chariot running, I was never quite sure if it would get us to our destination. Carl, on the other hand, had total faith in his "lemon" yellow sports car. And his faith, though sometimes misguided, was always contagious.

With barely enough room for my bags, we somehow stuffed one behind the seats and then crawled in. "Do you think it'll start?" I asked.

"Oh yeah, the chariot won't let us down," Carl said confidently. However, right before he turned the key, he requested we say a short prayer. After an eternity of cranking the starter (nearing the point of the battery's last rites), the little car answered our prayers by living up to its name. Coughing a couple of times it finally "spit fire" out the exhaust pipe and rumbled to a start.

The engine clanked a little pulling out of the parking lot. However, we accelerated onto the freeway like a patriot missile, zooming along in his convertible. As Carl yelled, "Yeee Haaa! You've just got to have faith!!!" he put the pedal to the metal. I knew then that the next two weeks would be an adventure worth writing home about.

"Enjoy The Time You Spend –
With Family And Friends."

Chapter 18

"Wake up, sleepy head," Carl said, jabbing me in the ribs.

"Already?" I mumbled.

By the time we had stopped at a few of Carl's favorite clubs, the night turned into morning. We had to, as he put it, "meet a few of his stranger-than-fiction friends." They were kind of weird I admit, but at the same time, interesting and fun people. Most of them were people who worked with Carl in the film industry or had met him in a bar. Either they were actors and actresses, sound editors, directors, or they got coffee for someone who was.

When we finally crashed at Carl's house, it must have been about six in the morning Texas time. Too tired to care, I didn't even get a look at his new place. He just pointed to the couch, and without even taking off my shoes I collapsed. He must have given me a blanket after I passed out because, when I awoke, I had one of those tacky, scratchy, army-green looking things sort of twisted around me. My arms searching out and finding several large holes now couldn't find their way back out. Last time I'd felt this tied up was when I was in Max's straitjacket.

Unwinding the intertwined mass from around me, trying to sit up in the couch, I asked, "What time is it?" My hair was standing straight up; my breath was so bad I could smell it myself. Still completely dressed, I must've looked like a person that stayed out all night drinking cheap booze and ended up sleeping in his clothes – pretty close to the mark.

"It's eleven o'clock, big Bro and we gotta rock, if we are going to accomplish anything today. Here man, have a cup of coffee," he said, setting a cup of hot coffee on the table in front of me. "I've got bacon and eggs cookin' in the kitchen. The shower is down the hall on the right," Carl said, on his way back into the kitchen.

I asked, rubbing my head, "Are you always this cheerful first thing in the morning?"

"What do you mean, first thing? It's late pal; I got up at nine, went down to get a newspaper, did a batch of laundry, and cooked you breakfast," he said. "Like Mom always said, 'You're burning daylight'."

"Who do you think you are, Felix Unger?" I said, pulling the blanket up over my head, feeling a lot like Oscar in the "*Odd Couple*." Carl reached over and pulled the blanket off of me. Leaving me no choice but to give in and get up, I took a sip of coffee.

Looking around, I was pleased to see a much nicer place than the one he had lived in last time I visited, over two years ago. Back then he lived in a studio apartment in downtown LA that rented for about six-fifty a month. For that he got four walls, a couch, a sink, a mini-fridge in one end of the room, and a cable TV hookup. (No cable, just the hookup) The real kicker was that the bathroom was down the hall – a public bathroom, down the hall (about three blocks). By comparison, this apartment was heaven.

After I showered and shaved I put on a pair of shorts, tennis shoes, and a T-shirt, eventually making my way into the kitchen for a plate full of lukewarm bacon and eggs. At home I would have simply nuked them back to sizzling. However, Carl informed me it was my own fault, I was "movin' too slow," making no apologies for his kitchen's lack of microwave technology.

Since he was moving faster than I had ever seen him move in the morning, I asked, "What's the big hurry?"

"We've got places to go and things to do, Bro," said Carl.

"Where do we *have* to go?" I asked.

"Today, we are going to do Olvera Street and Westwood. That'll give you a chance to rest up. Tomorrow, I figure we go to Universal Studios, followed by a day of rest down at Venice Beach; Thursday, we do

Disneyland or Knott's Berry Farm. Friday, we can go to Hollywood and walk the streets with the tourists."

"Slow down, where is the part where I rest and relax?" I asked.

"You're just saying that. I know you better," he said. "You may think that you came here for some R&R, but what you're really looking for is some F&E, fun and excitement. And that, big brother, is exactly what you're going to get."

The first day at Carl's was much better than I expected because I was able to forget my real life for the entire day. At first, I tried convincing myself that I was just plain too tired to do all of the "fun things." But with Carl's almost annoying exuberance and enthusiastic push, I found myself having a terrific time in spite of myself.

First, we drove down to Olvera Street, a great place to begin a vacation. Olvera Street is like a little Mexican marketplace in the heart of Los Angeles. It reminded me of going to the flea markets with my father when we were just kids. Checking out all of the pottery, statues, paintings, sombreros, and junk, along with devouring some great Mexican food, made me feel as if I was a million miles away from real life.

From Olvera Street we continued our journey across town to Westwood where Carl said we could watch a few of the oddball street performers and later take in a movie. Having never been to Westwood before, I looked forward to what Carl called a "real experience in the making."

First we took a drive through what Carl referred to as "the drag." Drag may have been the correct word choice, because we could have been *dragged* through the streets and moved faster. The traffic was absolutely unbelievable, horrendous. Even though it was late in the evening, the area was packed with people. They were all over, walking the sidewalks, spilling out into the street. It reminded me of Mardi Gras with people also stopping to watch the street performers. We couldn't really see much of what was going on from the car. It was just too crowded. Seeing all the performers though made me wonder if we might possibly encounter Max tonight. Perhaps he'd be doing his act on the next corner.

Carl informed me that we would never find a parking space in the center of town. We'd have to drive out to a parking lot and walk back to

Westwood. The walk wasn't too far and the parking spot was always available, he explained. He was obviously right about finding a space close to the action. Also, since it was one of those obscure lots, not that convenient, the price for all-night parking was only two dollars as opposed to seven. This I just imagined was a major factor in Carl's decision.

We discovered that Carl's parking place was available just as he predicted. And because we filled the time with talking, the walk back to Westwood didn't seem to take long. Contemplating some of the strange people, we toured around the streets for a couple of hours, ate a gyro sandwich, and took in a few street performances. I dished out a couple of bucks to a comical mime whose show we watched from start to finish. Normally, I think mimes are worthless, but since this guy was actually funny, I thought he deserved a donation. Carl was right, the street provided plenty to see. On one block alone, a clown made balloon animals on one corner, some kids danced to a boom box in a store front, while a musician played requests on his piano from the back of his pickup truck. He was pretty talented, so I slipped him a dollar, too.

One of the most interesting things I'd ever seen in my entire life was the man with the psychic cats. A dark-skinned bearded man, wearing a colorful Indian costume complete with a turban was sitting on a table cross-legged next to a large wooden box. On his table hung a sign that said: "Psychic Cats $2.00." Of course, I was too curious; I just had to pay the two dollars. When I did, the bizarre street performer drew back a curtain on the rather large box to reveal four cats, sitting politely still on a wooden shelf. Like the performer, the cats themselves were dressed in colorful costumes, each a different color, but sitting perfectly motionless.

In front of the cats was a gold fish bowl containing little rolls of paper. The man clapped his hands twice and stepping forward, one of the cats reached his little paw into the glass bowl and delicately attempted to pull out one of the tiny scrolls. When he finally got one out, the cat took the paper roll in its mouth, walked over and dropped it into the man's open hand – an amazing feat to watch. Never having seen anything like it, I didn't even realize that you could train a cat. What Max had said seemed to hold true, I guess, "With the proper training, dedication and attitude, *anything* really is possible."

THE MAGIC LIFE

When I opened up the little fortune paper, I half expected it to say something like "You will learn your true destiny tonight," or "You will learn the secret of life's meaning from a magician." Nothing quite so dramatic, the scroll simply read: *Enjoy the time you spend with family and friends.* Simple, but it did make a valid point I guess.

Of course, we eventually did encounter a magician. Though not nearly the performer that Max was, he was fair in his own right. He did one particular trick that I remembered seeing a long time ago – the cups and balls trick. Performing with three silver cups and three cloth balls, the magician passed balls invisibly from one cup to another. I could almost see through the trick's methodology; however, he completely fooled me at the end when he turned over the cups to reveal that they were all filled with lemons. After his show, I tipped him a five dollar bill and asked him his secret.

"A lot of people ask me how I do these tricks, more often they ask me *why*," he replied with a smile.

Once more, the tingling sensation rattled me, and I felt I had to know. "Why, then?" I asked.

The magician looked at me inquiringly and asked, "Do you really want to know?"

"Yes, I really want to know *why* much more than *how*," I said.

Suddenly, as if we had made some kind of psychic connection, his face lit up. *Why* somehow linked these magicians together and they knew that it contained the real secret.

"Well, it certainly isn't for the money," he said, picking up his hat to reveal that he had made about ten dollars – including the five I had just given him.

"Then why do you do magic?" I asked.

"I guess that it's sort of my reason to get up in the morning, my passion. May sound weird, but I live to do this stuff. I love conjuring more than anything else," he said. "Kind of silly I know, but since I was a little boy, I've wanted nothing more than to be a magician." He continued picking up his tricks and placing them into a pine box which lay at his feet. "Now, I am a magician – don't make a lot of money, but I'm content. Of course, I hope to make the big-time someday. Sure, I dream of being a headliner in Las Vegas, having a traveling show, my name in lights on Broadway. But, the truth is that I really like entertaining people. The other things would just be gravy. If you really like doing whatever job you chose, then as far as I'm concerned, you're already a success in your own right. You kind of look kind of like a magician," he said. "Are you?"

"He's a great magician," Carl chimed in. "You two should get together and exchange some secrets."

"I'm not really a professional, like you. It's more of a hobby, I've been interested in magic since I was a little kid," I said. "but, I'm really just an accountant."

"You should join some magic organizations. Are you a member of the West Coast Wizards?"

"No, I'm from Texas – just visiting."

"Oh well, I'd be glad to get together with you and swap trade secrets, but I'm taking off to San Francisco tomorrow morning. Here, take my business card," he said, digging one out from under the brim of his hat. "Call me in a couple of weeks and we'll talk magic. Right now I've got to do a few shows to make enough money to pay for my flight."

I would have liked to stay and find out more, but Carl was nudging me, trying to stick to his tight schedule. We continued down the street, stopping off at an outdoor cafe for a quick bite to eat. After looking at the menu, Carl complained that it was too rich for his blood. So, I told him the snack was on me. We sat there relaxed, ate a sandwich, drank cappuccino, and watched half of the sociological misfits in California wander by.

Out of the blue Carl comes up with a question. "Are you happy?" Carl asked, "I mean happy about what you are doing with your life?"

"Boy, that sure is a heavy question."

"I'm sorry, I didn't really mean to get heavy on you. It's just that sometimes I don't think you seem to be getting what you want out of your life, James," he said. "Sometimes I wonder if you shouldn't move down here and hang out with me. You could get an accounting job at any old accounting firm, you know."

"Hey, don't worry about me. I'm all right," I said, wishing he hadn't asked. Once again, I found myself remembering Gina, and questioning if I would ever be happy without her. Could I ever move on with my life? I had no other choice.

Later that evening, Carl dropped me off at a cinema, asking me to pick out a movie and then to wait for him afterward at another restaurant until he got back from rehearsal. Rehearsals, it turned out, could last for about two to two and a half hours, depending upon the mood of the director. Not really that excited about attending a movie by myself, I really didn't know what else to do. The movie turned out to be just okay, nothing worth writing home about. After the show, I waited in the restaurant, as we agreed, over a cup of decaf. I was only there for a short time before Carl showed up again.

"How was rehearsal?" I asked.

"It was pretty short, the director has the flu, so he decided that he wouldn't work us too hard tonight. The show is really shaping up and he wants me to add some more magic. Maybe you can help in that department."

"Sure, I might know a few things; a while back I found one of my old magic books in Mom's attic."

"Did you get anything to eat for dinner?" he asked.

"No, how about you?"

"Me neither, might as well eat here before we go."

The restaurant's food wasn't too bad for a greasy spoon. As we both wolfed down some huge California cheeseburgers (loaded with bean sprouts, thus the '*California*' title). We discussed his show and some of the cast members' idiosyncrasies. Carl and I had similar personalities, so conversation was always easy between us. We talked for quite a while about very little.

It was getting late, about two in the morning when we headed back to the car. Parking in the obscure lot and walking to the strip, I was concerned if we would be able to find our way back. But Carl assured me that it was his regular parking space, also mentioning that because it was so far from the beaten path, no one ever bothered his car. (If someone *would* steal it, he would be doing Carl a big favor.)

After walking the whole day, I was worn out. Because I did so little walking at home, my feet were killing me after just a few short blocks toward the car lot. Carl, noticing my discomfort, suggested that we take a shortcut through a back alley. Not exactly my idea of level-headed thinking, cutting through a back alley in the middle of the night in Los Angeles, but I was just tired enough and my feet hurt just enough to go along.

"Hey, it's not like we are in New York City," Carl said. "I've cut through here a thousand times."

"Well, I'm too tired to argue with you," I said, and we headed through the alley, consisting mostly of back doors to restaurants, bars, and nightclubs. For a dark back alley, it seemed pretty well lit – most of it. However, the farther we proceeded into the alley, the more the lights seemed to fade. A few of the bars were closing, shutting off their lights as they did. The darkness seemed to be creeping in rapidly.

As we walked down the increasingly dark alleyway, in between the garbage dumpsters, I heard a splash behind us. It was the distinct sound a car makes when hitting a pothole filled with water. A car turned down the alley toward us and we stood directly in its headlights' path. Instinctively, I turned back to look. However, all I could see was the glare of a pair of headlights, which the driver then clicked up to bright – blinding me. Carl and I both stepped to one side, assuming that the driver wanted to go by. But when the car didn't just move on around us, I began to feel uneasy. The hair on the back of my neck stood on end. Something was strange about the way it followed us. The car was creeping along, hanging just behind us, almost stalking us. It reminded me of a black panther prowling in the tall grass along a herd of antelope, as if he were waiting for one to run, trying to size up the slowest and weakest. Maybe he was deciding which one would be easiest to kill before making a move.

My heart rate increased as my mind started working double time, listening intently to the sound of the gravel slowly crunching under the wheels, trying to notice any change. Suddenly I wasn't tired at all anymore. I was prepared to run just like an antelope in panic, only my fear kept me from running.

I wasn't the only one who felt apprehensive. "Just keep walking, don't act afraid," Carl said, hitting me on the shoulder. "He probably just wants to sell us some drugs."

"Oh, great," I said sarcastically, "I'm sure glad that this isn't New York City."

We both walked over on one side, single file, to insure the car had ample room to get around us. But it just kept following us, stalking, always staying back just far enough to keep us from seeing what kind of car it was, or who was driving. This went on for a long minute or two, but it seemed like a lifetime.

"You still think that he wants to sell us some drugs?" I asked.

With that Carl came unglued. Turning around, he flipped off the car shouting, "Get the hell out of here, you @$%&* # pervert!"

Wrong approach.

The driver punched the gas pedal to the floor. The tires squealed, sending black smoke billowing up mixed with wet flying gravel as he whipped around in front of us blocking our path. Now in the dim light, for the first time I could actually see the car and the driver. I didn't like what I saw. The car was a big, black two-door Cadillac El Dorado, and the driver was even bigger.

This moving mountain of a man opened the door and stepped out. About six feet five, three hundred pounds of angry muscle and bone now stood between us and the rest of our lives. Sweat dripped from his forehead down around his white glaring eyes and past his teeth, shining like a mad dog's. This man was not glad to see us and evidently he didn't like being called names.

I considered looking for some distinguishing mark to describe to the police. But I figured that, after he had beaten us to death, my testimony wouldn't make much difference. I felt sick.

Carl looked over at me, eyes glazed, saying below his breath, "Holy shit!"

As I recognized what Carl had seen, I understood his sudden change of attitude. Subtly, the man revealed the cold blue steel of a 38-caliber handgun.

"I don't want to have to shoot you pretty boys, but I will. You two just put everything you got in the bag." With that he threw a gym bag with the Raiders' insignia on it down in front of us. Somehow the insignia of a pirate fit.

Carl didn't hesitate for even a second. As if he had done this many times before, he pulled out his wallet, removed the cash, and placed it in the bag. Never taking his eyes off the gun, he demonstrated to the thief that there was nothing more in his wallet by holding it open for him. He then showed his empty pockets, turning them inside out, and slipped off his watch, adding it to the bag.

I reached back for my wallet with my hands shaking so badly that I could hardly get them into my pocket. Just as I finally grasped my wallet, I couldn't believe what happened.

Out of the blue, Carl rushed him.

"Run!!" he yelled, diving, attempting to tackle the immense pirate.

Not about to run, with no time to think, I turned to help Carl – a second too late.

The gun went off, "KABLAM!!"

It was pointed into Carl's heart.

Time slowed down just as it had when the car hit Gina. Everything was running in slow motion. The sound of the gun shot echoed down the alley. Carl screamed, grabbing his chest in pain. A look of horrifying disbelief came over his face as his legs lost the strength to hold him. Smoke curled out from the barrel end of the gun as Carl's body fell backward into the darkness of the alleyway. Frozen, I watched the killer's white glaring eyes turn from a look of cold enmity to that of pure shock as he realized he'd just shot a man.

In that few seconds my thoughts focused on Carl, but when my eyes glanced upon the assailant's neck I was hypnotized by something else which caught my attention. Hanging against this huge mass of bone and muscle, a steel chain glimmered in the light. As my eyes focused upon the object pinned to that steel chain, the tingling sensation shot through me like I'd been electrocuted. There, hanging around his neck, in stark contrast to his ebony skin, was a familiar square of tattered white cloth – the same necklace as worn by Max Vi.

*"The Trick's Not To Make A Living Out Of Magic –
The Trick Is To Make Magic Out Of Living."*

Chapter 19

Blanks, they're just blanks – I didn't want anybody to get hurt," yelled the assailant, obviously shaken by the sudden change of events. He was truly concerned with Carl's well being. The picture began to get weird, almost surrealistic.

Carl, meantime, was cussing up a storm, "It burnt the shit out of me!"

I was concerned, but tremendously relieved when I saw Carl stand up with only a powder burn mark on his chest. Not having to worry immediately about Carl's health, I had to know. "I'll gladly give you everything I've got. And besides that, I won't even consider telling the police," I said, pointing to his necklace, "if you'll just tell me the meaning of the piece of white cloth around your neck."

What happened next was nothing short of miraculous. This gigantic mountain of a man became weak as he reached up to his chest to take the small piece of cloth in his left fist. Visibly trembling, tears formed in his eyes. He had been so overpowering and threatening just moments ago. Suddenly he began whimpering and sobbing like a harshly scorned child. I could see him trying to gather enough composure, but he couldn't. His lips were trembling too much for him to speak.

The mention of the small piece of cloth had unnerved him; the same cloth I had seen around Max's neck, the same cloth I had seen in my dreams. I didn't know what powers that strange object possessed, but somehow it had altered this man's life and somehow I knew it was going to affect mine.

His tears turned into an expression of anger against himself. "God damn it!" he cursed, throwing the gun halfway down the block into the darkness.

Ripping the chain from off his neck, "I can't believe this," he said, holding the cloth in front of his face. "I'm so sorry," he sobbed as he tossed the chain and cloth to the street. With that and a deep breath, he wiped tears from his eyes, climbed back in the El Dorado and drove slowly down the alley. Stopping only a moment, halfway down the block, I barely saw his silhouette as he opened the door, silently leaning out to pick up the gun. He then proceeded slowly around the corner and out of sight.

Carl looked at the bag still laying in the street with his valuables in it, then at me in disbelief. Bewildered, I stared back.

"What in the hell was that all about?" he said. "I can't believe what just happened."

"Huh, yeah – unbelievable," I said. "Unbelievable."

"Why did you ask him about the cloth?" he asked, perplexed.

"I don't know … I mean I'll tell you later, it's something that I've seen before," I said. "It's really a long story. It has to do with Max." I walked over and picked up the chain and cloth from the street.

"Well I'm all ears, Bro," he said, picking up the gym bag, reclaiming his money.

"Why don't we get to the car first; I'll tell you when we are safely on our way out of here."

It didn't take long for us to get into the car and make our way back to Carl's house. Even though I wanted to call the police, Carl talked me out of it saying that nothing would come of it but a waste of our time. "Besides," he said, "that guy was truly sorry. How many crooks do you know who would put blanks into a gun just to make sure no one gets hurt? We need more criminals like him." He took off his burned T-shirt and rubbed some aloe vera onto his chest burn.

With a just a hint of the sarcasm, I asked, "Do you mind if I ask you something?"

"What?" asked Carl.

"What were you thinking when you attacked that guy?" I asked sarcastically, then couldn't help laughing. "Are you out of your mind? He was as big as a house. Carl, you've been watching too many movies. You could have been killed!"

"I was saving you! What are you complaining about?" Carl asked, a bit put off.

"You damn near got us both killed," I said. Then seeing that he was a little bruised by my comment added, "But, thanks."

"I'm just glad to be alive," responded Carl.

"Me, too," I said, "I have to tell you, when I thought I was going to lose you – I felt just the same as I did when Gina was hit, like I was going to lose everything again. It was so strange. Life's so strange," I said.

"Yes, it is – but you know what?" he said. "It's the best thing we've got."

Carl and I, both running on pure adrenaline, stayed up most of the night jabbering away. In particular, we covered in detail the strange occurrence with the mugger and my strange relationship with the magician. I also told him about seeing the white cloth in my dream at the hospital and around the magician's neck. You'd have thought that, because Carl was an actor, he would have been more into "new age" stuff. But Carl concluded that it all had to have a logical and rational explanation. After a thorough discussion of just the facts, though, he decided that it was all a bit too metaphysical for him. He then suggested that I give the psychic's hot line a call. He was only joking, of course, but he claimed he was half serious.

Our experience would have sounded pretty farfetched to anyone from the outside; however, I couldn't get the images out of my mind. Here was a huge man brought to his knees by the mere mention of a small piece of white cloth. Something magical did happen there, something to do with Max, something to do with real magic, I just knew it.

The next morning I got up early. Carl was still sleeping. Figuring that he'd probably had a pretty rough night because of the burn on his chest,

I quietly poured myself a bowl of cereal and opened up Carl's morning paper, the *Los Angeles Times*.

Nothing much to see in the financial section, the one page that I always turned to first – out of habit. Bond prices were on the decline; stocks were maintaining a steady upward climb. I don't even know why I looked. My stocks never changed; like the rest of my life they were "low risk." There was really no need to look, but checking the paper was just one of those routines I had built into my continuously humdrum life.

It wasn't long before Carl got up, mumbled something, and turned on his TV. When I turned to the front page of the newspaper, I had to take a second look. I couldn't believe what I was seeing. There, on the front page, was a picture of the man who had attempted to rob us. Adjacent to his picture, the headline read: "Former LA Raider Josh Wooten Drug Related Suicide Attempt." It was him. Josh Wooten was the man in the alley.

"Carl, come here," I said, motioning for him to get out from in front of the TV and take a look at the paper. "You're not going to believe what I'm seeing."

"What?" he asked. Carl came over and looked over my shoulder at the paper. We both read the article in amazement. Stepping back, Carl took a deep breath and said, "That's him, that's the son-of-a-bitch who shot me!"

"Do you think that in some way he was looking for help from us? I mean more hoping to get caught or something?" I said, thinking out loud, not really expecting Carl to answer.

"He must have been losing it," Carl said.

Reading further, the article answered some of my questions, but I wanted a complete answer. "I don't know, but it says here that an addiction to crack cocaine led to his subsequent removal from the NFL and the recent divorce from his wife. I can't help feeling sorry for the guy. After he even failed as a thief, he must have just given up. He just gave up on life," I said, really feeling pity for the man, wondering if in some way my question about the piece of white cloth was responsible for his suicide attempt. "I feel a little responsible," I said.

"You are too strange sometimes, Jim," Carl said, not really meaning anything by it. "This is all just some strange coincidence."

I was beginning to understand what Max had told me about when a person loses his reason for living. If you don't have a reason to live, then you simply don't go on. I suppose when it came right down to it, Josh Wooten couldn't find his reason to live, or his circumstances were such that he wasn't able to complete his life's contract – no, if that were true, he would be dead right now. Maybe he didn't know his *why*. That wasn't the right answer. Maybe Josh did understand what he needed from life, but was one of those persons that Max had described. Josh Wooten knew his *why* but was unable to live it! That must have been it.

We must all have a reason, I suppose; that's the ultimate puzzle for man to solve. But I still didn't know what *my* own reason for living was. The confusion made me wonder again about Gina. I wondered if she still had a reason for living. Thinking of her made me feel a little weak, heavy hearted – was I ever going to see her again? For a moment I was completely lost in negative thoughts. Then I got an idea that would take my mind off her.

"Why don't I go down and see if I can help Josh Wooten?" I said to Carl.

"What? The man tried to rob us. If he had bullets, I would be dead now."

"Yeah, but he didn't and you're not," I said.

"Well, we could, I suppose, but you won't be able to see him today."

"Why not?"

"They always keep suicide attempts under wraps for at least twenty-four hours. I had a friend that tried to kill herself one time, I know," Carl said.

Carl, still objecting, sensed my determination and said, "We'll have to plan on going down there tomorrow – hey Jim, how about we go down to the Hollywood Magic Shop today?"

"Yeah, that sounds like a winner," I said, shaking it off and smiling, knowing that he wanted to change the subject to something more agreeable. I didn't give him enough credit sometimes; he really was a great brother.

Together we cleaned up the breakfast dishes and then headed out for the bright lights of Hollywood. When we got there, I was a little disappointed that there weren't more bright lights. Hollywood was not quite up to the standards that I remembered. It was really kind of dirty looking and smelled heavily of car fumes. Also, Hollywood seemed to have more than its fair share of bums wandering the streets collecting lunch from the overburdened trash cans that lined the streets. I guess I really shouldn't have called them bums, though. I felt for them. Most of them were simply lost souls. Watching them, I realized that they were a lot like the football player. They too seemed to have lost their reason to live. Or maybe their reasons were much simpler. Maybe a reason could be simply to get a half of a sandwich out of the trash, or collect enough cans to buy a bottle of wine. Maybe for them the quest was as simple as just making it through the day.

When we passed one old man who was talking to himself out loud and staring into space, I told Carl to wait up. Probably sixty or seventy years old, the old man was wearing some dusty, old, gray slacks with holes in the knees, stained and caked with dirt. Down in front of his tanned-as-leather wrinkled face, hung his dirt-matted and knotted hair. His long, brown beard, containing patches of grease and white, grew high into his cheeks and seemed to turn into his crinkled, squinted eyes. A reflection of his reality, his eyes were not clear, but cloudy with cataracts. I could have seen him as a backdrop, something to fill the space. However, that day I choose to see him as a person.

For some reason I was intrigued by his dementia. I wanted to listen. He was completely lost in another world. *"What is it like where he is? Where he exists may be the place we all end up,"* I wondered. Listening for a few minutes, I was not surprised to find that he didn't make much sense. Looking down where his toes stuck out of his old worn-out army boots, I felt almost compelled to buy the man a decent pair of shoes. He must not have had any family, or surely they would have gotten him off the streets.

"What do we do about Pinochle? How can you play if you have no cards?" the homeless old man muttered.

Obviously, he wasn't directing the question at me or I probably would have supplied an answer. He was talking to someone whom Carl and I couldn't see. Yet, I almost felt convinced, by the way he looked into the space and talked, that he was having a complete conversation with someone.

"Move the plates, and we'll have some cake after mother comes down," he continued. "Damn it, move the plates! How can we dance?"

I could almost make out the semblance of a story. He seemed to be talking to someone in his past. But I couldn't decide if he were actually making any sense in an imaginary world or if he were just muttering a string of unconnected random thoughts.

"They don't know about you," he said, turning suddenly to look me square in the eyes, sending a cold chill up my spine. "They don't know that you are magic. They don't know that you are the one. I know. You are the one." Totally focused on me just for that split second, he then turned away.

"What?" I asked looking back at him, but he didn't reply to me; he simply vanished back to his own world.

Once again lost and oblivious to Carl and me, he asked, "How can you dance with the plates on the table?"

Wondering exactly what would happen if I tried to enter into his world, I don't know why, but I looked right into him and said, "We can take the plates off of the table if you want to dance."

I was astonished when he answered me.

"Son, I don't really want to be a dancer; I want to be a cook; that's what they told me. They said I didn't want to be a dancer. That's just the way it is, I'm a cook. Some things will never change. Don't you believe them, though, I'm not a cook, I'm a dancer." He began to cry. "They never let me dance because they had plates on the tables."

"You are a dancer?" I asked.

"Damn straight I am. I know Fred Astaire personally," he said, blooming a big toothless smile. Cane in hand, he made his exit, dancing a respectable soft-shoe down the street as we watched and wondered in amazement. Somewhere in his world, the derelict old man was performing on a stage, perhaps to a cheering crowd. Not just stepping to a different drummer, he was dancing to a different orchestra.

Carl spoke to me, "Jim, do you always have peculiar things happen to you?"

"Lately, weird seems to be the course of events, doesn't it?" I said, to which he didn't reply. I knew why the man had spoken to me, though. He informed me of his reason for living. Just like the rest of us, he had his reason. His reason was that he was a dancer. His fight to be who, what, and why he was, must have been a losing battle – so he switched battlegrounds.

In his world he controlled the crowd, the band and the extras. He turned the lights off and on, the orchestra volume up or down to his liking. Maybe the old guy wasn't as bad off as I had originally thought. In his reality, he was truly in control. Maybe that was why he was dancing. It was sad. In a queer way, he had much more control over his world than I did over mine. Thinking about him made me remember something Max had said when we first met. "The trick's not to make a living out of magic. The trick is to make *magic* out of *living*." Could the old man possibly make magic out of that kind of living?

We walked on down the street and Carl suggested that we not stop and talk to any more of the "street people," as he called them. That was, if we wanted to reach one of my favorite places in the world, The Hollywood Magic Shop, before dark.

What a place – an ample supply of whoopee cushions and rubber barf awaited any kid at heart. When we arrived, a couple of magicians were working behind the counter, too. We browsed around, checking out all the magic apparatus and novelties. Then a true professional magician demonstrated a few tricks for us. Transfixed, as I watched him perform I was transformed into a kid in a candy store. Performing all of the tricks I wished that I could do, he shuffled cards with one hand, rolled a coin across the back of the fingers, and pulled lit cigarettes out of the air. This magic shop had all of the tricks that I'd ever wished I had, and the demonstrators were almost as good as Max, the first that I had ever really seen in his league. After he finished the tricks, the magician turned to me and asked, "How many do you want, Jim? Your name is Jim, isn't it?"

"Yes, it is. How did you know?" I asked.

"Magic," he said, "I'm a psychic."

"Come on, I don't believe that," I said. "You must've heard my brother talking to me." That seemed the only reasonable explanation; however, I really didn't remember Carl saying my name since we had come into the shop.

"Well, if you must know," he said with a grin, "I've been on the look-out for you and your brother, Carl, ever since Max told me a big spender would come in today."

"Max was here?" I asked. "When?"

"You just missed him by ten minutes," he said.

"You know him?"

"Sure, everyone knows Max. We've all had to deal with him at one time or another," he said.

"You sure we are talking about the same guy?" I asked.

"Max Vi, the magician with the salt and pepper hair, beard, right?" said the magician. "I'm sure, all right. Believe me, I don't know how he does it either, unless you two guys are just putting me on. Nevertheless, Max told me that two guys would show up this afternoon, and he described one of them as an actor and the other would look like – how'd he say it? Oh yes, like a kid in a candy store. Sure, we're talking about the same Max. 'Amazing Max,' we call him around here."

"He's about the most amazing magician I've ever seen," the other magician chimed in. "And believe me, when a magician comes in here and messes with our minds, he is good, damn good. I've been doing magic since I was ten and I've never seen a magician do so much with a person's perceptions. Sometimes I really think he's supernatural."

With that the tingle ran up my spine. I said, "Oh yeah, we're talking about the same guy."

The first magician continued, "He hardly ever buys anything, mostly he just tries out a new trick he's working on. As if he needed practice, his tricks are so good that it gives me chills to watch him. Are you a friend of his? If you are, tell him to join our magic fraternity. We could learn a lot from a guy like that."

"I really don't know him that well. In fact, I was going to ask you how to get in touch with him."

"No luck there, compadre. He never gives us a card or leaves his address. We ask, but he tells us that he doesn't even have an address; says he's homeless. Well, since you came in to purchase a bunch of magic tricks, I guess I should demonstrate some, so you can hurry up and buy."

"I hate to be the one to prove Max's predictions wrong, but I really didn't plan on spending much. I really only do magic as a hobby and not that much of it. I might buy a couple of tricks, perhaps if I thought they were really good."

"Oh, I'm sorry. I didn't mean you would buy. No, Max made me write down the name, Carl. He said that Carl would be the one doing all of the buying, even though Jim would probably be doing all of the talking."

Carl's mouth dropped open, "How did he know? I have never even met this guy. I didn't even tell you."

I turned to Carl and asked him, "What are you talking about?"

"The production company sent me down here to buy the magic supplies for my part for the run of the show. Remember, I told you that they wanted me to add more magic. Well, I thought that you could help me pick out some easy tricks. They gave me a seven-hundred-dollar budget."

"I told you," said the magician behind the counter. "Max never misses."

After a moment's pause he continued, "Oh, Max did say that there would be one thing that *you* might be convinced to buy. Let me go in the back and get it. Just a minute and I'll show it to you." With that he slipped behind the curtains into the back room only to return shortly carrying a large white box which looked like a shirt box, only quite a bit larger. He set it on the counter for both Carl and me to see. Opening it up revealed a starched, white canvas straitjacket, so new and shiny that I could smell the leather on the straps. Pulling it out, I held it up for Carl to see.

"It's a real one," said the magician. "A lot of magicians use those fake ones with the gaffed straps. But this is the real McCoy. Look here, the label even has a doctor's warning. '*To be applied only in the presence of a qualified physician,*'" he read from the tag.

"Wow!" I exclaimed, shoving my arms into the sleeves. The jacket was exactly as I remembered Max's, except this one showed no wear, no frayed straps, no scarred leather, no scratched steel buckles from years of use. "How much is it?" I asked.

"It's two hundred dollars, but we'll give you a professional discount – twenty percent."

Digging around in the box for some sort of instructions, I found a small folded paper, but to my dismay these directions only explained how to properly apply the jacket. There were no explanations on how to get out. "How am I supposed to get out of it? If I buy it, you will tell me how the escape is done, won't you?" I asked.

"I don't know," admitted the magician, reluctantly. "No one has ever told me how to get out of a real one. Unfortunately, as you can see, it doesn't come with instructions. The straitjacket is the only thing in this shop that doesn't. I suppose though, like a lot of things, it's just a matter of practice."

The other magician, who had been working with another customer, joined in, "Yeah, I know an escape artist named Matt Cooper. He told me that it's just a matter of positive thinking, using your mind over matter. According to him, 'If you don't *mind* a little pain, then it doesn't *matter* how you get out'"

Remembering my dreams, I wasn't sure where my owning a straitjacket would lead. Spending the one hundred and sixty dollars alone would be proof that I was just about crazy enough to need one. Escape was an art that I really wanted to learn, anyway. It sounded kind of fun. Besides, too many coincidences pointed toward my owning it. I had to buy it.

"Well, I guess I'd better get out my credit card," I said to Carl and the magician.

"Cool," said Carl.

That evening we returned to Carl's house to have some fun with our new toys. Carl had purchased plenty of magic tricks and supplies for the run of the show. One of the most fun items was the flash paper – paper that seemed to be made of gunpowder or something extremely flammable. When you touched it with anything hot, like a cigarette or match, the flash paper would burst into a bright flash of light and flame, entirely consuming itself, with not so much as a trace of ash left. Incredible!

Most of the tricks were self-explanatory. However, for a few of them, we took a while figuring out exactly what the instructions were telling us to do, and practicing to get the trick to work. After a while, we both became reasonably proficient. After all, one of the criteria for buying them was that they be simple to perform.

We'd decided from the outset to save the best for last. So, the final thing we tried to figure out was how to get out of the straitjacket. Carl strapped me in. Having seen it done, at least I had an idea of what it was supposed to look like strapped on. When he pulled the straps around to the back, I asked that he not strap it too tight, thinking that might help me. Even though it wasn't really tight, I was still trapped. I tried to pull my arms around and over my head, as I had seen Max do – no way. Tugging and pulling as hard as I could, sweat pouring from my forehead, I still couldn't get the necessary slack. My shoulders ached and my arms cramped. After only ten minutes of the ordeal, I found myself becoming extremely uncomfortable.

"Okay, Carl," I said, feeling like a trapped animal, "I give up. Take me out of this contraption – unbuckle the back." Too tired to care about my defeat, I took off the jacket and tossed it on the couch.

"Let me give it a try," said Carl.

"Okay, you just tell me how tight you want it."

It didn't take long before Carl threw in the towel, too. I had to let him out just as he had me. And just like me, by the time he gave in he was sweating like a pig. Maybe there was more to getting out than just a little practice. Maybe you needed to be a magician.

"Well, that was a hundred and sixty bucks for nothing," I said.

"Don't sweat it, you'll figure it out," said Carl. "Maybe you can ask that ghost-magician friend of yours."

"Oh, shut up – I should've left you in the straitjacket."

"Remember, My Friend –
The Illusion Is The Reality"

Chapter 20

Whether you're in a hospital ill, or just visiting someone – it really makes you focus on life. You can't help but feel your own mortality at some point – at least that's the way it is for me. As I walked down the hall toward the admissions desk, I really didn't know what to expect. I hoped Josh Wooten would be able to shed a little light on the mystery of Max Vi and his cloth medallion. More than that, I wanted to help him out somehow. Or rather, we might be able to help each other. Our lives must have become entangled in that back alley for a reason.

Carl decided to stay in the waiting room and I agreed. This pilgrimage was more of a personal mission for me anyway. When I reached the admission's desk, the nurse on duty said she was sorry, but Josh had asked that no visitors be allowed. However, I knew Josh would see me once he was shown the necklace he'd thrown into the street two nights before. After a little persuasive pleading, the nurse agreed to take the necklace to him and ask if he would see me.

"What is your name?" she asked me.

"He wouldn't know me by name. He'll know who I am, though, when you give him the necklace," I answered.

She was a bit confused, but she complied, asking for me to wait at the desk. Then she stepped down the hall and round the corner. Not surprisingly, she returned just a few seconds later and stated, "Mr. Wooten said he would see you now. He's right around the corner in room five twenty-seven."

"Thank you," I said, walking toward the door. Pausing in front of it, I took a deep breath, not knowing what I would say or what he would say to me. Flying by the seat of my pants, I felt second thoughts beginning to creep in; maybe this was a stupid idea.

I opened the door anyway, led by fate, and for once trusting in my own intuition. Josh was sitting upright in a hospital bed when I entered. Sitting there in his hospital garb, wounded, he didn't seem very threatening. Bandages were wrapped over his head and completely over one eye. His face was swollen and bruised – so much so, that his uncovered eye only retained a small slit for him to see. He leaned forward trying to focus his impaired vision on me, but he couldn't. Giving up, he lay his head back far in his pillow. If he could see me at all, I'm sure it wasn't very well.

"I figured you would show up eventually," said Josh.

"Why?" I asked.

"You always seem to appear whenever I'm really looking for you."

Wondering what he meant, I asked, "You've been looking for me?"

"I've needed to talk to you. I know it's not your fault I'm in this mess, but I just can't seem to live up to your expectations." Josh said.

"You don't have to live up to my expectations. What are you talking about?"

"I've committed the ultimate sin in your eyes – haven't I?"

"Hey, nobody got killed the other night. Nobody died. If you hadn't had the foresight to put blanks in the gun – it may have been a different story," I explained.

"You know about that?" asked Josh.

"Of course, I was there."

"You always know everything, don't you? You're always there," he said. "You were probably there even when I put the gun to my head."

"What do you mean?" I asked.

"I was pretty shook up the other night. Ha! That I had thought to put blanks in the gun, was a downright miracle. Something or someone told me to, though. That little voice you have told me, so many times, to listen to – well, I listened for once."

This conversation didn't feel right. Something was really screwy. I asked one question and he answered something else. About to ask if he knew who I was and why I had come to see him, his next words explained exactly what was going on.

Josh continued, "I'm sorry, Max. That wasn't me holding a gun in a back alley – that wasn't me. It was the coke – Jesus, when I think about what almost happened. I couldn't take any more, I'd messed up one too many times. I just wanted to end my misery. Now look what I've done. My picture was in the paper today, those boys are gonna see me and they're gonna press charges. Next time you visit I will probably be in prison. Jesus, I deserve it. I'm worthless," he said as he reached up and rubbed his forehead, wincing in pain.

It was clear to me now – he thought I was Max. Probably Josh had enough drugs in him to believe just about anything. I'm sure his hearing had been affected by the gunshot, just as much as his sight. I considered telling him who I was and why I was there, but he continued, and I didn't really get a chance to speak.

"I'm sorry," he said sobbing. "You have been here for me and my family, always, and I have let you down big time. I really do deserve this."

In a state of anguish, the big man couldn't catch his breath. Telling him that he was talking to the wrong guy would just add to his misery, but I didn't know exactly what to do. Anyway, what would it hurt if he thought that I was Max? – I'd just let him continue believing it.

"Don't worry, the boys won't be pressing charges," I said. He paused and started breathing evenly again. I reassured him, "I know that for a fact. But what about you? Are you going to be all right?"

"The ringing in my ears won't stop. The doctor said that I'm damn lucky; I might even be able to see out of both eyes again. But you and I know that luck had very little to do with it."

"Tell me."

"I don't know what to tell you, Max. When the Raiders drafted me, life looked so good. You know, I was livin' the life, let me tell you – party, party, party. Give a poor dumb SOB like me two-point-five million and what do you think I'm gonna do? Drugs and women, Jesus, I'm a stupid jerk!" he said, pounding his fist into the back wall.

"Martha forgave me for the drugs. But she won't forgive the time Melissa came home from school, sick, to find her Daddy in bed with another woman. Nope, she's never gonna forgive me for that; her love ain't that unconditional. You talk to me about your defining moments that change the course of a person's life – that was the mother of all moments.

"When Martha and I divorced, I lost more than just half my money, Max, I lost all of my self-respect. In a way, I guess I was lookin' to get caught when they kicked me off the team. I wanted to punish myself. But the final straw came when she called me, night before last, to tell me she was taking Melissa and Colin to Atlanta, to live near her relatives. She wanted them away from Daddy's *fast* life.

"That's when I freaked out and went out for a score. Hell, I didn't have two bucks to my name ... I couldn't even handle a simple rip-off – almost killed one of them. But the strangest thing happened. Instead of running, yelling, and screaming – well, I don't know what is supposed to happen in a situation like that – but whatever it is, the man didn't do it. He just stood there, looked into my eyes, and asked me about that cloth you gave me. But you know that 'cause you was there, right?"

"I was there all right," I said.

"I'm telling you Max, if ever I felt your presence, *that* was the time. I knew I had let you down; I knew that I had let everyone down, because I'm so stupid. I drove home and decided life just wasn't worth living anymore. First thing I saw when I got home were the bullets lyin' on the kitchen counter. I loaded the chamber and put the gun to my head, right up to the temple. Then something happened – damnedest thing. When I started to pull the trigger – someone pulled my hand away. If I'd shot straight, I'd be dead right now. But I swear, something pulled my hand, so all I did was shoot off my eyebrows. No one was there; maybe I just imagined someone pulling my hand back. Maybe my aim was bad, but then, maybe some power was with me. I don't know what it was. Was it you, Max?"

I didn't know what to say, but there had to be something. There had to be a way that I could help this man, the way Max was helping me. Where was Max now that Josh really needed him? Why was I here? Looking desperately for an answer, I thought, there had to be a reason. I couldn't just pretend to be Max. I didn't have all of his infinite wisdom and answers. Should I just tell Josh that I pulled his hand away? Leading him to continue believing that I was Max and I saved his life? Then somehow the right words tumbled out of my mouth.

"Does it really matter if it was me or not?"

"What do you mean?" he asked.

Something inside of me clicked. This man thought that I was Max, so to him, I was more than a man – an angel, something great. My own experiences had taught me what Josh felt. I had believed the same things about Max, and I knew that whether I was Max or not, whatever I said now was going to change this man's life. I knew that, and that's what really mattered. Josh Wooten had been given another chance.

"I mean that you've been given a second chance."

"Since Martha took the kids to Atlanta, my life is worth nothing."

"Josh, think! Would you get a second chance at life if your life were worth nothing? Would I be here if you had no greater purpose to your life? Would Max Vi help you discover yourself if you weren't meant to do something great? And I don't mean win the Super Bowl, either. I mean something really meaningful, something that will change the lives of others, something that will make the world a better place."

When I saw Josh wipe his eyes, I really felt his humanness, his reflection of all of us. "No, I guess not. I suppose I've got a reason to live, or you wouldn't be wasting your time with me," he said.

Even though physically his body was large and powerful, even though his background and life were far from my own, inside he was a human being with all the frailties, self-doubts, and regrets that go along with living. "But what do I do now?" he asked.

"You tell me, Josh. What will you do? What can a person with the guts to make it to the top of one of the toughest sports, toughest businesses in the world, do? What would a guy, who loves the grass beneath his cleats and who can lift over three hundred pounds over his head, do? What could a person do with a knowledge of football and a passion to be with his kids? Josh, a man like you can move mountains if he wants to. Listen to your heart and do what it tells you."

I could almost see his thoughts as joy filled his face. Tears rushed from his swollen eyes. His answer had been hidden by his own self-pity. In figuring out his path, he reached a defining moment in his life's contract.

"I can coach. That's what I'll do, I'll move to Atlanta and I *will* be with my kids. I want to be in their lives again. To hell with all of this LA bullshit; I don't need it anymore." He was sobbing; his life had truly changed direction. Somehow I was instrumental in changing his course, but he was the one achieving the real magic.

The time had come for this "Amazing Max" to leave, disappear, so I just turned and quietly slipped out the door. As I rounded the corner I heard him yell out to the sky, "MAAXX, THANK YOU, Thank you – you son-of-a-bitch wherever you are!"

An indefinable feeling rushed over me, as if my helping Josh had somehow returned to me as pure positive energy, real energy, more than just a great feeling. Beaming, I walked smiling around the corner. Stopping for a moment, I closed my eyes, and basked in the positive spirit. This positive feeling grew and grew until it finally transformed itself into goose-bumps – I opened my eyes. There stood Maximillion Vi.

"You performed well in there," Max said to me.

"Thank you. I take it you listened to the whole conversation," I said, not even the least shaken by his appearance.

"I listened to enough to tell you that you are coming along just fine in your quest for your true purpose. James, when an experience becomes this complex, in a cosmic sense, it means something unique, something significant. This is what I call a cosmic triangle – three people whose lives have become intertwined by fate, with no apparent reason in sight. Tell me, did you learn anything from this experience?"

"I don't know," I said. "I guess that there are defining moments in a person's life which can change its course. But his life is being completely changed by a big fat lie; I mean: I'm not you, but he believes I was."

"James, let me tell you something about the world around you. Do you know what matter is?"

"Well, I don't know if my explanation would be that scientific, but I guess – it's stuff. You know, it's what everything's made of, atoms and molecules, uh, protons, neutrons and chemicals. That sort of stuff is what matter is."

"Basically, you are right. Everything is one of three things in the universe: matter, energy, or empty space. Since empty space is nothing, there are the two kinds of stuff, matter and energy. Einstein showed us that the two are also interchangeable in '$E=mc^2$.' Energy is equal to mass multiplied by the speed of light squared. Really, everything we know of as reality is this mass and energy mixed with a lot of empty space in between. You and I, everything else, we are all the same basic stuff mixed in different ways. I hope I'm not losing you here.

"The illusion of reality is created when one realizes how little stuff there is and how much is just empty space. You see, James, when you start breaking the solid things around you into their atomic particles, you find that the actual mass is something of an illusion. Actually the world we see and feel is just very tiny, sub-microscopic particles moving back and forth very fast.

"It's as if I took a tennis ball and moved it back and forth fast enough to create the illusion of a football field. It would look and feel like the ground. You would even be able to run on top of the field without falling through, because the ball is moving so fast. For all practical purposes you would 'know' that the field was a solid object. But your perception is deceiving you; it is not a solid object. In truth, it is just a little object influenced by a tremendous amount of speed and energy.

"Now do me a favor. Say the word 'magic' in your mind, not out loud, just in your mind," said Max.

I did and then said, "Okay, what's your point?"

"Did you hear the word?" he asked.

"What do you mean, of course I heard it."

"But I couldn't hear it," he said. "Yet, you hear it. It doesn't make any sound – yet you hear it. A dream doesn't make any light – yet you see it. And you can hurt when no one is touching you, yet you feel it."

"Every time you create a thought in your mind, you are creating something real. You just created 'magic' as pure thought energy. That energy, as Einstein suggested, is really only mass in a different form. In fact, it was Einstein who proclaimed, 'Imagination is everything; it is the preview of life's coming attractions.'

James, there's an ancient Latin proverb which says, 'If you believe that you have it, you have it.' Buddha said, 'All that we are is a result of what we have thought.' Christ probably said it best when he said, 'If thou canst believe, all things are possible to him that believeth.' The great minds of history knew about the limitless power of pure thought energy."

"You don't mean that I can do anything that I can imagine, do you?" I asked.

Just then Carl arrived from down the hall and called out to me, "James, how did it go with the big guy?"

I looked away. Of course, when I looked back, Max was gone.

"*Incredible,*" I thought to myself.

Not even mentioning the incident to Carl, I simply told him I was finished here. We said "thank you" to the nurse and walked out to his car. Somewhere in my mind I recalled something that Max had mentioned on the plane.

"Do you know where Almedia is?" I asked.

"Sure, its about twenty minutes east of here. Why?" Carl replied.

"Something I just remembered," I said. "Just begin your quest and the universe will rush in to help you."

"Opportunities Often Disguise Themselves As Tribulations."

Chapter 21

The sign on the door said, "Bien Venido – este casa es su casa." Welcome – this house is your home. The clean well kept adobe-style hostel seemed out of place and in stark contrast to the falling down brick facades and painted cinder-block storefronts which lined the streets around it. While the other buildings had pull-down metal gates covered with graffiti and iron bars covering the mostly broken windows, the little stucco building showed no evidence of the fear that pervaded the streets of the broken-down neighborhood. It was clean, bright white, freshly painted – no broken windows. The only iron bars were on the small decorative iron fence surrounding a flower bed filled to the edges with red and gold poppies, standing fearlessly tall in full bloom. The only broken glass being pieces now leaded together creating the mosaic stained glass Madonna over the entryway.

There was something very special about this place, you could almost see an angelic circle of light around it, as if the place were under the protection of the divine. Even though the neighborhood itself felt somewhat threatening, Carl and I felt safe once we passed through the wooden gate entering the small yard.

Pushing the doorbell, Carl leaned his ear against the rustic wooden door making sure that it rang. "I don't think it works," he said giving the door a couple of hard raps with his hand.

We waited for a second in silence; the door opened slightly as a little boy stuck his head out. A short Hispanic woman, wearing a brightly colored dress, stepped out behind him. She was probably in her late forties, slightly overweight, with long black hair. After quickly inspecting both Carl and me with her crystal clear brown eyes, she then smiled asking, "Si'?" After which, she said something in Spanish to the little boy who quickly turned and vanished behind her skirt, back into the house.

Since she seemed to have focused her question on Carl, he answered her, "Yes, my brother and I are looking for Mrs. Annabel Rosa Saldana."

Not able to speak a lot of Spanish, I did speak just enough to realize that we were in trouble when she answered us, "Lo siento mucho, pero no hablo Engles." I didn't know if she understood the name Annabel Rosa Saldana, but I did know that she didn't speak English. My quest to discover my *why* was suddenly becoming more difficult.

After Carl and I stared blankly at each other for a long moment, not even knowing how to tell her that we didn't speak Spanish, she seemed to intuitively understand our blank looks. "Uno momento, por favor," she said, then she walked back into the house, motioning for us to follow, yelling, "Sylvia, Sylviiiiiaaaa!"

Sylvia came from the kitchen, holding a bowl full of cake batter in her hands. Wearing remnants of her battle with the flower, cocoa, and eggs across her white apron, she was still stirring the mixture as she conversed in Spanish. She then removed the apron, handing it, bowl, and spoon to the first woman who disappeared with the mixture, back through the kitchen door. Sylvia turned to us saying, "Is one of you the clown?"

"I'm sorry," Carl asked, "what did you say?"

"Oh, you're not the clowns, then," she said. "I'm sorry, we're about to have a birthday party for the children and we are expecting a clown to show up. What can I do for you then?"

I stepped up and answered, "Hi, my name is James Carpenter and this is my brother, Carl. We are looking for Annabel Rosa Saldana."

Sylvia defensively cut me off, "What is this in reference to? And who sent you?"

"I'm sorry, let me explain. No one really sent us, I heard about her from a magician friend of mine named Max Vi," I said.

Her recognition of the name changed her countenance from distrust into one of distinct pleasure. "Max Vi?" she smiled, "That's a name that I haven't heard for a long time. Come in, please, come in." As we followed, she cleared a path through a sea of toys, tricycles and plastic wagons, to a sitting room where everything was in stark opposition, immaculately kept. The room looked as though it stepped right out of the Victorian era with ornate carved furniture, many silver-framed pictures and lace doilies draped over lamps and chairs. Immediately one could tell that this room was off limits to the children. Carl and I both took our seat on a comfortable sofa set at the far side of the room, Sylvia sitting across from us in an armchair. "Do both of you know Max?" she asked.

"Actually, just James," Carl said, "I'm just along for the ride."

"Yes, I have known Max for some time now," I said, "I wanted to see if Mrs. Saldana could answer some questions about him for me. Max kind of sent me on a quest."

"I'm sure that when I tell Anna that you know Max, she will be more than glad to talk to you. Do either of you speak Spanish?"

"No, I hate to say it but neither of us do," I said.

Before she could reply the other woman's voice called out from the other room.

"Sylviiiaaa, Sylviaaaaaa!"

Excuse me, that's Anna calling me back into the kitchen. Annabel can do a lot, but she is a terrible cook," she said, "I'll be right back, momentito."

From the living room, we could hear Anna shouting in the kitchen. Although we couldn't understand, we could guess that she was very upset. Sylvia and Anna both came into the room. Sylvia spoke to us.

"I'm sorry, gentlemen but Anna says that you will have to leave. She feels that she doesn't have time to talk to you today. You must understand that with the children's party going on, today really isn't a good time for us," said Sylvia.

"Okay, I understand," I said, reluctant about giving up on my quest, "How about if we come back tomorrow?"

Sylvia turned, spoke in Spanish to Anna for a moment, then returned an answer, "I'm sorry, but Anna says that she doesn't wish to speak to you at all."

"What? Why? Did we say something wrong?" I asked. Anna just turned her head, let out a huff, and stomped back into the kitchen.

"I'm sorry, but she is just upset because of the party. She doesn't really mean to be rude. It's just that today isn't turning out the way it was supposed to," Sylvia lamented. "We have twenty-five children sitting in the den waiting for a show from Dynamo the Clown. He was supposed to be here a half-hour ago. And it looks as though Dynamo isn't going to show. This is not that big of a catastrophe, I know. Anna usually doesn't get that upset when things don't go smoothly. She knows the kids will get over it. They will still have their cake and ice cream. By tomorrow they will have all forgotten that the clown didn't show up. I can't understand why she is so upset today."

The lights seemed to come on in Carl's head. "I've got an idea," said Carl. "Do you think that the kids would like to see a magician?"

"Of course. Do you know someone?" asked Sylvia.

"I know one who is here, right now. His name is the great '*Jamesini*'," Carl said slapping me on the back.

How original, I thought.

"Carl, I can't do that," I said.

"Sure you can, James. We have all the stuff we bought in the car."

"We will gladly pay you," said Sylvia. "How much do you charge?"

"It's not the money," I said, "It's just that... well I haven't done magic for a long time. I don't think that they'd like me."

"Oh, I'm sure they would love you," she said. "Let me tell Anna that you have come to save the day." With that she disappeared into the kitchen.

Turning to Carl, I prepared to give him a little reprimand. "Carl, what are you thinking? I can't do a show for these kids. For God's sake, I'm an accountant," I barked.

"Not today, you're not. Don't worry, I'll help you. We have all those tricks that I bought for the show, remember? You've been practicing, right?

THE MAGIC LIFE

Besides, you wanted to talk to this Anna woman didn't you? Well, I'm positive that once you do the show for the kids she'll tell you everything she knows about this Max guy," said Carl.

"Just begin a quest and the universe will rush in to help you," I said.

"What?" asked Carl.

"Nothing, just something Max said on the plane," I said.

"Well, I'll rush out to the car and get the tricks. Is that *rushing* enough for you?" Carl said jogging backwards quickly out the door laughing to himself.

Anna and Sylvia soon returned. Anna, much more affable, appeared completely overjoyed that we were going to help with the children. I couldn't tell exactly what she was saying, but I was able to make out the "muchas gracias" that fell from her lips at least ten times.

When Carl came back in with the bag of tricks, the ladies took us into the den. There, ranging in ages from 3 to 14, were twenty-five kids: some rambunctiously playing with toys, some screaming, and a few crying. They all stopped dead in their tracks, turned and stared at us as soon as Anna spoke to them, "Hoy tenemos una sopresa. Tenemos un Mago."

"She is telling them that you are a magician," Sylvia said to us.

All the kids listened intently to her as she gave instructions and then they scurried around the floor, ending up sitting in rows, cross-legged in front of me. Sylvia improvised an introduction in Spanish for which all the children applauded.

Then it dawned on me. They don't speak English. "I can't do this, they don't speak English," I said, to Sylvia, "and I don't know hardly any Spanish."

Then something surprising occurred. It was Annabel who turned to me, smiled widely and in perfect English, without a hint of an accent, calmly stated, "Don't worry, if you need us to translate, we'll jump in to help. But I'm sure that you won't need us, because magic is part of a universal language. It is like music and love. No one needs to teach you these things, James. They are part of life that everyone seems to understand intuitively, from birth. I'm sure you will do just fine."

"I thought that..." I started to say something about her speaking English.

But Carl immediately started the show by throwing a lighted ball of flash paper into the air that burst into flame and then disappeared without a trace. The kids were all in awe for a moment and then began to applaud and cheer. Carl then handed me the rope and scissors, saying, "Knock 'em dead, Jamesini. I'll hand you the tricks."

Before long, without a word of Spanish, simply using a few hand signals, I had all of the children yelling, "Abracadabra!" laughing and clapping. Bringing up several of them as volunteers to help me, I discovered that they caught on very quickly to anything I told them in English. One particular little girl made great facial expressions as she helped me do the linking rings. Linking the rings of steel together, I would make them seem to pull apart like smoke right in front of her eyes. She stood there with her mouth and eyes both wide open for a moment. Then she covered her eyes saying, "Es imposible'!" I knew what she meant.

They all loved the magic show. It took me about a half an hour to go through all the tricks we had purchased: cups and balls, linking rings, color changing scarves, pencil through dollar, torn and restored newspaper, and the break away wand. Taking my final bow, I was sad that I hadn't bought more. The straitjacket was still out in the car and Carl asked if I wanted to give it a try. However, knowing that I couldn't get out, I told him to leave it there. The little girl, who had been my assistant for the linking rings, came up to me after the rest of the kids all ran off to the dining room; she hugged my leg, saying in a thick accent, "I love you, magician."

This *was* indeed one of those magical moments that Max had talked about.

"They all loved you. I want to thank you very much," whispered Anna, "I apologize for not speaking English. But I knew when you first answered the door that you had come as a solution to my problem. I decided that it would be best if you and the universe just worked out the details. Come, let's go into the parlor and I'll gladly tell you all I know about the amazing Max Vi."

She led us back into the Victorian room, sending Sylvia and another helper to be in charge of distributing the cake and ice cream. After we were seated, she spoke commandingly, "James, I can tell that you are getting close to your destiny. After being on a similar quest of my own, I can see the signs.

THE MAGIC LIFE

To someone who has been through the lessons of Max Vi, it becomes easy to see it in a person's eyes. You have been touched, haven't you?"

"What do you mean?" I asked.

"Max has a way of touching a person so that they look at life in an entirely new way. You have been touched. He is truly magic, that Max," she said, "Has he given you one of these yet?" Anna walked across the room to an armoire where she opened an ornately carved box and withdrew a chain with the small piece of white cloth attached with a safety pin.

"The cloth," I said, "What does it mean?"

"If Max gives you one, it means that you are close to reaching the end of your quest," she stated. "You must not have yours yet, because if you did, you would know what it signifies. I'm sorry, James, I can't tell you the meaning. That wouldn't be fair. Besides the cloth means different things to each of us. And besides, there are some things that a person shouldn't know before the proper time. Knowing certain things can sometimes make a person run away from his or her own destiny," Anna stated, "That is what this is about, isn't it? Destiny, I mean. James, you are trying to discover your true destiny, aren't you?"

"Yes, I guess that is what you might call it. I'm searching for a meaning to my life," I said.

Anna continued, *"The meaning of life is the reason for every moment that we live.* If you think about it, we are all here, right now, for a reason. James, you may believe that you came here to discover some secret, but I believe you came here because I needed you to come and fill the hearts of my children with joy. The children needed you to be here. And why do you think you are here, Carl?"

Carl was taken by surprise by her question. "I don't know, I am just trying to help my brother, I guess," he said.

"And wasn't it your idea that made your brother become the magician today?" she asked.

"Yeah, as a matter of fact it was," said Carl.

"Well then, maybe you had a greater purpose than the rest of us today, without your even knowing it, Carl. Without you the rest of this wouldn't have happened. Sometimes it's difficult to discover who is the student and who is the teacher," said Anna with an air of wisdom. "Maybe you and I both have something to learn from Carl today. However, since you helped me out of a jam, James, I will tell you the most important things in life, my life, and you can learn from them whatever it is that you decide to learn."

"That would be great," I said, "I'd really appreciate any information about Max that I can find out."

"Okay, I met Max about nine years ago. Back when I was a well respected attorney in this county. My husband, Cid, and I had just gotten our divorce finalized after a rocky eight-year marriage. We believed at the time that we had just grown apart. Cid was a beer-drinking highway construction superintendent, and I was living a totally different kind of life, drinking martinis in amongst the legal eagles. I don't tell a lot of people this, understand, but under all the superficial excuses, the real reason we divorced was that I couldn't bear him a child. We both wanted a family. That was tearing both of us apart. After one too many arguments, we decided to call it quits.

"Then one night, I was out with some friends at a night club, over in Hollywood, called the Magic Castle. Maybe you've heard of it?"

"Yeah, we've got it on our list of places to visit," replied Carl.

"Anyway, appearing on stage that night was a rather distinguished-looking magician, you guessed it, the amazing Maximillion Vi. Most magicians to me are kind of obnoxious. Before seeing him, I wasn't that impressed with magic or magicians, knowing that it was all just simple tricks. That was until he asked me to come up on the stage and assist him with an illusion. I really didn't want to go up there, but there was something about him that I just can't explain.

"Like the Pied Piper?" I asked.

"Yes, like that. He had an amazing power over me. Like I said before, I was touched. First, he hypnotized me and told me to put my arms down at my side and become stiff as a board. Then he had two men pick me up and lay me between two chairs, my head on one chair and my feet up on another. Then he did the most incredible thing that I've ever seen or felt. One at a time, he pulled the chairs out from under me. Believe it or not, I remained floating in the air. I didn't just stay there, either. He levitated me up ten feet and out over the audience. I don't really expect you to believe me, but I mean I was actually suspended there. This wasn't a trick! There were no wires, no strings, no mirrors, nothing for me to lay on at all. No, I was actually defying the law of gravity.

"After the show was over, I just had to meet him, so I sneaked back stage. He was very nice to me and very easy to talk to. We eventually went into the bar for a drink. Making a long story short, Max told me that he would be back in six months to do another show, and that he'd teach me the meaning of life if I was interested. He pulled a gold coin from my ear, which he gave to me. He then said to bring it back to him, if I decided to come see him in six months."

"This is sounding very familiar," I said.

"Well, then you know how it works," she said matter-of-factly. "He disappears and reappears at the blink of an eye, giving me little insights into myself and telling me to search myself for the answers.

"Did he tell you that he thought you were the '*one*'?" I asked.

"No, I don't believe so," said Anna, "but he told me so many things. Did he tell you that?"

"Yes, never mind. I'm sure it's nothing. Please go on," I said.

"James, when I was young I wanted to be an attorney, because I believed that it would bring my family respect and admiration. Coming from a very large family, nine brothers and sisters, only two got a college education. My father and mother made huge sacrifices so that I could go on to law school, more a struggle for them than it was for me. My father was so proud of his little girl who passed the bar to make it out of the barrio. Don't think that I wasn't grateful either. When I left this neighborhood, I took them with me, moved them into a house in Gardena. James, I believed that I was following my destiny. When you are making a lot of people happy, how can you be off track?

"But Max taught me something very important: *it is never a person's destiny to be unhappy*. I was very unhappy. My marriage had failed; I had no children; my mother had become ill, and both she and my father were dependent upon me to pay the bills. Even though Max showed me that I had to discover my *why* in order to be happy, I couldn't because I was trapped by circumstance. Well, I kept searching for the answer and kept coming up empty. Until one day Max appears and tells me, 'If you want things to *change*, Anna, you've got to change *things*.' Those words changed my life.

"Deciding to give a little back to the old neighborhood, I opened a legal clinic, giving free legal advice one day a week. It ended up that I spent most of the time defending teens who were caught up in gang-related crimes. The time was emotionally draining, but giving something back made me feel a lot better about myself and my chosen career. But I still wasn't happy. What I really wanted was a family.

"One day I had an opportunity-in-disguise appear. *Opportunities often disguise themselves as tribulations.* Without going into detail, the court had asked me to assist them in taking an abused child away from his parents. Probably, that was the toughest thing I'd ever had to do in my life. Not that taking him away from the parents wasn't the right thing to do, the little boy was only four and had been severely beaten by his alcoholic father. But, the boy was so sweet and innocent," Annabel started showing tears, "and afraid. That little boy hugged me so tight. When we got to his foster home, I just didn't want to let go. That was a defining moment in my life. That was the day that I changed things."

Carl and I were mesmerized by this woman's heartfelt story, her voice overflowing with the emotion and tears held back.

Anna continued, "When I told my father that I was giving up law, and was going to become a full-time social worker, I truly believed he would disown me. He had given up so much for me to be who and what I was. Believing that both my parents wouldn't love me anymore, I was surprised to discover that they wanted nothing more than for me to be happy. My mother even told me that she had a love without boundaries, an unconditional love, for me. Whatever I did with my life would be right as long as it was right for me. James, the only boundaries that had been imposed were the ones I'd set by my own mind. All along it was me holding myself back.

"Today I have twenty-five children, one hell of a family. Believe it or not, once I was happy, somehow my ex-husband and I discovered that we hadn't grown so far apart as we thought. Cid and I happily remarried, after only a year apart. We both look on these children as our family."

THE MAGIC LIFE

Two young boys ran up to the doorway to the room and stopped before crossing the threshold; speaking Spanish to Annabel, they made the motion to "come here."

"James and Carl, I have told you my story, it's up to you to learn what you will from it. As for Max Vi, I really don't know much about him. I never saw him again," she said, standing up and saying something in Spanish to the children then turning back to us, "I wish that we could spend days together but I am being called back into the party. Would you please join us for some cake and ice cream?"

"We'd love to," said Carl.

"Sure," I said, "And thank you."

Carl and I walked with Anna and the boys to the dining hall where twenty-three of the happiest kids in the world were up to their ears in cake and ice cream. The rest of the afternoon we spent playing with the children, Carl and I giving piggyback rides, pushing swings, and pulling wagons. The language barrier turned out to be no barrier at all.

One feisty boy, about six years old, came up to Carl holding out his index finger, giggling; many of the other children had stopped to watch. We could tell that something was up. Carl quickly caught on, reaching out and pulling on the boy's finger. The little boy farted loudly and proudly, giggling as he did the deed and running away laughing. Carl and I couldn't hold back, bursting into the belly laughs. We lost it. A laugh pandemonium filled the room. Even Anna, Sylvia, and the two other adults who were trying not to laugh, could only cover their mouths, tears running down their cheeks, as they laughingly chastised the boy.

"You see, James, this is what destiny will do for you," Anna said, picking up the child and giving him a big hug.

Becoming time for us to leave, while saying our good-byes, Anna gave us each a hug saying, "James, there is one thing that I know you should take with you today."

"What is that?" I asked.

"You should learn that there is a language that is spoken throughout the universe, one which crosses all boundaries and borders, a language found in music, dance, art and even magic. It is a language of unspoken passion. It is praise without words. It is silent intuition. James, life's language is the universal language of love. Learn that language and you will understand everything." Those were the last words I heard from Annabel Rosa Saldana.

Of all the time I'd spent on my vacation, just playing with those kids who didn't even speak our language, was the most rewarding, the most magical time of all. When we said our good-bye all twenty-five kids each gave Carl and me both a hug, one after the other. Then they stood in the yard and waved to us as we drove away.

Carl and I spent that evening sitting by the ocean discussing the events of the day, listening to the surf pounding rhythmically against the sand. There was a cooling ocean breeze and the beach was almost deserted as we watched the sun set and took the opportunity to reflect.

"Some people can explore the oceans and learn nothing, while others can gather a sea of knowledge from a simple grain of sand," Carl said.

"Where did you hear that?" I asked, thinking that Carl had become quite profound in the last few years.

"I don't really know. It's just something I remembered."

"Do you ever think about your reason for living, your *why* as Max calls it?" I asked. "Do you think it's about being an actor for you?"

"Sure, I've thought about it, but I don't think it's that simple. Maybe some people live just to be something, but I think there has to be more to the meaning of life than an occupation," Carl said. "Otherwise, I'd just tell you to get over it and become a magician."

"Why do you suppose I'm so afraid of giving up being what I am? Of losing everything I've got?"

"Everyone is afraid of losing what they have, whether it is property, possessions or wealth. I suppose that the more you have, the more fear you have of losing it. That's why I don't worry about it very much; I don't have much to lose."

I added back to Carl, "Yeah, I had a professor once tell me that poor people only spend *half* their time worrying about getting money while rich people spend *all* their time worrying about losing it."

"The truth is that the fear of losing your possessions is much worse than actually losing them," concluded Carl.

"I don't know if I agree with that statement," I said.

THE MAGIC LIFE

"Well, if you lose everything, you eventually get over it and go on with life. However, the fear of losing everything always stays with you."

I asked, "So how is someone supposed to get over the fear?"

"I haven't given it much thought, but if you believe that life has a purpose, then you must be ready to accept whatever it has in store for you," Carl said, stumbling on to the answer.

"You know what, Carl? You're not as dumb as you look."

"Thanks," he said.

"Of course you couldn't be as dumb as you look," I said with a laugh.

"Bite me, Bro."

"If You Want Things To Change –
You've Got To Change Things."

Chapter 22

No more than five minutes after Carl got his new telephone installed, it rang. "Jim, it's for you," Carl said, and he handed me the phone. "It's your office." How in the world could anyone have gotten my number here, or why in the world would anyone be calling me?

"Hello."

"Jim, this is Greg. I need you to get back here as soon as you can."

"What is it?" I asked. "What's going on?"

"I don't know how to tell you this, but, Gina, she woke up, and spoke to Linda. She asked to see you," he said, his voice quivering with excitement.

"May I talk to her?" I asked. "I want to talk to her."

He continued, "It was just a quick thing, she slipped in and out of consciousness for just a few minutes, we don't know what's going on but we've taken her back down to St. David's for some more tests. Anyway, Linda and I would really appreciate your coming back early. Maybe there is a chance that something..."

"I'll book a seat on the next plane out, and I'll see you at St. David's," I said, my mind whipping into a frenzy. Suddenly *my* life had completely changed course. Now that everything was going to be all right with Gina, I no longer had to search for the meaning of life; I had someone to live for.

"What's up?" Carl asked.

"I have to get a flight out ASAP. Gina woke up from her coma for just a minute, she called for me, and her parents want me to come back to Austin," I said, smiling.

"Well, I guess there isn't really anything else to say about the subject," Carl responded, showing some remorse for a rather abrupt end to our vacation, but he was careful not to say anything to upset me.

I called the airline to switch my return flight to the first flight that I could get: 1:30 that afternoon, getting me into Austin around 7:00 P.M. after a connection in Phoenix.

At the airport Carl said goodbye, "Good luck with everything, Jim. I want to thank you for everything you did for me. I didn't get a chance to tell you, but you saved my life, too; I love you, Bro," he said and gave me a hug.

"I love you too, Bro. Thanks for an amazing time," I said. "You're right; my life *is* changing for the better."

On the plane I had some time to think and reflect; my life would now get back to normal with Gina's recovery. I wouldn't be so compelled to chase silly dreams, I would have *my* reality to hold on to – Gina was my reason enough. We could make life everything that it needed to be, just by being together. I just had to hold on to the faith and everything would turn out all right. The first thing I was going to do, as soon as she was conscious, would be to kiss her and tell her that I loved her. No longer waiting for the right moment, from now on I was going to make the moment happen. From now on, I was going to live without regrets.

When I walked into the hospital room, something wasn't right; there was an anxious feeling in the air. The Lees were there, looking remorseful, standing by the bed. Linda had been crying – mascara streaked her cheeks. Greg hugged Linda tightly to his side with his right arm. His left hand clutched onto Gina's. He and Linda both had their heads bowed down and were quietly praying for Gina as they stood over her.

Not as peaceful and serene as she had been at home, Gina was completely motionless, yet somehow she seemed unhappy. With all kinds of machinery hooked up to her again, she didn't look as though she might just sit up and talk any more. The feeling of optimism that I expected to receive was nowhere to be found in that room. Evidently the Lee's had been waiting for a sign from her for hours, and it was no doubt beginning to take a toll on them. They were very frustrated and tired.

Greg turned to me and spoke. "Jim, we're glad that you're here," he said, shaking my hand.

Linda, turning to face me, letting go of Greg's hand for a moment, hugged me, not as much a welcome-back hug as it was a hug for her own support. "Thank you for coming. I did speak to her," she said, as if someone may have suggested that she only imagined the conversation. "Gina said she loved you and knew that you had been there for her. James, she heard every word you said. Then, all of a sudden, she just told me good-bye, closed her eyes and went back to this."

Greg continued, "Unfortunately, she hasn't responded at all. The doctors don't know what to think, in fact they are concerned that her blood pressure is down and that her vital signs are weak."

I walked to the bed and took Gina by the hand.

She looked so weak and frail that I prayed silently for her. My heart skipped for a moment when I felt pressure from her fingers clasped around mine. "Gina," I said excitedly.

She squeezed my fingers. Her eyelids fluttered and then slowly opened. Looking up at me, she smiled and her lips parted. Suddenly her body shuddered, then became still. She stopped breathing and the heart monitor resounded that flat-lined *eeeeeeeee.*

"Call for the doctor," I yelled. "Someone get the doctor!"

The room became filled with pandemonium. A nurse screamed for a doctor and then started administering CPR. Immediately, doctors, orderlies, nurses filled the room, asking us to please step into the hallway. Instead, I retreated back into the corner, out of the way. In all of the commotion, they became oblivious to me. Wrapped up in the seriousness of the moment, they weren't pressing for me to leave. The doctors wheeled some more equipment into the room, ripped her robe from her, shoved a needle into her chest, pounded on her and administered shocks making her body convulse. It all seemed to last for a long time, but eventually all of the commotion slowly ground to a conclusion.

THE MAGIC LIFE

When I saw the doctor look at his watch, I knew that was the end. Gina was gone. I felt her spirit leave the earth, tugging at my heart, taking a piece with her. A nurse covered her lifeless body with a sheet, turned, and putting her arms around me, walked me out of the door.

The Lees looked at my blank face for an answer, which I was unable to give. The doctor standing at my side said, "I'm sorry. She has passed away."

"No, she can't be dead," I said, tears running down my cheeks. With no strength left in my legs, I collapsed on the bench in the hall. I could hear Mrs. Lee sobbing. Mr. Lee had his arms around her to keep her from falling. He guided her to a pair of cold metal chairs and sat holding his wife in his arms – wiping off a tear running down his own face.

My mind in a fog, I sat there for what may have been hours. The Lees finally left and the orderlies rolled the empty gurney from the room. Finally getting the strength to lift my head up, I spied the same old janitor I'd seen there before – the man that I'd seen when I imagined Gina had spoken to me. Maybe she had spoken to me. I didn't know what to think – certainly I wasn't going to have the life I expected, however briefly. Gina was the only woman that I'd ever really loved. "I never even had the chance to say *I love you* to her," I said to myself.

"She heard you, you know," commented the janitor after overhearing me, walking down the hall pushing his cleaning cart.

"What?" I said.

"I said she heard you, you know," he repeated. "I remember you and that girl. You know she will take everything you told her with her. When you give someone love, that goes with them."

He put his hand on my shoulder and then continued speaking to me. "You listen to me. I may not be a youngster anymore, but I know about life because I've lived it. Sometimes life has to give us a new plan. Now it's your time to learn what your new plan is. You can't live with the past. She heard you. She knew. You gave her what she needed to go on."

"Thanks," I said.

"Oh yeah, there is something that I meant to give you," he said. "Come with me. I wanted to give you this – it might be important."

He led me down the hall, onto the elevator, and then to his locker. There he dug out a crumpled up piece of paper, just an old envelope. I could read the name that was written on the front: "James."

I opened it where it had been torn open once before. There was nothing inside.

"It's the envelope to that card that you threw away. You know, the sunrise? The man told me to keep it and to give it to you, if I ever saw you again. I don't know why he thought the envelope would be important. I almost forgot about it, but he was such an interesting guy. He made me promise, not just say it; he made me raise my hand and swear on my mother's grave. I knew that I wouldn't forget you. I had dreams about that guy for a week. What an interesting man – you know, he kind of reminded me of Jesus, or an angel – something like that. Well, does it mean anything to you?"

"I don't get it," I said, not understanding the importance of the envelope at all, "Did he tell you anything else?"

"No, I don't think so," he said. "He just said that this would be something you would want."

Then I turned the envelope over and I realized why Max had thought that the envelope would be significant. There on the back was an address: 2243 Syringa Dr. # 234, Austin, Texas.

"Thank you. Thank you very much," I said.

*"In Each Of Us Is Hidden –
The Ultimate Magician."*

Chapter 23

Max Vi opened the door of his apartment and smiled. Standing there in a T-shirt, a pair of gray and black sweats, and tennis shoes, he was not the mystical Max that I had come to know so well, but understand so little. His hair was somewhat out of place. His beard needed a trim. Max looked like a just regular guy. The apartment was nice, but simple, nothing out of the ordinary. I could even hear his TV running in the background. The only thing different about the place was that it was just so plain.

"James, you have been very patient with me," he said. "Come in and we'll talk."

Entering and glancing around, I observed all the trappings of an ordinary, commonplace person. A coat tree with an assortment of old coats stood by the front door. A sports duffel bag lay on the floor in front of the coffee table with old newspapers sitting in a stack under an end table. A plant stand held a raggedy looking potted plant near the window, some of the leaves falling off from lack of water. This was as if I had walked into anybody's place. These were not fantastic, god-like angelic things. These were common things, human things.

Max had been reading a book on card tricks, which lie open on the coffee table. A deck of playing cards was stacked neatly to the side of it. A mirror had been leaned up against a short stack of books on one end of the couch, turned and propped up so he could practice his tricks in front of the mirror. He was good because he practiced, not because he was magic.

After returning the mirror to its place on the wall, Max walked up to the nineteen-inch TV. Turning it off, he said, "You look a little surprised by my surroundings."

A voice came from the back room. "Who is it, honey?"

"It's James Carpenter," he called back to his wife, Kristin.

She walked into the room. I remembered her well, a truly beautiful woman. Even so, she too looked sort of plain-Jane wearing just a Polo shirt and a pair of jeans.

"Hello, James," she said. "It's good to see you again. Stuart has been telling me a lot about you. He told me that you have been living through quite an ordeal. I know that you two have a lot to talk over. It was nice to see you again, James. Honey, I have to run to the store and pick up something for the baby."

"Stuart?" I asked. "Baby?"

"Oh, I mean Max to you," she said. "I'm sorry, honey. Am I spilling the beans too early?" She gave him a kiss, grabbed her purse and adding, "Keep an ear out for Amy. Bye, guys. Have fun," she said as she made a quick exit.

Max chimed in saying, "The jig is up; my real name is not Max. It's Stuart – Stuart Haycock. Yes, I really am a human being, not a ghost, not an angel, not the devil, and certainly not a figment of your imagination. I'm just an ordinary person like you. Only, one major difference – I am happy. Here, James, I've got something to teach you." He reached into the duffel bag, pulled out his straitjacket, and tossed it to me in one fluid motion.

Still awestruck by the bizarreness of the ordinary, I caught the jacket by the sleeve without thinking, in an automatic reaction.

"I can only hope that I don't lose too much credibility with you – now that you see me for *who* and *what* I really am. However, remember that who and what aren't nearly as important as *why*; and believe me when I tell you that the *why* I possess will help you in ways you can't even begin to imagine – the best surprise is yet to come. Here, put your arms in the straitjacket and let me strap you in," he said.

"No thanks, that's all right," I said, lowering the jacket by the sleeve to the floor. "I didn't come here to learn tricks."

My world had collapsed; Max was just an ordinary man. Even though in my heart I always knew that he had to be just a man, I'd deluded myself into believing he was more. At a loss for words, I felt empty, as if betrayed by my best friend, like the vacant feeling I experienced when my father died. Naively, I had actually believed that Max would be able somehow to magically bring Gina back to me. Now that magic was gone.

"James, you may not believe in me now as some sort of greater-than-life being. You may not see in me, now, whatever your mind led you to believe before. But, beyond your perceptions of me, and the reality that I presented to you, I know something that can help you move on with your life," Max said. "Something about reality, about magic and life. I have learned the one secret to life – I am that secret. You are that secret," he said, placing a hand on my shoulder. "*In each of us is hidden the ultimate magician.* I am going to teach you something more than tricks. I am going to teach you the philosophy of the magic life."

He held the jacket open in front of me, saying, "James, just think of this jacket as my visual aid. Here, let me get you strapped in."

There was really no point in arguing, so reluctantly I placed my arms into the sleeves.

"You see this piece of cloth hanging from around my neck?" Max said as he tugged at the steel chain that seemed to pass right through his neck. The clasp was still attached, and the chain still intact.

"That's a good trick, isn't it? I'm going to give this necklace to you after you've freed yourself; sort of a medal," he said. "In reality, it's just a piece of an old shirt of mine, my way of giving you the shirt off my back."

"I'm not so sure I want it," I said. "It's just a piece of cloth, isn't it?"

"It is much more than that," Max said as he set the necklace on his coffee table in front of me and then stepped behind me to pull the straps and buckles together, "Think of what the cloth did for you and Wooten. What a tremendous coincidence that was, and quite frankly, I was really impressed with the way you handled that *opportunity.*"

He kept on talking as he buckled me in, "Remember, I once told you that the most difficult thing in life was to know your *why* and not be able to live it. Wooten's *why* was more than to be a football star, much more: family, football, and teaching. He thought that fame and fortune would make him happy. But like so many opportunities that lead us, he was just misdirected away from his true calling. Two and a half million dollars can lead a person just like a sugar cube leads a jackass! Sometimes things that appear positive can actually be leading a person down a rocky canyon path. Fame and fortune led Josh down a canyon away from his *why*, and he slipped off the edge. You have a great deal to learn from Josh. I know this doesn't all make sense to you, but in time it will – you will understand."

The jacket constricted my breath. Max reached under my legs to latch the final strap into place, still talking to me as he did. "We all find ourselves in difficult circumstances at one time or another in our lives, a lot like this straitjacket. Struggle is a life imperative, the test. Without struggle there would be no puzzle to solve. Death, too, is integral to life, the ultimate test, the last solution piece to the puzzle. Jim, try not to be too remorseful for the people who fit the last piece, filling in their picture. Remember, unconditional love goes well beyond the grave," he said, as he again picked up the cloth from the sofa table.

Completely confined by the jacket, I was now strapped in tight.

"Everyone we touch, have contact with, or listen to in our life, has meaning – like a piece to a puzzle. Sometimes the messages may seem unclear, some pieces lost because we are talking when we should be listening, teaching when we should be learning, or even trying to learn when we should be teaching ... But believe me when I tell you, there is no such thing as a coincidence.

"We may not even be aware of it – but we *always* teach and learn something from everyone we meet. Whenever you cross paths with someone and exchange a few words, ask yourself, *'What did I just learn?'* You may be astonished. If you can't figure out the lesson, ask yourself what you may have taught the other person. You can always find meaning in life's little *coincidences*.

"Why aren't you trying to get out?" Max, asked.

"I can't," I said, refusing to even try.

"Don't you recall anything I told you about life? About reality?" Max said of my statement of submission. "You must have learned a lot about life from your love for Gina," he consoled. "Death is not the end, James – simply an actor making an exit off a small stage. What lies behind the facade we don't know, but the true reality of the actor goes way beyond her moments in front of us. What she creates is a living, breathing person for us, but what she really is continues well beyond the makeup and lights." He paused for a moment, then he continued, "There was more than prose to it when Shakespeare wrote: 'All the world is a stage.'

"I don't claim to know *all* the answers to this enormous question we call life, but let me explain the riddle to this small piece of cloth that has meant so much to me. This piece of your puzzle, I am more than glad to place for you.

"Not too long ago, I found myself in a situation similar to yours: well off in the physical sense, but bored in the emotional sense. Life hadn't really presented enough conflict to help me discover the ultimate truth, or at least I hadn't been paying enough attention to discover it. Strife is a necessary part of a person's life if he wants to discover ultimate truth, or reason for being – especially if he's not attentive. Sure, we can get along just fine without problems. But, conflicts such as tragedy, poverty, or disease force us to ask life's tougher questions – like, 'Why am I alive?'

"Go ahead, James, struggle to get out of your straitjacket and I'll tell you a story about my struggle against the straitjacket of life. You really should give it your best shot, because, just like life, I'm giving you no choice in the matter."

Reluctantly, I started jerking back and forth, pulling against the jacket as Max looked at me, smiled approvingly, then went on. "James, I was raised in a different sort of household. Both of my parents died when I was very young, so my grandparents on my mother's side of the family raised me. My grandparents were very good people, and I loved them very much. They had taught me the true value of a dollar and the time-honored family traditions of saving for the future, honoring the Puritan work ethic – blah, blah, and blah....

"Like you, I'd been put through school, got my MBA from Harvard – la tee da – and was pretty well set. Living the MBA fantasy, I moved to New York, got a job with a big Wall Street brokerage firm, and was on my way to the top. I was happy, too. I mean, I thought I was happy. You only think you're happy, if you have to stop and think about it. I had surrounded myself with all the trappings that people who know nothing about living tend to: fast cars, great clothes, a big high-rise apartment – lots of girl friends. Lord knows I wasn't about to get close to any one woman, because they wanted nothing more than my money anyway.

"The only *real* positive aspect of my life was my relationship with my grandparents, which, unfortunately, I took for granted. Unfortunate because life learns these things and eventually gets around to teaching you.

"Early one October evening life decided to teach me an important lesson. I had just been given a promotion and was making big money in the market; I heard about this growth opportunity ... in plastics. Well, I decided that the best thing I could do for my grandparents, was give them an early Christmas. After investing my grandparent's money for years, and always being careful to diversify to protect them, I took a risk. Using the family savings, I rearranged the portfolio very heavily in one particular high-return plastics stock, even though I knew better.

"For the first three days my grandparents were doing great, triple the ordinary earnings. Then the bottom fell out. The stock, which I had played as a long shot, had been built up on a rumored buyout. A buyout would mean that the company's stock would go through the roof. However, the company created the rumor itself – total fraud. When the rumors dissolved, the truth hit the stock really hard, virtually disintegrating it down to zero.

"That day, I lost everything. Playing the margins, borrowing really heavy, when the day was over I owed over a hundred thousand dollars. The next day the securities exchange commission started investigating my investments; I was told that my services were no longer needed at the firm. By the end of the week, I'd lost my apartment, car, girl friends – everything but my freedom.

"However, the hardest thing in the world, for me, was taking the call from my grandfather. I remember most of the conversation exactly.

"'Son, Mom is pretty worried, but I know we'll be okay,' he said, 'Won't we?'

"'Pops,' I said, not being able to keep from bursting into tears, 'I lost big time – I will get it back for you. Somehow – I promise.'

"'Don't sweat it, we can bounce back,' Granddad said, trying not to reveal his own shaking voice. 'We didn't have anything when we started last time.'

"The next day he called again, this time to tell me that Grandmother, who already had a weak heart, had just passed away. He said not to blame myself, but I knew that the added stress from my stock fiasco was just too much for her. Stress was taking its toll on my Grandfather too. At the funeral, he looked terrible, the funeral costs adding still more strain.

"Three weeks later, I was back in New York packing up my belongings, getting out of my high priced apartment, convinced it was all my fault. Fate dealt me one more card – a call telling me Granddad had also passed away. His reason for living had ceased.

"I felt I had nothing to live for either. Tears were streaming down my cheeks. Unable to breathe, I stopped packing and walked over to the windows to get some air. I opened them up," he said, demonstrating with his arms, "like this."

"The windows were an old type, with metal hinges, that swung out. I felt a cool breeze from the outside. James, I could hear the sound of Manhattan – that sound of struggling to the middle. Twenty-three stories off the ground and windows big enough to stand in; so I stood up on the window sill just to take a long look down at the street below. My vision was blurred with tears; I could see only hopelessness in the people walking and driving by on the street below.

"I wasn't really thinking clearly, but I knew that I was about to end my life. Weak from overworked emotions, I slowly leaned out toward the street, out to the very limit of my balance. Knowing that this was my good-bye, I closed my eyes and said a prayer. I am not really a very religious man, but, I said, 'God help me' and let myself fall.

"As I fell forward off balance, far beyond the point of returning to the window, a miracle changed my life. Leaning way out beyond my own center of gravity, I should've fallen to my death. Instead I was actually stopped, suspended in the air by a power I didn't understand – the hand of God. An invisible force rescued me. Even though I'd given up on life, life hadn't given up on me. At that moment, I truly believed that I was being held up by my guardian angel.

"James, I got goose bumps. For the first time, I realized how much of life's potential I'd missed. I understood the true meaning of life. Life is about living! Believing that I'd met with a higher force, that something or someone greater than myself had saved my life, I leaned back into the window. If God had decided to save my life, my life must have been worth living, I must have a reason to live.

"Wiping a few tears from my cheeks, choosing life, I opened my eyes and hopped down from the window sill. When I jumped back onto the solid floor of my apartment, there was a sudden jerk at my shirttail as it tore away from me. There – caught on the metal window hinge – was the torn white cloth from the tail of my shirt.

"It was my *hand of God*.

"You see, I realize that it was more than just my shirttail, catching on the window, that saved my life. Belief is what saved my life, the belief that something metaphysical or spiritual had happened. If I had known just my shirt was saving me, I would've just torn it loose and jumped. Belief made me change the course. To this day, I don't really know that it wasn't the hand of God. Maybe the way that God, whoever or whatever it is, works is through such small things as that small piece of cloth – no coincidence.

"That little piece of white cloth is still with me at all times. Not because I believe that it is some mystical talisman that has magical powers – the cloth is a reminder that true belief changed my life. True belief changes people's lives, James.

"You believed in *my* magic the same way that I believed in *that* magic, when *you* actually created the real magic all along. Your belief changes things – not what is presented to you. I could only do the tricks. You made them magic."

So intrigued by his story, I completely forgot my struggle against the straitjacket. Standing there still completely bound I asked, "But how did you do all of those things? Like when you first appeared in my apartment, how did you even know where I lived?"

"Remember when I opened your wallet at the festival, when you were my assistant? I simply got your full name and address off of your driver's license. Besides you are listed in the phonebook," he said. "And by the way, you really ought to start locking your patio door."

"What about the money, you knew exactly how much was in the hat. How did you do it?" I asked, now working at escaping from the jacket again.

"I switched the hat with one that I had in the trunk that contains exactly one-hundred seventeen-dollars and forty-seven cents."

"And the cards in Gina's purse," I said, suddenly realizing that everything he did was an illusion. "You put them in there before we went out, didn't you?" For some reason, I had completely forgotten that Gina had hired him to come do magic at the restaurant; he had ample opportunity to hide them in her purse.

"You were on the elevator, too, weren't you?" I asked, as the pieces of the puzzle fell into place and the full picture came into view. He was the ultimate magician, his magic so well done that I believed it to be true magic, even though I knew otherwise.

"What about the elevator?" he asked.

"When it stopped and I heard you say, 'nothing will happen unless you make it happen?' Why me? Why am I the one?"

"James, relax. Don't struggle so much. As with life, your mind and heart in unison is the key that will set you free. The jacket will move if you simply relax and concentrate on being free, not setting yourself free. Let your breath out, relax, and slowly inch your arms over – I have a lot more to tell you about the power of coincidence."

*"When Your Heart Beats To The Rhythm Of The Universe –
Listen To Your Heart."*

Chapter 24

Just as he suggested, I relaxed and concentrated. Wow, as I did, I could feel one of the arm straps gain a half inch of slack. Slowly I moved my right arm toward my head, again concentrating on relaxing. Trying to think about being free versus getting free, I listened intently.

Max continued his story where he had left off. "Afterwards, I got down from the window ledge and packed my bags. I sold everything else that I had, which was easy since I had lost most of my possessions anyway. Selling everything gave me a freedom that I hadn't felt since I was a child. I could go anywhere and do anything I wanted, no longer having to live up to anyone's expectations – except my own. From that point on, I lived, really lived, my own life.

"I began by going to the train station and buying a ticket to Springfield, Missouri. Don't ask my why I picked Springfield; it just sounded like something very different from New York. It's just another strange coincidence that brings you and me together.

"Sitting in a park in Springfield, determined to start a new life, I saw a guy doing some magic tricks with his little boy. Actually, the little boy was showing the trick to his father. Perhaps you know the trick, the '*cut-the-rope-in-half trick.*' As I recall, you didn't exactly know how to put it back together yet. Sitting, watching you, yes you, James, I was taken back to my youth, to the time my grandfather had given me a magic set. I had locked away a childhood dream for years. Like you, I once dreamt of being a magician.

"James, my seeing you, my meeting you – was no coincidence. You created Max Vi, because you appeared at a defining moment in my life. Without knowing it – you, as that little boy, at that very moment – changed my life forever. You gave me the opportunity to choose my direction. You caused me to remember when I possessed a child's innocent outlook. You made me realize what it is like not to prejudice life with one's own past. *You* – just a small unknowing child, struggling to perform a magic trick – were *my* greatest teacher.

"Seeing that you and your father shared a special kind of love, I decided that if that love could be shared by magic – well, that was what I wanted from life. I actually introduced myself to you and your dad, John, that day – a wonderful guy who told me many things about the art of living and loving life. After that one meeting, I dedicated my life to creating magic in the lives of others. From that day on I set out to discover the secrets of both magic and life.

"At first, I just enjoyed being, traveling the country, doing magic, talking to a lot of people about the meaning of life. Eventually, I uncovered some real magic. Performing magic made me discover *why*, my reason for being. I had the ability to create true belief in people – not just the kind that a person gets by watching a good card trick. I mean, people really believed in the magic I presented. I discovered that, with a little magic, I could make people believe in life's possibilities, not just think about life's possibilities, or wonder about the possibilities. I mean believe in them – know them. James, I felt a calling to use this unique ability to help others follow their heart, discover their own destiny.

"Vowing to maximize, not only my life, but the lives of the people I touched, I adopted the stage name, 'Maximillion Vi.' You see, 'vi' means *life* – 'Max Life.'

"From the time that I crawled down off that window in New York City, I went back to my beginning, putting the past behind me. I was an empty slate, open to all the possibilities. Then without the prejudice that life gives us as we grow up, I learned to walk. After I decided who, what, and why I was, I learned to run. In return for living my *why*, life granted me happiness and fulfillment. Then, when I made the greatest discovery of all – an unconditional love for life – something incredible happened. I learned to fly!

"When you learn to love life unconditionally, it will embrace you. You and life become one – energy and matter. You gain a knowledge that few ever find, creating whatever you believe to be possible. You are the one that controls life, all aspects. There isn't a thing in this world that you can't do. It's all perception, James. You determine how you perceive each and every moment, how you live each and every moment. You can choose to see either the future filled with hope, or the past, empty with broken promises. But *you* make the choice.

"You have control over only one thing of in your life. Can you tell me what that is?" asked Max, but he didn't wait for an answer. In the meantime I was beginning to make headway against the straitjacket. The straps neared my head and I knew that if I could just get my head down through my arms I might be able to free myself. Finding listening to Max and concentrating on the jacket difficult, I discovered that if I simply relaxed, I was able to do both.

"Just one thing, James – if you think that you have control over anything else, you are mistaken. You can't make Gina come back. You can't make Carl become a famous actor. You can't make Josh become happy. And you can't get out of the straitjacket around you. You have no control over these things. You have control of only one aspect of your life. You have complete control over it and no one else can ever command it. Listen carefully to this because it's going to confuse you.

"While it's true that you have total and complete control over only one thing in your life, in that one thing, you have control over all things. The one thing you have control over, James, is your thoughts. The one thing that controls everything else in your world – your mind, your body, your will, your soul – is the one thing you've been given complete dominion over. You, James, are the master of your own thoughts.

"James, I was never on the elevator. I probably didn't perform half of the miracles you credit me with, but because you lived them, they happened. Only if you believe in magic, does it exist. You have to know it in your heart of hearts. That's the secret.

"People often say that you can achieve what you believe. This is only a half-truth. Do you know that you can walk on water, James? No. Do you know that you can fly? No! Belief only creates reality when you know it to be the truth. James, we believe only what we perceive. In life we are given perceptions – limitations which we occasionally have the power to overcome. Like when we rely upon technology to overcome the limitations – such as a radio allows us to hear messages from out of thin air. Imagine how magical a radio is to someone who doesn't understand it. It's not magic for us to hear music from a radio, because we know it's possible. But you and I, we have the ability to manipulate people's perceptions and take them into a level of thought allowing them to create their own reality. We can allow them to set their perceptual limits aside. You will learn these same things in time, now that you are discovering your *why*. You will learn to create reality from your thoughts.

"The time I met you at the festival wasn't just another of life's strange coincidences. I believe – in fact, I know – the power of such a coincidence. When I first heard your name, immediately I remembered you and your father, and I knew that there must be a special reason for me to see you again. My intuition was telling me that you were someone special in my life. Intuition is something you should never ignore. Intuition is when your heart and the universe are beating in rhythm. Listen to your heart, James, and you're listening to the universe.

"Listening to my heart, it didn't take long to figure out what the universe wanted me to do. I was to teach you to gain the wisdom of life that I have uncovered. Life wanted you to know its secrets, my secret. As Max Vi, I created an illusion to teach you the power of the illusion, James. Remember, my friend, the illusion *is* the reality. With it you can create true belief. Once you believe you can change the world, you begin to change things for the better."

Still working on the jacket, I listened.

"James, when your father died, life challenged you with its most difficult lesson. Unfortunately, you haven't yet learned the lesson life is trying to teach to you, and in order for you to move forward, you must.

James, you can't let circumstance outside of your control, control your life. You can't let someone's unconditional love, the universe's most positive force, play such a negative role in your life. Life simply won't let you."

Everything was coming together, starting to make sense. When my father died, I couldn't let go. The straitjacket that held me was not the one around my shoulders, it was the one in my mind. When he died, my joy for life died with him. All these years I'd thought that I'd moved on, that I'd gotten over it, but I'd only repressed my feelings. The evidence was there in the empty pages of my scrapbook and the forgotten trophy I'd tossed into his grave. At the time I believed that I loved him too much to let him go. But then my love was immature. Giving was not enough. Loving him unconditionally would have meant that I'd have been able to let him go, knowing that my love would never cease, and trusting that his love for me would also never end.

Suddenly the jacket slackened, I pulled my hands over my shoulders and I placed one arm over my head. This was going to work, the jacket was coming off – *I knew it!* Then I had a flash of brilliance, as though the universe had suddenly harmonized with everything in my being. The philosophy of the magic life crystallized in my heart. All of the events that had passed since meeting Max somehow pointed to the same thing.

Unconditional love knows no limit – that is its power, its secret! The only limits were those set in my own mind. My thoughts were my life's straitjacket. In my heart I knew that I could let Gina go without placing limits upon life. Love in the highest form places no limits. Unconditional love would go beyond all boundaries, even the boundary of death. Suddenly I understood why Gina had died and I realized that even her death could never lessen the love between us.

Within this realization, I saw myself released and free! Pulling my shoulders down, the jacket loosened as I slipped my head up between my arms. My heart synchronized to the beat of the universe. Love, intuition, magic, they all made sense. My *why* was not just a matter of simply changing my job from accountant to magician, it was...

"James, you are just like me in many ways. We both had to learn a tough lesson: in spite of what life conjures up, you have the ability to transform it. That *is* the magic life. You have the ability to do what I have done; I know it. When I saw you with Josh Wooten, my suspicion was confirmed. You are the one! The one who created me. The one who can make a difference in the lives of a million others. Each person you meet – every person who listens to you – you can touch with the magic! You can teach them this philosophy, just as I have begun to teach you. James, unconditional love for life is the secret."

I understood exactly what Max meant; at that moment I was free! My mind was no longer holding me back. Reaching down, I grasped the crotch strap with my now freed hands. All I had to do was to force the jacket over my head.

Max explained, "This small piece of cloth that kept me from ending it all *is* something magical: whatever people wish it to be, whatever they believe it to be, whatever they *know* it to be. This ordinary piece of cloth changed my understanding of life. It will change life as you know it, too." Max winked, smiled and said, *"Every second conceals within it, a lifetime -- every minute, an eternity. Remember, James, the illusion is the reality."*

My love for my father was unconditional! My love for Gina *was* unconditional! My love for *life* was unconditional! I'd discovered the love that could let go of her while still loving her. My heart and mind let her free at that instant, as I felt the unconditional love pour from me, I felt it fill me. With it came a feeling of peace, of warmth, of freedom, which I'd never felt before. This was what Max meant by the love that would come back from giving unconditionally.

Tossing me the chain, Max Vi said, "Congratulations, James, you've passed the test. You are here to take my place."

Freedom! Springing free from the jacket, flinging it into the air and catching the chain in one continuous motion, I yelled, "I did it!!!"

The jacket never even reached the floor. When I looked around – something totally impossible had happened. My surroundings had vanished and I was no longer in Max's apartment. I don't know how, but I do know that it was real to me. Even though I had finally learned not to question the magic as to *how*; still, I had to ask myself *why*.

"Why was I standing once again in the midst of a crowd, on the street corner, at the Pecan Street Festival?"

"Each Second Conceals Within It A Lifetime –
Every Minute An Eternity."

Chapter 25

Just the same as the first time I'd met him, Max was escaping from his straitjacket, the crowd bursting into an ovation as the straitjacket flew into the air. Once again, I found myself holding Max's magic hat; people were applauding, with some already giving up their hard-earned cash.

Holding the red satin sheet over his head, exactly as before, Max ended the act. Turning around in a circle, calling to the audience, "Ladies and gentlemen, please take this one small bit of magic into your lives. Learn that life itself is the magic! *Each second conceals within it a lifetime, every minute an eternity.*" He winked at me, then said, "Learn to live each moment as though life itself could suddenly just disappear." Lifting the sheet over his head, he vanished; the sheet drifted slowly to the ground, silencing the crowd.

Then again, just exactly as in the past, the white-haired woman walked forward placing a dollar into the hat, saying, "You two fellas put on one heck of a show." The crowd applauded and strolled up randomly, placing money into the hat. I felt that I had dreamed this, or lived this all before, as though time had not passed and it was the first time that I watched Max perform.

THE MAGIC LIFE

Walking over to the old trunk and lifting up the top, I peered in; I felt the tingling sensation shoot through me as never before. But this time, I knew *why*. This time, the Amazing Max was not inside. All the props were still there, but in his place there was a spiral bound notebook. The notebook was titled by Max's own hand. It said, "The Philosophy of the Magic Life, By Max Vi." Instinctively, I opened it to the first page and read:

Dear James,

Learning and teaching are two of the three most important things in life. Loving life unconditionally is the most important. You know your 'why' – congratulations, you've learned to run. Now give life all your love and you will learn to fly. Fly and fly high, learning from those who will teach, teaching those who will learn, and loving life in the process.

Prepare yourself for a wonderful journey, taking each step along the way with enthusiasm, without fear, and always staying true to yourself. Where I am going you cannot follow now, but learn the philosophy of the magic life and your path to your own truth will slowly unfold.

James, you are the one. You are the greatest magician of all time, because it's all in your mind.

With unconditional love,
Max

Somehow my heart tapped into the universal language and a feeling of love surged from me like the rays of the sun. Loving life unconditionally meant loving all of it: all of the ups and downs, the tragedies, and the victories. They were all life. Whatever my life was going to be, was whatever I made of it from this moment forward. This was what I had learned.

My *why* was to help others discover the secrets to the magic in life – the joys, the sadness, the celebrations, and most importantly, the love. In that defining moment, I began to exist in the present, knowing exactly what "Max Vi" meant. What a challenge – to maximize life – exactly what I intended to do. Not only did I know the possibilities of the future, I knew exactly what was next. Without hesitation, my days of mourning my father and Gina over, I started to live my *why* – to maximize my life.

Dumping the money into the trunk and placing the hat on top of my head, I closed up the trunk and jumped up on top. Dropping my voice lower, almost automatically – as if I had done this a thousand times – it boomed out like a ringmaster, "Ladies and gentlemen, children of all ages, step right up – the show is about to begin! Come see the incredible, amazing, astounding … (What name would I use?) … the magic man himself, James Max – attempt miracles beyond the concepts of human imagination!"

A crowd gathered quickly around me. They were about to watch me escape from a straitjacket – one that I had struggled against for a long time. As I looked into the faces of the curious audience, I felt an unconditional love for each and every one of them. A startling sensation came over me; I felt Gina's presence, as if she were right there with me. Then at the back of the crowd, my eyes met the eyes of a beautiful young woman smiling a coincidental smile.

I felt a tingle.

"Nothing Is Impossible — Absolutely Nothing."

Final Chapter

Years have passed since my last lesson from Max Vi. So much has changed since that time. Leaving accounting to become a magician was a little scary, at first, but very liberating. Resigning from Lee, Fellers and Gadheart was in reality more difficult for my Mom to swallow, than it was for me. However, after many long, heartfelt talks, she's learned to accept both Carl's and my need to realize our dreams.

This particular dream of mine, however, she is still a little uncertain about. Certainly, I understand her concern. Sitting here on this hard metal chair, after being meticulously strapped into my straitjacket, I find myself looking up at the end of a two-hundred-foot crane that is about to hoist me into the sky. I can't help marveling at the wonders that Max revealed to me. Knowing the future, versus half-hearted believing it, had made many things possible in my life. Now, I am about to become one of only five magicians in the world to have ever escaped from a straitjacket while dangling from a burning rope over two-hundred feet in the air – a feat that even Max never attempted.

Stepping up onto Max's trunk at the festival was certainly a defining moment in my life. Max was right about everything. Yes, I escaped from more than just that straitjacket that day. Seems those magicians were right –

like most things, the escape has more to do with knowing you can than anything else. That's why the insane can't get out of them, they simply don't know they can get out. In fact, most people don't really understand that they can get out of whatever straitjacket they are strapped into. That's why we see so many miserable people; they just don't know that they can get out.

One of the police officers is now locking my ankles into the inversion boots. The buckles are similar to those on ski boots and I ask him to make sure that they are snapped tight, latched to the last position. Once he has them tightened to my satisfaction, I instruct the other officer to wrap the lead duct tape completely around them to make absolutely certain they don't fly open during my ascent.

The music starts playing. Taking a deep breath, trying to relax, I am drawn back to the impossible events surrounding Max's last disappearance. You see, after my first real show that day at the festival, I passed the hat and then headed back to Max Vi's apartment, wanting *him* to count my huge new income (thirteen dollars and thirty-six cents) and perhaps to thank him for changing my life. With great anticipation I drove back over to his apartment complex and knocked on the door. An old man, wearing a pair of jeans, a flannel shirt, and a fishing hat, answered. Looking confused, as though he thought I was selling something, he asked, "What can I do for you, today?"

"May I speak to Max?" I asked, mistakenly thinking that maybe this old guy might be another of Max's *works-in-progress*, like myself.

The rather pleasant old guy scratched his stubble-covered chin and said, "You must have the wrong apartment, son." When I explained, showing him the envelope with Max's address written on it, he just smiled and said, "Well, I don't know what to tell you because I've lived at this address for goin' on ten years."

At first I thought he was putting me on, another of Max's tricks, so I glanced inside. If it was an illusion, it was an incredible one. Everything inside was different: furniture, television, even carpeting; I had no reason to doubt the old man. To tell you the truth, I almost expected it. Let's just say that I wasn't *that* surprised.

As for Max Vi, I haven't seen or heard from him since. He's never even shown up in a dream. Quite frankly, I wouldn't believe that any of it had ever happened except that I still have his necklace, props, and books.

But, I don't know if he was *"real"* to this day. Max did tell me that he created the "illusion" for me to learn. Now, when I look back to seven years ago, the whole experience seems as if it were just an *illusion* – an imaginary tale, or perhaps a misguided memory. For all I know, Max could've hired that old guy to be there to answer his door. Maybe it was all some kind of hypnotic trance. Maybe Max hypnotized me somehow when I first met him and the whole adventure had been just a grand hallucination of some kind.

Checking back on reality, I hear the announcer begin his voice–over to the crowd. I don't have to listen because I know the words by heart – after all, I was the one who wrote them. "Ladies and gentlemen, children of all ages, you are about to witness one of the most daring escapes…"

What I want to believe, or rather, really do believe, is that Max Vi was a man who learned the secrets of the universe and wished to share them before he moved on to a different dimension. Reading Max's hand-written philosophy has convinced me of that. In his *Philosophy of the Magic Life*, Max wrote about the power of thoughts and unconditional love, of the importance of learning and teaching. He wrote about the importance of family, friends, and the people that one doesn't even know. He discussed the powers of patience and persistence. Most importantly he included how life gives us constant clues to its meaning and direction, and information about the recognition of defining moments.

Max believed that life places its greatest secrets right in front of you, if you only choose to look. But what really convinced me that Max had moved on to another plane was that Max's philosophy contained information on how to achieve impossible things. There were things like the creation of matter from pure thought energy, continuing with impossibilities, such as levitation, time travel, de-materialization, and thought projection – what Max referred to as "learning to fly." *Had Max learned to fly?*

The announcer is just finishing up, "… does not release himself before the rope burns through – he'll either have to *learn to fly* – or he'll plunge two-hundred feet to his death!"

Max's philosophy is somewhat difficult to understand and even more difficult to live up to, like trying to live up to the writing on the walls and the signs in the sky. I haven't yet learned how to de-materialize, levitate, or walk on water. However, I have learned that, where there is love, passion, and knowledge, there is the possibility of a truly magical life. Ever since Max disappeared I have tried to live life according to this philosophy, always attempting to help others discover that magic life while savoring every moment of my own.

Right now I'm about to live a very special moment in my life. The three policemen give the restraint a quick look over (everything checks out), and then they attach the diesel-soaked rope to the end of the crane. One of them also gives a tug on the safety line, which will hang next to me in the air, giving me something to grab hold of once I have made my escape.

Remember the girl from the crowd, at the Pecan Street Festival – the one who caught my eye and caused the tingle seven years ago? Well, Max certainly taught me not to let opportunities like that pass me by. As she walks onto the stage carrying the burning torch, her long red hair blowing in the breeze, she says, "While you're up there hanging around, don't forget who loves you," giving me a quick kiss before stepping back to light the rope.

"I won't," I say as the flames leap from the torch, engulfing the rope. "I love you, too."

Time to concentrate, relax. My heartbeat quickens as I watch the rope transform into a roaring flame. With a quick jerk, the crane kicks into high gear, the cable hoisting me upside-down, skyward. Looking downward, I see the ground pulling quickly away. Higher and higher I travel. Concentrating intensely, I'm not afraid.

Twenty feet – looking down at the audience, I realize that there may be a young boy or girl in that crowd who is dreaming of someday becoming a great magician, or perhaps something much greater. Maybe today's escape will help inspire him or her, somehow, helping him or her believe that, in this world, nothing is impossible – absolutely nothing. Beginning my struggle against the straitjacket wrapped so tightly around me, forcing my arms away from my body, I realize the tremendous potential of that one thought, *"Nothing is impossible."*

Sixty feet – the rope sways back and forth slightly with each blast of the wind. Smoke billowing into the air, my heart pounding, I am working diligently, gaining more slack with each second that passes.

THE MAGIC LIFE

Eighty feet – my body weight pulling down on the hemp, the fiery rope starts to untwist slightly. Spinning slowly in a circle, I am aware of every motion, every slight twitch and pop of the burning fibers. Drips of flaming diesel blow away from the rope, and as I watch them disappear, falling slowly to the pavement below, I realize the scene is playing out exactly as I had dreamed.

"See yourself out of this," I say to myself. "You're going to get out!" Wrenching sideways, I feel the rope make a sudden lurch, frightening me just a little. Time is ticking by. "Fear will not enter this picture!" I shout to myself. This isn't a test of physical strength as much as mental clarity – if I can just clearly see my way out.

One-hundred feet – the blood rushes to my head, creating a false sense of euphoria. My mind wanders a bit, thinking about the vastness of the universe and my unique place within it. Looking over the horizon, I sense that I exist within all that I survey, as though I am truly one with the universe. Suddenly I am overcome by that strange tingling sensation – one that I haven't felt for years, but a sensation that is as recognizable as the first time I felt it.

One-hundred-fifty feet – a voice, as plain as you or me, whispers into my ear. "Don't worry, nothing will happen unless you make it happen." My struggle relaxes as a feeling of calm envelops me.

"*Max?*" I ask.

One-hundred-eighty feet – the sleeves slacken. I'll be okay now, after I just force my shoulder out of place. Pressing forcefully and steadily against the jacket, my shoulder pops along with a minor pain, giving me the necessary slack. A heavy sigh of relief – just one more second and I'll be free.

Two-hundred feet – my arms are now freed. All that remains is to pull the jacket off over my head. The defining moment has come – I know in my heart that I will be free. Then in one brief flash, I catch something, someone out of the corner of my eye. Twisting my body around, for just an instant I see Max, like a ghost, semi-transparent, floating in mid air next to me. Grinning his mischievous smile, he winks at me and then holds the safety rope out for me to take hold.

In that exact same moment, I burst free from the restraint, tossing the straitjacket into the air. The burning rope separates, with a crackling burst. The crowd gasps, believing I'm about to fall to my death. However, in virtually the same instant, I make my lunge for the safety rope. It is almost as though Max guides the rope into my hands. My legs swing downward, bringing me upright with a jerk, but somehow I manage to maintain an iron grip on the rope.

"I'm free! I've done it! I've made it!" I shout out, tingling all over, my heart pounding wildly, my eyes filling with tears of joy. "I'm living the magic life!" Max looks at me; he smiles, and then fades into the clouds.

Still feeling the rush of adrenaline, I begin my descent. For the first time, I can now hear the crowd applauding, cheering, and whistling. Looking down, I see my Mother and Carl rush from out of the stands to greet me on the platform far below. As the crane slowly lowers me toward the ground, I wonder if anyone else could've see Max. Of course no one else saw him. He appeared only for the twinkling of an eye, only in my mind, but in my heart I know he was really there, watching out for me and showing his approval. "Thanks, Max," I whisper to myself.

Then, in confirmation, his voice calls out to me over the applause and cheers of the crowd, saying, "Congratulations, Jim, you've made your dreams become reality. You've learned to fly!" Then I hear his voice as though it is moving far away, shouting back at me, "Goodbye, James."

"Goodbye, Max," I say as I near the ground.

Before I get back down to earth, literally and figuratively, there is just one more thing that you should know. Some of you will believe it was possible, some of you won't. Some will say this is just a work of fiction, others will *know* that it's much more. But, what I need to tell you about is that girl in the crowd, (that later became my wife) the one whose smile caught my eye that day, who is now running over to give me a congratulatory hug and kiss.

I'm not going to hang here, trying to convince you that I actually went back in time that day and that Max somehow gave me a second chance to not let life pass me by, because, you wouldn't believe me anyway. After all, we all "*know*" that we don't get a second chance at life, right? And when you "*know*" something, that *is* reality – isn't it? So, I'm not going to tell you that that woman, the one now pulling off her long red wig and shaking her short blond hair, running over to me, is the same girl I'd dreamt of marrying when I was just a teen.

The police officers remove the boots and rigging, before I plant myself, both feet firmly on the ground. My wife wraps her arms around my neck, gives me a warm kiss and says, "Did ya miss me?"

"You'll never know how much," I reply.

"I love you," she responds.

"I love you, too."

You don't have to believe that she is Gina, the same woman whose love I'd once traded away for security. I don't expect you to; because, after all – that would be impossible – wouldn't it?

My mother and Carl are both here, too. Mom takes her turn and gives me a hug, "James, I sure am proud of you," pulling Carl into the hug. A small tear comes to her eyes, as she adds, "I'm awfully proud of both of you boys."

A small blue-eyed boy sticks his head out from behind his uncle Carl, grabbing tightly on to my leg, asking, "Daddy, can I be a magician when I grow up?"

Recalling the words of my own father, I answer him, "Son, you can be anything you want to be ... except unhappy."

About the Author

When Ace Starry was a small boy, his father bought a discarded trunk at a junkyard, intending to turn the trunk into a coffee table. Upon opening it, he discovered several books on magic and a few old magicians' props. It was from that moment on that Ace dreamt of becoming a magician. Today he has realized that childhood dream and lived many more. You can see and read much more about his escapes, magic and the magic life philosophy at his web site: www.starry.com.

Mr. Starry has a diverse and interesting background. Though he now resides in New York, he grew up in the western United States. Born the son of a carpenter in a small agricultural town in Idaho, experiencing both poverty and affluence, he spent his childhood in Utah, California, and Texas. His formal education includes the unlikely combination of an Associate Degree in education, a Bachelor's degree in theater, and a Master of Business Administration Degree in marketing. Growing up in the numerous towns and cities, attending seven different grammar schools, a junior high, two high schools, a jr. college, and two universities has given Mr. Starry many insights into life. Today, in spite of all that education, Ace believes that *"life itself is the greatest educator."*

More than just a professional magician, Ace has worn many hats: a ditch digger, a burger flipper, singer/songwriter, a standup comedian, a carpenter, a plumber, a salesman, a real estate executive, a computer consultant, and even a CEO for a software company. He also spent a short time as a security guard for "The Greatest of All Time," Muhammad Ali. From these diverse life experiences and education, Ace Starry has developed a philosophy about life he calls "The Philosophy of the Magic Life." Knowing the secrets to magic has given Ace a unique perspective on the secrets to the *illusion* called life. In this, his first novel, he shares that secret.

MORE INFORMATION

Rare Bird Press is a small press publisher, dedicated to delivering works of uniquely creative first-time authors who demonstrate a positive philosophy to the public. If you enjoyed THE MAGIC LIFE please help spread the word by sharing it with your friends and family. If you would like more information about The Magic Life Philosophy and Rare Bird Press please visit our web site, http://411webs.com/rarebird or contact the author at:

Internet: E-mail to ace@starry.com or visit the www.starry.com web site.

Postal orders can be placed at:

Rare Bird Press, 240 Pennsylvania Ave., Yonkers, NY 10707

Please send _____ copy (ies) of THE MAGIC LIFE at $19.95 each to:

_____

_____

_____

Sales Tax:

Please add 8% for books shipped within New York.

Shipping:

$4.50 for the first book and $2.00 for each additional.

Payment (circle one):

Check Included   Visa   MasterCard   American Express

Card Number: _____Expires: _____

Name on Card:_____

Signature: _____

Look for other titles coming soon from author, Ace Starry:

THE PHILOSOPHY OF THE MAGIC LIFE

THE SECOND -- A Novel Possibility (1999)

MATRIXING -- A Handbook for the New Millennium (2000)